ENDGAME

AHMET ALTAN

Translated by Alexander Dawe

CANONGATE

Edinburgh · London

Published in Great Britain in 2015 by Canongate Books Ltd,
14 High Street, Edinburgh EH1 1TE

www.canongate.tv

1

First published as *Son Oyon* in 2014 by Everest Yayinlari

British Library Cataloguing-in-Publication Data
A catalogue record for this book is available on
request from the British Library

ISBN 978 1 78211 259 4

Typeset in Bembo by Palimpsest Book Production Ltd,
Falkirk, Stirlingshire

Printed and bound in Great Britain by Clays Ltd, St Ives plc

I

The town was sleeping.

Someone is always up in a big city but in a small town everyone goes to bed around the same time. That's something I found out after I got here.

I was sitting under a towering eucalyptus tree on the main street, on one of those old-fashioned benches with names and hearts carved into its dark wooden planks.

I'd wanted to sit there ever since I came to town, but that night was the first time.

I leaned back.

I looked up at the sky.

They were all sleeping, dreaming. Dreaming together.

I watched their dreams slip out through windows, doors and chimneys. I watched them rise up into the clouds, flaunting their colours; I could almost see them, talking, laughing, sobbing, making love. There they all were, entwined in deep embraces on velvet-curtained stages, in stables and on dark streets, in sitting rooms and by the sea. A neighing horse, two women kissing, a tearful child racing through the night, a horde of golden coins, a glistening knife. Sometimes I caught sight of a man or a woman vanishing from their own dreams to haunt the dreams of others.

I watched the town dreaming.

I wasn't drunk, or at least not from drink.

I had just taken a life.

I remembered it like a dream.

But I couldn't remember much. I remembered an arm – my

arm, though somehow it was severed from my body, wandering far away, beyond my grasp. It was holding a gun. I don't remember pulling the trigger; I only heard the shot. And then I saw a mouth opening, as if to speak, a face contorted, one hand in the air, the other clutching the wound. And then a body falling, but no blood.

What is it people feel when they kill another human being? My body was taut, seized by a fear I had never known before, and then it seemed I had drifted off to sleep.

I left the house and made my way here.

I don't remember thinking about anything in particular.

I sat down. What a careless novelist I was, no different from God.

A good novelist doesn't build on coincidence, or stoop to coincidence to get out of a corner.

But God has a savage sense of humour. And coincidence is his favourite joke. And life is nothing but a string of coincidences.

You see, I was a stranger in town.

I came from a big city, far away.

I stayed there to write a book about murder. And so what if I turned out to be the killer? I'll simply put it down as God's work, another one of his cruel coincidences, taunting his own creation.

The entire town was steeped in dream.

I was the only one awake. Or was I dreaming?

The time has come to tell you what happened.

But the story isn't really mine, and if it is savage beyond belief it is because it comes from the hand of a cruel and indifferent God.

II

I remember everything about the day I first saw her.

We met at a little airport nestled between low hills and the sea.

At first I couldn't really make out her face, blurred by a faint, gauzy light, and I was transfixed.

Later I came to appreciate its beauty, and an almost blinding brightness in her eyes. She knew she was beautiful. When she was a young girl she learned how to use the enchanting powers of her eyes.

I could imagine what happened: she was chased and showered with gifts, which she would accept almost disdainfully, and then, grateful for the attention, she would only receive more – I've met men who gave away their lives.

I never saw her grieve for anything that slipped away; in fact she seemed to collect people and things so that she could throw them away. And I never quite understood how she could collect so much without ever lifting a finger, and when in her heart she really never dreamed of holding on to anything for very long.

She was calm, her serenity drawing people to her. Sometimes it even seemed like she moved objects.

It was raining that day.

Through the window I could see an endless grove of olive trees, turned greyish-green by the rain; their gnarled trunks bursting from the earth, they looked like an ancient army, waiting for the command to march.

Our little plane was late for take-off.

The departures lounge was on the first floor of the building.

The control tower was on the second. Four other people sat behind the broad glass windows that looked out over the tarmac: a crop-duster pilot, two wealthy locals with badly knotted ties, and the woman.

She was sitting alone, listening to the pilot a couple of seats away from her. They seemed to know each other well. And I saw her nod to the other two men.

Then she stood up and walked over to an old coffee machine in the corner, slipping past me like a flash of light.

I was reading a newspaper but I could feel her passing behind me.

On her way back she stopped and put her coffee down on the table in front of me. Then she leaned over and picked my raincoat up off the floor and draped it over the chair beside me.

'It was on the floor,' she said.

Her voice was soft, almost a whisper, demanding attention, and I was caught off guard.

She treated people, and men in particular, as if they were children who needed special attention. Sometimes I got the feeling she thought men were disabled in some way. I didn't know that then.

She picked up her coffee, flashed me a smile and then she left. I watched her go.

These are the moments we can later appraise with hindsight. Reliving the moment now, I feel clairvoyant. But at the time I had no idea what would come to pass.

Sifting through the past on that bench, I could see how my life veered dramatically in the direction it did.

I dashed through the rain and boarded the plane.

There were only three rows of two seats on each side. Big cardboard boxes had been carefully stowed in the back two rows.

I sat down by the window in the front row and watched her walk unhurriedly towards the plane, oblivious to the rain, her head buried in the upturned collar of her coat.

She seemed amused by how we had raced to the plane.

Through the curtain of raindrops that ran down the scratched and pitted window, I thought I could make out a smile on her face.

She was soaking wet by the time she boarded the plane and she really was smiling.

Before she could sit down next to the pilot she had been speaking to earlier, a young man with headphones around his neck emerged from the cockpit and called out, 'Come on, we can talk on the way.' And he saluted the young woman with a nod before the two men disappeared into the cockpit.

She hesitated for a moment then sat down beside me.

She felt like she had to explain herself: 'I'm afraid of flying.'

'But you seem to know all the pilots,' I said.

'I do. They're actually teaching me how to fly. The pilot you saw in the airport is giving me lessons in his crop-duster. His name's Tahir.'

'Aren't you afraid then?'

She shrugged.

'I am.'

The plane lurched forward as she took off her raincoat and placed it on the seat behind her.

As the plane lifted off the runway, I saw her clutching the armrests; her knuckles were white.

'Don't be afraid,' I said.

'I'm getting used to it. I actually like the feeling. It's just that I talk a lot when I'm scared. Is that going to be a problem?'

It was hard to hear her over the roar of the engine.

'No,' I said.

'What do you do?'

'I'm a writer.'

'What do you write?'

'Novels.'

'And your name?'

'You wouldn't know me.'

'Probably not. I don't read much any more. Though I read a lot when I was a kid.'

She paused and then smiled: 'Everyone you meet probably says that they read a lot when they were a kid. Is that true?'

'That's right,' I said. 'I don't meet many who read any more.'

'Is that heartbreaking?'

'What?'

'That people don't read your books?'

'I'm getting used to it. I like feeling disappointed.'

She laughed.

Now I realise it was the way she laughed just then that hooked me. I liked her quick reaction to my joke about her fear.

The plane shook and she grabbed my arm.

In that moment I knew my life would never be the same. It's hard to explain, how that laugh and then the way she held my arm seconds later was the beginning of it all. I could just feel it.

There are those moments in our lives when we feel that nothing will ever be the same again. In retrospect we say that somehow we could feel the surge, the sudden change in direction, though sometimes it is a false alarm and we forget about the moment altogether.

But this was something seismic.

That moment I knew I had succumbed. I could feel myself being swept away, dragged into an abyss. And I wanted to be taken.

For me, exhilaration is the most dangerous emotion, and I felt it then: the expectation that she would teach me things more perilous than love.

I was drawn to excitement, leaping at any opportunity like an animal taking the bait, though fully aware of the impending disaster.

I thought I was the only passenger on the plane on the evening flight back to town. But drifting off to sleep, I saw her reflection in the window. I turned and saw her standing above me, holding all the novels I had ever written. Otherwise I might have forgotten all about her.

They constituted my Achilles' heel, pinched by God when he dipped me in those magical waters. My novels, the weakest and most sinister aspect of my person.

I looked at her hands wrapped round my books and the letters in my name between her fingers. I looked up at her lovely face, like an inlaid Seljuk coin. I could almost feel the warmth of her breasts beneath her blouse and cotton jacket, the warmth of her navel and her thighs.

Seeing my books in her arms made me feel pathetic – a forgotten prophet prepared to worship anyone who will follow, building temples, shrines and altars for the few disciples, and drinking magical elixirs.

'Where did you find those?' I said, like we were old friends.

'In a shop that sold books,' she said, laughing and then sitting down beside me.

'Do they still sell my books there?'

I had assumed they were out of print. I couldn't remember the last time anyone had read one of my books.

'I'll read at least one of them tonight,' she said.

'Do you think you'll like it?'

'Let's see.'

'How about this. You read one and if you like it meet me tomorrow afternoon at the old restaurant near the station.'

'All right,' she said, buckling her seatbelt. 'I'm exhausted. I'm going to sleep a little. Is that all right?'

'Of course.'

Laying her head on my shoulder, she was asleep within minutes.

She trusted me and felt safe on that trip, and I never would have thought that a woman sleeping on my shoulder would have such a profound effect.

III

Vineyards and olive groves blanketed the mountainside above the town. Pale-green olive leaves, flickering in the wind, blazed like a giant lamp, and a yellowish light from the vineyards fell over the hill. Cypress and plane trees cast long, dark shadows, their wisdom and dignity lending the setting a solemn air.

At the foot of the mountain there was an old, brick-built wine factory with wisteria cascading over the walls. Locals grew contraband cannabis in the fields behind it – everyone around here seemed to smoke weed – and everything in the area bore the faint scent of marijuana.

Below the factory wealthy residents lived in large, two-storey, sand-coloured houses with broad terraces that looked down on the town through flower gardens. The town itself was a cluster of stone houses and walled courtyards veined with narrow streets, built on the plain at the base of the mountains. A row of palm trees ran along the coast where the town met the sea, and between the palms grew oleanders with red flowers that seemed to have been planted by a tasteful gardener. Then there was a golden beach that stretched along the shore.

In the centre of town there was an old train station with a yellow brass roof, but the tracks had been torn up. I always liked that station no longer visited by trains. There were little shops inside, which smelled of tobacco and steel. Next to the station was the Çinili restaurant, with its shaded garden. The tables were covered in white tablecloths – it catered to the grandees in town – and it always smelled of anisette and dried mackerel.

I arrived late one summer afternoon. I'd been on my way to the Taurus Mountains, hoping to find a mountain village where I could live for a while.

Through the heat haze rising from a stretch of highway, I noticed a narrow road, and a piece of wood hammered to a stake. The faded letters on the sign read: 'sea for sale'.

I turned without even thinking.

I like driving down roads I've never seen before. There is almost always an adventure that lies ahead. In the end I usually find my way, but then again, that never really happens, and the adventure lasts a little longer than you expected.

I was hungry and so I stopped in front of a köfte restaurant on the road that ran through the centre of the town. There was no one else there. I sat down under a willow tree in the garden and ordered something to eat.

I was tired and restless.

I had been wrestling with ideas for a new book, a murder mystery, but I hadn't managed to start. I was wondering if I would ever write again. I needed a miracle to jolt me back to life, and back to writing, something that would stir the creative juices that had grown still in the dark cave of my soul. I was dead to the world, and no one knew. Writing would bring me back to life.

I was served a plate of grilled meatballs, a bowl of hot sauce and a tomato salad. The food was actually quite good.

The proprietor came over to my table and asked me if I wanted anything else. He made me feel a guest in his own home.

'Thank you. I'm fine,' I said.

He hovered over the table, a bored look on his face.

'Where to? Your car's filthy, by the way.'

'I'm heading south.'

'It's burning up down there.'

'Burning up right here.'

'Much hotter there.'

I agreed with him in the hope that he would leave me alone.

'A cold beer is what you need,' he said. 'Goes well with the grilled meat.'

'Why not,' I said obligingly, and in a flash he was back with two beers.

'Beer's on me,' he said, sitting down at my table. 'I hate this time of day. Everyone's at home, avoiding the heat, cars hardly ever pass by and if they do people aren't hungry, and I can't just close up and go home, and if I stay I get bored so I wait, hoping someone will stop by . . .'

'Ah yes, now that's it,' he said after taking a swig of beer and nodding to an imaginary friend in approval.

A burly young man, neatly dressed and with his hair combed back over his head, lumbered into the garden. 'How's it going, Uncle Remzi,' he called out to the proprietor.

'Slow and steady, Sultan,' he replied.

'Uncle's called me over.'

He greeted me with a nod and left.

'Not a bad kid,' said the proprietor.

'Seems like a polite fellow,' I replied.

'Polite, eh? A real killer.'

'What?' I said. I thought I had misheard him.

'A murderer,' he said, as if telling me the young man was a cobbler.

'Did he shoot someone?' I asked.

'Shoots them all the time,' he said, 'but he never gets caught. He's Oleander Ramiz's nephew.'

I looked him straight in the eye, but the expression on his face was grave, almost sad. 'When he was a kid, his uncle ate the oleanders in their garden and poisoned himself. Imagine that. That's how he got the name.'

'What's his uncle do?'

'Him? He's a killer too.'

I leaned back and looked at him again. Sad and tearful eyes. He seemed troubled by stories he had never shared and mysteries that would never be solved. His shoulders were hunched, like a man resigned to his fate. I felt that he would either become a good friend of mine, or a calculating enemy.

'I saw a sign back there, sea for sale,' I said.

'Oleander wants to sell the beach.'

'It's his?'

'How could the beach be his?' he said, looking at me as if I was a fool.

'Well, how can he sell it then?'

'He can't . . . But he wants to.'

'Give me another beer, will you?'

The expression on his face brightened and then I knew that we would become friends. 'And one for you,' I said. 'This round's on me.'

Over the second beer, he told me about the killers in town. Yugoslavian refugees had come 'eons ago' – as he put it – and fought with the locals, even killed each other.

'What's the issue?'

'Land, marijuana sales, women . . . This place now has a real reputation. They even go elsewhere to kill people.'

'But it seems like such a peaceful place.'

'It is,' he said.

'I'm looking for a quiet place. Any places for rent around here?'

'We could find something for you. Not many people are looking to rent around here.'

That evening I rented a two-storey house with a large veranda that overlooked the town.

That's how it all started.

IV

Sitting on this bench I'm wondering how I ended up at this dead end. What's left? Am I here because I befriended a pot-smoking restaurateur? Or was it that strange sign along the road that started it all? I marvel at how the seemingly impossible is precisely what I was dealt.

If I had only ignored that sign, or left the restaurant without saying a word, I would now be leading another life. I might be living in a mountain village, working on a novel, my only real concern labouring over the right words for the last sentence of a chapter.

But now I'm sitting on this old wooden bench, listening to the breathing of a slumbering town. I am watching all the dreams up in the sky and considering all my options: I could run, spend the rest of my life in jail, or I could take my life.

What if I hadn't seen that sign along the road? What if I hadn't stopped at that restaurant? What if I had just finished my meal and quietly left? How believable is a story that begins with a plate of köfte and a pot-smoking restaurateur? But then consider God. His stories are beyond belief.

I confess that I'm a little jealous of God.

He's killed millions but not once did he ever stop to consider the consequences. No one ever blamed him. Or at least he was never tried in court.

Years of human history but not one of his chapters was ever truly criticised or judged, all his coincidences never challenged by the law.

How does he get away with so much?

By killing off the unbelievers?

I've also taken a life.

But this doesn't make me a lesser God. I am a murderer.

I can see the walls of the houses swell and fall with the breath of those who sleep within them, I can see the entire town as if under a thick cotton quilt. I know most of the people there but I can no longer imagine what they are dreaming. No one knows what another dreams, and even the dreamer doesn't know what lies ahead. The hidden meanings in the dark world of dreams have always frightened me, images fluttering ceaselessly through my mind, indecipherable, only partially revealed to me in sleep, perhaps veiled to my waking eye but wandering quietly in and out of my mind, leaving behind a trail of crippling devastation that I can hardly comprehend.

The town is silent.

Everyone is sleeping. Sleeping together.

Do they know that they will wake up in the morning to the news of murder?

What will they say about me?

What now? I should leave now. With every passing minute they're more likely to catch me. That is if I want to get away.

I'm paralysed.

Exhausted.

God must be exhausted. Killing takes so much out of you.

But does he ever feel remorse? Regret for having brought me into this world. Or was I created expressly for this purpose? But why choose me for the crime? Why give life only to later snuff it out?

I am alone tonight, with only God to grapple with or blame.

What would I say to him if he came and sat down here beside me?

'Why did you do it?' I would ask. And he might say, 'The crime is yours. You took that side road, stopped at that restaurant, settled in this town, and then you committed murder.'

But who really took that life? Me? Or was it God?

Why should I go to prison for his crime?

And why worship God if he granted me the power to kill? It is the eternal question: 'Why me?'

And is the answer simply: 'Because I had a plate of meatballs'? That's hardly satisfying.

Our lives are made up of moments, like seeds we choose to water and that sometimes sprout and grow. Later we're surprised to see what they have become, and we call them God's coincidences because we believe God scattered these moments, these seeds, over the course our lives, and that he watches to see which ones we choose to water. But then again, doesn't he already know so much from the very beginning?

I watered the wrong seed.

Are you amused?

Are you suffering beside me? Steeped in the same fear? In the same overwhelming tide of helplessness?

But can you feel these emotions?

Or do you only know them by observing this mortal plight?

You created us so you could taste emotions that you would otherwise never know. To see and feel desperation, weakness and fear from your own creation.

So here is my description of helplessness, something I now know all too well: a human face pressed against a wall by a thousand hands, fixed in place, unable to breathe, no escape and no salvation.

But how can I convey these feelings to you? I am dying to do so but these are things you will never know.

I am God's teacher but this pupil of mine will make me pay with my life.

He knows my suffering.

And my fear.

A fear that makes me cold, like a block of ice on my back. I am shivering from the cold.

But it was a magnificent journey that led me to this moment of abject terror. No one would have believed it. I never would have expected so much if not for that black speck of foreboding that took shape in my heart, laying there in the shadows, and I chose not to watch it grow.

Nobody wants to see the truth, so why should I?

But now I was face to face with it, and it was staring me in the eye.

God was revealing inescapable truths.

I saw the truth.

Horrified and full of fear, I saw the truth.

V

I rented a really nice place. It was fully furnished, and decorated like the home of a nineteenth-century aristocrat, with carved cabinets, large mirrors, velvet wingback chairs and beautiful carpets. But it didn't feel overcrowded and the arrangement of furniture lent the place a peaceful air. A mountain breeze was always drifting in through large, bright windows, fluttering the curtains.

I always had breakfast on the veranda, between carved wooden columns, looking out over the sea, which was light green where it met the golden sand of the beach. It grew darker in the distance, occasionally flecked with white. The palm trees and the red oleanders and the station dome shimmered in the sunlight.

The caramel-coloured floor tiles helped keep the house cool. In the morning I would walk through the house barefoot, looking out every window, gazing at the olive groves, the mountains, the vineyards. I would look out over the town and the sea, taking in the palm trees and the oleanders, and then I would wander among the jasmine, the roses, the bougainvillea and the lemon trees in my garden; it was a paradise without an Eve.

Remzi and I became good friends and he rushed over whenever I needed help. He even found a woman to take care of the house. As Hamiyet fluttered about the house, cleaning and cooking, she wore a smile that was always changing but never absent, one of those smiles that I could never quite define, a smile that intimated a secret sin, never shared in either happiness or grief.

But she spoke to the furniture.

She would whisper to cabinets, tables, chairs, sharing her secrets with them. Once I caught her arguing with a broom. But when she wasn't talking to the furniture she would give me all the gossip from town. More and more I started to feel like I had come to a den of sin, and as I got to know the people I could put faces to the stories.

Hamiyet was a tall, powerful, busty woman, and she wasn't shy. She'd roll her skirt up over her calves when she mopped the floors; and when she leaned over to pick something up, her breasts sometimes slipped out of her blouse. She never seemed to mind.

I was full of energy when I woke that morning.

Hamiyet was prattling away with the plates and the tablecloth, and the eggs she had made for my breakfast. It had rained the day before but the sun was shining in a bright blue sky, and the scent of wet grass and dirt, the fruit trees and the flowers was in the air.

I'd told the woman to meet me if she liked my books but I was beginning to have regrets.

I hadn't had a meal with a woman for such a long time. I was a lonely man. It seemed like no one in the world knew I still existed. And there wasn't even a splash when I released a new book. I was unhappy and angry, but I did my best to stay in touch with people. I tried to make peace in the hope of driving away a grudge people didn't even know I carried in my heart. But I had walled myself up in a monastery, and I was reluctant to venture outside. I had settled into a life of seclusion.

I was weak and fragile and this made me angry. I was full of anger and self-loathing, and I felt sorry for myself. Swinging back and forth between two very different states of mind, I either wallowed in defeat or I was drunk on the dream of an imminent victory, a commander setting out on one last adventure, rallying the troops, crying 'I'll show the world yet!' But then I would suddenly find myself steeped in the sadness that comes with inevitable defeat.

'If you like the books . . .' I had said to her, because I wanted her to read them, someone to read them, someone to say something. I wanted to end this oppressive silence. A buried resentment drove me to say it.

Normally I'd never mention my books to a woman before the first date.

I was frustrated for having told her, but no one notices the anger that rages inside me, the ungrounded fear and loathing. The bravado of a beaten man.

It wasn't easy facing these truths. I was on the verge of giving up and just not going.

But I was dying to see if she'd come.

I wanted her to like my books, and I missed those conversations you have on a first date, when every word is loaded, and anything can happen. I wanted to feel alive again, I wanted someone to admire me, someone who could lead me back to the world of people. I wanted to break down these walls built by arrogance and fragility. I needed someone, but I was afraid to admit it.

In her presence I knew that I'd become another man, whose confidence would rise with every sentence. A woman's voice would change me. I would become a garden swirling with all the scents that come after rain. I knew that much.

If she came everything would change.

The hours dragged by. I followed Hamiyet around the house. I collected fruit in the garden, watched the doves build nests above the veranda and flicked snails off the trees.

I arrived early and sat down at one of the tables under the magnolia tree in the garden.

Slowly the place filled up with customers. Bigwigs in dark suits alighted at tables like black birds. They were both a frightening and comical sight to behold, with their dark suits and loosened ties and enormous bellies, sweating in the heat. From time to time they'd look over at me suspiciously, making me feel like an outsider. I felt like a zebra among lions.

Then everyone turned to the door. She was there, looking out over the garden.

The black birds were staring at her hungrily. But she didn't seem to notice.

She greeted everyone in the garden as she came over to me, even exchanging a few words with some of the men, and for a moment it seemed their lust was compassion. They were calmed by her innocent expression, the coy and child-like look in her eye, her grace and the polite distance in her voice. They even seemed a little ashamed, and they wanted to protect her.

I felt the same compassion too, and the lust.

She had the power to tame these savage birds. In an instant. It was impressive to watch.

But I saw something else.

She wore two different smiles on her face, one on top of the other, and when she moved her lips you could almost see the other smile – a self-satisfied, ironic and belittling smile, the real emotions hidden beneath a gentler smile.

That's when I understood her most dangerous ability: to suddenly inspire compassion. Unhappy with his creation, God sent prophets to spread compassion and to preach against the dangers of lust. It was one of their main messages. But it went unheeded because God, master of contradictions, planted in the human heart a wild desire, a spark left by his awesome powers, that humans were destined to battle – God wanted so much to happen – and most were overwhelmed in the face of this power; if only in their dreams, the most pure of heart, committed the sin in their dreams. And although we could not obey the prophets' words we learned how to act in the face of sin, we learned how to face it down or take flight, if we do not eventually fall prey to it.

Compassion is another story.

Closing the doors on lust, God flung open a door to compassion. We travel easily on the road to compassion, with no doubt in our heart, determined and never afraid.

The enigmatic smile on her face told me she knew the power of compassion. Her compassion was a kind of Trojan

Horse – a God's compassion – and doors were flung open and she rode in with a conscience veiled. All lustful thoughts had been banished.

God wouldn't say it but I will: 'Be careful of the compassion of a beautiful woman.'

Some conceal selfishness and beauty with compassion, and they have the power to devastate and destroy.

It was an idea I wanted to include in my new book, a new message from a prophet, and I wanted God to know.

On second thought I realised that if I did a reader might issue his or her own Godly declaration.

'Mortals, beware the conceit of authors.'

A lust that inspired my conceit, and her compassion.

We were gladiators in the arena. I knew so much. But knowing so much did nothing for me.

I was helpless.

She was wearing a white dress with dark blue polka dots and chic sandals, red nail polish on her toes. I wanted to have her.

Then and there.

My emotions were locked away behind stronger walls but she could portray a range of emotions on her face whenever she wanted. That was something I simply couldn't do.

And her counterfeit emotions were displayed so brilliantly that hardly anyone could detect the smallest trace of what she was truly feeling.

When she flashed that innocent, vulnerable smile, even the truth behind was blinding.

As she sat down whispers rippled through the garden like a breath of wind. They were trying to work out who I was.

'I'm starving,' she said.

She had a beautiful smile.

The waiter hurried over to our table and she ordered nearly everything on the menu.

'Is all that for both of us?' I asked.

'Oh no, I'm just really hungry.'

'Hard to believe you're that hungry,' I said.

'I love to eat.'

'Seems so.'

She put her bag down on the chair beside her, a small leather bag with a little golden chain on the handle.

'Did you read the book?'

'Yes.'

'And?'

'I'm here, aren't I?'

'It wouldn't be a sin to say you liked it.'

'I'm not a real reader. I don't think my liking it would really mean anything. Does my opinion really matter?'

I wanted to reach out and grab her by the shoulder and say, 'Tell me.'

'Did you like it?' I asked, calmly.

'I did.'

'You hesitated. Did you really like it?'

'I loved it.'

'Then why don't you just say it? Say it like you just ordered all that food. You're allowed to speak about books in the same way, with the same appetite. It's not bad manners.'

A bashful smile fell over her face and for a moment she looked like a little girl.

'I really liked it. You write beautifully. And you have a thing about writers and women. You know a lot about them.'

'What did you like most?'

I wanted to talk about it, her favorite parts, memorable chapters and sentences. I wondered if she had specific comments to make. Did she really think that I was a good writer? Was she a real fan?

I'm not satisfied with light praise.

No writer ever is.

It is easier to accept a flat-out rejection than faint praise, which is much harder to bear.

Beneath a writer's confident and tough exterior, there's a fragile heart ready to break when there's even the slightest absence of excitement in someone's voice.

I can be with a woman who hasn't read my work, I've been with many; but I could never be with someone who finds my writing mundane; and I certainly couldn't make love to a woman who felt this way.

'There were some very touching moments.'

'Which ones?'

As she looked at me I wondered if she pitied me or if she understood that I valued her opinion deeply. I didn't know. But she had really read the book.

'Did you finish it?'

'I was up all night . . . I was very impressed. How can you do that?'

I leaned back and felt the stress leave my body. I had become desperate. I desperately needed this woman, who hadn't read a book in years, to praise my work.

It was pathetic but I was overjoyed to hear what she had to say.

'I undress, stick my head in the fridge and then I write.'

'What?' she said, incredulously, her eyes wide open in surprise.

'No, that's not how I write,' I said, laughing. 'That's what Marquez said. But it seems like a terrible method.'

The waiter arrived with our food and soon the table was covered with salads, stuffed mussels, chicken liver, meatballs, pastries and fried aubergine.

'Are we really going to eat all this?' I asked.

'I'm hungry.'

And she really was. She had an incredible appetite. We settled into a comfortable rhythm as we ate. Almost in a whisper, she recounted what she remembered from the book, as if sharing a secret with me, something that had really happened, speaking about the characters like they were real. 'If you liked it that much, why don't you read more?'

She leaned over the table and said conspiratorially, 'I'm too easily swept away. I get the real world and the fantasy world all mixed up. I can't distinguish what happened here or there.

It's a jumble in my head.' Then she added, 'You know, it really scares me sometimes.'

I was beguiled by her innocence and her vulnerability and I felt something like love. But at the time I had no idea what had prompted the feelings. She had the power to erase all the preconceptions I had about her. The moment she stepped into the garden she had made me forget.

She could do that.

'I read all the classics when I was a kid. My mother encouraged us to read them. I was lost in *Anna Karenina*. For a while I really believed I was living in a Russian palace.'

It occurred to me that I didn't even know this woman's name. She'd never told me and I'd never asked.

'I don't even know your name,' I said.

'Zuhal. My grandfather chose it.'

There was a ripple of movement and I looked up to see a man walking into the garden. He was wearing a dark suit, long black pointy shoes, a loose tie, and a tough but serene expression on his face. He wasn't handsome but he had that rough look many women found attractive. There was a certain confidence in the way he walked and the look in his eye told me that he was a ladies' man. A group of men trailed behind him, their heads lowered. He was clearly a powerful man and respected in a man's world. Although he was younger than most of the other men in the garden, they all greeted him with respect. Waiters rushed over to him.

He suddenly stopped at our table and put his hand on Zuhal's shoulder, as if I wasn't even there, and asked: 'How are you?'

Zuhal had sensed his arrival before I had and she knew who he was – that was all too clear. And though she didn't look up, she blushed when she felt his hand on her shoulder.

'Fine,' she said, looking up.

'You're eating a lot. There won't be anything left for us.'

They were roughly the same age, maybe he was a year or two older, but the self-assurance in his voice gave me the feeling that no one there could have questioned his authority; he had the air of superiority an older man shows a younger lover, almost a fatherly love.

Zuhal had just tamed a garden of savage birds with a smile but now she was a shy little girl.

'I was hungry,' she said, like a student giving a teacher a bad excuse.

'Be careful now or you'll put on weight . . .'

He looked me over for a moment, memorising all the details of my face and the way I looked at him. He would learn everything there was to know about me in less than five minutes, at least everything that was known about me in town.

'Who's that?' I asked, after he had left, unable to conceal the distaste in my voice.

'The mayor.'

'Why does he treat you like you work for him?'

'We were lovers. We met at university,' she said, pushing her plate away.

'And now?'

'We're not together any more.'

She narrowed her eyes.

'But I'm still in love with him.'

Her frank and sudden confession was devastating; I was reduced to nothing. But then again I knew that a woman would never share such a thing with a man she'd just met unless she felt something for him. In that moment she seemed so pre-occupied that she wouldn't have noticed if I got up and left.

We were silent.

I couldn't know what she was thinking, apparently about the man. I wanted to ask her why she'd just told me her feelings for him. A moment earlier she'd been my greatest fan. How could she betray me so suddenly?

She had stopped eating. I asked her if she was finished and she nodded. 'I'm full,' she said.

'I wouldn't take him seriously.'

'I know. I just don't feel like eating now. Ready to go?'

We paid the bill and left.

She walked straight out of the garden, looking down at the ground.

Not one of the men was looking at her now. It was strange. They acted like she wasn't even there.

There was a nervous energy in the air.

VI

'He has a heart of stone,' she said.

Sunlight was shimmering off the train station dome, washing the street in a shower of light, the oleanders glimmering red.

I am fascinated by women. I listen to them like a treasure hunter, poring over a newly discovered map. I listen for clues between the lines, deciding which path I should take and where I should stop to rest, and where I need to dig.

But I had suddenly lost interest.

'Are we just friends?' I asked. 'Telling each other love stories?'

She was silent.

I wanted to show her that I could be as rude as that man who had treated her so badly in the restaurant, and when I was there with her. I wanted her to understand that she didn't have to allow people to get away with so much.

'I'm in love with him but I like you too. Isn't that possible?'

'Of course . . . Why not? But I'd rather you loved me . . . That's more fun. But why do you like me?'

'Weren't we together last night?'

I didn't know what to say. She laughed at the confused expression on my face.

'I was reading your novel. While you slept. So we were together in a way. I was thinking of you, thinking of you writing, wondering what kind of person you were in real life, and which characters were like you, and I was curious to know if those women were your lovers in real life. Were they?'

'No.'

'You're lying.'

'I never lie.'

'Then you're a real liar,' she said, laughing.

It was like nothing had happened at the restaurant, like she'd never seen that man. Books can work miracles. They create a powerful bond between reader and writer.

'I want to know how you make love.'

'That's easy enough to find out.'

'But I'm leaving tonight.'

'When are you coming back?'

'I don't know.'

I was silent, feeling the heat rising up from the streets. Little shop doors were ajar, like the entrances to dark caves. I was disappointed.

Suddenly I was a complete stranger in town, like a child dropped off at a boarding school by his mother. I thought about leaving too.

She had told me she was leaving like it was the most natural thing in the world, without hesitation, and with the intimacy of lovers. It made me feel like we would have made love that night if she didn't have to go, and that we would when she returned. I was falling in love with a woman in love with someone else. But she was closer to me in so many ways.

'Why is everyone so afraid of him?'

'They think he's had people killed.'

'Has he?'

'I don't know.'

'You never asked?'

'I did.'

'And?'

'He thought I was mad.'

'And you said?'

'Nothing.'

Now sitting all alone on this bench in the dark emptiness, I can hear the way she said those words: 'I'm leaving tonight.'

I remember that moment as sheer bliss. Moments like these are unforgettable. They forge an unbreakable bond between a man and a woman, and nothing can overshadow or undermine them. It is an intimate moment that reminds us of animal warmth, the warmth of a woman's skin.

I am a man and my desires are both a blessing and a curse, at least that's how I see it. I have hunted after carnal pleasures, never hesitating to leap into catastrophe. What did I find there? It was always that 'moment' when a woman surrenders. And I'm not afraid to admit that I savour these moments of surrender. That dark maze of lust and sheer desire has nothing to do with the modern world; it is primitive and savage.

I cherish these moments.

Moments when a woman becomes a mermaid, slipping out of a mother-of-pearl oyster shell silvered by the light of the moon, casting off all her other roles. Then she is only female, surrendering naturally in a soft light. For the most part these moments unfold far from the prying eyes of others, in quiet corners, in bedrooms with the curtains drawn; but some women can surrender in broad daylight, oblivious to the crowds, and with just a glance, a smile, a word; it is a miraculous moment of pure intimacy, a moment of unforgettable joy. These are moments made by God.

Earthly moments that belong to the natural world and to God.

Innocent. Pure. Untainted.

In those moments you enter a world of sin but wearing all your innocence. I have never felt as happy or as innocent any other time. Then I feel the strength of being a man and the complete absence of power that comes with surrendering to another human being. This was such a moment.

Those words changed the direction of our relationship.

We would have a secret life together, in a secret organisation: dangerous and exciting.

We both knew it. There was nothing for us to say. That moment had come and gone, changing us and the world.

Her love for another man had melted in the heat of the moment and I was only saddened by the thought of her leaving that evening.

Suddenly I felt so terribly alone.

Loneliness. God and I know the feeling all too well. It's like he's trying to teach me the feeling, choosing to teach the emotion to select individuals, and using horrific coincidences to make his point. How could someone's mother, father and wife all die in different traffic accidents? You couldn't get away with that in a book. Only God can. I know because I have seen his work with my own eyes. Did he simply want to instil in me a fear of driving? Well, then he got it wrong. I'm afraid of people.

Sometimes I feel like I'm standing at a dangerous crossroad, and I fear that anyone standing next to me could be hit by a car.

Loneliness has taught me this.

But it's really not so bad.

You get used to it. You even start to like it.

It's a luxury to be free from all concerns, living like a turtle. Your home on your back. No worries in the world. Sometimes I think that our desire for possessions has to do with our bond with other people. In the end we have no choice but to leave all these things with someone. I never wanted to own more than I could carry on my back. I never wanted more than that. But I could have more. It's strange to think that I'm rich. Another coincidence. I didn't earn any of my fortune: I inherited it. I simply can't work for money. I like to spend it but I don't like to work for it.

I suppose if I hadn't come into money I'd be a beggar or a con man. You see, writing is a mix of the two: you fool people with your lies, take their money and then beg for their admiration. Sadly I was never very successful. I wasn't able to deceive anyone. I won no adoring fans.

Zuhal was my first and only fan.

My head was spinning with conflicting emotions. I was on

a fast-moving swing: soaring forward, I felt grateful and I wanted to keep her for ever; then swinging back, I felt nothing but disdain and I wanted to belittle her. She wasn't interested in literature, and I knew that I shouldn't take her opinion seriously, but she was the only person I knew who actually liked my books.

As we walked arm in arm through the back streets of town, bright yellow light bounced off the walls along the narrow streets. Some were no more than two metres wide. Women sat on throw rugs they'd spread out on the doorsteps in the shade.

These were houses from another time, with tall, carved wooden doors, and red geraniums bursting out of oriel windows.

Almost everything in the town seemed from another time. We walked in and out of a little square with an enormous tree and a fountain in the middle, children racing about in all directions. Miracles sometimes happen between a woman and a man, and as we walked together I felt us growing closer, as if with every step we knew more about each other, and without even speaking.

Was it real? It didn't matter. I could feel it and that was what was important. An emotion strong enough to make its own reality.

We were both willing to walk those streets together, lingering in each other's company, confessing something, forging a strong and lasting bond.

I suppose that was the day I discovered that this was love: wandering through the streets with someone, side by side. In one of the little squares we sat on stools at a shaded coffeehouse.

'Aren't you afraid of him?' I asked.

'Sometimes. But not the way I fear others. His heartlessness scares me . . . He's playing with me. And there's nothing I can do about it except try to make him angry. Sometimes at night I ask God to save me from him. With all my heart. You know, it's really strange. It's like wishing for death . . . It's like I need to love him to keep on living. I'm pathetic.'

These confessions didn't make me angry any more. Just the

opposite: the more she told me about her love for this man, the closer I felt to her; every word she said about him brought us closer. As she talked it seemed any fear she might have had of being close to me was slipping away. 'Actually I'm afraid of you too,' she said. 'Maybe even more than I am of him. I read your book. You're heartless too. Somehow I just know it. But I don't know how.'

She paused for a moment, a puzzled look on her face.

'Is it that I only fall for heartless men? I can't be that pathetic.'

Before I could come up with an answer the proprietor arrived with Turkish coffee in the handle-less cups you see in miniature paintings, and Zuhal was fascinated by them. She turned to the man and asked where he'd got the cups. They seemed like old friends. He said he'd bought them from a woman in the street market.

And then she started bargaining for them, and having a great time with it. I can't remember now, but in the end she bought the cups for a ridiculously low price, far lower than the proprietor ever would have expected. Then she stood up and walked over to a woman sitting on her doorstep. They exchanged a few words and then she was back at our little table with a gift box and wrapping paper.

After wrapping up the cups, she said, 'All right, let's go. I don't want to be late.'

She left that evening.

Towards midnight, I got a message from her. Just three words. 'I miss you.'

VII

Sometimes I listen solely to my instincts, like an animal.

After that night we corresponded almost every night on the internet, an infinite universe beyond reality, where everything is possible – fantasies forever unfolding – and there is nothing to stop you or ever slow you down.

Every day and every night you are born again online to live a completely different life. Hurtling through endless space, far from the rules of the world, its standards and routines. Seeds sprout faster there, relationships develop more quickly.

I was new to this world but I soon discovered the possibilities. Although we became more intimate day by day, I never suggested that we should see each other in person.

My instincts told me that we should first spend time in 'space' before we met again in the real world.

So I led a double life.

At night it was a life with a woman I never saw and never touched, sharing secrets, nourishing an intimacy – a life that was ours alone.

I spent my days in the coffeehouse next to Remzi's restaurant. It was the heart of the town, absorbing stories and then pumping them back out.

The proprietor of the coffeehouse had a limp and wore a perpetual frown. They'd given him the nickname 'Centipede'. I never learned his real name.

At first they kept their distance from me. They didn't reject me altogether – I suppose because of what Remzi had said about me – and they certainly weren't hostile, but they didn't invite me into their circle. And I didn't try to ingratiate myself with them. I just sat there on my own, reading my newspapers and books.

My first real contact with them was through the newspaper. They'd come over one by one to ask if they could see the newspaper I had just finished reading. And I was always happy to pass them along. Every day I bought new ones. I would read through one, put it down on the table then wait for someone to come and pick it up.

They weren't in the habit of buying newspapers, but if they came across one they would flip through it. They especially liked reading the paper the day after a football match. They would pore over the sports pages, exchange papers with each other and then lose themselves in a heated discussion. Eventually they even started reading the front pages, and the magazine section.

Coming into the coffeehouse every morning with news-papers under my arm, I could sense they had been waiting for me. Centipede would scamper over to me with a coffee. There was silence until I had finished my first paper, but as soon as I'd put it on the table the person closest to me would ask if he could read it.

I used to enjoy watching the way they would read, studying their movements and reactions.

Soon I had my regular table – it seemed they had made some kind of agreement, because no one ever sat there – and when I came and sat down people would scramble for tables near mine. The person closest to me always got the newspaper first. Tables near mine were like prime opera boxes. I was start-led to see how I'd become the most esteemed customer in the coffeehouse just because I bought newspapers.

Later they started to ask me questions when they discussed politics. I gave them brusque answers and they could never quite work out what I really thought. But there was a sea change when they discovered that I knew more about football than they did. I told them I used to play for the Beşiktaş youth team but had to give up football because of a knee injury. It was a lie. But they didn't doubt me for a second.

I had become the coffeehouse sage.

They consulted me about almost everything.

That's how I managed to seep into the inner workings of the town.

They told me all the gossip: tragedies and trivial misfortunes, sumptuous weddings and fiery disputes over land – some even said that the entire town would be razed to the ground and rebuilt – the project for a monumental hotel on the beach, the church on the top of the hill, supposedly built by an apostle of Jesus Christ, whose body was rumoured to have been buried there, and how there was a vast treasure beneath the church; they told me about promiscuous women and the strained relations between various gangs, murders and blood feuds, now and then stopping to roll a joint and offering me a drag. I would smile and politely decline.

One night I imagined the town rising up on a cloud of marijuana smoke before it vanished into the sky. I wanted to stay sober so I could see that day.

Everyone was always a little stoned. Even the women in town. 'What do you expect, abi? Even the kids smoke,' they would tell me.

But they were always guarded – even when they were a little high – and only gave me half the story, repeating the same rumours over and over, never touching on what really piqued my curiosity, never telling me what was happening on a deeper level.

Then I met someone who would lead me to the other world.

He was a young man who occasionally came to collect Hamiyet in the evening. I wasn't sure of their relationship, but he called her his 'aunt'. And supposedly he was staying with her.

I often saw him at the coffeehouse. He hardly spoke to anyone there. He would sit alone, never joining the discussions or arguments, never laughing at other people's jokes. He just sat there and smoked. They used to say that he was smoking away all the money that I paid his aunt.

He always gave me the impression that a chasm lay between him and all the other regulars in the coffeehouse. He wasn't cowed or sheepish; he was a strong and powerful young man. He didn't seem to need other people. He was content with whatever it was that separated him from the others and didn't want to share it with anyone.

It was the first time I'd seen a state of happiness so completely independent.

Then I realised that every afternoon he disappeared for a couple hours. And not just him: all the other young men disappeared too.

One afternoon I stood up and said that I was going for a walk, and I followed the young men. I didn't have to go very far: they were all packed into an internet café on the street just behind the coffeehouse.

It was a dim and clammy little shop that reeked of marijuana.

I only had to go to the place a couple times when it wasn't busy to work out just which chat rooms they were visiting.

Then I started going home in the afternoons. It wasn't long before I tracked down the young men in different chat rooms, and I would strike up conversations with them using various fake identities. Soon I knew just how each person communicated and I could put a real face to a persona in the virtual world. I got to the point where I had infiltrated the town's entire online network by tracking everyone's online address, their usernames, the groups they belonged to and the chat rooms they visited. For the most part, they were chatting with women.

In the afternoons nearly half of the town vanished into this virtual world where they changed their identities and searched for people with whom they could share their secrets, people who were like them, and they would make love.

Over time I came to know who was looking for a man or a woman; and when people found each other they engaged in a conversation full of all kinds of unimaginative sexual banter.

Some had specific proclivities and stronger imaginations; they were looking for someone like them with whom they could share adventures they would never tell anyone.

Discovering all this, I felt like I was in the underworld.

I could see the invisible.

And it tore my life apart.

In the evenings, I chatted with Zuhal and in the afternoons I chatted with the people of the town in a boundless world of realities nothing like the world above ground. The solitary life I led in town was calm and mundane in comparison. The virtual world was dramatically different, full of colour and excitement.

But the unexpected thing was the way the unseen, unspoken and indiscernible truths of the real world cropped up in the virtual world, which was surprisingly familiar.

Looking back, I'm amazed how the half-stoned inhabitants of a sleepy town were able to sink so deeply into sin.

Whose masterpiece made these people? In a small town they lived like kings, openly baring their sins.

Who created all the sins that caused so many books to be banned?

Who is responsible for the sins that people have committed since not long after their creation?

Tonight, on this bench, I see God all around me, and in my mind.

Why were human beings created with souls capable of these sins?

Is the sinner more sinful than the creator of the sin?

Is God a sinner?

If God created sin when he made us, then why punish us for it?

And if God didn't create sin, is there something in this universe that he doesn't know? Is there a limit to his power?

Why make me a murderer?

Why have me kill the person he wanted dead?

I see the first light of dawn rising up over the hills behind the town, reminding me that my time is dwindling, and I am restless.

How long would it take them to find out?

I had to do something.

I was so tired. It seemed easier to bury myself in the past than to come up with a plan. When the future was so frightening the past seemed that much more alluring.

Though I spent so much of my time searching for reality in an unreal world, I kept going to the coffeehouse every morning. Sometimes I'd have meatballs at Remzi's place for lunch and sometimes I'd go to the Çinili restaurant and eat with the bigwigs in their black suits.

They always look at me but never approach me.

I can feel that it makes them tense to see a stranger in town. They have many secrets and every stranger is a threat in their eyes.

One day I was sitting at the Çinili restaurant when there was a flutter of movement and I realised that the mayor had arrived. I had already learned so much about him. But did he know that? Stepping into the garden, he spotted me almost immediately and came over to my table.

'Hello. Mustafa Gürz,' he said. 'I'm the mayor.'

I stood up and we shook hands. Looking him in the eye, I didn't know what to say. For a second it occurred to me that he could snap his fingers and someone in the restaurant would have jumped up and killed me. I'm not sure where I got that idea but I clearly remember the chill that ran up my spine.

'If you don't mind, I thought I might join you. We can eat and have a little chat.'

'Please, have a seat.'

Waiters arrived at the table with food before he had even ordered.

He smiled. It was a warm smile that offset the harsh contours of his face. Clearly he was one of those rare types who seemed both gentle and cruel. But more surprising than his smile was what he said as he leaned towards me across the table: 'I've read your books.'

I'm ashamed to admit this now but I think I blushed. I could even feel my ears burning. It was so unexpected that even in the depths of my unconscious there was no appropriate response, no right answer. 'Is that so?' was all I managed to say. And still smiling, he said, 'Yes.' For a moment I thought that he was mocking me.

'When did you read them?'

'Over the weekend.'

'Just recently, then . . .'

'Yes, I just read them. It took me a little while to get around to it.'

I stammered out another 'Is that so?', feeling like a boxer being pummelled in the ring, staggering to stay up on my feet.

'I really liked them. For whatever reason I just can't get into contemporary novels, I like the classics. I like writers who make you think, but I think books that analyse people are something else altogether. I think literature should be more about people than events. But then again what does my opinion matter, you're the writer. Let's just say I can personally relate to those kinds of books.'

'So you enjoy reading,' I said.

'Is there anything more important? I think literature is one of man's most praiseworthy pursuits. Greater than science. Consider Jules Verne. He took us to space before science did.'

He paused for a moment. 'Would you like something to drink?'

'I'll have a rakı,' I said. Drink was undoubtedly invented for just such times.

The conversation was so unexpected, I felt lost.

He ordered two glasses of rakı.

'So how do you know Zuhal?' he asked, politely, but a shadow fell over his face.

'We met here,' I said. 'On the plane. Why does a small town like this even have an airport?'

'People here are a little bit mad. Mahmut Amca, former president of our Chamber of Commerce, was always coming and going and he got fed up with the bad roads, which you can imagine were a lot worse back then. First he wanted to repave the roads but he found out how expensive that was going to be so he decided to build an airport. People thought he was insane, and they protested, but he insisted, saying that the airport would be cheaper than new roads. So he did it and he bought a little propeller plane. His son, Teoman, bought a new plane, for personal use and commercial flights. Then he bought a crop-duster and in the end it turned out to be a profitable investment. And we were happy to have our own airport. We travel by plane and not by bus.'

Raising his glass, he toasted my health. Then he asked, 'So have you come to our town to write a new book?'

'Let's see. I was looking for somewhere quiet, and there was something about this place.'

'I wouldn't call this town quiet,' he said, looking me in the eye.

'I've heard,' I said. 'All the murders.'

'Oh not so many really, just a couple of cases, but they talk as if someone's shot every day.'

'Why the killings?'

'It's all about land. Property values are only going to rise. Everyone knows that. So people are racing to get their hands on land. Then it quickly becomes a blood feud. And people here are a little behind the times. Revenge is still a powerful emotion. If you ask me, money is a stronger incentive than revenge.'

'You have a difficult job,' I said, beginning to feel the rakı. It was just what I needed; I was pulling myself together.

'Of course. That's inevitable but I'm used to it now.'

'Do they ever threaten you?'

'Me?' he said, surprised. The sincerity in his voice was real; clearly he had never considered someone actually threatening him. 'No, people here would never go so far.'

'Are they afraid of you?'

'Oh no, please, it's not that, it's just that my family has been here for such a long time, and there are a lot of us, so let's just say it's respect for the family.'

He had such a calm and natural confidence and I realised he was condescending to me in the same way he did to everyone else. He had already ruled me out as a potential rival.

He treated me like a valuable but useless antique vase, never offending or threatening me. I was faced with a dilemma. If I were to submit to his courtesy, which was gift-wrapped in pride, he'd place me among the bigwigs and he'd speak to Zuhal about me with a sort of affection; but if I were to counter with the same indifferent air of arrogance, he'd never speak well of me, and prevent me from learning more about the people in town.

I was caught between curiosity and pride.

I decided to take a step back to a place where I was safe from a sudden attack of kindness or his insolent aggression. But it wasn't really a conscious decision, rather an action seemingly independent of my thoughts.

'Are you and Zuhal old friends?' I asked.

I knew that on the subject of Zuhal it was best to feign ignorance. Surely both of us would talk about our meeting with her separately, reshaping the scene in our own way.

I imagined the way she would laugh at us.

'We're friends from university,' he said. 'We went to the same college in Minnesota. You wouldn't believe it. Someone from here must have discovered the place because there were a lot of students from around here at the time. Zuhal majored in economics . . .'

'And you?' I asked with a smile. 'Literature?'

'No,' he said, laughing. 'We own all of these olive groves here, so my dad wanted me to study agricultural engineering.'

'Why the interest in literature?'

'My uncle. There's a black sheep in every family. He loves reading.'

Then he paused: 'Black sheep in the positive sense. I don't want you to get the wrong idea.'

He had a polite and cultivated side: and the courtesy was genuine.

'No offence taken,' I said. Then I laughed and added: 'In my books the "black sheep" are almost always portrayed in a positive light.'

'Then let's drink to them.'

At that moment I sensed that we might actually become good friends, despite the strange tension between us. One of the strangest friendships is the one between two men pursuing the same woman and we seemed to be heading in that direction. I was both excited and a little nervous. 'You were telling me about your uncle . . .'

'He wasn't interested in the family business. We have a little house up in the olive groves, which was built so we could spend summers there but no one ever really went. I used to go up there with my uncle. Like I said, he wasn't interested in working, but he was a really fun guy, always making fun of people − you'd like him. He'd bring me books and the way he'd talk about them inspired me to read them. And I really enjoyed them. Introverts like reading, but you already know that.'

I didn't take him for an introvert and the look on my face made him laugh.

'One can be lonely in a crowd,' he said. 'It's a bit of a cliché I'm afraid but, well, sometimes clichés are true.' So he had some intellectual modesty. His overdone confidence had been undermined by the thought that he'd said something silly. So there were subjects in which he didn't feel entirely comfortable. I was pleasantly surprised to see that on matters in which he didn't see himself as the sole authority he was sensitive, even shy.

In my contentment I ignored the clear indications of my own malice. There are times when I can't see what I'm doing, and this was one of them.

'Life would be that much harder without clichés,' I said. 'Clichés constitute the courtesy that life has taught us. And it's true that you can be alone in a crowd. Unfortunately crowds are no cure for loneliness. Loneliness is an illness that can only be cured by one person. There's another cliché for you . . . But who could deny it?'

'Some might. But then they probably don't know anything about loneliness.'

We looked at each other.

Then we both burst out laughing and everyone in the restaurant turned to look at us. It was the last thing I had expected.

I don't think we really knew why we were laughing but something about our situation and the conversation we were having was suddenly incredibly funny.

He looked at his watch.

'I should get going. There are things I have to do.'

Standing up, he said, 'Some friends are coming over this weekend. We're going to roast a lamb on the spit. You should come over if you have the time. Zuhal's coming.'

Checkmate.

I was completely thrown. I was chatting with Zuhal every night (we knew the most intimate details about each other) but she'd never told me that she was going to the party.

She had told Mustafa.

So while she was leading me on, she was also speaking to him and even planning to see him.

The blow was devastating. I could hardly control myself.

'Zuhal's coming too,' I said, without concealing my surprise.

He looked at me intently. He'd hit me just where he wanted.

'That's right. You should come.'

'Thanks,' I said. 'I'll try to make it.'

I had another drink after he left. When the other people in the restaurant got up to leave they nodded when our eyes met.

I had been accepted into high society.

But the initiation ceremony would be far more painful.

VIII

The moment I got online I couldn't help but ask.

'are you coming to town this weekend?'

The answer was brief and to the point.

'no.'

'mustafa said you were.'

The screen was blank.

'you talked to mustafa?'

'he came and sat with me at the Çinili restaurant. we had lunch together.'

'he wants to get to know you. what did he say about me?'

'he's roasting a lamb on his farm this weekend. he said you were coming. i was surprised. you never told me you were going.'

'well i'm not. he sent me a message about it, asking me to come, and i'll try.'

'then i suppose he assumed you were going.'

'he only hears what he wants to. he's got a special talent for that. what else did he say about me?'

'nothing. but then he did say you went to the same university.'

'anything else?'

'no.'

'what did he want from you?'

'he'd read my books. wanted to get to know me.'

'where did he find them?'

'i assume he ordered them.'

'so he saw us together and had someone look into you . . . be careful, he's dangerous.'

'we talked about books. he likes reading. we had a nice lunch.'

'he's well read. he actually reads a lot. knows a lot too. history, philosophy. and he can be nice when he wants to be. but that's just what's dangerous about him. i could never tell who was the real mustafa. was it that bright and loveable man or that rude and savage one . . . did he say anything else about me?'

'no he didn't.'

'he was trying to lower your guard, get you to talk . . . he's crafty.'

'he asked me where we met.'

'what did you say?'

'on the plane.'

'and what did he say?'

'nothing.'

'he'll check at the airport to see if it's true . . . he's trying to work out if there's anything between us . . . he's jealous . . . i've never met anyone so jealous . . . but he never shows it.'

'if he doesn't then how do you know he is?'

'he's doesn't let on right away but he gives me hell later . . . it went on like that for years . . . at first i never knew why he was angry. then i made the connection. the more he upset me the more i made him jealous. we destroyed each other.'

'why was he so jealous?'

'i didn't have to do much. if i wore something sexy when we went out or if I smiled at a man he would go mad. on the way home he would start an argument with me about some-thing . . . he would say i was acting like a whore. he was more in love with me before. then somehow he got over me and i fell in love with him.'

'he doesn't seem to be over you. look at the way he's looking into me. he's read my books. still checking up on you. then he has lunch with me.'

'he's not in love with me but we were lovers for a while. now he acts like he still owns me.'

'you're exaggerating. he doesn't seem like that kind of guy.'

'so one lunch and you know the man i'm in love with better than I do?'

'maybe.'

'he's bright. he can seem however he wants to seem.'

'is he that bright?'

'very. brightest person i know.'

'if he's so bright then why is he the mayor of a little town and not doing something else?'

'why should he? he's the sultan here. no one can challenge him. you should see the gangsters who hang out with him. they don't even look him in the eye when they talk to him. he was offered a seat in parliament several times but he never wanted it.'

'why?'

'I'm in charge here, he says, why should I go and serve someone else?'

'bright.'

'like i said.'

'so no one can challenge him?'

'something would happen to anyone who did . . . he'd have them arrested for drugs, or shot, or he'd catch them with someone and create a scandal. he's got eyes and ears everywhere. knows everything. can do whatever he wants.'

'does he have ties to the police?'

'have you seen the police chief's mercedes?'

'no.'

'you will. he goes to crime scenes in it.'

'doesn't anyone complain?'

'no one wants any trouble. what can they say? he's the sultan of the land. you should be careful.'

'we had a nice chat. no animosity.'

'he doesn't have any friends. too proud.'

'he was polite enough to me.'

'he knows how to be. he's from a good family. his mother was quite the lady. then she got ill. she raised him well but he's a black sheep. takes after his father.'

'doesn't sound like a man you're really in love with.'

'i love him despite everything i know. that's the problem. i know he's the last person i should be in love with. but i am. i'm pitiful. an idiot. are you bored of me?'

'no.'

'why not?'

'i suppose because you're beautiful.'

'i'm not. he says that too but I don't think I am.'

'but you are.'

'all right, let's say that i am. is that enough?'

'it is.'

'really?'

'really.'

'how?'

I could sense the tone of her voice in that last word. She was getting bored with conversation and wanted to make love.

We would make love in words.

The internet is one of the strangest things invented by man.

There is a different kind of pleasure that comes with making love like this. In these flights, Zuhal spoke an entirely different language, using words she never used before, pushing away the idea of physical appearance. In her desire she stepped out of herself and became someone else. And without ever touching her I was electrified by her words.

But I wasn't driven out of my mind. It was the idea that she was writing them. And it was more than just a jolt of joy. It was immense. And habit-forming. I was hooked. And so was she.

It soon became an addiction.

We had learned how to make love without carnal knowledge. We knew what we liked, we knew the words that stoked desire, and we knew the words to use as we came to a climax. We knew each other.

In that realm we knew each other well.

Perhaps better than anyone could know another.

There were no obstacles, no boundaries, no rules. We were

not even there. We had vaulted above the constraints of our own bodies.

We were infinite.

Immersed in a terrifying freedom where everything was possible, a realm of ambiguity that cast everything in a brilliant light, a darkness that made everything brighter than it really was.

The sky above us had receded and the world was devoid of life.

It was only us.

The only two people alive in this universe.

All our secrets were revealed, out in the open space, and there was nothing left to contain them.

My instincts had served me well. I was on the right path. Giving voice to her secret, unspoken desires, pent up for so many years, Zuhal was able to let herself go in this seemingly infinite world. If we had physically made love, I doubt that she would have experienced such freedom.

Most people in this world make love, and they do it well. They reach an understanding, and they know joy, but some experience more: they seek dishes not on the common menu; they are curious about the specials; and when they meet others seeking to satisfy their passions with exotic fare, they leave the world behind, taking refuge in a shared intimacy, creating a new life for themselves in which they are Gods and Goddesses of a universe all their own, in which the map of lovemaking is redrawn to match their desires. Travelling to distant lands on an unparalleled adventure, they savour new delights.

Zuhal said we shared the same 'pathologies'. Perhaps she got the idea from one of my old books. For reasons I cannot fully understand she derived a perverse pleasure from injecting words I had written in the past into my present life. Messaging with her, I also came to know pleasures I had never known before.

If we hadn't met in that world, our shared pathologies would never have emerged; and they were ours, impossible to explain to anyone else. But we knew that anything was possible.

We never held back: we told each other everything, discovering our shared desires. We believed it was a miracle.

Knowing this brought us the kind of pleasure that others only know after having made love for a long time.

And that night, as on all the other nights, we drew long and hard on the wellspring of pleasure that came from our shared pathology.

I lost myself completely.

Everything could be forgotten.

But I knew so much.

I had learned so much.

In this unreal world we experienced a reality more freely than we could ever have in the real world.

If I had to make a choice between the virtual and the real I would choose the former, because it is that much more real.

IX

When I woke up the next morning Hamiyet was on the veranda, chattering with a bird as she prepared my breakfast. It seemed they were having a lively conversation.

Later I wandered down into town along narrow, stone-paved streets lined with jasmine, rose bushes and tangerine trees. I arrived at the coffeehouse and I sat down at my table under an enormous olive tree. Centipede brought me my coffee and the tables around me began to fill up.

I started reading my papers.

When I finished one someone came over and took it away.

Just across from me I noticed a man I had never seen there before. He was wearing a black shirt and black trousers, and he was intently reading through the horse racing pages. Though he seemed outwardly calm there was something about him, perhaps the way he was dressed, or his posture, or the way he glanced at the other customers from time to time, that gave me the impression he was trouble.

I looked him over and then went back to my paper. A little later one of those yellow minibuses that run to neighbouring villages pulled up in front of the coffeehouse and a short man stepped out onto the street. I looked around for Centipede, hoping to order another coffee. The short man calmly walked over to the man in the black shirt, pulled out a gun, pointed it at his eye and pulled the trigger. The man in the black shirt had just looked up to see who was there.

The shooter had stepped aside before the blood splattered.

The victim's head flew back and a brown liquid exploded

from the socket that once held his eye, which seemed to have burst from the back of his head.

Then he toppled to the floor in his chair.

The short man fired another shot and then calmly walked out, smiling at me as he left. I think he even winked. The minibus was waiting for him outside. He hopped in and the engine roared into life and they were gone.

Everyone in the coffeehouse seemed frozen in time. It was years after a massive volcanic eruption and we had all turned to stone.

Nobody moved. Nobody said a word.

It was like we had all been shot dead.

Then suddenly we all surged back to life and people rushed over to the victim.

Centipede leaned over and took a good look.

'He's dead,' he said, almost serenely, as if it was the most natural thing in the world.

I was still in my chair.

I was trying to work out how the man's eye had burst out the back of his head. It had to be the bullet, but then I was convinced that I had seen an eyeball. That's what I saw but my mind wouldn't accept it. A little later there were sirens and the police arrived. They pushed the crowd away but told everyone to stay, explaining that they would take statements from all the witnesses.

Then a steel-blue Mercedes stopped at the door.

The local police chief stepped out of the car.

He was a stocky man with broad shoulders and short hair. Dressed in a black suit, he wore a disdainful expression on his face. Everyone made way for him as he stepped over to the body. He had hardly looked at the man before he said: 'Anyone know this guy?'

He seemed a little disgusted. No one answered. Clearly no one wanted to get involved. But later Remzi told me that the victim was 'one of Oleander's men'.

'Get a statement from everyone here,' said the police chief.

It seemed like that was all he was going to do. As he made his way back to his car, he recognised me, or perhaps pretended to see me for the first time; I couldn't be sure.

'Are you the writer?' he asked, imperiously.

So he knew who I was.

'Yes,' I said and he briskly sat down at my table.

'Good material here for your books, don't you think?' he said.

'Why was the man shot?' I asked.

'I don't know. Mafia fighting over land. The dogs are always killing each other. We'll find out soon enough.'

'Seem to be a lot of murders around here.'

'Not so many really. People exaggerate.'

'Can't you stop them?'

Slowly leaning back in his chair, he looked me carefully in the eye.

'Now, I am responsible for public safety. Am I not?'

He was expecting an answer and so I had no choice but to say, 'Yes, that's right.'

'That's right,' he said, nodding his head. 'These people are animals, are they not?' And this time he went on before I could answer. 'Where do animals live? In the jungle. Isn't that right? Yes, it is. This is a jungle. How do you keep order in the jungle? You can't stop animals from killing one another, can you? You can't. So then what's my job? My job is to prevent the forest from going up in flames. Isn't that right? To make sure people here are safe. Now can anyone harm the people here? No, they can't. If they did, we would take care of them. Isn't that right? No theft, no muggings, no harassment here. This is the world's safest town. But yes, animals will keep killing each other. It's the law of the jungle. Can you change the law? You can't. Not even worth trying. If we tried to control them they'd just burn the jungle down. Would that be any better? No.'

I'd never heard a man describe his own corruption so eloquently, justify himself so completely.

I admired his brazenness. So much impudence required courage.

'But of course you need to be careful when you're surrounded by so many dogs. These beasts wouldn't touch locals but they do disturb them. Isn't that right? So be careful. I wouldn't live the novel you set out to write.'

And he laughed heartily at his own insight.

'Well, that's that then,' he said. 'I'd better go and work out which animal is responsible for this. And remember what I told you.'

He got into his Mercedes and was gone.

The police took statements from everyone in the coffeehouse. None of them had seen the killer. And no one knew the man who'd been shot.

All the statements were the same. Everyone said the same thing.

Then the prosecutor came and the statements were repeated to him and he had a quick look around before he left.

Not long after that an ambulance came for the body.

Then Centipede mopped the floor and everything went back to normal. No sign that a man had just died there.

As a child I was taught that death was a kind of majestic darkness and since then I always feared it. But now it seemed simple, even mundane.

The shooter took the crime so lightly that he winked at me just minutes after putting a bullet in someone's eye. The man had died in an instant and three hours later there was no trace left of his death.

Was this death?

Was it that simple?

You're sitting there reading the horse racing pages and some guy comes and blows your brains out.

A brain picturing galloping horses was suddenly splattered over the coffeehouse floor, sending imaginary horses racing through the grass. I could see the jockeys in colourful outfits riding on their backs. All of the hopes and schemes, frustrations and desires, jealousies and passions that had resided within the folds of that brain were then washed away with a bucket of water.

The sum of a man's memory had been destroyed.

As the denizens of the coffeehouse excitedly rehashed their memories of the murder, I found myself wondering what images the bullet had pierced.

What images had been rent asunder?

Were the memories of people in that brain blown apart by that bullet? Which memory was lodged in that part of the brain? The memory of his mother, his wife, his lover, his child, his enemy?

I imagined the broken images of people crushed by that bullet.

When a man died an entire horde left this world with him; he didn't die alone.

I was overwhelmed with the feeling of having witnessed a massacre. Not just the killing of one man.

I was horrified by the thought of the collected memories of his life being blasted away in a single moment.

Remzi sat down at my table with a glass of tea. 'Dead and gone,' he said.

'The man's actually dead,' I said.

'The sultan's soon to be on the scene . . . He was one of their men. They won't let this go.'

'Do you know the shooter?'

'No, those guys are just hit men. Not from around here.'

'But then why did he come by minibus?'

Remzi smiled.

'These hit men are too much. They'll take someone out as long as you pay them. But then they take a minibus to the job. And they can never track down the minibus because the drivers change the plates. I hate to say it but I don't think the police even want to find the killers. Everyone needs them. And you know that on their way to the crime they even pick up passengers, just like any other public minibus. But of course they have everyone get off at the stop before the crime scene. Everyone around here uses those buses to get to local villages, and you never know if you'll get on a hit man's bus.'

It was as if the hit men were openly trying to belittle death.

They take a minibus to a murder, put a bullet in someone's head, and then laugh about it later.

These murderers had a sense of humour.

I'd seen with my own eyes how easily people were killed.

But I wasn't scared.

Though I had every reason to be.

X

Hamiyet believed that Jesus was buried in the church on the top of the hill. She said some nights you could see a flash of light over the hill and supposedly lightning never struck the church. Once a fire ravaged the olive groves along the hillside but went out just ten metres from the church. Then there was a terrible flood but the waters split in two just before the church and streamed past on both sides.

'Sometimes they come to dig over there. And whoever tries ends up dead. Have you heard about it?'

'Are there any stories in this town that don't have to do with death?'

She flashed a coy smile.

'Of course, but I couldn't tell you.'

'Why?'

'Because . . .'

'I wouldn't understand?'

'Oh, you'd understand . . . That's for sure.'

Sometimes I think that the world is made up of cages built for two, and when a man and a woman are inside they slip on identities entirely different than the masks they wear outside. From the outside, Hamiyet was a woman who spoke to the furniture and believed in all kinds of superstition, a woman who danced to the beat of her own drum. But when the two of us were alone together she was flirtatious. It seemed so natural. She flirted with such flare. She was a master. Though she was openly seductive, she always was careful to protect herself with double-entendre. I suppose she felt she could let go with me because I wasn't from town; she didn't have to follow the local codes. I caught myself watching her with desire.

I had come to know a secret she'd kept hidden from the world, and this changed my perception of her and the way she flirted. I was one of three people who knew who she was, or rather what she was, and what she had done.

But she would never discover this.

Knowing someone's secret gives you an upper hand; a kind of voodoo doll. I knew the subtext of everything she said, and was able to manipulate her if I wanted. But she had no idea I was doing it. Hamiyet fascinated me.

And I flirted with her too.

I wondered whether I could ever manipulate her into feeling close enough to me to share her secret. The covert sexual games we played served my plan. And I enjoyed them.

I have always enjoyed such games.

Everything was a game for me.

What is life if we don't play it like a game? Nothing but an overwhelming stretch of anxiety and boredom.

But now, sitting on this bench, I can see that making life a game is the easy way out. And still the players want to be taken seriously. But there is a power that makes this desire a reality, and this night has shown me this power.

It has crushed me, ripped me into pieces.

The dreams have voices.

I hear the voices of the dreaming town, how loudly they moan and wail. Imprisoned sounds, ever encaged in dream, forever jangling in their jails. Voices that can somehow never emerge are condemned to resonate within. They must be filled with voices. How can they live with so many voices, stand so many unrelenting voices?

How do these people, who in their dreams unleash such a cacophony of sound, bounding through unimaginable adventures, wake up to lead such mundane lives?

There's so much more I wanted to learn about the people here. But I suppose I'm out of time.

That weekend, full of the same curiosity, I went to Mustafa's farm. I was curious to see how these people in a town steeped in marijuana and death really lived, how they had become so intimate with death, how they had turned death into a game, just as I'd turned life into a game.

I was playing with life to amuse myself.

Were they playing with death for the same reason?

The fine sand on the beach, untouched for years, piled into little dunes and studded with the tips of shrubs and glittering with seashells, was like a desert that stretched as far as the eye could see. And so it was surprising to see the deep blue sea just beyond it.

Mustafa's home stood on top of the rocks at the end of the beach. I suppose it had once been a Byzantine fort. Now it looked more like a palace that overlooked the sea. At the back there was a large garden and in the front a broad terrace made of granite that stretched out over the beach. It blended well with the castle walls.

Tables had been arranged in the back garden. I was surprised to see that they weren't using the terrace. It seemed like hardly anyone in town was even interested in the sea – maybe because the water wasn't for sale.

When I stepped into the garden, I was horrified to see most of the men dressed in tracksuits. Were they on their way to the gym? They looked like beached seals. I wished they were wearing their daunting, dark suits. They looked far less comical in those. Lambs were roasting on spits at the end of the garden.

Mustafa was quick to find me. He was wearing pressed black trousers and a blue shirt. He'd taken off his jacket and tie.

'I'm glad you came. Let me introduce you.'

It was like we were old friends.

Wading through the crowd, I asked, 'Zuhal didn't come?'

'Something came up,' he said.

I've always enjoyed knowing other people's secrets. And when they don't know that I know. They hide them behind walls, never imagining that someone may have scaled them. But then I suppose I suffer the same fate. I am unaware of the intruders. Our secrets intersect like ripples on the still waters of a pool.

'You have a beautiful home.'

There was a mixture of joy and pride in his expression, even child-like innocence. 'We worked really hard,' he said. 'But I suppose everything came out all right.'

'How did you get permission to build here?'

'I'm the mayor. I give the permission,' he said, laughing. 'Why do you think people want to become mayor in the first place?'

'To get their hands on historical forts?'

'Of course.'

'The government doesn't object?'

'By government you mean someone they send here, some random committee. They say the same thing I say. And they're happy with what they get in return. Isn't that better than everyone being unhappy?'

'Everyone's happy?'

'Of course they're happy.'

'The other day they killed a man right in front of me. He didn't seem very happy.'

He turned and fixed his eyes on mine, his face darkening and the muscles in his jaw contracting. Then suddenly the features softened, changed, and a grisly smile emerged.

'But you're happy,' he said. 'It wasn't you.'

'It could have been me?'

'It could have been anyone.'

'Even you?'

'Possibly, but my blood would cover this entire town.'

This time his smile was for real.

'You're lucky,' he said. 'How many novelists get the chance to witness something like that? I'm sure you'll capture the scene beautifully in your next book. Come on then, people are dying to meet you.'

'To meet me?'

'Certainly . . . You'll be the first writer they've ever met.'

He led me through the crowd.

Some of the guests had actually ordered my books from the city, but most of them confessed they hadn't read them yet.

Most of the young guests had studied at universities in America but they reintegrated into the town's social fabric. It was like the education they had received abroad had been washed out by what they'd learned in childhood. As for the older generation, few had finished secondary school. They were in good spirits, laughing and joking with each other in various groups, as comfortable as their gym clothes, and their local accent had a light and lovely lilt.

Raci Bey was a short and portly fellow who had a monopoly on wine production in the district; he also owned several olive oil factories. 'Cooking lamb is no walk in the park. Mustafa will have us dying of hunger soon enough and then he'll get his hands on our land,' he said and burst out laughing.

Raci's wife was different. At first I wasn't sure what it was. She had a sharp face and there was a faintly ironic smile that lingered at the corners of her mouth. Something about that and the angles on her face was strangely arousing. I couldn't quite work out why.

Her name was Kamile Hanım and she was an honest, shrewd, authoritarian woman; I suppose the authority came from her quick wit and loquacity.

'Are you the writer?' she said, as if asking a vet if this was the ailing cow.

I laughed and said that I was.

'Can you make enough money as a writer?'

'Some do, but I don't.'

'You drive an RV. How is that if you don't make any money?'

Her daughter interrupted: 'Come on, mother, why in the world do you care about his RV?' She was a tall blonde.

'It's all right,' I said, calmly. 'I came across some buried treasure.'

'Listen to that,' said Kamile Hanım, laughing. 'Quick on his feet.'

Everyone in the town said they had come into their money

the same way; whenever I asked it was always the same answer, 'The guy's dad found buried treasure.'

Kamile Hanım had got my drift.

'Well, you should at least register your treasure at our Chamber of Commerce,' she countered. 'That's where the people who find treasure go. Are you married?'

Embarrassed again, her daughter said, 'Mother, please.'

'It's all right,' I said, again in a conciliatory tone.

'I was married . . . But I lost my wife in a car accident.'

'How terrible. I'm sorry to hear that . . . And you never married again? I'm sure she would have wanted you to remarry.'

'She would have, but it hasn't happened.'

'I can find you someone here . . . I arrange most of the marriages around here.'

'Oh, mother,' her daughter said again.

Kamile Hanım was quick to respond: 'She's the only one I couldn't find a match for. Her husband left her because she's a whiner and now no one wants her. Enough of this Oh mother, oh mother, leave me alone.'

Her daughter blushed bright red and said, 'Don't pay any attention to her. She can be so rude sometimes.'

As she stomped away, Kamile turned to me and said, 'The little minx is ashamed of me. She's busy trying to fix my life when she should be busy fixing her own. So what do you write about? Love and romance and all that? Someone said you depict women well.'

'Love and romance and all that,' I said and smiled.

'I was a big reader when I was a kid. Reşat Nuri and Kerime Nadir's books. They always made me cry. Why do you writers have to make people cry? You should make us laugh too. Then when the kids came, and with all the problems at home, I wasn't able to read any more.'

She glanced around the garden then conspiratorially flashed me a womanly smile and said: 'Now, tell me. Have you been with many women? Is that how you know them so well?'

Beneath her authoritative confidence there was a flirtatiously mocking tone. Most of the other women in town spoke the same way. Hamiyet spoke this way, in a tone of voice steeped in sexuality. The unseen world I had discovered online was in fact run by women and, like water running underground, it was never clear when their sexuality would suddenly emerge, usually when they felt safe in the presence of a 'stranger'.

Above ground the men were engaged in disputes over land, power struggles and murder while women ruled the town with their urgent, uncontrollable sexual desires.

'I've known many women,' I said.

'Did they love you?'

'They did.'

'Did you love them?'

'I did.'

She lowered her eyes and then looked at me.

I could swear that she was thinking about how I made love, how it would be if we made love.

In that moment she was far from everyone in the garden, looking off in the distance, her eyes now fixed on the horizon, her irises darkening.

'You're lucky,' she said.

'I was lucky,' I said.

'And were they lucky?' she asked.

'They were.'

Lightly touching my arm, she said, 'I can imagine.'

I looked up to see a tall young man in his thirties standing beside us. 'And this here is my son, Rahmi,' Kamile Hanım grumbled. 'Did Gülten send you here? Haven't they got anything better to do than pester me? Mother this and mother that, following me around. What's the problem now?'

'Mother dear, why not leave the man for a little so that he can talk to the other guests?' He seemed unmoved by his mother's moods.

'Oh, for crying out loud,' she said. 'Go on then and speak with those idiots. They'll bore you to death, tell you all about their properties and what's going to be renovated in town, the prices of land by the sea, treasure at the church . . . Now, Rahmi is going to pick you up and bring you to our house on Thursday. I'm making lamb stew . . . Don't come with a full stomach and don't you forget.'

'How could I?'

Rahmi put his arm in mine and as he led me over to the other guests he asked, 'Did she do your head in? Sometimes she can really go too far, but you should forgive her. Gülten told me about it. My sister, the one you just met.'

That evening I planned to ask everyone there about Zuhal and gather as much information as I could. I was sure these people would have some entertaining stories.

The garden was tastefully designed. There were olive, kumquat, lemon and tangerine trees with glistening ripe fruit, and enormous magnolias and oleander that were clearly not from the region. In the corners there were pergolas draped with honeysuckle and jasmine vines. The ample open space in front of the house (more of a castle or a château) was divided by two flowerbeds filled with tulips of all colours. Mustafa said that flowers for every season were planted there.

A broad, flowing staircase, also made of granite, led to the entrance of the stone house. There was a large veranda decorated with the capitals of columns salvaged from ancient ruins and the sun streamed in through large windows. At night, when all the lights were twinkling, you could see the palace from town. It looked like a giant lantern.

An air of intimidating magnificence lent by the black stone and the bright light that streamed in through the windows seemed to reflect Mustafa's double nature; he had built a house in his own image.

Rahmi took me over to a group of men.

I always get the same feeling when I'm with a group of men. A man inhabits two extremely different worlds: he is either a savage or a child. There is nothing in between. He jumps from one extreme to the other, from childishness to savagery and back again. The savagery manifests itself in different ways

– straightforward physical violence, wit, intrigue, curses and peacock-like displays – but the childishness is always the same: an exaggerated display of playfulness and pain, a feminine side.

During this festive roasting of the lambs, these men were like children in a bath tub, talking about football, women and the expensive prostitutes they knew in the big city as if they were playing with rubber ducks.

They were superficially respectful towards me, and distant, because in their eyes I wasn't sufficiently childish or savage – and perhaps because I was a writer. In fact I was both. But I chose to hide these emotions behind a smile. I didn't want them to see either.

True, I wasn't one of them, and that wasn't a problem. But if I tried to seem like one of them I would only lose whatever esteem they might allow me. I knew that sooner or later one of them would start talking about what I was really interested in. And indeed someone did.

With a polite smile on my face, I asked: 'Where does the legend about that church come from? Who came up with the idea that Jesus is buried up there?'

Poor people in town believed that Jesus was buried at the church, but for the rich it was a different story altogether: they saw money where the poor saw Christ.

Hamdullah Bey, who owned a famous resort outside the big city, said: 'Probably a Roman general came up with that story.'

Then each of them told me their version of the story, picking up where the last person left off. 'There's a deep, intricate maze under that church. A Roman general buried the pirate treasure up there, and to be sure no one would ever find it he built a church over it and spread the rumour that Christ had been buried there.'

'Well, then who does it belong to?'

Silence.

Rahmi finally answered. The others assumed a serious and solemn air.

'No one knows who owns it now. They say it once belonged to an Ottoman Pasha. But no one knows who has the deed now. It has to be someone in town, and whoever has it is afraid to come out and say so.'

'Why's that?' I said, interrupting him.

'There's an enormous fortune up there, more than you could even begin to imagine. You could buy a country with that kind of money. It's treasure collected from hundreds of pirate ships. They would never let just one person have that much money. That amount of money is dangerous. So the holder of the deed is afraid and keeps anonymous while he plots how to get away with the money. Or else . . .'

'Or else . . .' I said and waited for him to go on.

'Or else the papers were lost when the Pasha died and the deed to the church went to a relative. Or who knows, maybe the butler, and then one of his children inherited the deed, but surely it was written in Ottoman and perhaps this person doesn't even know what it means. Or it's packed away in a chest in someone's attic.'

'Hasn't anyone ever excavated the place?'

'You would have to dig secretly, and that's not easy. It's full of mazes and deep wells. And it's bad luck to dig in such a place. There were a few archeologists who got government permission but in the end they all died. And that's the truth, my friend, they are all dead and gone.'

'How did they die?' I asked, astounded.

'Traffic accident, drowned in the sea, shot over a dispute.'

'But then how do you explain these deaths?'

'I don't. But I do know that the entire town keeps a close eye on that place, and probably not just people here. If someone even goes near the church there's talk about it in no time.'

'So it's dangerous to go there?'

'Well, I wouldn't advise it. People are willing to let the treasure be, but no one wants anyone else to have it. People would blacklist anyone who went near the church.'

Then he warned me again, 'Everyone in town keeps a close

eye on the place,' and for a moment they all turned and glared. That's when I understood why no other outsider was living in town: everyone here was rife with paranoia that stemmed from a rumour going back a hundred years. They saw each other as treasure fiends and anyone new in town was only treated with hostility.

They were all looking for that deed and secretly conducting research and manoeuvering, gathering people from local gangs to act as spies, watching each other all the time. A newcomer in town was eventually forced out, and if he didn't go, there was an accident.

The endless search had become a way of life. As Rahmi said, 'Everyone is willing to let the treasure be, but no one is willing to let anyone else have it.' In this town, even thinking this was tantamount to losing a grip on reality.

On this bench, I can see how the treasure drove everyone out of their minds, poisoned generations, and cut people off from the outside world. For them, outsiders were always enemies.

They were civil amongst themselves but when an outsider entered the mix they went mad.

It was a madhouse.

At first it frightened them to hear that I was a writer, and they doubted me, but when they found my books they came to the conclusion that I was naïve, like all other writers.

My books saved me from a freak accident; they kept me alive in this town; books no one else had ever read had kept me alive.

Looking at their faces from the base of the granite staircase, I could see just how dangerous it was for me to be speaking about the treasure, and I changed the subject. 'Do you ever swim in the sea?' I asked, and their faces softened, and they were children again.

'Only the kids do,' they said. 'Older folk find it indecent.'

Olive Oil King Seyit Bey, who had dyed his hair but left streaks of white around his temples, said, 'Sometimes we sneak in at night. Someone says it's indecent to swim in the sea and like idiots we believe them. And we never challenge them. But I swear one day I'm going to strip down bollock-naked and plunge into the sea in broad daylight.'

Seyit Bey weighed at least a hundred and fifty kilos. Someone quipped, 'There would be a tsunami. Anyone else could have a try but it's off-limits for you.'

And they cracked up laughing.

For them the most mundane jokes were the funniest, the ones they used over and over again. They knew them all by heart. They had no interest in new and subtle jokes, and if you tried one they would hang their faces and then shoot you an angry look, no doubt thinking that you were making fun of them. But aggressive or personal jabs were fair game. The women had sat down at the head of the table and were talking and laughing. I knew that I shouldn't sit with them. And although no one came over to speak with me, occasionally someone would look over in my direction. It really did take a long time for the lamb to roast.

But it was delicious.

I found Mustafa after we had finished and said goodbye. He walked me to the door.

'Be careful on the roads,' he called out to me as I left.

I had never imagined that such well-intentioned words could be so terribly frightening.

XI

'gülten? she fell in love with haldun when they were at university and then got married. they had a big wedding. he's a dentist. his dad's an olive man. they're loaded. had two kids. but haldun started hitting the drink. why . . . i don't know. and i think he started beating gülten. then they split. now she has a lover in the city. he's married. what does he do? he's a dentist. strange. they say that kamile's a lesbian. she's got a sharp tongue. that's why everyone stays away from her.'

When Zuhal was chatting with me online she had this way of answering her own questions, and that day she told me a lot about the people she knew in town.

'but it was like she was flirting with me,' I wrote.

'they say that when she goes to the city she calls a gigolo. i don't know. anything's possible with kamile. i'm afraid of the woman. and her husband raci bey. but it's like he's blind to it all. or he has no choice but to turn a blind eye. there's nothing he could do anyway. they say that raci is close to the refugees. he's probably the most powerful man after mustafa. some people say he has the deed to the treasure. but then again everyone says someone else has it.'

'does the deed really exist?'

'i have no idea. that's what everyone thinks. if not for that church the town would fall apart. talk about that treasure keeps everyone together. or at least it seems like that to me. strange. mustafa is convinced there's treasure there. why . . . i don't know. babies know about the treasure before they're born. take serhan abi. who? the pharmacist. with the quiet wife. she never says a word, always knitting. he's a sweet man. he says nothing's there, it's all just talk. how does he know? i don't know. but everyone's looking for the deed. you'd be amazed to see how much money people spend trying to find it. they are all watching each other like hawks. sometimes i wonder what will happen if they really dig up the place . . . if there's nothing there. the next day everyone would be dead . . . strange.'

'when did all this talk of the treasure start?'

'i don't know. nobody really knows. people hear the story from their fathers, grandfathers, their great-grandfathers.'

Then she changed the subject.

'i saw mustafa in a dream last night. he was driving in some kind of roman chariot. but he was wearing a black suit. he said he was going to war. then he disappeared through a hole and popped out in the olive groves. god, if only I could forget this guy. i can't get him out of my mind. he sent me a message last night. asking where i was. i told him i was in the city. and then he said he would come and see me. i was about to tell him to come but then i knew he would just make me cry. i told him not to come. why, he asked. i said i had work. what work, he asked. meetings, i said. i'll come later, he said. but i won't meet him. i hate it when he gets drunk and calls me. he only wants me when he's drunk. and when he sobers up he's the same mustafa.'

'maybe when he's sober he can't bear the pain of losing you.'

'i'm the one in pain. he suffered in the past. now i'm suffering. he got over it. have you ever been in love?

'of course.'

'have you ever been heartbroken?'

'no.'

'i woke up in tears this morning. i was crying because i didn't ask him to come. but i'd cry if he came. sometimes he can be so cruel. such hurtful and poisonous words. then i attack him with my own words. and we always hurt each other. it was so wonderful before. we had such a good time together. are you angry with me for loving him?'

'no.'

'i will never be able to love you the way i love him. you know that, don't you?'

'i do. that's fine.'

'why fine?'

'what do you want me to say?'

'don't know, just not that.'

'all right.'

We were both surprised by our own indifference. I wasn't jealous.

And I didn't really know why.

I knew that Zuhal loved another man so passionately that she would never be able to let him go. She belonged to him, loved him with all her heart. So perhaps it was the thought that I would never lose her – because she never was mine – that kept me from being jealous.

Maybe I was satisfied: she was betraying her great love with me, and this stroked my ego.

Jealousy was a damaged soul, a painful crack in the wall around our sense of self. But Zuhal wasn't a part of my life, she wasn't a part of who I was and so I didn't feel jealous at all. Though I felt strongly connected to her, in a strange way she wasn't a part of me.

As much as I tried I just couldn't understand it.

Why wasn't she a part of me? How was I both so intimate with her and so distant?

I didn't want her to be mine. No. I wanted her to entertain me. To excite me. I wanted to win her heart. I wanted her to betray her love with me. That's what turned me on. I confess that I felt a kind of malevolent joy as I challenged an overwhelming and absolute love that had nothing to do with me. I wanted to break it apart.

Lacerating her love and the man she loved gave me a feeling of triumph; but I didn't really understand that I was also hurting myself – conquering them left me cold.

But if the wounds were opening, I still couldn't feel them.

Sometimes I can't solve even my own mysteries.

Was there any reason for me to feel jealous? I know the emotion. It's easy to describe. But not to be jealous in this situation? It was inexplicable. If she left Mustafa and gave herself to me, but still loved him, would I be jealous? I suppose so. Was I not jealous because she didn't give herself to me, didn't choose me? Mulling all this over, I hadn't noticed the words flashing on the screen.

'do you miss me?'

'yes.'

It was the truth. I missed her.

'what do you miss?'

'i miss everything about you.'

'everything? tell me.'

I knew straightaway where the conversation was going. I was already aroused. We were going to make virtual love.

Our relationship had two principal foundations: the pure love she felt for another man and the pure lust she experienced with me through written words.

The former was such a powerful bedrock that it seemed as if the relationship would be shaken if she were to one day leave Mustafa; something would be missing.

We began to make love.

I don't know if it was because of this virtual lovemaking, or because we're all born with the need to feel another living being, or because of the darkness in the unseen face of my life, or my fondness for the prostitutes who eke out their existence in darkness, but it wasn't long before I discovered Sümbül. That was her real name. She was honest about that and the kind of life she led. Between the wealthy neighbourhood where I lived and the lower part of town where the middle class had settled there was a belt inhabited by the very poor.

The neighbourhoods had not been arranged in hierarchical order.

The poor had settled between the rich and the middle class. In fact the middle-class homes that extended as far as the centre of town were the newest and most unattractive. The rich lived in vast old mansions and the poor lived in little old stone houses, while the middle class lived in short apartment buildings.

Sümbül's home was in the poor neighbourhood. But I never went there. She came to me. She had a pink telephone with sparkling gems (something I'd never seen before), and music for a ringtone. She was always getting calls. But I was usually her last customer, calling her around midnight.

It was strange the way people in town looked after Sümbül; they never let anything bad to happen to her. Once a drunk teenager was rough with her and the next day they broke both his legs and left him on a street corner. The kid never even went to the police and hobbled around on crutches for months.

They called him Sümbül's gimp.

I suppose people felt that her presence offered some security, stopped the young kids in town from pestering other women and provided an outlet for their wild desires. She had friends and neighbours. Like the other poor women, she carried her groceries in a mesh bag and covered her head with a scarf when she left home.

She wasn't beautiful but she was cheerful – she had a good sense of humour.

'I'm this town's lightning rod,' she would say. 'Lightning always strikes me first. I keep this place honourable.'

It's not easy for me to make friends with other men but I can quickly befriend women. For me talking to a woman is like wandering into a gift shop filled with a thousand different ornaments. There are so many different things to talk about – gossip, secrets, petty jealousies and personal troubles – that speaking with a woman is like playing with little ornaments that you can pick up and look at without getting bored and without having to buy them. If you don't bore women by over-selling yourself, you can talk about things that will entertain you for hours.

They have none of the boring, ostentatious self-satisfaction that men have, and to those men who proclaim themselves able to solve all problems they say, Well, go ahead and solve it then, and seem to leave all kinds of problems on the sideline as they have a good time; they know that these problems can be solved easily and believe they can solve them much better than men, and they do. I enjoy them most when they're putting men down but they really have to believe I'm a true and close friend to do that. Sümbül and I quickly became good friends.

She came to me around midnight. Somehow she'd picked up the habit of drinking whisky and cola – she must have had customers from the big city who met her in fancy hotels.

'Take off your clothes,' I would say to her, and she would undress and sit in front of me. She was completely comfortable naked.

Unlike the other women in town, she was fascinated by politics, and she never missed the nightly news. Occasionally we'd discuss popular issues. I always found it amusing to talk politics with her when she was naked. I suppose because I was a writer she always enjoyed talking with me and in time she started telling me about her other clients, though never disclosing names. She pitied men's hang-ups but was never surprised.

'Write about prostitutes,' she'd say, 'there's great material there.'

'Now I'm not the type of girl to just finish the business and send a fellow on his way. But that's not to say I can't finish a guy off in five minutes – they just can't last any longer – but that's not my style. There was the miserable guy who came to see me, his wife never listened to him, no one ever listened to him, but I did, which is why he even called for me when he was out of town. There's nothing I won't do, I never say no.'

Men can never really know other men and that's why I was curious to hear about what these men did with her. And she told me. There was one I'll never forget. She didn't give me his name but I assumed he was one of the town's better-known gangsters.

'The man would come and just sit down opposite me, look

at me and then start crying. We would never speak. Never did anything either. He'd just look at me and cry. He'd bawl his eyes out. Then he'd pay me and leave. Once I asked him why he was crying and he said that if he told me he'd never come back. I didn't push him but one day I'm going to ask him again, I'm dying to know.'

One night I asked Sümbül what the people in town thought about me.

'You got off lightly.'

'Got off lightly?'

'One of Oleander Ramiz's men was going to beat the living daylights out of you.'

'Why?'

'So you would leave town.'

'How do you know?'

'Everyone knows.'

'Everyone knows?'

'Of course they do,' she said. 'The whole town was talking about it.'

A sadness suddenly swept over me as I realised how much I cared about the people in town, and it broke my heart to think that as I chatted and joked with them, believing them to be friends, they could look me in the eye knowing that I was going to be beaten and not even tell me about it. I felt betrayed. This feeling only proved how much they meant to me. I was fond of them but they had betrayed me; they had never cared for me.

Sadly I said, 'No one ever said a word about this to me.'

'No one could tell you. They were afraid. One day you'll leave, but they have to stay. I'm sure they dropped hints, though.'

'No, they never did.'

She raised her eyebrows, pursed her lips and said, 'Didn't Remzi ask you if you were bored here, tell you to try somewhere a little more fun? Didn't Centipede tell you the mountains were beautiful this time of year, that you should spend some time up there? Doesn't Hamiyet wonder why you don't go back to the comfort of your own home? Didn't you ever stop to think why they were saying all these things?'

'No.' But I was pleased to think that they were trying to warn me, which means at least I hadn't been betrayed. 'But why didn't they beat me up then?'

'Mustafa said you were harmless and that they should leave you alone for now. That's why.'

'Mustafa got me off the hook?'

'He's got something in mind. He always does.'

'Do you know him?'

'I've known him since he was a kid,' she said, laughing. 'But I haven't seen him for a while. I don't really see much of those guys after they grow up.'

'But then why were they planning to beat me in the first place? What was the problem with me? Is it because of the treasure?'

'Of course. They don't like strangers poking around here.'

'Do you think there really is treasure there?'

'God, I don't know, but that's what they say. And even if it's true, what use is it to me?'

'It's like Schrödinger's cat,' I said, softly.

'Whose cat?'

'Schrödinger's.'

'Who's that?'

'He says put a cat and poison in a box, and the cat is both dead and alive until you actually open the box.'

'So you're saying that the treasure is either there or it isn't?'

'No, I'm saying that it's both there and not there . . .'

She took a deep breath.

'You're the cleverest man in the town and now you're saying that the treasure is both there and it's not there. The damned thing is enough to drive even the cleverest people insane.'

She stood up and ran her hand up her inner thigh. 'Come over here and I'll show you Sümbül's cat. Now, that's definitely there.'

Sümbül's cat was no match for Schrödinger's and between

her legs the last thing on my mind was quantum physics.

She downed the last bit of whisky-cola before she got up to go. As she was stepping through the door, I took her by the arm and said: 'But you never warned me.'

She looked at me, a forlorn expression on her face.

'Didn't I tell you to come and say goodbye before you left town? I was putting the idea in your head.'

That's when I realised that in this town certain topics were never openly discussed, and when they were you had to pay careful attention to catch innuendo and subtle signs to understand just what people meant.

Now, thinking back on it, I wonder why I didn't just leave then. What was keeping me there? When there were so many dangers, warnings, the strange happenings, when I always had the feeling that something bad was just around the corner.

Maybe it was simply curiosity.

I was curious to see what would happen. A writer's boundless curiosity.

And maybe a little pride.

I had the feeling that I would win over the entire town.

To somehow know the truth behind the people there without them ever suspecting me, to see what they were hiding, to let slip details to do with the dark sides of their lives, it didn't just quench my curiosity but gave me a strange and exhilarating rush of power.

And like all forms of power, it is a pleasure that comes at a price, a pleasure for which you pay later on.

And now I know the price I had to pay.

XII

Two days after that strange conversation with Sümbül, I was sitting in the coffeehouse reading my newspapers when Mustafa's enormous black car pulled up in front of the garden and his thickset driver, who was also the mayor's official bodyguard, walked over to me. 'Mustafa Bey is expecting you.'

Everyone at the tables around me seemed blown back by a sudden gust of wind; but then they were still; it was like a ring of energy had pushed them away from me. For the coffeehouse denizens I'd gone from being a friendly writer to one of the bigwigs.

They gazed at me with admiration, fear and respect.

It annoyed me that Mustafa had sent his driver to order me to come and see him. But there was nothing I could do.

It would have caused a real commotion in town if I'd refused him.

Anyone refusing a summons from the mayor would have upset the order in town, and even my good friends at the coffeehouse would have been angry with me.

This was the way things worked; it was unfair and meaning-less but everyone had a place in the order of things, and they were accustomed to this. No one wanted to disturb the delicate balance. Though it was a balance full of threats, oppression and fear, it was a known element; they wouldn't know what to do with themselves if the scales were somehow tipped.

I got up and walked over to the car.

We drove to the town hall.

I loved the building. It's a broad, three-storey, sand-coloured stone building with oriel windows and dark blue tiles over the cornices and delicate columns at the entrance.

Mustafa's office was on the top floor. It was a large room. Two leather armchairs sat in front of a long desk and at the far end of the room there was a round conference table. Between them was a wooden coffee table surrounded by a set of leather armchairs.

Two people I'd never seen before were sitting in the leather chairs and talking to Mustafa. When I entered the room he stood up to greet me.

One of the men seemed carved out of wood; he was a tall, thin, tough-looking man; the contours of his face, like those of his body, were harsh and taut, no flesh and blood, only bone. Under his thick, woolly eyebrows were dark little eyes fixed in a steely gaze.

'The honourable judge,' Mustafa said, and the man nodded his head without extending his hand. The other was a stout, young, informal man. A little rosary dangled from his left hand, and he was stroking the glimmering beads. Mustafa introduced him to me as the honourable district governor. Nonchalantly, he reached out his hand, which was soft and fleshy.

Mustafa chatted with me as if we were old friends, ordering me a coffee, and the others listened to us without saying a word. But before long they got right to the point.

'We would like to ask you to write a speech for us,' Mustafa said.

'Me?' I said, surprised.

I would have never thought I'd be called to a town hall to write a speech.

'Aren't you a writer?' Mustafa asked, laughing.

For the first time since I'd been in town they saw my true face. I was suddenly incensed by all their disparaging jokes about being a writer. I felt the muscles in my face tighten.

'You're confusing literature with petitions,' I snapped. 'Call a clerk. You're talking to the wrong man!'

In the heart of every writer there lies a murderer.

Writers spend their lives struggling to conceal this murderous desire from other mortals.

Like God, they ruthlessly destroy the people of their own creation, drag them from one cruelty to another, meting out punishment, and with the callous indifference of a serial killer. And no one knows when he has taken a life from the solitude of his room. But when a writer is enraged the walls of his refuge come crumbling down, revealing his true identity.

In that moment those men caught glimpse of a killer, and they recognised him straight away because of who they were and what they did.

They stirred slightly, moving forward in their seats, and respectfully uncrossed their legs as if they were sitting before their superior officer. They hadn't expected such a reaction from me. They were flushed with fear. And they didn't know why.

'No, that's not what I mean,' Mustafa said. 'We're asking you to do us favour.'

'A favour?'

'I'm due to make a speech before the municipal assembly. Later, copies will be posted around town. So it's important that we have something that's well-written. We're not persuasive writers. We'd only come up with something dry and official, and unclear.'

'Well, then what do you want to say?'

'We're going to forbid people from going up the church hill. And we're going to present this decree to the public. You see, there are far too many old wells and dangerous ruins up there. We're concerned that someone might fall and die.'

'Do you have the jurisdiction to issue such a decree?'

The judge spoke for the first time, in a gravelly but authoritarian tone, like sandpaper running over a wooden board.

'When it comes to public safety it is within our jurisdiction to make any decision,' he pronounced.

The district governor reiterated: 'It is of course a matter of public safety.'

'Is restricting people from going to such a place really a matter of public safety?'

'God forbid if something were to happen to someone there,' said the governor. 'It is our duty to prevent such a tragedy from ever happening in the first place. Now, if someone were to tumble into one of those wells we would be the ones responsible.'

'Why not put up a sign? You could simply warn people that way.'

Sensing the discussion could descend into argument, Mustafa cut us off.

'A sign is out of the question. Someone will go up there at night and not see it . . . It's simply not practical. A restriction is the easiest and surest way to handle this.'

'But then how will you enforce it? How will you stop people from going?'

Running his fingers over his rosary, the governor explained: 'We'll post a watchman there.'

Clearly they already had everything planned out. No doubt the governor drove the enormous Mercedes parked at the door.

'What do you want me to do?'

Mustafa flashed me a smile, and for a moment I felt like he might shoot me right then and there. 'Instead of a dry, boring speech on the new restriction we need a speech clearly explaining the danger of moving about among the wells and ruins. People must understand both the danger of going there and the rationale behind the prohibition. You see, people here like to gossip now and then and such a speech would serve to cut the rumours . . . And so we are kindly asking for your help. Of course you are in no way obliged, but we imagine it would be quite simple for you to do. And if you did we would be eternally grateful.'

To agree meant becoming their partner in crime. But I also knew that after my sudden outburst they would be more careful and respectful towards me.

I took a long sip of coffee.

They watched me intently.

Then, with a smile, I said, 'Fine. I'll do it.'

I had agreed so that I could stay in town.

The judge and the governor rose and respectfully shook my hand and Mustafa saw me out of the building.

I was breaking the law and, what was worse, it amused me. I was also excited about infiltrating the power struggles in town. I would be able to learn so much more. I might also be killed.

I was dropped off at the coffeehouse.

The people there greeted me with curiosity but also with respect. I was now a powerful and respectable figure in their eyes.

And all this because of a single page I had agreed to write.

As my closest friend there, Remzi had the courage to ask me what had happened.

'Why did they send for you?' he said.

'They are officially prohibiting people from going up the church hill. And they want me to write the announcement.'

Silence.

'Oh God help us,' said Remzi. 'Mustafa Bey is going to dig up the church himself. There's going to be a war in this town.'

XIII

I feel a strange trembling sensation.

It's a hot night but I can't stop shivering.

I'm hungry.

The hunger came over me with such sudden ferocity; how strange to feel hungry under these circumstances.

This adventure began with Remzi's köfte but could I really eat a plate of them now? I probably could.

Remzi made the most delicious meatballs in the world.

Branded with dark strips from the grill, they were carefully laid out on bread that soaked up the sizzling juices. This was served with sliced onions in sumac and a little cup of hot sauce on the side. I always told Remzi to hold the onions and the hot sauce. Just the meatballs, lightly flavoured with cumin, and bread.

I sat and ate meatballs in Remzi's garden almost every afternoon. I always praised him for making better meatballs than anyone else. He enjoyed the attention. Maybe that's the main reason we became friends.

Then I'd drink cold beer he brought me in a thick honeycomb glass mug and listen to the town's secrets before heading home and going online.

It was a pleasant life and I was happy.

I feasted on mouthwatering meatballs and sin.

Thinking about it now, I was a strange kind of freak in a strange town; but like everyone else I seemed completely calm and ordinary on the surface. Sometimes I used to wonder if I would ever find a town to match my personality. So did I really end up here by chance?

A coincidence.

But there's form, an internal coherence, unseen connections in God's divine order, and perhaps that is why his work is so compelling. The way he tightropes between accident and control.

Anyone else but me would have left. He would have shrugged off these strange twists of fate and left. But I chose to stay. A chain of coincidences. God creates them, but lets you decide how to live through them.

Sitting on this bench this hot summer night, shivering with fear, I feel that I've made my life with God as my accomplice.

He created coincidences as if they were empty houses for me to furnish. We choose a home and make it ours. But he provides the inspiration.

Maybe God isn't the only one to blame for everything that has happened.

God is my accomplice.

We have committed the crime together.

We have sinned together.

He opened the door to chance and I walked right through.

Did he know in advance that I would? He did. He knows me. I don't know him but he knows me.

I didn't speak to him but he spoke to me.

I perceived him as a silent, untouchable accomplice. But I would be punished and my accomplice would go free.

What a wonderful talent. To create all those sins and remain innocent.

Is that why you're great, God?

Because you remain innocent amidst all your sins?

I understand God.

I know his secret.

Who can condemn me for a murder in a novel that I have written? Who can blame me for bringing suffering to the characters in my books? Who would think me evil?

The more evil I create, the more I'll be praised.

And I am one of God's novels.

We are all the same.

He is praised for everything he does to us and everything he makes us do. Buildings are overflowing with his books. They are read far more than anyone else's.

He's a talented colleague.

I write better than you. Your language is inconsistent. Your narrative structure is in disarray. But you're more believable than I am.

And your inventions are truly wonderful. This magnificent idea of sin. We can't overcome it; we are forever entangled in it. At the end of the day it is always there, lodged in everything we write.

So you are peerless.

Only you can draw the limits of this novel.

Only you could have discovered sin, and then made sinners of all your heroes.

There's no escape for me now.

I suppose I'll wait until morning and then turn myself in.

I don't seem to have any strength left, or I'll pull myself together a little later, I don't know.

Speak to me, why don't you.

You know they say that people who talk to you are mad?

So are you driving me insane?

Look, I say this as a friend, you're going too far. You'll lose all your credibility. 'He was already mad,' you'll say, and the truth is they'll believe that too.

You don't like criticism, do you? Who does? I don't like it either. You relish praise. But let them withhold it from you and then see. Now, this is just between you and me, but you like to advertise – you call out to people every day, encouraging them to gather and sing your praises. And they do. I envy this.

After all you've done to me there's nothing more you can do. That's why I'm not afraid of your wrath.

Truth is, however, I really do enjoy your 'there's more to come' game, always creating a little suspense, and just when we think the adventure is over the hereafter starts, keeping the reader engaged.

But let's face it: your early work wasn't so great. What was the deal with all those dinosaurs? And everything else. That chapter was roughly made and boring. Surely you agree, since you tore those chapters up and threw them away.

Did you burn them?

Some say you did.

What came after that wasn't so great either.

So you created nature first.

Believe me, the plot was simple.

Survival of the fittest.

No complexity, intrigue or surprise. It's dull. You repeat yourself again and again.

I suppose you're tired of the monotony. You say, This novel will never get off the ground. I need more action and dramatic twists. Something left hanging. Something to shock and surprise. I should pick up the pace. Something to pique the reader's interest.

I'm sure you said this.

So, look, humans are sound characters for a big book like yours. That's where your mastery can flourish. How did you come up with this?

How did you come up with a character so complex and full of contradictions, who can even work against himself, who can't even guess what he's going to do next, full of more emotions than you could find anywhere else in nature?

They appear much too late in the novel, that's my only criticism. You only thought of people three hundred and fifty million years after you created the shark. But don't tell me, My time is different from yours, because you really should be more composed in the face of criticism, and I still say that even for you three hundred and fifty million years is quite a while.

Are you about to send a police car around the corner, sirens blaring, because I've said all this? Are you going to have me caught just like that? Don't be angry. We're speaking like two friends in the same line of work. Two friends in the business of murder.

If indeed the main subject matter is humankind then you dithered some time before getting to the heart of the matter. You have, for example, given much attention to the birds. And insects too. You created so many different kinds of them and I'm curious to know why.

But of course you know your greatest discovery. It is the human mind. You made human emotions as lively and complex as the events that swirl around them.

How did you dream up the human mind?

If I actually believed I could speak to you after death, I would pull out this gun and put a bullet in my head and then ask you this:

'How did you come up with the human mind?'

There lies your tremendous creativity.

You went through a momentous transformation at one point in your novel, bringing the book to life with the human mind, an entirely new type of character.

We are competing in describing your creation.

That's what makes you different.

Your story is utterly ruthless.

How many hours until dawn?

It's still dark outside. A naked mannequin stands in the dewy light in a shopfront across from me.

The weather is warm.

The scent of jasmine and eucalyptus fills the air, a hint of lavender drifting down from hillsides in the distance.

The town is breathing it in deeply.

A treasure horde of diamonds, gold and emeralds is a constant in some corner of their communal dream; every night there are people in town who have the same dream, perhaps they've been dreaming it for centuries.

I remember the conversation I had with Sümbül about Schrödinger's cat. Whenever I went on about that sort of thing my uncle always said I sounded like a fool, but quantum classes with Sümbül unclothed on the existent and non-existent treasure were somehow just right.

It's warm outside but I'm shivering.

You're making me shiver.

Tonight it is just the two of us.

I shouldn't be so frightened with you here, you shouldn't put such fear in my heart.

You could have been a little kinder.

But you are right. It's a writer's work, killing off characters of his own creation.

XIV

According to Sümbül, Oleander was the guy who was going to rough me up. One day I ran into him in Remzi's restaurant, and I wasn't convinced it was a coincidence.

While I was eating, three black Mercedes pulled up in front of the restaurant and there was a flurry of activity as enormous men in black suits jumped out to open one of the back doors.

A stocky, slightly shorter than average, olive-skinned man with broad shoulders slowly stepped out and moved casually through the men as one of them threw a jacket over his shoulders. Remzi raced to the door to greet him. The man stepped right past him, saying, 'How are you, Remzi?'

He walked with such conviction he seemed unstoppable, almost pulling his destination towards him.

A table was quickly set.

I continued eating but watched them out of the corner of my eye.

A little later Oleander stood up and walked over, and for a moment I thought of the man who had been killed in the coffeehouse and involuntarily shut my eyes.

Oleander stopped at my table.

'Brother, would you do us the honour of joining us?' he said, respectfully.

I looked at him in disbelief; a display of respect like this wasn't something you encounter often and I didn't know what I owed it to. Was it because I was a writer or because I was friends with Mustafa?

'Of course,' was all I could say.

I've always been fascinated by people who make a living from death. I find the brutality repugnant but have always admired the courage it takes to put your life on the line. Perhaps this is what led me to murder later on. I always loved listening to their stories.

I stood up. Oleander stood aside to let me pass. I was confused and I felt a little unsure. This was the first time I was meeting someone like this. I knew that this kind of person was dangerous; they could suddenly fly into a rage, become another person altogether, and shoot down a good friend.

I was holding a scorpion and I needed to be careful not to anger the beast.

When I reached their table they stood up to greet me. I sat down first, then Oleander and the others.

'Could you bring my meatballs over here?' I asked Remzi.

Oleander said, 'Those are cold, make him another plate.'

His courtesy was laced with authority, a confidence that allowed him to make decisions for me. I don't like the attitude. But I kept quiet.

'How are you, brother?' he said with respect. 'I've wanted to meet you for some time but it wasn't our fate until now. How do you find our town?'

He was sitting upright in his chair, his jacket draped over his shoulders. As he spoke only his lips moved. Stunned and a little afraid, I was listening to an iron statue. I knew that I was speaking to someone who could kill me at any moment. Behind the courteous façade was a man who ordered people killed. A stern look on my face, I sat stiffly in my chair.

I knew that I had some kind of immunity ever since Mustafa had posted the declaration I'd written, that no one but Mustafa could easily take my life, but there was a glint in this man's eye, the size of a needle, a steady, dark glimmer, reminding me that he didn't spend too much time thinking things over.

'It's a beautiful town. Peaceful. I'm very happy here.'

'Peaceful, yes,' he said, gravely. 'Why did you come, brother?'

It wasn't a question. This was a cross-examination. He posed the question with a dangerous level of curiosity that left me no choice but to answer, provide some kind of explanation; he was gracious but also powerfully persuasive.

I knew he wouldn't let me avoid the question.

I couldn't simply say, 'None of your business.' He was threatening me.

For a moment I thought of asking him if he was the one who sat in front of Sümbül and cried.

For a moment.

His attitude was getting on my nerves. To ask him such a question meant being prepared to shoot him or be shot. But in that fleeting moment I thought about taking the risk. I could have shot him. I would have done it in self defence. I suppose at that moment there were similar shadows dancing in my eyes. He had seen them.

It was an animal instinct. He had sensed the thought passing through my mind and he shifted in his chair. If he wasn't surrounded by so many men, if we'd been alone together, I would have asked him. I would ask him, and one of us would have to die. Or maybe he would laugh, albeit a little fearfully, and take it as a joke. Which one of us would it be? That's what was running through my mind just then.

I knew he wouldn't have hesitated to kill me but my animal instincts were telling me that he feared death more than I did.

Then I smiled. I leaned back in my chair.

'To write a novel, Oleander,' I said.

There are moments in a conversation when a tone of voice or a single word can shift the dynamic. I had just used his first name and he had chosen the formal 'you'. Did I now have the upper hand? Oleander was the kind of person who'd understand this difference immediately. He was always tightrope-walking over these nuances.

He would either respond to me rudely or he would have to accept me as his 'elder brother'.

I felt a sharp sting on my tongue and I nearly shivered. But I was having a good time.

He conceded.

'What kind of book, brother?'

'A murder mystery.'

Everyone there seemed to sway like barley in the wind as they turned to look at Oleander. His next question was steeped in irony.

'Do you know anything about murder, brother?'

'I'll learn.'

I swallowed a meatball, took a long sip of beer, looked them over and said, 'Dig in, gentleman. These are getting cold.'

Oleander turned and said, 'Eat.'

I now had control of the table. And no one there could believe it.

Nothing about the way he held himself, sat or spoke had changed but something else had. Now he believed he had to show me a certain respect. In his relationships with men, Oleander only knew fear and threat; all other emotions were suppressed. I was the kind of man he should be able to frighten easily, but he had failed, and this put him off his stride.

Now he was keen to win me over.

'Late one night, brother, these dishonourable refugees had me trapped on the road into town. I remember there was a full moon and the olive trees were flickering in the light. I remember it all so clearly. I swear to God I took three bullets before I could even draw my gun. One in the lung. But I took down three of the bastards before the rest of them left me in the middle of the road, three dead bodies lying next to me. I spent two months in the hospital. But Mustafa Bey, what a guy, brought a doctor from who knows where to come and look after me. They said he saved me.'

'How are you now? Are you in pain?'

'No, brother. Not even a scar. The lung's still working, you see!'

His men flashed approving smiles.

Then he relayed more of his adventures, making fun of his enemies, praising Mustafa, and the police chief, but he kept asking me little questions, eager to find out more about me.

Then he stood up and said, 'If you'll excuse us, brother, we have important business to attend to.' And in the local parlance, I said, 'But of course.'

He shook my hand and walked out without looking back.

And one by one his men stood up, buttoned their jackets and said, 'Respects, brother,' before they left. It was quite a sight to behold.

I thought of all the stories I could tell Zuhal. Remzi came over to me.

'What's happening, brother? First Mustafa Bey and now Oleander – you're rubbing shoulders with all the bigwigs in town. God, I've been living in this town for years and only once was I in Mustafa's car, and I only ever ate with Oleander once before . . .'

'Why do you think he came?'

'He comes to eat here every once in a while.'

He paused, and it seemed as if he was ashamed of having lied, or at least of having been evasive.

'He came to see you. Everyone wants to know more about you.'

'What do they want to know?'

'You're an important man, brother. You're a writer. You're a friend of Mustafa's. Soon enough you'll be eating at the Çinili.'

'Would I sell you out like that, Remzi?'

'Everyone does, brother.'

'But would I?'

'No, you wouldn't, brother.'

'And you wouldn't sell me out.'

'No, we wouldn't, brother.'

Sadly I wasn't so sure.

XV

I didn't get a chance to tell Zuhal anything that night.

Because I finally got the news I was waiting for.

'i'm going to the hotel on the mountain tomorrow. come along.'

We didn't say much more.

But she was curious.

'will it be as good in real life as it's been online?'

'it will.'

'are you sure? what if it isn't?'

'it will be.'

'i'll message you my room number when i get there.'

'ok.'

'see you tomorrow night then. goodnight.'

I didn't turn off my computer. I stayed up, wandering about the room. I read her words over again and again.

This woman was closer to me than anyone in the world and I'd only actually seen her twice; and she was in love with another man.

I had no one else.

I knew her life story. Her family. Her childhood. Her friends. How she made love. What she liked. What she said when she made love. I knew words no one else knew she knew.

But I'd never seen her naked.

I knew how she cried without ever having heard the sounds.

Our relationship was nothing more than words on a screen, our fantasies.

We were close there.

As for reality, I had no idea what our relationship was. I didn't know what went on in her real life and what she didn't tell me. I knew she was hiding a lot from me.

She was hiding me from people in her real life.

For her I was a phantom.

I was nothing but words flashing on a screen late at night.

We were nothing but words.

Now we were both worried that reality wouldn't live up to those letters on the screen.

We shared a life that was made up of letters and we were afraid to jeopardise the virtual world if we mixed it with the real. Maybe we wanted nothing more than to remain there on the screen.

But we were curious.

We wanted to know if a man and a woman got the same pleasure physically touching as from words, the same thrill and passion.

The world we'd created in our imaginations would overlap with another world: the world of our senses.

Was the world of our minds better than the one of our senses?

Was it more pleasurable to think of caressing a woman's body than it was to actually touch it?

When we draw on the experience of our five senses we speak of reality but then what are emotions set in words on a screen?

If what we cannot see, taste, touch, hear or smell is not real then how should I explain those ecstatic evenings full of mad desires?

Before the advent of the screen our lives were dictated by thoughts and senses alone, one influencing the other, but the screen had managed to separate the senses from thought; and now it was time for us to see which one was stronger, which one truer.

We felt that we could trust our imagination more than we could our senses.

The life that we had created in our minds was perfect.

We had thrown out all excess, the broken pieces and the distasteful aspects of the real, and made a flawless life that was our own.

Could we create the same perfection through our senses?

Our thoughts or our senses might clash or come to a startling agreement.

It was something that had confounded human beings for years: mind over matter or matter over mind; and the debate would come to its conclusion in the bedroom of a hotel in the mountains.

I tried to whittle away the time with these strange thoughts, calm myself down, muttering, 'Everyone has made some contribution to philosophy with the mind but now I will make a very different kind of contribution.' Once I even caught myself smiling as I gazed out over the lights in town.

It was a restless night.

I woke up several times.

In the morning I was tired and in a bad mood. I stayed at home and read my papers, keeping a close eye on Hamiyet. I watched her mopping the floor with her skirt rolled up over her knees. I knew that she knew I was watching.

Both of us enjoyed the little game.

Zuhal's hotel overlooked a valley leading up into the mountains. Village-style bungalows with two rooms were scattered throughout a forest overlooking a lake. It was about a forty-minute drive away.

By evening I managed to settle down.

Indeed my movements seemed heavy and deliberate.

I left the house as the sun was setting. I didn't know how long I'd be staying but I prepared a little bag with a change of clothes for a couple of days.

As I travelled along the narrow road that wound its way up into the mountains, I looked out over the steep cliffs, sometimes catching a glimpse of the sea that suddenly leapt out from behind a patch of trees.

I received a message as I was close to the hotel.

2B.

I arrived at what was probably the best time of day: the sun had already sunk over the horizon, and everything seemed as if it had come to life in what some call an empire of light. Weary of the bright sun, the mountains, plains and trees seemed ready to walk off into that peaceful blue light; a magnificent serenity, a magnificent feeling of power.

I left my car in the little car park next to the main building.

The lights along the paths were lit, and the colours of the forest seemed darker.

In the sky there was a single, almost imperceptible cloud, hovering there like a little lamb.

I made my way down the path.

I found 2B on the door of a bungalow with white walls and calico curtains in the windows.

The door was open.

I stepped inside.

The lights were on.

She was sitting by the window with her back to the door.

It had gone dark outside and the lamplight was reflected in the window; I could see her reflection watching me.

She was wearing a long white nightgown. It wasn't transparent but I could sense she wasn't wearing anything else.

I closed the door and stepped over to her.

She turned when I was just beside her.

There was an almost sorrowful look in her eye.

I put my arm around her waist.

Her body quivered, like olive leaves in the wind. She was shy, but she wanted to make love.

I led her to a downy mattress on a low bed.

Silently we took off our clothes and began making love. We made love without saying a word.

It was a bubbling stream, and the rushing waters knew intuitively how to slip round the rocks, and surge over a cliff; we weren't even there, only bodies intertwined, unthinking, yet sensing of every twist and turn, two bodies navigating curves for the first time, glistening and glowing in a rush of pleasure.

When we finally stopped night had fallen and the forest was a swell of darkness.

I heard her whisper for the first time, smiling, the sadness gone. 'Are you hungry?' she asked. 'I'm starving.'

She ordered enough food for five. But I knew she could eat it all.

Wrapped in sheets like Roman senators, we ate and gossiped about everyone in town. I told her all about Oleander Ramiz. But I never mentioned Sümbül. I imitated the way the men left me saying, 'My respects, brother,' and as she laughed the sheet slipped out of her hand, exposing her breast. She rushed to cover herself, as if we hadn't just made love, and I took her hand and said, 'Leave it that way.'

She switched on a filter coffeemaker on a little table in a corner of the room.

We'd made love the way everyone else does.

But now we would do it our way.

We would do it with all our hang-ups, our violence, our savagery, our perversion. That's the way we were. After weeks of making love without touching, we knew how to complete each other.

Sipping her coffee she ran her foot up my leg. A gentle touch was the signal for a new beginning.

We started next to the table.

I devoured her like an animal. I loved having her that way. And she loved it, too.

I left no part of her untouched.

Now we spoke to each other. I asked her what she wanted. And she answered. She listened to me, writhing.

Soon her face, her nipples and her thighs were bruised and swollen but she only wanted more, a little more violence, more pain, and more pleasure.

We cried at the top of our lungs.

Wailing, she pleaded, 'Don't stop.'

Soon dawn was breaking over the horizon.

I was lying on my back, one of her legs over mine, her head buried in my shoulder.

She was crying softly.

I didn't ask her why.

'I was afraid,' she said. 'I was afraid it wouldn't be so good.' She looked up at me. 'We're lucky we found each other, aren't we?'

'We are,' I said, feeling that we were truly fortunate.

I felt the warmth of her smile.

And we drifted off to sleep.

When I woke up it was close to noon. She was already up. She was standing in front of a mirror, wrapped in a sheet. She turned towards me, dropped the sheet and said, 'Look at me. You're an animal.' I smiled, feeling strangely embarrassed but content. 'What am I going to do about my face? I'll have to cover it with foundation,' she said, almost proud.

We had breakfast on a wooden balcony overlooking the trees. Below us the lake shimmered like a blue diamond on a ring. That's what I said to her and she answered:

'Couldn't be a blue diamond. There's no such thing.'

'There is now,' I said. 'I just said it and so there it is. And not such a bad thing really, perfect for the lake. Something God must have missed, never got around to making one. If he could make a lake like that, surely he should have made a blue diamond too.'

We hungrily ate breakfast.

'I feel closer to you now,' she said. 'But isn't it strange to feel so close when I'm in love with another man?'

'Everything about us is strange.'

'But you know if Mustafa came here right now, and I had to make a decision, I'd choose you.'

'Tomorrow?'

'I don't know about tomorrow.'

Her answer made me laugh; I don't know why I found it funny but I just couldn't help laughing.

'Don't laugh. It's embarrassing.'

I leaned over and touched her cheek. 'Don't be. There's no need to be when you're with me. I'd never do anything to hurt you.'

'I feel comfortable with you. As if I could do anything. I feel like you would never be angry with me.'

'You can do whatever you want with me.'

'Anything?'

'Everything.'

'You won't ever forget saying that?' she said, looking me in the eye.

'I won't.'

'And I won't fall in love with you?' she said.

'No, you won't.'

'Promise?'

'Promise.'

'If I fall in love with you then you're the one to blame. Agreed?'

'Agreed.'

After we finished breakfast she brought me inside. We made love again. This time it was calm and simple, like a glass of cognac after a rich meal, sending a pleasant glow through our bodies, lending a peaceful air to a savage night.

When I came out of the shower, she was putting on make-up in front of the mirror.

'I'm going to the city,' she said.

'I'll get dressed and leave then,' I said, 'and you can take your time getting ready.'

'Fine,' she said.

I got dressed and left.

I could never stand staying in a hotel room after making love; I don't think there's anything in the world more heartbreaking. I don't think I've ever felt as lonely as I have in hotel rooms.

I walked cheerfully up the path.

I knew she was happy we weren't leaving at the same time.

She didn't want anyone to see us together. She was afraid Mustafa might hear about us. This wasn't a source of sadness for me; in a strange way I even enjoyed the secrecy, the hiding, holding on to a secret that was ours alone. Mustafa's mere existence gave us a secret to share, and brought us that much closer.

After such lovemaking you feel something like a passionate love, an exalted feeling of happiness, gratitude, joy. I thought about sending her a message but I held myself back.

I knew it was something I shouldn't do.

I sensed that I needed to keep the relationship the way it was. It was a perfect statue – nothing could be added or taken away.

Touching it would only upset its symmetry.

I took a side road into the forest, winding down the mountain road among the villages and fields.

I had lunch in a village restaurant.

Then I had tea in a neighbouring village.

I chatted with the locals.

Towards evening, as I was approaching town, I received a message.

So there is such a thing as a blue diamond.

Thank God, I wrote back.

XVI

It was already getting dark as I approached the town.

I missed her. And the darkness seemed a part of my longing for her, and the darker it became the more desperately I wanted to see her. Then I panicked. Was I falling in love? That would be disastrous. I would ruin a beautiful relationship, leaving nothing but pain and agony.

I had to struggle not to call.

Experience can come to the rescue at times like these.

I'd been through similar relationships before, swept away by similar fits of desire.

Maybe it was only to be expected after such intense physical intimacy.

So I decided to wait until morning, wait for the emotions that had been blown up the previous night to settle.

Only when the aftershocks had ended could I assess my true feelings.

I was shaken.

I had to wait for the feelings to settle.

I sped up with the desire to get home as soon as possible.

Not far from home I saw lights at the church on the hill. The site was officially off-limits. Who was up there? How could anyone be up there without being shot or apprehended?

But full of my own troubles, I didn't think much of it.

I went home.

I was exhausted.

I had a drink.

Then I drifted off into a deep sleep, wondering how I would feel in the morning.

I felt much better.

The panic of that emotional storm had passed and there was the same pristine relationship, glimmering like a fairytale city in an immaculate crystal globe.

Hamiyet had set out my breakfast on the veranda.

She was softly humming a little tune.

'You seem in an especially good mood,' I said, already knowing why, or at least harboring a strong suspicion, but I waited for her to answer.

'Oh nothing,' she said. 'Just singing.'

'I saw lights on the hill last night. Do you know what they're doing?'

'No. I went to bed early last night. No idea about that.'

I looked her in the eye. She looked away and I saw that she was blushing. I knew she hated when I looked at her like that but I enjoyed it.

If there were ever a shop selling sins, the flickering light in Hamiyet's eyes would be right in the middle of the display window. Hamiyet didn't know what I knew about her, but she became restless and rushed off into the kitchen, caught her foot on the edge of the carpet and cried: 'Oh, you're always like that.'

I wandered down into town through the narrow streets of the poor neighbourhood, streets paved with stones of all sizes. In one of the little squares I saw a bunch of low, little wicker stools in front of a coffeehouse and I decided to sit down for a moment.

I asked a scrawny boy in a faded Barcelona football shirt for a coffee and leaned back against the wall and looked across the street. Three metres from me was a shop with wooden cradles in the front window, roughly the size of a normal house window. The sign above it read: 'Woodwork'.

In front of the shop a man with a long beard and a moustache draped over his lips sat on a carpet. He wore a thick leather apron up to his chin and in his lap was a cradle he was carving.

He lifted his head and our eyes met. Despite his imposing beard, his face was bathed in a warm light, and there were crinkles around the corners of his eyes.

'How are you, saint?' he said, whimsically. 'Worn out by the hill?'

'No. Just coming down. Going up is a different story.'

He looked me over for a moment.

'They're both difficult. Master Rumi said all roads go up and down because people always lose their way when the road is flat. Roads are never completely flat. And when they are, well, then you lose your way.'

'You're carving cradles?'

'Why, yes I am. That's my job. We ask permission from the trees, then we use the wood to make cradles for those who are about to join us.'

'Is there a market for so many cradles?'

'People are just popping them out,' he said, smiling under his bushy moustache.

'Who?'

'The people who live on the hill here,' he said, waving his hand in the direction of the poor neighbourhood.

'Are you from around here?' I asked.

'Born and raised.'

'Any trouble round here? People harassing you, that kind of thing?'

'No, that wouldn't happen to me.'

'Seems anything can happen in this town. Just the other day they shot a man dead right in front of me.'

'I know the kid. Knew him since he was a little boy. He was hanging out with the wrong crowd. He was a good kid but he went and got involved with the wrong people.'

'Why are they killing so many people?'

'Driven mad by all the rumours about the treasure on the hill. Talking about it endlessly, they start to believe that it's really there and then they're fixated on the money. They all want to get rich quick. The rich are thinking about how they can buy the entire town . . . That's wealth, you're born into this world and then you die, doing whatever kind of work God has given you, settling with what you have, that's wealth, no greater wealth than that. We're all a part of this world and when you kill another human being you're killing a part of yourself, and so consider the cost. When they shot that boy, they shot the creator. Did they stop to think about that? What is man? God is in that tree over there, and then consider human beings . . . They've lost their bearings, drifting further out to sea.'

'Do you believe there's a treasure up there?'

'Hardly, wise one. That's the devil talking.'

'Then what's the story behind the church?'

'It was built by a monk back in the day. It's just a little thing, could hardly even call it a church.'

'I saw lights on the hill last night.'

'Me too. The mayor's digging. No one else would go up there, considering the new decree.'

'The mayor seems like a decent man.'

He raised his eyebrows and said, 'Well, now that's going a bit too far.'

'Don't get me wrong,' I said, a little embarrassed. 'It's just that I met him a couple of times and he seemed decent enough.'

'Well, he puts on a good face for you. You aren't a competitor and you're not an enemy either.'

I remembered the previous night. Mustafa was a potential enemy and a competitor.

The carpenter went on: 'He's not the type of person who chooses to do wrong for the fun of it but when it comes to a foe he's merciless. People are strange. They know both good and evil but how do they choose between the two? And stranger is that sometimes they choose both, never thinking, Oh I'll go for good over evil.'

'God made us that way, wise one,' I said, picking up his lingo. 'Evil is profitable.'

He was clearly in his element.

'Would you cut off your arm for a profit? What is worth more than your arm? Nothing, correct? And so with every evil act you cut off a piece of yourself, and the creator grieves. Where's the profit there? People aren't even aware that when they opt for evil they're hurting themselves. But they're not evil at heart, they're blind. They can't see the truth shining brightly right there before their eyes.'

It was about time to leave.

'All right then. They say that Jesus Christ is buried up on that hill,' I said.

A sardonic smile lit up his face.

'Last I heard he flew away, and I have no idea if he ever came back . . . Never heard a thing.'

I put money for my coffee on the table and stood up.

'So long, old man. Hope to see you soon. God be with you.'

He called out after me, 'Be careful on the hill.'

I turned and said, 'You're the one sitting on it.'

'No harm just sitting. You're the one going up and down.'

When I turned to look back he was hammering away at his cradle, his head bowed.

Surely Zuhal knows this guy, I thought.

When she decided to buy a place in town she opted for an old stone house she renovated. It was in the poor neighbourhood on the hill and it had a secluded garden. She was friends with almost everyone there, and she knew all about their lives. Every time she came to town she spent most of her time with them.

I really didn't know why.

Maybe it was because she knew they would be pleased to have someone like her around them. She was charitable and I'd seen her do some amazing things to help the poor. Maybe she liked how they treated her like a queen. Maybe she'd moved there to annoy Mustafa. Whatever the reason, she'd settled in that part of town against his wishes. But they liked having her there. And she told me all their stories.

I took a shine to the old man.

There are some people who are truly good at heart, clear as spring water, and when you see them you feel glad. He was one of them. I also enjoyed his sense of humour.

I decided that I would come back and see him again.

When I arrived at Centipede's place the tension in the air was palpable, with people speaking passionately amongst themselves in hushed tones.

I signalled to Remzi and he came over.

'What's going on?' I asked.

'They started digging up at the church last night,' he said, lowering his voice.

'Who started digging?'

'No one knows. But who else but Mustafa would try?'

'Mustafa might very well try, seeing that he's the one who made the place out of bounds.'

'Normally he wouldn't dare, because everyone would go mad, but who knows? If he's really lost his mind . . .'

He stopped, thinking he'd said too much.

In a faltering voice he added, 'You know, just an idea, otherwise things would spiral out of control . . .'

'You're afraid, aren't you?' I said. I was amused by it all.

Suddenly a grave expression fell over his face. I had expected him to say something to the effect of 'Of course not. Me, afraid?' but he leaned closer and said, 'You should be too, brother. This is no laughing matter.'

'What will happen if you speak to Mustafa about it?'

'The best you could do now is to watch the match play out from the sidelines.' He could see I hadn't understood from the look on my face. He explained: 'They put the wheelchairs on the sidelines.'

'Mate, it's just the two of us talking. What's there to be afraid of?'

'Brother, they're listening. He's got men everywhere.'

'Who's listening?'

He shrugged.

Suddenly I realised I wouldn't have a friend left in town if I kept asking these kinds of questions.

They were all terrified.

And the fear was like an enormous tree, alive and powerful, its roots spreading through all corners of the town.

I couldn't really understand why they were so afraid, but the fear was like an infectious virus, spreading with every exchange, growing a little more with every hushed conversation.

Fear fed more fear, it seemed, and it only took one of them to start a new fire and it fanned out in every direction, consuming anyone in its path.

Since arriving in town I'd come to understand that these people eventually forgot the source of their fears, but continued to relish the emotion. There was no need to even question why.

Hearing a new bit of information, they would take flight like birds, even if they had nothing to do with the incident; and because they had nowhere to go, they would always come back to perch on the same tree. The town was a giant cage, full of frightened little birds.

Just as the carpenter had said, the treasure was driving everyone insane.

And no one knew if it was even there.

People at the coffeehouse didn't know what was going to happen next, but they were convinced it was going to be big.

No one came over to me and I felt restless sitting there with them.

So I got up and left without saying goodbye. I decided to go the Çinili. I thought it would be more peaceful there.

It was full of people. But now there was hostility in the air. Looking for an empty table, I spotted Kamile and her son Rahmi. They had just arrived and we sat down together.

After wading through the usual social niceties, I said, 'So what's happening? Everyone's on edge this morning.'

'Mustafa Bey started digging at the church last night,' Rahmi said.

I couldn't help but smile. The affluent set in town would always address each other with the formal Bey, even if they were childhood friends. These people are like porters in a restaurant, I thought to myself. I suppose that's how they were brought up. They had a real, low-brow sense of humour but whenever they were talking about someone they always addressed him as Sir, using the word Bey.

'Are you sure?' I asked.

'They had excavators working up there all night.'

'But there's a court order prohibiting anyone from going there, and they plastered the decree all over town.'

'That means a prohibition for everyone except Mustafa Bey,' Kamile said, flashing a sarcastic smile. 'It's open season for him.'

From what Rahmi was saying I sensed that something was going to happen, because he wasn't just afraid, he was angry. Mustafa had clearly crossed a line: he wanted to be the sole leader of the entire town, the rich and the poor. And considering Rahmi's state of mind, I could see that Mustafa had effectively declared war.

'What will happen now?' I asked, curious.

The answer was short and to the point.

'Nothing but trouble from now on.'

He sadly nodded his head. 'I have no idea why Mustafa Bey has gone and done this. He knows the traditions around here better than anyone.'

As we were speaking I could hear people whispering at the other tables; news had just blown through the restaurant. Rahmi called over the head waiter, who said something in his ear. For a moment I could see a slight smile on Rahmi's face but it quickly disappeared.

'What's happened?' I asked.

'Muhacir's men shot two of Oleander's in the main square. One of them is in critical condition. He's in the hospital now. I said there was going to be trouble. And there you have it.'

It wasn't long before people in the restaurant were leaving

and gargantuan bodyguards emerged from the Mercedes parked outside. Everyone was taking precautions.

I also went home early.

That night there was a knock on my door. No one ever came over so late. It was Mustafa's driver.

'His honour the mayor wishes to see you,' he said.

'Now? What's happened?'

'I don't know.'

The town was silent. We raced along dark roads. In the distance Mustafa's palace looked like a forest on fire, lights thrown up into the sky.

He met me at the door.

'What's the matter?' I asked. He was frowning.

'Things aren't so great, but we're going to fix it,' he said.

The judge, the district governor and the police commissioner were all sitting quietly in the living room. They nodded to me without getting up.

Mustafa asked a servant to prepare me a coffee.

No one said a word until the coffee arrived. I was brimming with curiosity but I said nothing. As my coffee was set down on the table I couldn't wait any longer.

'So what's happened?'

'They shot Muhacir's man in the hospital last night,' Mustafa said.

'And?'

The police commissioner chimed in: 'Now the dogs will go to war. The animals will burn down the jungle. Disturb the peace.'

'Do you know who the shooter is?'

'We have a pretty good idea but there were no witnesses. No one saw a thing. And if they did, they wouldn't speak.'

'Was it Sultan?'

The words just slipped out and the four of them glared at me and I thought they might kill me right then and there, but in his gravelly voice the judge rumbled, 'How do you know Sultan?'

'I saw him once with Remzi at the köfte restaurant.'

'It probably was him,' the police commissioner said. 'But we have no witnesses.'

Turning to Mustafa, I said, 'Why are they killing each other? Does it have to do with the treasure?'

Mustafa twisted his face angrily. 'Those dogs have nothing to do with any treasure,' he erupted. 'They're fighting over marijuana sales. That's why they're fighting it out like wild dogs.' He stopped and then added, 'And the worst of it is that everyone thinks they're killing each over the treasure. All these people are village idiots. What do these brutes have to do with the treasure? The imbeciles in this town go on about the treasure if a flea flips up into the air.'

'That's the way they all think,' I said.

'I know, and that's why we need to calm them down. They're acting as if it's the start of a world war. If this madness spreads to the general public we won't be able to get it under control.'

I looked at them as if to ask, 'What does any of this have to do with me?'

Smiling, Mustafa said, 'We would kindly ask you to write a statement saying that the construction work there last night was to do with the closing of a dangerous well and that there will be no future work. I will read the statement in the municipal assembly and then we'll post the announcement in town.'

On the one hand they were telling me that the murders had nothing to do with the church, but on the other they were trying to stop them by making it clear that there would be no further digging at the church.

I wasn't a fool.

And I was getting fed up with them calling me in every two minutes to write something for them, although it did elevate my importance in town. But again, I really didn't want to have anything to do with these men.

Then it dawned on me. I should never have accepted their initial offer. I didn't really have a good excuse but now I had no choice other than to carry on helping them.

I'd made the wrong decision the first time around.

Standing up, I said, 'I'll send you the document tomorrow.'

'Have you seen Zuhal lately?' Mustafa asked me as he saw me out. It seemed like an ordinary question.

'No,' I said without any hesitation.

For a moment I thought I saw the muscles in his face loosen. and then a faint smile, but it quickly disappeared.

The next day the announcement was posted all over town.

Mustafa had taken a step back, putting the conflict on hold for the time being.

XVII

'do you want to know how i feel when i'm with you . . . now i know you'll think i'm exaggerating . . . and maybe i am . . . i don't know . . . in a strange way i know you won't misunderstand me and you won't get angry at what i do or say . . . and you know that i trust you . . . and this gives people an incredible sense of freedom and the chance to reveal all your secrets . . . it's such a warm feeling . . . i feel the same kind of feeling in God . . . i know that he'll understand my choices and that he'll forgive me . . . for two people to share the same feeling . . . it's strange.'

When I got back from Mustafa's late that night I found Zuhal waiting for me online. She wanted to speak about the night before. I was happy to think of returning to that world of only us, our world, a blend of the real and the unreal. I had tumbled down the rabbit hole and found myself in a fantasy world that was ours alone.

'when i make love to you i feel such emotions . . .' she began. 'parts of me break off and become part of you . . . i don't know what you feel . . . whether you feel this . . . sometimes i'm afraid . . . i think that whatever it is in me that i surrender to you won't ever come back . . . i don't want you to think i'm exaggerating . . . this is different from making love to the man i'm in love with . . . i suppose the laws of nature have changed . . . or this is just something i never experienced before . . . maybe others have felt the same way . . . i'm not talking about sexual satisfaction . . . yes, that's there and so much . . . but i'm talking about something else . . . at the height of it i feel something altogether different . . . i love you, i become a woman, i create you and i am your child, you're mine, i'm yours and then everything is chaotic and something shifts . . . please tell me i'm not insane because i really am starting to think that i'm going insane . . .'

I understood what she was saying because I felt the same way.

'we're not just making love,' I began. 'at the same time we're changing our identities, our personalities . . . in this sense we're tasting a freedom unlike any other in this world . . . something inside us is cracked open and another person emerges . . . a person that belongs to no one . . . a person whose very existence depends on the other, who cannot live without the other . . . because it's only when we're together that these aspects of ourselves emerge . . . but it's an addiction . . . we need each other to experience that split inside . . . and in a way it is only at certain times and situations when those people inside feel a particular kind of love . . . it is the moment of birth . . . and the attachment and the dependency of a child on their mother . . . and the love . . .

'it is another life running parallel to real life . . . a different kind of love parallel to real love . . . it comes alive with love-making and finishes there, but doesn't disappear, only goes into hiding . . . but its presence is always felt . . . this bond turns us into so many different things, a woman, a man, a mother, a father, a child, a lover . . . we become many and the multitude and this makes it so hard for us to leave each other . . .'

I wrote all this from the heart. And when we physically made love again we had the same feeling, as if we were creating each other, drawing out other aspects of our personality.

It was true that making love seemed like love itself, and perhaps it really was, but the feeling was later repressed.

But when we returned to that hidden refuge there was a physical upheaval, a frenzy of desire.

This is what I went through every time we made love.

Some things I will simply never know: why was it that the

love we made together did not take shape in our real lives, despite the way it grew and gained strength in our fantasy world?

What was the answer?

You might say it was because of her love for another man, or my own fear of falling in love with her, but I don't think that was it. Those truths had been toppled by a powerful swell of emotion.

We had prevented the love from reaching into our real lives. The reasons for doing so were hidden deep inside us.

Thinking about it now, maybe neither of us had the courage to channel the dual nature of our relationship, the flux between fact and fiction, into one life, because neither of us was willing to let go of the strength that came with this duality, the mystery, to even consider exposing all those hidden aspects.

Maybe both of us wanted to keep this thing we had – whatever you might call it – hidden, so as not to damage it in any way, to preserve it. We couldn't let it out into the open.

I told Zuhal about what had happened in town.

'i heard,' she said.

She always knew what was going on.

'sometimes mustafa goes mad . . . i don't know why . . . and when it happens there's nothing he won't do . . . i know him . . . be careful.'

'but he's a friend of mine now.'

'don't trust him . . . he's actually a good guy but when he loses it he's pure evil . . . you have no idea what he's capable of . . .'

'he's after the treasure?'

'no . . . he doesn't need money . . . his family's rich . . . but now he wants the entire town . . . and he won't suffer anyone standing in his way . . . he wants everything done his way . . . that hill where the treasure is, if it's even up there, well it's become a kind of obsession . . . it's strange . . . i suppose he thinks if he can take control of the church then everything else will follow . . . once when he was drunk he told me some mad things . . . i don't know why he thinks that way.'

'will the others let him do this?'

'no . . . i suppose they all think the way he does . . . . i mean the rich crowd . . . that hill is some kind of legend for them.'

'tomorrow night i'm having dinner with raci bey and his family . . . kamile hanim invited me when i was at mustafa's party . . .'

'you'll have to tell me all about it . . .'

'i will.'

'i miss you . . . i can't stop thinking about that night . . . strange.'

'me neither . . .'

The following evening Rahmi sent a car for me. His place was in a housing estate at the edge of town in the middle of an olive grove. I thought of Mustafa's palace on the opposite side of town, one of those old sandstone houses. And the biggest one there.

Rahmi met me at the door. The whole family was in the living room. Rahmi's wife and his two little boys, sitting there as if posing for a family photograph.

I was surprised to find the living room tastefully decorated. The furniture was a little gaudy but everything seemed well placed, giving the room a natural, comfortable feeling.

Despite their enormous Mercedes, the crude jokes, the funny tracksuits and the black suits and loose ties, the rich set in town actually seemed to have some taste. Like the furniture in this living room, they had settled in town and were a natural part of the habitat, living by their own customs and traditions.

From the way his wife and sister fluttered around him, I got the feeling that Rahmi was more important among the rich than I'd thought. In their eyes I was nothing but a new toy. I felt there was a kind of unspoken competition set in motion as they tried to capture 'the writer', possess him like they did everything else in life. They were competing all the time and I suppose I was just another object that they were fighting to have as their own.

Admittedly Kamile Hanım was the only one who fascinated

me. Raci Bey was a quiet man, and his children Gülten and Rahmi were like all the other rich kids in town, but there was something about Kamile Hanım, something that sparked my curiosity. I couldn't quite put my finger on it. It was an attraction that inspired you to take a second look, an allure that called for a second glance.

I imagine she was in her early fifties.

She was a little plump but in good shape. She hadn't let herself go; indeed she was very much alive, full of life and a desire to live. I think most people would sense this energy in her but would have a difficult time explaining it. Maybe it had something to do with the agile way she moved, maybe it was the teasing, flirtatious smile that every so often flashed across her face.

She was like a radio broadcast with secret signals that could be heard and understood by anyone who took the trouble to tune in. If you listened carefully, and you had the talent to pick up such tones, you would hear another voice altogether. I didn't fully understand these signals, but I could receive them; my ears had been tuned to them since childhood. And I could hear them loud and clear.

A long table was covered with all kinds of food. There were elaborate salads with greens I'd never seen before, vegetables in olive oil, pickles, salted bonito and a plate of little fried fish.

Gülten and Rahmi's wife Nuray were having white wine, but Kamile Hanım had joined the gentlemen, pouring herself a glass of rakı.

'I've read all your books,' Nuray said, excitedly.

'Me too,' said Gülten.

'If only I'd come to this town sooner. My books have never been so widely read before.'

'Everyone's reading them. All the women in town,' Gülten said.

Raci Bey and Rahmi listened to the conversation with distressed expressions. I found it all very amusing.

'How do you do it?' asked Gülten.

'You get women just right. You get the way we think,' Nuray said. Then, shooting a glance at her husband, she added, 'I told Rahmi to read your books but he won't.'

Rahmi mumbled something about not having enough time and was clearly angry at his wife for having put him on the spot.

Kamile Hanım listened quietly without saying a word.

She was waiting for something. I was waiting for something too.

I was still speaking with the others at the table, and as I turned my head from one person to another I slowed down for a fraction of a second, levelling my gaze at her, pausing for enough time to catch her signals.

Then it happened.

In that split second we caught each other's eye and looked deep inside. I was right. She was right too. Now we knew what was bound to happen next.

I had been tense as I waited for this moment, but suddenly the stress left my body.

I have always sought the dark side of a woman's heart, and when I find it I indulge, prepared to pay the price later on. I do it over and over again. I had discovered a new dark side; I was on the verge of doing something I definitely should not do. But I knew I could never hold myself back.

Kamile sensed the change in me and asked: 'Why do you always write about women?'

'They're far more entertaining than men.'

'But more dangerous,' she said, challenging me.

'And thus entertaining, no?'

Rahmi seemed lost. 'Women more dangerous than men?' he said.

I pitied him, along with the other women there. They ignored him. This man's wife is up to something, I thought. The devil in me was working overtime.

I looked at Nuray. Her husband was behaving like a fool in front of a man he barely knew, and the rage and condescension in her face was tangible. He must have felt it too, because he'd lowered his head.

'I've always wondered what people think to themselves when sitting around a table like this,' I said. 'What if we all shared every thought?'

'What do you think? We'd kill each other,' Kamile said.

Raci Bey didn't say a word but glanced at his wife and I thought, This man is brighter than his son. I shouldn't under-estimate him.

I decided to address the men at the table.

'What happened to the man shot in the hospital?'

'He died,' Rahmi said. 'He was Muhacir's son.'

'I met Oleander but I've never met Muhacir,' I said.

Seemingly uninterested in the world around him, Raci Bey quietly shifted in his chair.

'Where did you meet Oleander?'

'There's a köfte restaurant where I usually have lunch. He came over once and we spoke for a while.'

'Hmm,' Raci Bey murmured and there was silence. Everything was silent. Rahmi looked over at his father.

'What did he say?'

'Not much . . . He told me about how he had been ambushed on the road into town. He seemed very proud of the incident.'

'He's a bad apple,' said Raci Bey. 'A nasty piece of work. If I were you, I'd stay away from him. You give him your hand and he'll rip off your arm.'

'So there's a blood feud raging between him and Muhacir?'

'For years.'

'What kind of man is Muhacir? I've never seen him.'

'He's a gentleman,' said Raci. 'Respectful. Not like Oleander. Of course he's involved in some shady stuff but that's none of my business.'

So I could clearly see the two sides in the dispute. Raci Bey and Muhacir were aligned. And Mustafa's real competitor in town was Raci Bey. It was surprising that this quiet, slovenly man, who was intimidated by his wife, was one of the main players in the power struggle. I hadn't expected it.

'That night they put up a fence around the church. Around the wells,' I said.

'I think you wrote the announcement?' said Raci Bey.

'I did. Mustafa asked me to.'

Raci Bey let out another hmm. 'Do you know Mustafa from before?'

The women were silent, quietly listening to our conversation. The roles at the table had suddenly shifted. Even Kamile was quietly listening to her husband.

'No. We met here. I first bumped into him in the Çinili restaurant.' Another hmm.

'And you wrote the announcement at the municipality?'

'No, we were at Mustafa's house.'

'I think the honourable judge and the district officer were there too.'

'They were.'

'The announcement was a good move,' said Raci Bey. 'Otherwise things would have spiralled out of control.'

I asked if there really was treasure there and Rahmi bleated, 'Of course there is.' But at the same time Raci Bey said, 'I don't know' and shot his son a look and said, 'It really isn't important if it's there or not. But if the people here believe it to be true then you have to believe it's really there. That's what this boils down to. You can't be high-handed.'

'Mustafa is being high-handed,' Rahmi said, angrily, forgetting to use the formal Bey. And his father shot him another look.

'Mustafa wasn't like this before,' said Raci Bey. 'He was more careful, more respectful, listened to what the people around him had to say, and he wasn't headstrong. But something's changed. May God put him back on the right path. But it doesn't look good, the way things are going.'

'Are you worried about more murders?' I asked.

'Anything is possible,' Kamile said. 'Once they go off the

rails and lose respect for the rule of law, anything could happen. I supported Mustafa when he ran for mayor, because he needed it. He's a pious man and was never disrespectful until now, not once, but he's been strange ever since this new district governor arrived, he's acting all high and mighty. Anyway, now it seems like he's come to his senses but no one can be sure of his next move. I don't want him to disturb the public peace. We owe it to our elders to protect it. We should leave it to our children in the same way it was passed down to us. We can't let him break us apart, unsettle the public peace, let it go to the dogs.'

She had captured everyone's attention.

Then came dessert. Kamile had made a kind of candied fruit that I'd never tasted. The raspberry ones were incredibly delicious.

'Oh my,' I said. 'These are divine.'

'We call them daddy fruit. I don't know what you call them in the city,' Kamile Hanım said. 'I'll make you more if you liked them that much.'

'Please do,' I said.

So she had a reason for us to meet again and no one seemed to notice except Nuray's mother-in-law, who glared at me out of the corner of her eye.

'I wonder if Muhacir will take his revenge on Oleander,' I said to Raci Bey.

'They're always fighting but now it's a different story. We're heading towards a real disaster, God protect us. Once the balance has been tilted there will be worse to come.'

There was a threatening tone in Rahmi's voice but Raci Bey's silence was far more unsettling than his son's anger.

That night I sensed he would never forgive Mustafa for disregarding them in his decision to starting digging at the church.

This matter wouldn't be easily set aside.

Mustafa had backed off but his actions were still fresh in everyone's minds – they would never be able to trust him again.

They all walked me to the door.

Kamile Hanım stood at a distance.

She was looking straight at me with a flat expression on her face

I knew exactly what she wanted to say.

XVIII

I don't quite remember now but it must have been two or three days after that dinner that I found myself looking for a jeweller in town.

Zuhal had asked me to get something for her. 'I don't want anyone to know it's from you, but I'll know and I'll always wear it.' I asked her what she wanted and she told me to choose.

I had decided to get her a ring, something stylish but simple enough that it wouldn't draw too much attention.

There was a famous kebab restaurant in the centre of town. I'd never eaten there but I'd heard a lot about it. There was a jeweller's just opposite.

Looking in the front window, I heard voices behind me and turned to see who was there.

Raci Bey and his men were standing outside the restaurant and a young captain, who led the town gendarmerie, was walking over to his car. I could see that Raci Bey was beside himself, his face flushed bright crimson.

'You dog,' he screamed at one of his men, who stood meekly before him with his hands clasped. Raci then slapped him across the face. The captain turned to see what was happening and Raci slapped the man again.

And then he left.

The man sat down at the base of the wall, covering his face with his hands. He must have been crying. No one went over to help him.

'This Raci Bey is bad news,' I thought, 'with no good intentions.'

I saw the extent of his anger in the way he'd shouted at that man, and then slapped him, but I had also witnessed an evil born of an unwavering confidence in his own power.

On this bench in the middle of the night, hopeless, and in the midst of a town groaning in a communal slumber, driven mad by its dreams, I consider all the shades of evil I've seen since I first arrived.

The cradle-maker told me people commit evil because they're blind but I don't think that's how it works.

God plotted his novel with this thought in mind.

Isn't that so?

Isn't that the way you did it?

You know better than me that this is how it is.

There's something deplorable in your need for evil, in how you resort to evil to move this novel along. You insist people should do good but place evil in their hearts.

We both know you have no choice but to shelter evil and those who dabble in the black art.

I agree that it's not a bad idea creating an opposite for everything, dramatic tension in your work swirling back and forth; it's simple but gets the job done.

But this is where your novel falters.

Because you created evil first and structured your narrative around it, giving your heroes an exceptional urge to sin; but to balance out the scales, you command him to be 'good'.

Allow me to explain.

You are incapable of meting out punishment to your evil-doers.

For if you do strike evil down with penance then no one would truly continue to commit the crimes, and you would get nothing out of the bargain. Where would you find the fools to fumble and receive their sentences? You could create them, of course, but then who would read your book if all its heroes were fools?

You must inspire and reward evildoers to perpetuate evil, to sustain the dramatic tension in your work.

Which is precisely what happens in your book.

Despite all injunctions for them to struggle against the dark, and the punishment you dangle above them, these evildoers are always rewarded in the end.

This is the result.

And if you fail to solve the problem in this book, you leave the solution for the hereafter, the book to come, a second volume.

But know that this is hardly an adequate solution.

No well-structured book will leave the ending for a sequel, but you have no other choice.

Speaking frankly, it seems like you just dashed it off.

Now, if you had managed to find a way to punish evil and still maintain a narrative in which evil exists, well then I would have said, 'Bravo, a true masterpiece indeed!' But evil unpunished only serves to hinder your novelistic efforts.

Of course you have powers that we will never have, and you can do away with naysayers when you wish, which gives you a tremendous advantage over us.

No one dares to say your novel is badly plotted.

I can, because you made a mistake, you punished me before I could criticise you.

'I have more in store for you if you keep on like that,' you say, that much I know, but let's save that talk for when I read 'the sequel', that is to say the book of the hereafter, so I now declare unapologetically that this book is flawed.

But praise where praise is due. The concept of good and evil was indeed a profound discovery – I will give you that. You are wonderful in the creation of concepts, it's just that you fail to entwine them in some kind of narrative structure, because there's always the sense of the blasé in the approach, a devil-may-care attitude if you will.

How did the idea of evil come to you?

Which one did you discover first? Good or evil?

I think you came up with evil first, because good is flimsy and attenuated by comparison, but you're aware of this because you're always sending people to the footnotes to bolster their good sides.

But then what I've lived through is there for all to see, which means these footnotes aren't enough to fix the book.

By rewarding good deeds and punishing evil you will not end up with evildoers. Who would opt for evil in such a scenario? And if you don't punish evil then you only end up encouraging people to engage in it, and then I have every right to ask you this: 'If your intent is to goad people to the heights of malevolence, well then why punish them afterwards?'

Between you and me, there is nothing duller than a hero with a good heart.

The alluring ones are all depraved, winners all have the devil inside.

Do you find it amusing?

Indeed I might ask of the creator of such overwhelming evil this: 'Are you good or evil?' But the truth is that I hardly have the strength to even broach the subject.

I too fall back on cliché: 'Let us never equate a writer's personality with his work.'

You know evil better than I.

But you are punishing me.

Not because I am bad but because I am questioning the very nature of evil. The gall!

Truth be told, I was expecting a little more compassion from a colleague.

No, I will not lie to you on such a night. I have also committed crimes, but my punishment is far greater than what others have received.

Observing people, hunting down their weaknesses like a hound, taking in the scent, just like a dog – these are my crimes. All I need is a faint scent in the air.

And I'm off.

Digging up their secrets.

I don't know why I derive such pleasure from these pursuits but for me there is truly nothing more enticing than the secret of another human being.

You leave them no choice but to hide these secrets, and I

then try to find what they are keeping from you, and from others.

You shouldn't have rewarded evil and forbidden it, there shouldn't be so many secrets, this thing called literature should never have been invented.

Is this my sin?

Am I at fault?

While all the secrets you know are hidden, isn't the greatest crime bringing them to light?

Or is it to show how hopeless and pathetic you have left your subjects?

Will Hamiyet's nephew burn in hell?

He's only twenty and he's committed the gravest sin.

I knew he was a sinner from the moment I saw him. Is it a sin for me to recognise a sinner like that?

But how can I explain how you leave a sign that allows me to identify them?

I don't want a secret sign for sin, a trace of your work, yet I see these mysterious clues, faint codes hidden somewhere in the eyes, the lips, the bodies, a blatant sign, a seal that you have pressed upon them, and I can see it.

That's when I watch them.

I've been watching Hamiyet's nephew for some time. His name is Yavuz, internet codename 'my aunt'. The moment I saw the username, I knew I was on the right track.

I started chatting with him.

I told him I was twenty-two years old and that I was attracted to my aunt.

Initially he was shy but I knew he wanted to share something with me. I'd come to know that for many the internet was a kind of confessional, a place where people wanted to speak and share the sins too heavy to carry on their own, and with people they would never meet in the real world.

My crime is pretending to be a stranger. Yes, it is a crime. And yes, I have done so many times. I have stolen secrets from people I know. I have lied to them. I have made them talk.

This kid sat alone in the coffeehouse, and never spoke to anyone, as if in another world, an absent look in his eye. Even on the internet he was reluctant to open up.

But slowly and over time, by spinning lies about myself, inventing sins, I was able to bring him to the point of confessing to me.

At first he only asked me questions. I liked my aunt? When did I first realise this? Does she know? How does she act when I'm around? Have I ever seen her naked?

In fact these were the very questions he wanted me to ask him.

That much I understood.

So among my own confessions I started to ask him the occasional question.

'Do you like your aunt?'

'Yes.'

It actually took us some time to get this far.

'Does she know?'

There was a long silence. I felt like he might close the chat.

'I suppose so,' he wrote.

'Have you ever seen her naked?'

Another long silence.

'Yes.'

'How did it happen?'

He started to explain.

'One night I came home and I thought she wasn't there. Then I heard the water running and I went to the bathroom. The door was open and she was in the bath, her eyes closed. She didn't see me.'

'Did you watch?'

'Yes.'

As Yavuz answered my questions, Hamiyet was a few steps away, speaking to the furniture as she dusted. I looked up at her as I read his words.

The people here were like the town itself, silent on the surface but sinful beneath the still façade. You can either drive right past without noticing a thing or, like me, you could stop and take a closer look. And eventually you would be drawn in.

'What was her body like?'

It was a difficult question, one that might frighten him, but I couldn't help but ask.

'Full, big boobs, a bit of a belly, strong legs, beautiful.'

'What was she doing?'

'Rubbing soap over her body.'

And then before I could ask another question he wrote 'I need to go now' and the screen went blank.

He was scared of what he'd just told me, of revealing his secret; he was scared of himself.

I knew he would come again but he needed time to let this initial confession sink in. People never get it all out in the first go; there's always something missing, lies wedged in along the way, doors left open to scramble back through. So you have to wait patiently for the final story, without ever pushing. But once they start they almost always finish.

The hardest part is getting that first confession out.

He was offline for two days.

I saw him at the coffeehouse, sitting quietly in a corner, not joining any of the conversations, not joking with anyone, only thinking with an enigmatic smile on his face, a smile that only someone privy to his secret would have known. I knew what he was thinking.

His sin had set him apart from the others and he was practically consumed by it.

As long as he didn't speak about it, he could revel in the pleasure it brought him without acknowledging it was indeed a forbidden act. But still he had to tell someone. He wanted to share the feeling, and listen to the sinful thoughts of others to know that he was not the only guilty one.

One day I went back to the cradle-maker and asked him why we were so drawn to sin. He responded, 'Indeed the creator endowed us with sin. But why?'

He looked up at me over his cradle.

Then he lowered his head and said, 'The sins of man bring us together. We gather to share our sins so that we will be stronger in facing them the next time, to know that others have sinned too. If not for these we would be forever isolated, stranded on our own mountaintops. We are united by sin.'

He looked at me with a broad, luminous smile and added, 'But we should gather to do good deeds. Sin brings us together and then we endeavour to do good only to purge ourselves of sin.'

For a while we were silent.

Then without looking up at me, he spoke: 'Don't doubt the creator, my friend. Whatever obstacles he has set before us it is for the good of humanity. You cannot attain perfection without passing through these trials of fire. Sins are there for us to purge ourselves of them, and passing these trials you come closer to the light of the creator. This is the difference between man and beast – the struggle with sin and then achieving salvation.'

Maybe he was right, maybe all these cities, towns and villages were nothing but vast fairgrounds of sin where we secretly gathered to share them with one another.

I wondered if that old man who whittled away at his cradles really knew the sins we so desperately needed to share. Does he know what will become of the little creatures that will soon sleep in his cradles?

I don't think so.

I was the one who knew.

I was the one who pursued them.

I was the one who studied sin and indulged in it.

And there were so many I had yet to discover.

The day after I saw Raci Bey I asked about the incident at the restaurant and they told me that the man he'd slapped was the driver of the digger up on the hill.

XIX

'why does a woman want to have children?'

I leaned back and smiled.

But the sentence that followed knocked me out.

'i decided to have a baby with mustafa . . . i won't marry him . . . i'm just going to have a baby.'

'why?'

The screen was blank for a few minutes, and just when I thought the connection was gone she started.

'i can't get over him . . . he's like no one else in my life . . . i call it love . . . but maybe that's not it . . . but the end result is the same . . . call it whatever you like . . . i just can't get over him . . . it's like a curse . . . the more i struggle to get free, the deeper i sink . . . maybe if just once i could really have him then i might not want to ever see him again . . .

'he's dangerous . . . but this only makes me more attached . . . i think you understand . . . he's so much a part of me that he gives my life meaning . . . i have no idea what i'll do when he's gone . . .

'to get rid of him i need to make him mine . . . that's the only way i can save myself . . . but there is no real way i can do that . . . marrying him isn't a solution . . . even then he won't be mine . . . it will only make the things that much more difficult . . . but if i have his child there'll be a bond between us . . . it will both bring us together and set me free . . .'

'are you sure that's what you want?'

'right now, yes . . . it's seems like the only way out . . . there's just no other way i can free myself . . .

'my parents and everyone else will probably be dead set against it . . .

'but the worst thing about it is that i know i have the courage to really go through with it . . . mum always says that i have a wild side . . . and i suppose she's right . . . i can take on this responsibility . . . i'll be a great mother . . . and when the time comes i'll explain everything . . . not the way i'm telling you about it now . . . there's just one problem left and that's the fact that he won't leave me alone . . .

'ok, i admit it . . . this is all insane . . . but everything has been so confusing recently . . .'

She was like a child playing on the edge of a balcony, trying to frighten me or just attract my attention. I didn't know if she really was going to go through with all this but I sensed she might fall. And if I tried to protect her I felt that I might only end up encouraging her.

'the decision is yours,' I wrote, 'why not . . .'

I wasn't really in the mood to chat and she didn't seem to be either. Signing off, she added, 'i'm coming to town tomorrow. neighbours are having a henna party and they insist i go.'

'see you then.'

'of course.'

The following morning I went down to the coffeehouse and found everyone in a good mood.

'What's up?' I asked Centipede. 'Seems everyone's feeling fine this morning. I haven't seen such high spirits for a while. Someone finally find the treasure?'

'Oh no, brother, hardly . . . We're laughing at Sultan.'

'What happened?'

'You know the big carpet shop at the back of the main market? Well, they had some kind of trouble with Sultan, didn't pay their protection money or something . . . So Oleander goes to Sultan and tells him to scare the life out of them, and Sultan goes and shoots the guy right in the face.'

Seized in a fit of giggling, Centipede kept saying the words over and over again, 'Go and scare the life out of him, and

Sultan goes and shoots the guy right in the face.' Almost everyone else there was repeating the words too, and nearly splitting their sides laughing.

'Go and scare the living daylights out of him, and then he goes and shoots him.'

I was the only one left out.

I asked if they'd caught Sultan and Centipede laughed even more loudly. 'No one even saw it happen,' he said. I didn't dare ask them how they knew it really happened. I had understood: no one ever witnessed this kind of murder, and no one was ever caught. The killer would lie low in one of Sultan's houses in the vineyards for a while before he came back into town.

They were merrily laughing away at the incident but I could sense an underlying tension. Clearly the town was on edge.

Of course not every criminal and killer walked away a free man. Some of them were caught and others got away. Two days earlier I was wandering through the secondhand shops near the minibus stop when I saw a passenger get knifed in the stomach. But by the time he hit the ground, the square was full of police and they dragged the driver off.

Just like the police commissioner had told me: they were 'keeping the peace', and so when there was a disturbance someone was apprehended, but the 'animals' – as he called them – were allowed to roam free. They were untouchable. Because they could burn down the jungle.

It might seem strange to an outsider but after living in the town for long enough you got used to the killing and the fact that certain killers go free. It even begins to seem natural for them to shoot each other in broad daylight.

The strange thing was the way the town could appear calm and peaceful despite all the murders and the growing tension and anxiety. What I really couldn't understand was this contradiction. I suppose the appearance of calm was because people had become accustomed to the murders and no longer found them unusual. Maybe the police commissioner was right: if the gangs' hit men were apprehended the balance would be skewed and the public would grow restless.

Towards evening, Zuhal sent me a phone message, *I'm here. Let's meet tomorrow.*

I sent one right back.

Tell me how it goes tonight.

I'll write if it doesn't go too late.

When I'm alone I never feel lonely. I've come to enjoy and even delight in solitude. In fact I normally choose to be alone. And I often miss it if I have been around people for too long. But it's more than that – I need to be alone. I've never quite understood why. It's not that there's anything in particular I want to do but it gives me the freedom to think of all the things I have in mind to do. Perhaps this is why I'm often willing to drop everything I'm doing to be alone, so that I can think before I act.

I've always had the strange belief that the mere existence of other human beings has tethered my freedom, for it isn't long before I begin to feel restless in society. I need to be in a space where I have the freedom of movement without having to say a word to anyone, but as I've said: it's not so that I can act, it's so that I can consider all the options. At those times I'm quickly frustrated with anyone who might block my desires or question my intentions, another force of will, a demanding presence.

Maybe this is why I've led a life of solitude for so many years.

To avoid another force of will that might challenge mine, another demanding presence.

I'm never bored when I'm alone; nor do I feel the need to talk to anyone, to be rescued from the solitude. I can walk alone for hours, sit alone quietly without saying a word.

I've never understood why people are so terrified of being alone. So many people arrange their lives so as not to be alone, giving up so many things they want simply to avoid solitude. This is something I can't understand because I have often sacrificed desires to be alone. I have sacrificed my happiness for it.

But that night was perhaps the first time I came to understand loneliness, feared by so many others.

When the light on the screen went out I felt it.

I suddenly felt as if I was in a dark cell and I longed for a human voice, a touch, a ray of light.

Even though I was close to Zuhal, this loneliness caused me to think that I might never see her again.

Thinking of the impossible has always been a torture for me. But solitude would lift all barriers and everything would suddenly open up in my mind. It was impossible to see Zuhal then. I imagine it was that one sentence – *I'll write if it doesn't go too late* – that brought on the loneliness and a strange kind of hopelessness that I had never felt before.

Maybe that was when I realised that what I was experiencing at that moment – indeed what we all experience – was an amalgam of reality and our dreams.

Like that wisp of a cloud I saw that day I drove up to the mountain hotel, faint dreams are blended into everything we experience. It is hard to believe that a trace of a cloud, a dream that seems so small and insignificant beside reality, holds within it a secret longing that can colour the real.

It wasn't Zuhal or her absence that brought on this feeling – I hardly ever saw her – but rather that little cloud in my mind, a dream not yet fully formed. The longing to love someone and to be loved had suddenly become a reality. Zuhal had become a woman I was in love with, a woman I could not live without. But though I was in love I still wanted to be alone, because love couldn't change my need for solitude. This woman had introduced me to loneliness and it was an unbearable emotion.

That little cloud drifting above reality had transformed Zuhal's absence, changed her in my mind, turned her into the figment of a woman I couldn't live without, a woman I had to be with right then and there, showing me her face, her voice, her touch.

I realised I was looking at myself from a distance, spying, and that gave me a bad feeling. I could see the truth even though I was under the spell of my dreams. I was aware of the illusion but I couldn't shed the emotions that came with it.

I needed someone to help pass the time, to fill the void Zuhal had pitched before me.

And it was strange that Mustafa and Sümbül were the two people I most wanted to see.

I thought about calling Mustafa – I know it's hard to explain. I usually talked to him about Zuhal or books. In a way, I was close to him because of Zuhal. It was a relationship we perceived differently, conjuring up contrasting emotions, but we both knew that it was built on our love for the same woman.

The relationship between two men who desire the same woman can be one of lifelong enmity, but also one of lifelong friendship.

I picked up my phone to call him.

Then I realised how ridiculous it would be.

If we talked that night Mustafa would only corner Zuhal the next day, ask her all kinds of questions, and insult her. In just one night our friendship would dissolve into hostility.

I called Sümbül.

I was afraid that she might be busy with a customer.

She picked up.

'What are you doing?' I asked.

'Oh you know, just watching a debate on TV.'

'Can you come over?'

'Sure. Just give me some time. I can be there in half an hour.'

Whores never come on time. They're always late. I don't know why. But Sümbül was different – she was always right on time.

Half an hour later there was a knock on the door. Sümbül was someone you could trust.

She was wearing thin, baggy slacks, a comfortable shirt, flat shoes, no make-up and her hair was pulled back in a bun.

'Whisky-cola?'

'My pleasure.'

'You need any help?'

'No, I'll make it.'

I poured a rakı for myself.

'Take off your clothes,' I said.

I loved watching her strip.

Without ever making a fuss she peeled off all her clothes and sat there completely naked, one foot tucked under her arse. Her breasts were just beginning to sag.

'What were you watching?' I asked.

'Oh God, one of those idiotic political programmes. I just watch them because I'm bored.'

'So, what's the state of affairs?' I asked, smiling. I always enjoyed listening to her take on things.

'As far as I can tell, these politicians do what we're doing right here but they're the ones who leave with the money.'

Then she laughed. She found the analogy amusing.

'So you're saying that the country is one big brothel,' I said.

'No, not like that. Whores are bright. They wouldn't do the deed and give money to have it done.'

Sümbül was never bothered by the word 'whore', and she used it freely herself, found it entirely natural.

'The truth is that a whore's pimp spends all the money on himself, but then again . . .' She stopped for a moment and then said sadly, 'I had one like that too. I was smitten, I spent the money I made on him. And he was only too happy to take it. Then I caught him with another whore. I gave him a good kick up the arse and felt much better.'

She was quiet for a moment. I suppose she felt it was inappropriate to show such sadness on the job and her face lit up. 'You can give someone a good kick, but as soon as you get rid of one another shows up.'

'Who are you going to vote for?' I asked.

'No one,' she said. 'They're all in the game for their own interests. They give you a little hope then you see they're all the same.' And she laughed again. 'You know how they say all men want the same thing? I swear politicians want the same thing too, they're no different.'

She took a sip of her drink and smiled.

'What's happening in town?' I asked.

'Same thing that's happening all over the country. It's really tense out there. I'm worn out from giving all these guys extra care. I have to loosen them up before they can do me. I swear everyone's petrified, and I can't understand what's happened. Pretty soon they won't even be able to get it up and I'll starve.'

'You'll never go hungry. You'll always have customers.'

'Of course I will, but the guys here are getting worse. They're frustrated.'

'Will there be more violence?'

'I think they're going to take out Sultan.'

She was quiet then, and when our eyes met I saw fear, and an imploring gaze. She knew she'd said too much. She was usually careful about what she said but the words had just slipped out.

At that moment I realised two things.

She'd slept with one of Muhacir's men and got the news from him.

And that Sümbül was probably passing the information on to the police, because otherwise they'd never leave her in peace.

For a moment I was overcome with sadness. I hated the idea of her being an informer but it seemed inevitable. It was a reality I didn't want to accept because if she was indeed relaying information, she wasn't doing it of her own free will, and she no doubt had to protect her customers.

She was able to establish friendships with most of them.

Sometimes she called me first and that's when I knew that work was slow and that she needed money. I'd then call her over even when I wasn't in the mood, we would just chat without ever going to bed together and I would send her on her way with the money. She knew that I called her over for her friendship. And I also knew that if I didn't have money she would let me have a go with her for free. We were friends.

She stood up.

'Well, I think that's enough politics for tonight. Come on, let's have a little fun. Let me show you a good time. I'll cheer you up.'

She made her way to the stairs and I followed.

'You won't be disappointed tonight,' she said, slinking up the stairs. 'Tonight everything goes.'

In return I would forget that Sultan was going to be shot.

Indeed I would forget everything altogether. Sümbül knew the tricks.

After I sent her on her way I slipped back into my sombre mood and turned on my computer.

Just three words.

'where are you?'

'i'm here,' I wrote back.

The next line came quickly. It was clear she'd been waiting for me online.

'i thought about you all night.'

'wasn't it a good night?'

'it was actually a lot of fun. if i ever get married again i'll definitely have a henna night but i missed you . . . a lot . . . i was thinking about you all night . . . thinking about you with my hand on my stomach . . . all night people kept asking me why i was smiling . . . and i couldn't help but wonder what they would say if i told them what i was thinking.'

'what was that?'

'about our night in the hotel . . . and what we did together.'

There was a pause and before I could write back.

'i'm getting hooked on you. i really missed you.'

'i miss you too.'

Then we started to make love in words. Once I asked if we should video chat but she told me she was afraid of the images getting around on the internet, so we only wrote to each other. Our fingers and our imaginations were enough to put us in a place where anything was possible.

Making love with Zuhal in words after having ravished Sümbül in reality was even more fulfilling and ecstatic.

This was a different kind of reality that was hard to explain.

As we were signing off she wrote, 'meet me at the hayati's creamery in the morning. we can have breakfast there. it feels like we're spending the night together. i'll think about sleeping in your arms.'

I was surprised. She was worried about being seen with me in that remote mountain hotel but now she wasn't at all concerned about being with me in town. Then I understood. She was afraid of 'mustafa knowing what was going on' but she wasn't the least bit afraid of 'mustafa worrying that something might be going on'. Indeed that was precisely what she wanted.

When I woke up in the morning she messaged me: 'leaving home now.'

'me too.'

Hayati's creamery was on a little hill not far from Mustafa's home. It was a popular breakfast spot, nothing more than a tent and low tables, overlooking the sea.

Hayati was a short man with a big head and a permanent frown, but the rumour was that he was extremely rich. He made homemade crêpes with fresh cream and a sprinkle of sugar on top. That was it. And freshly brewed tea.

But his crêpes were unforgettably delicious.

Zuhal was there when I arrived, sitting at a table. She'd ordered breakfast for both of us.

Though we'd both gone to bed late, her face looked refreshed and peaceful. There was an incredible innocence in her expression. She was a young lady, a princess, a queen, a little girl – all of them in one.

'You're killing me,' I said, smiling.

'How so?' she said with a smile that betrayed her true feelings.

'You just look so innocent. But I know what happened last night, and what you said, what you wrote . . . It's hard to imagine the two together. It's driving me mad just thinking about it.'

'Do you know what happened the other day?'

'What?'

'I was going through my wardrobe with a friend, planning to give some of my extra clothes to the poor. After looking through what I had my friend said, Zuhal, do you know how many different styles you have here? And at that moment I understood. I had all these different kinds of clothes, as if many different women shared the same wardrobe. But I always wore the same style. I'd bought all the other dresses but I never actually wore them.'

'You can wear them with me,' I said. 'All of them.'

'I know,' she said.

Her eyes . . . those enormous eyes set in her innocent face bore that infinite darkness. Her face was the same but her eyes had changed.

It was a beautiful day. The scent of lavender and jasmine hung in the air. And that little, lonely cloud was hovering up there in the bright blue sky. It was as if it followed us wherever we went.

'I saw that same cloud up at the hotel,' I said.

'I know. I saw it too.'

'If it keeps up like this, we'll have to adopt the guy.'

I expected her to laugh or say something.

But she looked at me without saying a word.

Even now I can't make out what it was in her eyes, the way she looked at me. I have no idea what she was thinking then. There was a sadness in her eyes that bordered on grief, an overwhelming loneliness that surprised even me, the desperation of someone who'd been abandoned – it was all there in her eyes. It was so brief that it almost seemed a figment of my imagination but I was sure of it, and it was the last thing I expected.

'We could only ever have a cloud as a child,' she said, and the look in her eyes disappeared. But I sensed a lingering anguish in her soft, whispering voice that contradicted her eyes, which had not changed as quickly, though the look was gone by the time she finished her sentence.

She smiled and took a bite of her crêpe, which cracked in her mouth and the cream oozed out from the sides. She hungrily took another bite. And we ate together, looking into each other's eyes, and when we finished she ordered another, and I ordered another tea.

'You love to eat but you never put on weight.'

'I do.'

'I've never noticed.'

She smiled in a familiar way. 'You'll see soon enough.' The sentence was full of promise and innuendo.

'You're turning me on,' I said. And that sincere smile again.

'There's no harm in that.'

When we finished breakfast she said, 'Today's the open market day. It's really fun. Should we go?'

'Yes, why not.'

'You won't be embarrassed to be with me?'

'Why would I?'

'You'll see . . .'

Walking to our cars, I felt truly happy. She gently put her arm in mine and I could feel the pressure of her grip.

'Last night Mustafa sent me a message asking me to come and see him.'

'And what did you say?'

'I said I couldn't, that I was at a henna night. Then he said I should come tonight.'

We walked side by side, looking straight ahead.

'Are you going to go?'

'I don't know . . . I hate going to that hotel.' Then she turned to look at me.

'You meet him in a hotel?'

'Yes . . . There's a hotel in town . . . You won't believe it but it's called the Amsterdam Hotel. Mustafa has a room there.'

'Why doesn't he invite you to his place?'

'I don't know . . . He says his mother's ill and never leaves her room. Or that's the excuse. But even though he knows I hate the place, he insists on us meeting there. He wants to embarrass me, make me feel bad about it. Even when he knows how I feel walking past everyone there . . .'

'Why doesn't he go to your place?'

'He says they'll see him . . . It doesn't matter if people see me at the hotel but it does if they see him at my place.'

'Are you going to go?'

'I don't know.'

More than sadness I felt disappointed: I'd hoped she would come to see me that night.

'Let me know,' I said.

'I will.'

We drove off.

Alone, I examined my feelings. I wanted to know if I was really sad. I wasn't. Disappointed, but not sad.

On the way there I wondered why I wasn't sad. I suppose I believed that she was drifting away from Mustafa and becoming closer to me, and this belief protected me until something actually happened or at least helped me hide the emotion from myself. I did that sometimes. I could bury feelings I didn't like. Later they would suddenly take hold of me in the middle of the night, waking me up. But until then I was fine.

By the time we parked our cars on a quiet street near the market I'd managed to suppress the feeling. I guess part of this 'ease' came from the idea that Zuhal was still 'Mustafa's woman'. She'd told me from the start that she was in love with him and our arrangement was based on that. I'd grown accustomed to the idea.

As we got closer to the market I could hear the mounting clamour of the shifting, murmuring, seething crowd, an indecipherable hum with the occasional cry that soared above the din. Turning the corner, we were face to face with it.

But the noise actually suggested a bigger crowd. It was

nothing like the teeming markets in big cities. People were comfortably wandering around the wooden stalls where all the different items were lined up for sale: lettuce, fresh greens and vegetables, knitted sweaters, fresh eggs, mounds of olives and bottles of olive oil, used furniture, knives, baubles, pocket torches, and even a stall stacked with used car tyres.

Strolling through the market, I understood why she said I might be embarrassed because she touched everything that caught her eye, even sniffing the objects as she turned them over in her hands, gazing at them for some time, chatting with the salesman, haggling and then switching right back to small talk. She bought five little brooms with mistletoe on the ends, and in response to my surprise she said, 'They're excellent gifts.' I'd be lying if I said I didn't hold my breath as we passed the stall with all the tyres but she managed not to run her fingers over them.

Winding in and out of the stalls, she tasted different fruits and chatted with nearly every salesman, making her way to the antique dealers in the back.

She was used to these kinds of places. She liked people and crowds, despite her strange and distant air, which was nothing like mine and which was far more alluring.

We went into every shop.

She ran her fingers over almost every piece of furniture: old chests and used clothes, lamps and broken plates, glasses, carafes and chains.

Seeing the puzzled look on my face, she said, 'I like to touch the things I want to remember. I can keep them in my mind that much longer.'

'You must have quite a bit of space set aside in your memory for all those tomatoes,' I said, and she laughed and gently slapped my face.

There was something like love between us.

In the back room of one shop she delighted over an embroidered dress made of cream-coloured silk, the edges lined with lace. It wasn't something she would actually wear.

They haggled for some time, occasionally fitting in the odd chatter about family, and in the end she bought the dress.

Then we left the market.

The streets became narrower and quieter. We walked in silence.

All of a sudden she stopped and lifted her head like a little dog catching a scent in the air.

'Come on,' she said, taking my hand.

Turning the corner we followed a winding street then came out on a wider one with several shops side by side.

She walked straight over to one of them.

The mouth-watering scent of salt, vinegar and garlic wafted out the door.

The smells were even stronger inside, where a plump woman with dyed blonde hair was sitting. Clusters of dried fish dangled from the ceiling. There was salted fish in vats. Cured beef hung over the counter.

The place was filled with all different kinds of dried or cured food: aged cheese, pickles, mackerel . . .

'My God, it's heaven in here,' Zuhal exclaimed as she touched and sniffed everything there.

The blonde woman told us how to cure mackerel. 'You grill them on embers first and then lay them in the vinegar.'

Together they separated the salted fish.

In the end Zuhal bought them all. She bought something I'd never heard of called 'kalyos'. She asked the woman what it tasted like.

'I don't know,' she said. 'I don't eat anything here. I have no idea what these things taste like.'

'How's that? You've never wondered?'

'I have but just never tried.'

'I can't believe that.'

'It's the truth. Not even the cured beef.'

The woman gave us her card as we left. 'You can always order more.'

'These people are mad,' said Zuhal after we had left. 'You

sit in a place like that all day long and you never wonder what the food tastes like.'

I thought, Everyone's the same. They sit through life never really tasting it. But I kept the thought to myself.

Arm in arm we walked back to our cars.

We loaded everything into hers.

'Let me know about tonight,' I said. 'If you're going to go or not.'

'All right,' she said.

She waved and then left, and I watched her go.

I had the same feeling after she had left me in the hotel in the mountains.

A heavy loneliness. The kind I never liked.

I went home too.

As night fell I received a short message from her.

I'm going.

XX

I didn't sleep well.

I think I woke almost every hour and checked my messages online.

But there was nothing all night.

And there was nothing from her in the morning.

In a bad mood I had breakfast on the veranda. I wasn't really hungry. I wondered what their hotel room was like. Was there a mirror? What had they done together? Did she do the same things to him that she did to me?

'Of course she did,' I said to myself.

As she still hadn't sent me a message, I assumed they were having breakfast together. Did they go to the creamery? Were they gazing out over the sea? Did she tell him she wanted to have a baby? Were they laughing together? Was there no longer a cold wind blowing between them?

Like a coroner performing a post mortem, I felt more and more removed from Zuhal, growing colder and more distant.

Hamiyet was busy mopping the veranda, her skirt rolled up over her knees. 'What's up? You're in a strop this morning,' she said.

I didn't ask her how she knew. Was it because I wasn't eyeing her legs? And though I didn't say so much, I smiled and glanced at her sturdy calves, which were fully exposed, and said, 'Oh no, I'm fine. I was just thinking.'

'Oh, I see. But why not smile a little. I've never seen you with such a long face before.'

I couldn't leave the house but I couldn't go and check my computer either.

I sat on the veranda and read my papers.

That's when I got a message from her.

Come home.

We used the word 'home' for chat, and our home was a place that was ours, a place that separated us from the rest of the world.

I dashed home.

'last night i went back to the city,' she wrote.

'what happened?'

'i couldn't stay with him . . . in that filthy room full of the traces of other women and scraps of food all over the table . . . it's a mess . . . and i kept thinking of you . . . so i left in the middle of the night and drove back to the city.'

'was he angry you left?'

'really angry . . . we messaged a lot on my way back . . . cursing each other . . . saying all kinds of nasty things . . . he even accused me of using him for sex . . . oh i was going to write him a really good response to that . . . finish it once and for all.'

I have to admit this made me smile.

'i went home and i read your books.'

'good.'

'i want to ask you for a favour.'

'what's that?'

'in one of them you describe a religious wedding with an imam.'

'i think i have several of those.'

'probably but i remember this one.'

'yes.'

'marry me in that kind of ceremony, with an imam . . . let's get married in a mosque . . . you choose the mosque . . . arrange everything . . . and marry me . . .'

'because i described something like that in my book?'

'it seems you write what you've actually experienced and

then you relive it in words . . . it's strange . . . i'm the woman you married in your book . . .'

'yes.'

'so we're going to get married?'

'if you want to.'

'have you ever turned down anything a woman asked for?'

'why do you ask?'

'it seems to me that you say yes to everyone and everything, and so sometimes i don't feel special when i'm with you . . . especially when i read your books.'

'don't read them then.'

'are we going to get married?'

'yes.'

'buy me a ring . . . and let's get married in a village mosque . . . you find the village and the mosque and the imam . . . and make me feel like you want to do it . . . more than getting married, i want to know that you want it.'

'all right . . . i'll arrange everything.'

'i had such a bad night . . . such terrible dreams . . . i woke up again and again . . . terrified . . .'

'don't be, i'm here.'

'you're teasing me but i believe you when you say it . . . don't say such things if you don't really believe them . . . i believe everything you say . . . don't tell me anything you don't really believe.'

'i won't.'

'i have a question.'

'go ahead.'

'you won't hurt me, will you?'

'no . . . i would never . . . you can be sure of that.'

'i'm sure . . . i need to go now . . . will we get married the next time i come to town?'

'we will.'

'promise?'

'promise.'

'are you going to make me feel like you really want it?'

'i will.'

'promise?'

'promise'

'ok, i'm going now . . . will you be my husband?'

'yes.'

'i've been fantasising about it all day.'

The screen went blank.

It was a strange conversation. I felt as if I'd spent the night with a different woman. I couldn't understand how the roles had changed but I liked it. I felt relieved. I felt somehow lighter.

Leaning against the door opening onto the veranda, I watched Hamiyet. Her legs even more exposed, I could make out thin veins in her calves. She turned to look at me, a fleeting, nearly imperceptible glance.

'I'm going into town,' I said. To be honest, I had no idea what might have happened if I'd stayed home. The strange commotion in me might have spurred me to act on those desires. Perhaps something I would do later on, inevitable but nevertheless delayed.

I tucked my papers under my arm and set off along the shortcuts that would take me to the main street. Crossing the street, Mustafa's massive black car stopped in front of me.

The window came down. 'Where are you going?' he asked.

'To the coffeehouse.'

'If you have nothing better to do, come with me. I'm swinging by the municipality and then I'm going to the Chamber of Commerce cafeteria for lunch. We can eat together.'

'Why not,' I said.

I got in.

He looked exhausted and his face was pale. Clearly he'd been up all night.

'You look tired. You must be busy these days,' I said.

'I worked late last night,' he said.

'You shouldn't wear yourself out like that. This town needs you,' I said.

I was making fun of the man, cruelly delighting in his defeat.

I knew everything about him, or at least almost everything, while he knew very little about me. If Zuhal wasn't fearful of him, she'd tell him all about me. Some women were double agents, telling both men everything they know. But Mustafa could only learn so much from her because he frightened her and was extremely jealous and mistreated her. All that came at a price. To remain in the dark. Never to know. And then to think you actually know it all.

We stopped in front of the municipality building. People flocked to the car. I stayed inside. Mustafa came back fifteen minutes later. 'I'm terribly sorry to make you wait like that. Let's get going,' he said.

The Chamber of Commerce was one of those old-style, three-storey buildings of sand-coloured stone which gave the town its charm. It was right on the sea. The cafeteria was on the third floor. The food wasn't very good, so the rich set usually didn't eat there, but it was full of high government officials who wanted to have a quiet face-to-face meal, and who usually didn't eat anywhere else.

We sat at a table by the window with a view of the sea. It was a little early and we were the only ones there. Waiters were all standing nearby.

'Shall we have a rakı lunch?' he asked.

'Why not?' I said and he signalled for the waiters, who hurried over to take his order.

'Rakı and a few things to go with it.'

Silently he looked out over the sea then turned to me and said, 'Life's tough, isn't it?'

'It is,' I said.

'Are you able to write?'

'No. Sometimes it seems as if I'll never be able to write again.'

'Write. You write well.'

'We'll see.'

'Do you know all the women you describe in your books?'

'Why do you ask?' I said, a little annoyed by the question.

He went on as if he hadn't noticed. Or was it that he didn't care?

'I've been with many different women. And I can't understand how you can know them well enough to write about them, know how they feel. I don't understand a thing.'

'What don't you understand?'

Shaking his head as if in pain, he said, 'I don't understand anything.'

I really felt for him just then, and for a moment I forgot that this woman he was desperately trying to understand had asked me to marry her only a little while ago.

'I don't know what I'm doing or why I'm doing what I'm doing . . . It's such meaninglessness. You want to make a woman happy because you love her and she gets it all wrong. Why does a woman keep telling you she loves you while doing everything in her power to make you sad and angry? Why does a woman suddenly turn and leave after she's cried in your arms? Why does she think you want to leave her just when you're about to propose to her?'

'Maybe you did something to upset her?'

'Maybe she did something to upset me and she can't forget,' he said.

He was quiet for a moment and I imagine he was considering what he'd just said. 'Now, tell me, can a woman really do something that stupid? Is it possible? I'm dying to know. Would she blame me or take it out on me for a mistake that she made?'

'I'm not sure what kind of mistake you're talking about so I can't really give you an answer.'

He looked out over the sea, took a sip of rakı, lit a cigarette, and all the while I knew that he was thinking about whether he should tell me, and suffering so deeply that I can't say I didn't pity the man: he had no one else in the world he could talk to other than the man who was sleeping with the woman he loved.

Looking into his eyes, I waited and the worst of it was that as I looked at him I imagined him making love to Zuhal, his words and his expressions.

Now, on this bench in the middle of the night, waiting for what I imagine will be a horrible end, I can still smile when I think of that moment.

Oh God, is that why you're punishing me?

Are you punishing me for that?

I agree I should be punished. What I did was unfair, cruel and sinful.

But am I the only guilty one?

This man has no one to talk to about the woman he loves except the man who is making love to her. You have condemned him to this. Are you not guilty for it?

Did you not condemn him to his loneliness and desperation?

What did you suppose I'd think when you dropped him at my feet?

How can you expect kindness from a man who's sleeping with his friend's girlfriend? Should he simply forget all about it?

Should I have erased all those passionate scenes from my mind?

Don't you know that's impossible?

What were you thinking when you made it clear to me that the woman who had just asked me to marry her had only but a few hours ago been shedding tears in his arms?

Didn't you ever stop to think that I might feel hurt, broken, enraged by such a confrontation?

What's the point?

To add a little more excitement to your book, and have a little fun putting me and Mustafa in such a bind, just to see what will happen when the emotions collide?

Did you expect these two men who had been hurt by the same women in different ways to lick each other's wounds like animals?

We are human beings.

Humans you created.

When you are so flippantly fiddling with our emotions, how do you expect us to react to the pain?

Don't you know that pain only becomes anger, hostility and revenge? How could you not? You're the author of this book, and if you know so much how could you expect anything else to happen?

And when you read the end result of your own work, just what you had anticipated all along, are you angry at what the heroes of your own design have done?

If you're the one writing then why are you angry with me?

And if I am the one writing then why am I suffering?

Shouldn't we decide who is responsible for what our hero has done and the pain that he is to endure?

There isn't anyone apart from us, another God making fun of the two of us, is there?

It's just the two of us?

Now, I don't mean to rile you up, but you're aware that you have abandoned all responsibility, piling it all up on my shoulders, aren't you?

I get all the responsibility and you get all the power.

You write it all down and then you punish me for it.

After it's all there on the page you find me guilty, a sinner, cruel?

But who is cruel?

Who is punished?

Here in the middle of this sleeping town are we going to declare this poor, ill-fated man guilty and a sinner?

As I listened to Mustafa speak of his troubles, I thought about how he made love to Zuhal. What do you think about when you listen to my laments? What do you know that I don't know?

What are all those things I will never know before I die?

Will you laugh when I die?

Will you grieve?

Won't you be bored without me here on earth?

You never will be able to find someone else like me. You

can write your heart out, but you can't come up with another like me.

Does this make you mad?

Indeed does the idea that I can write all this down make you angry?

If I have something else in mind as I write all of this, and you're aware of it, then yes, you have every right to be angry.

Is there any doubt in your mind as to the real author of this book?

How much more time till morning?

Are you going to save me?

Can you come up with a means of salvation when there is no way out? Can you create a way out of this trap?

But neither of us are capable of so much at this late stage, are we?

From this moment on, both of us are condemned to what we've already written.

We can't change that now.

There are limits to our power, limits to your power.

I am at that limit now.

Is this not the very thing we know as hopelessness, to be at the limit of one's power, to hit a dead end with no way out?

The only chance for this unresolved problem of yours is to say you'll fix it in the sequel, in the hereafter.

That's not enough for me right now.

I need a solution to unfold in this book.

And it doesn't seem like I'll find one in the middle of the night.

In fact it seems a bit strange to think that I'll be killed here tonight because that day as I was listening to everything Mustafa had to tell me I was thinking about how he made love to Zuhal.

But what isn't strange?

After thinking quietly to himself for a while, Mustafa made his decision – he no longer had the strength to bear the pain alone, and there was no one else in town he could talk to.

'I fell in love with her when I was at university, and she loved me. Those were wonderful days. We travelled together and had such good times. I'll never forget how beautiful she was when she laughed, I've never heard such a beautiful laugh. Back then I was different, I didn't have a care in the world. You know how people are when they fall in love. Nothing else matters. I assumed we would get married when we got home. I don't know why I never told her that. Maybe because I didn't want to scare her or I wanted to surprise her later. Maybe I just wanted to be sure that she loved me as much as I loved her. I can't really say. Love isn't easy, you love someone but then you have such silly suspicions. Anyway. You know, I was even thinking about the names we could give our children. We finished university. She came back. My dad wanted me to stay there another year to do an internship and so he arranged for me to work at his American friend's company. I didn't want to do it. He really pushed me. It got to the point where it nearly broke us up. The thing is that I could have written off my dad, and my whole family, and then I considered how difficult it would be for us to live and how I would have trouble providing for her, and in fact in a way I did it so the two of us could live a happy, affluent life. I stayed. And she came back. You know, I cried for the first time in my life when I dropped her off at the airport. I cried for her. She never knew about that but I never forgot. Then we started to write letters. But over time we wrote less and less. I couldn't ask anyone about her, I was too embarrassed. I was afraid I would get the wrong answer, put myself in an awkward position. When I got back she was already married. To a kid from the city. Good-looking guy. His dad owned an olive oil factory. I didn't call her after I heard about it. I just came back to this damned town and I never left.'

He paused then said, 'What should we eat?'

I was lost in the story and confused. 'Ah . . . I think I'll have a steak.'

He laughed. 'Good idea. This place has always had terrible

food. Best to have grilled meat. I'll have one too. How do you like it?'

'Well done.' And he laughed again.

'Turkish style,' he said and turned to the waiter.

'Two steaks well done.'

He took a sip of rakı and seemed a little more relaxed.

'I also married someone from town. My mother arranged it. I agreed without even thinking about it. But it didn't work out and we separated. I wasn't working. Then some time went by. One day I went into town for business. I had a lover at the time, and I went into a shop to buy her a gift. Zuhal and I met again there. You know, I was really nervous even though so much time had passed, and I didn't know how to hide it. We ate something together. She had also recently separated from her husband. And then we got back together again. She came back to town and bought a house. Sometimes she would come here and sometimes I would stay with her in the city. But I could never forget the fact that she had married someone else. I didn't feel like I could ever be that close to her again. I loved her, but not like before, I couldn't trust her. But you know I really wanted to. I truly did and I pushed myself. But then there were these strange times when I would think about her married to some other bastard, a worthless dog, and I would go mad. I couldn't stop myself. I suppose I said some pretty hurtful things when I was angry, and I did things to disappoint her. There were times when I left her. But when I did, I was full of regret and when I came back she behaved in a way that made my suspicion and rage flood back again. She did every-thing she could to make me angry. She knew how to do it. You see we really tore each other apart, left each other to lick our wounds. I tried other women, to get over her, but it didn't work and I just couldn't leave her. In the end I said to myself, I just can't give her up and if I do I'll either be at war with her or myself, so just let the past be the past. And whenever I thought of her, whenever she crossed my mind, I would go into a room and trash the place until I calmed down and then

I could go back to her. So I called her. I was going to ask her to marry me. We were so good before. Talking about it, she started to cry. Then she started an argument about something that had nothing to do with it. And in the middle of night she gets up and leaves. It was like she wasn't the one who had married someone else and was blaming me. As if I had made everything happen. In her mind, it's all my fault.'

He stopped and looked at me, and a bright smile spread across his face, a young, innocent smile, and he took my arm like a young man horsing around with a friend and said, 'This would make a great novel, wouldn't it?'

'Depends how you write it,' I said.

'No, I don't mean that. Believe me, it wouldn't work, nothing would come of the diary of two madmen, but something would come of the diary of two fools. Even if I told the whole story to Gogol, it wouldn't work.'

Sometimes he could really surprise me.

He sighed and asked, 'Is it that she can't forgive herself for what she did or that she can't forgive me for what I did?'

Mulling over an answer, I heard a languid voice behind me. 'Oh, so you're here too, I see.' Mustafa and I turned around to see the judge and the district governor standing over us. Making a considerable effort to conceal his disdain, he said, 'Please join us.'

'If you're having a private lunch, don't let us disturb you,' the district governor said as he pulled out a chair for himself.

'Of course not. We just met on the street and we're talking books,' Mustafa said.

Unforthcoming, the judge sat down at our table. I had never before seen such a thin man: his shoulders, chest and head looked two-dimensional. He face was fixed in a permanent frown. You would never expect the man to ever smile.

They ordered.

'So how have you been, Mr Mayor?' said the district governor. 'I've been hearing things.'

Mustafa furrowed his brow.

'What kinds of things?'

The district governor looked at me, no doubt wondering just how much he could share with me before deciding that I wouldn't understand.

'It seems Muhacir's men are getting ready to do something rash.'

So clearly they'd heard about the planned hit on Sultan. Either Sümbül had talked or there was another informant inside Muhacir's team.

'Ah,' Mustafa said, and a shadow fell over his face. He was now a very different man. 'So it seems we need to speak with Raci Bey before those dogs turn this place upside down.'

The judge weighed in with his wooden voice. 'If you could issue an outstanding warrant for Muhacir, we might be able to arrest him for the public good. To keep the public peace.'

'The public peace' was a magic word in this town, bandied about for any kind of 'benefit'.

'Things could get even more out of control then,' said the district official.

I listened to everything they were saying with an innocent expression on my face, as if I was entirely unaware of the situation.

'The trouble-makers will be arrested,' said the judge.

'Oh, esteemed judge, it seems you'd like to lock them all up and be done with it,' said the district governor, laughing as he stroked his prayer beads.

'If required for the public good, of course, and why not?'

'And will you have Oleander arrested as well?' I asked innocently, and all three heads swivelled in my direction.

'No,' said the district governor. 'Oleander is a nationalist, a patriot, and you shouldn't pay attention to the rumours about him. He's a tough fellow but he'd never betray the government or his country.'

A range of expressions moved the faces of the other two.

'Muhacir isn't that kind of man. I'm sure he has ties to foreign powers. He has family that comes and goes. They say they're relatives but who knows if they really are. What do they do? What kind of work? No one really knows. They might be trying to prepare the treasure as a gift for them. It would be a betrayal of the country if they sold a national heritage treasure to them. That's what I am concerned about.'

Hearing mention of the treasure, I felt that I could interrupt without arousing too much suspicion.

'Why not establish a shared foundation in the name of the town and move ahead that way? The state would most likely seize the treasure but at least a part of it would remain with the town. And you could then set up a museum and tourists from all around the world would come to see it. It would only enrich the town.'

'Out of the question,' Mustafa said so sharply and abruptly that everyone snapped to attention and he felt compelled to explain himself.

'First of all, there's nothing fit for a museum up there, only money and jewels. Hah, a museum. Someone will find that treasure. No one would accept the idea of a joint foundation that would let the loot go to the state. They're all after the deed. And one day it will come to light.'

'If the deed is ever found, it will only benefit the holder. What about the others?'

'We'll think about that then,' said Mustafa.

The district governor turned to me with his impertinent smile and said, 'It seems you have an interest in antiques.'

I gave him a quizzical look and he went on: 'You spend quite some time in the antique shops. Looking for something for the home?'

'I like antique shops. You never know what you'll find there.'

'Maybe you'll be the one to find the deed,' said the governor. 'Beginner's luck . . . It's just might turn out to be you.'

'I'm not looking for it,' I said, sternly.

'In any case only bad luck will come to whoever finds it. It's not wise to be looking for something like that,' said the governor.

Our coffees arrived. The governor turned to Mustafa and

said: 'So what are we going to do about Muhacir. I don't want any trouble.'

'Let me talk to Raci Bey first and we'll take it from there . . .'

When they finished their coffees, they stood up. We sat and smoked in silence for a while.

'We were having such a nice chat,' said Mustafa. 'And they ruined it.'

Then I couldn't help but ask. It was pure evil to do this.

'Could there be another man?'

Mustafa shook his head.

'No, she's not like that. She'd do anything else, but not that. Sometimes she tries to make me angry and jealous but she would never sleep with another man unless she married him. And if she was going to get married she'd tell me first. In that respect I trust her. It's just not possible she's with another man.'

'A little while ago you said you didn't trust her but it seems you really do.'

'I trust her a hundred per cent in this regard. You could put her in with a regiment of soldiers and she'd come out with her virtue intact. I don't trust that she won't up and leave me again. But I don't worry for a moment that she would sleep with another man. She would never do that.'

'Are you two together right now? Are you lovers?'

'Look, I don't even know what we are, lovers or not. Sometimes we are and sometimes we aren't. It depends on her mood that day. And that's just what makes me so angry.'

'It seems to me that you two have a strong bond, one that would last. So don't think that things will fall apart for any old reason, because looking from the outside you see an ongoing, healthy relationship, one that will last, albeit a little painful but that surely stems from the strength of your connection.'

'Is that what you really think?'

'That's what I really think.'

He put his hand on my shoulder.

'I suppose you're right. Look, it was good that we had this talk. You're not tired of me?'

Suddenly there was a flush of colour in his cheeks and his face was radiant.

I knew that I would call Zuhal the moment he got back to the municipality building, and learn what they'd talked about last night. They were keeping an eye on me, watching my every move. But I was watching them.

'I'll walk back to the municipality. But my driver can take you wherever you're going,' he said.

'I'll be fine,' I said but he insisted.

We parted at the door. I got in his car.

I'd made a good friend.

And that was because I'd lied.

XXI

Heading home in his car, I was lost in thought. If they knew I'd spent the entire day with Zuhal, and where we'd gone together, why did Mustafa tell me that long story? Did he already know about us?

I knew he didn't have anyone else in town who would listen to his story and offer consolation, I knew he had no choice but to keep his shortcomings and his troubles from the others, but that still wasn't an explanation.

I presumed he didn't see me as competition.

He had such confidence in Zuhal that he could never believe she would betray him or sleep with another man, despite all the jealousy, restlessness and doubt. This was a weakness shared by most men; for them, believing such a betrayal was possible, and accepting it as a part of their lives, wounded their male ego. They could never expose such a blow in public, and unless they were convinced of a wrongdoing they persevered with blind confidence. Indeed sometimes when they caught a woman *in flagrante* they were willing to believe her if she denied it. They were fools caught in a miserable contradiction: ongoing suspicion combined with an inflated sense of trust.

Most important was the fact that Mustafa didn't perceive me as a threat. He just assumed that all women were impressed by money and power; it was in fact a firm conviction, and in his mind a writer didn't fit the bill.

But if he still had suspicions, our chat today had allayed them.

He was the kind of man who'd kill me if he ever found out but my lies had made us the best of friends.

Who could ever be honest in a world like this?

Not me.

Of course at times I've been reduced to the same miserable condition. I could become one of them at any moment, a woman could trap me, drawing on my weaknesses, blinding me, but at least I would always have a slight sense of what was really going on. When I'm blinded like that I can feel it. I slip into that warm and soothing pool, accepting the illusion but not without a slight awareness of the game.

Although I am a man I tend to find men in that state amusing, not pitiable.

That much I confess.

I believe that the occasionally astounding audacity of some women is born of their ignorance of these simple truths.

Poor men. They aren't really after money and power but they feel they can fill the void, a product of their self-deception.

When I got home, Hamiyet told me she'd made my favorite tamarind sherbet. 'It's in the fridge. Would you like some now?'

'I'll have some later,' I said, still a little lightheaded from the rakı and hoping I might soon extract the big confession from Hamiyet's nephew.

As I sat down in a large armchair beside the window the phone rang.

No one knew my number at home. I didn't even know it.

Hamiyet picked up and handed me the phone. 'It's for you.'

Before I'd even put the receiver to my ear, I had an inkling who it might be and that voice tinged with flirtatious authority said it all. From 'Hello' I was sure who it was.

'How are you, Kamile Hanım?' I said.

'I'm fine. How are you?'

'Fine, thanks.'

'Who was that woman who picked up, a maid?'

'Yes.'

'Does she live in?'

The condescension that slipped into her voice whenever she spoke of another woman was astounding.

'No, she's leaving in a little while.'

'Good. I made you some of those sweets you liked so much, and I'm coming to town so I thought if you're home I could stop by and give them to you.'

'I'm here. See you then.'

I love women and the way they are oblivious to the fact that they can be so alike, taking every man for a fool. Hamiyet was a woman, and she assumed I was naïve, and though she was about to leave she kept coming up with one last thing to do. I watched her quietly. She couldn't stop a woman, whom she assumed thought little of her, from coming to my home but she could certainly make her uncomfortable by making her presence felt.

But she didn't know that Kamile Hanım would deliberately be late to make sure she'd gone by the time she arrived.

That's what I expected to happen.

And it did.

Hamiyet spent some time pottering about, coming up with yet another little task to do, but soon it became impossible for her to justify staying any longer.

Flustered, she said, 'I'm going. Do you need anything?'

'No, thanks. See you tomorrow,' I said, a grave expression on my face.

She left with long face.

Half an hour later a black jeep pulled up in front of the house. Kamile stepped out of the car, opened the back door and took out a box. I watched her from the window.

She was wearing a jacket and skirt.

She looked good.

It was professional but with a sultry side.

And she would choose which side would dominate.

I opened the door before she had a chance to ring the bell.

'You were watching me from the window?' she said.

'Yes.'

She put the box on a coffee table in the entrance.

'Your favourite sweets. I made a lot. But they go stale if you let them wait too long, and then they're no good. Let me know when you finish them and I'll make you more.'

'Thank you. Have a seat.'

She stepped into the living room, taking everything in.

'You haven't done anything with the furniture.'

'No, I haven't.'

'It's a beautiful home. One of Sabit Bey's places. He's a good man. He had a young boy, a sweet little bundle of joy, but one day he went swimming with his friends and drowned. Maybe a cramp, I don't know, but they couldn't save him. Then they couldn't bear to stay here any longer. His wife Selime Hanım always said, How can I bear to look out at the sea every morning, Kamile Hanım, my heart just can't stand it. The poor thing. How could she get up every morning and look out at the place where her son died? So after they buried him they were gone the next day. And they never came back. This is the first time I've been here in years. How time flies.'

She wandered about the living room, looking out the windows facing the sea, then turned and sat down in a wing-back chair, taking off her jacket and throwing it on the settee before leaning back and crossing her legs. As her skirt came up just a little I could see a sliver of her thigh where her legs were crossed. I couldn't help but look. Her blouse was taut over her upper body, accentuating the curves.

'So, what are you up to then? Visiting our pretty town with friends? Making the most of it, are you?'

So she had also heard about my visit to town yesterday. So that's why she'd come. For a moment I thought that I could conquer this town not through secret liaisons but by doing just the opposite and exposing everything I did. I could manipulate them that way. Kamile had come to my house because I had visited a street market with Zuhal.

'I've been taking a look around. It really is a beautiful town.'

'Especially when you have a beautiful guide.'

I laughed.

'Why would I choose an ugly one?'

'You're going to make Mustafa mad,' she said, smiling.

Opening my eyes and mustering an innocent expression, I said, 'Why would that be?'

She pulled a cigarette out of her bag, attached a small cigarette holder and said, 'Stop pretending to be so innocent. You might fool our dumb brutes with your act. You really are too much. You know everything that's going on.'

I didn't say a word.

I looked at her breasts and then ran my eyes over the rest of her body. That was my answer.

I wondered if she would stay or go.

She didn't move.

The two buttons right above her breasts had come undone and I could see a little skin.

She wasn't young, and she wasn't very beautiful. But she was voluptuous and the way she sat there was incredibly enticing.

'Would you like something to drink?' I asked.

'I'll have a coffee,' she said. 'Do you have coffee?'

'I do.'

'Good. But you mustn't make it. You'll get it all over your hands and your face. Let me do it. Where's your kitchen?'

We went to the kitchen together.

As we opened the cupboards our bodies touched. I caught her scent. A pungent scent that matched her style. We didn't say anything but both of us knew that just one word would have ruined the pleasure of the moment. I noticed her breathing and she was blushing.

We took our coffees back into the living room and she sat down and crossed her legs again. But this time revealing more.

'Would you like something with the coffee?'

'Such as?'

'A cognac?'

'Oh, why not then. You can manage that yourself, can you?'

'Of course,' I said.

I poured two glasses. I set hers down next to her coffee and I sat down across from her.

We drank without saying a word.

From then on I knew that I was in dangerous territory and that every move would have to be made carefully. I let her lead. She would decide just what we were going to do. I wasn't going to initiate.

'Why so quiet?' she asked.

'What would you like me to say?'

'What do you want to say?'

'A lot of things.'

'Well, then say them.'

'Ladies first. Please go ahead.'

'Are you wise or just terribly afraid?'

'Let's just say I am wise enough to know when I should be afraid and when I should be bold.'

'That's true,' she said, smiling. 'You're something else.'

She lit a cigarette. 'I have something in mind, but I just can't decide,' she said.

'Let's wait until you do then,' I said, looking at her legs again. When I looked up our eyes met. She had followed my gaze and wanted me to know.

'Draw the curtains,' she said in a tone of voice that was almost cold.

I stood up and drew the curtains. An inspiring, muted light fell over the room, the color of cognac. An intoxicating glow. I could smell the cognac in the air.

She took another drag on her cigarette then stubbed it out in the ashtray beside her.

She stood up and walked over.

She stopped right in front of me. I didn't move.

Then she surprised me.

Pulling up her skirt, she sat down on my lap with a glazed expression on her face, her legs against my knees.

Her breasts were right in front of my eyes.

I took her by the hips, stood up and put her down.

'Come,' I said.

We went upstairs together.

She undressed and got into bed.

She led the way, familiar with all the motions. But she seemed rushed, in a hurry. I followed at her pace, letting her do everything she wanted for a while, and then I took her savagely by the wrist.

'Just relax,' I said. 'Let yourself go.'

She looked me in the eye.

'You're going to bruise my arm,' she said.

'So?' I said.

Then we fell into the heat of passion.

She had surrendered the lead.

I was drunk on her mature body, full breasts and ample curves, driven out of my mind, drunk on her selfish and insatiable desires, driven out of my mind by her sheer desire for pleasure, and her willingness to do anything for it, moaning as if I wasn't there.

Something about the way she made love reminded me of Sümbül.

There was nothing but this animal urge.

Afterwards she lay on her back for a moment or two, looked at the watch on the bedside table, and without saying a word she got up and dressed, and I accompanied her downstairs.

'I'll call you,' she said to me at the door. I wasn't supposed to call her.

For a moment I thought she might slip me some money.

I suppose she considered it.

From behind the curtains I watched her get into her car.

It was as if nothing had just happened.

I went back into the living room, sat down in the armchair, lit a cigarette and drank the last drop of cognac.

And suddenly the reality dawned on me.

I was sleeping with the women of the town's two most powerful and most dangerous men.

'They'll destroy me and no one will even know what happened,' I thought to myself.

But the thought only made me smile.

There was still quite some time before Zuhal would come 'home'.

I got dressed and went into town.

I went to a little working-class meyhane frequented by shopkeepers and minibus drivers.

I had them give me a full rakı spread with all the mezes.

I drank alone.

I wanted to relish the recent experience; I had expected something like that to happen.

On my second rakı, I said, 'If they kill me, they kill me,' because I knew that I was going to sleep with both women again before they did, and the two of them would drive me insane in dramatically different ways.

XXII

The station's golden dome quietly shimmered like the shell of a giant tortoise, promising a beautiful day, but storm clouds were gathering over the sea. Someone at the coffeehouse told me that rain was on the way and there followed a heated discussion as to precisely when it would come and go, people drawing on past experiences and any scrap of information on the topic they could muster.

Centipede's nephew was getting married that evening. And I was invited. The ceremony was going to be held at a coffeehouse in a neighbouring village.

The groom's father sold chickpea pilaf from a cart he pushed around town. His son was an orderly at the hospital, the bride a 'homebody', as they put it.

In the afternoon the skies suddenly went dark.

And rain poured down.

I'd never seen rain like it. Streaming down almost as if in a rage. Big drops smashing onto the ground like bullets, exploding into fragments before falling back down onto the earth.

I stood there at the door to the veranda, watching the rain strike the earth, as if the clouds were hurling down a million glass marbles. It was a tremendous noise. I breathed in the scent of the rain. A strong, refreshing smell. Pure. The scent of the sky.

Oblivious to the downpour, Hamiyet was busy cleaning and chattering away at the furniture. In front of the mirror I heard her remonstrating with something or other. 'Now you just stay put and don't move,' she said, so sincerely angry that I really thought for a moment the little object taunted her, leaping a little up into the air.

I thought of Kamile Hanım.

Her insatiable concupiscence had seized my imagination. I loved the way she selfishly quenched her own desires.

I felt like a toy, an inconsequential naked body only there to provide her pleasure. And I liked it. Her selfishness stripped me of myself, sweeping away my past, my memory and my preconceptions. It didn't matter who I was: a shopkeeper, a porter, a gardener or a scholar of physics, as long as I provided her pleasure, she didn't care. I was a man. And a man who could provide the kind of pleasure she wanted. She wanted nothing more. This gave me a rush I could never forget.

Considering her crude and selfish sexual desires, I sometimes found it distasteful; but the actual act of ravishing her was a fountain of pleasure. When I made love to her the mind was trivialised and the body exalted and I felt like a man bursting with confidence.

She would come again.

I wanted her to come.

I wondered if most of the women in town had the same selfish sexual desires. It was a rough-hewn sexuality, alien to men, oblivious to the partner's emotions, solitary and distant. There was something about it that drew me in.

I remembered the surprise and rush of pleasure I saw in her face when I took her arms, pinned her down on the bed and said, 'Don't move.' And just like me she felt the pleasure that came with being used by a crude and selfish desire, and she liked it.

The rain suddenly stopped towards evening.

And once again sunlight shimmered off the station dome.

I started out early.

I would take my time getting there. I wanted to look for a village mosque along the way. A beautiful mosque. The mosque in which I would marry Zuhal.

She wanted to live the novel I'd written. She wanted to

become that woman. Perhaps she was fonder of her fantasies than of reality. I think that's probably one of the reasons why she was so happy with our home, a fantasy world. There she could experience love the way she really wanted to.

We shared a love that existed only in a virtual world. Both of us feared it might turn into a reality.

I wondered how many more times I would get married in a mosque, and how many more times I would write about it; maybe I would write it into every one of my books. I liked the idea of a marriage in a mosque.

This made me feel closer to her but it didn't relieve the lingering loneliness.

I suppose this was just one of many contradictions. Despite my need for solitude, I enjoyed getting attached; it made me happy to share a special bond with a woman. It was ours alone and she endorsed it. But when that happened I was goaded to give up my solitude in return.

The approval then came from a higher power, asking me to relent, and if I did not a punishment would be waiting for me in the 'other book', which I accepted because I wanted to have it both ways. I was willing to burn in volume two.

Everything has a price.

If you're willing to pay, the sky's the limit.

I don't know God's thoughts on the matter but to my mind the greatest sin is not paying for it after the fact. God slipped sin into the rules of the game. It is there for you when the mood takes you. But you must pay the price either in this book or the one to come. Eventually you will have to pay. You can't fool people, and you can't fool God.

I have always been willing to pay, and though I've deceived people I've never deceived God. I've never tried to hide my sins in hypocrisy.

'Look and see,' I said to him. 'Look and see. You're reading your own book, already aware of everything that will come to pass. You have the right to know.'

I idled along the way to the wedding, letting these thoughts run freely through my mind. As I passed through neighbouring villages I searched for the mosque that would unite me and Zuhal, and the punishment that would be meted out to me in the book to come.

I was going to marry her.

A fantasy wedding for our fantasy love.

I passed through a village called Şeftali, or Peach, and soon realised how it got the name: there were peach trees everywhere. It truly deserved its name.

Then among the verdant landscape I saw the humble white dome of a mosque and its slender minarets.

I would marry her there.

I had found the door to the fires of the second book. And it was beautiful.

I didn't linger in the village for very long.

I wanted to come here with her so we could discover the village together.

The sun was just setting when I arrived in the village where our wedding would take place. I had some time to kill.

There was a small, green tomb at the entrance.

It stood there alone and peaceful among the cypress trees.

I stopped there.

It was surrounded by a green fence and stepping inside I found myself in the middle of a rose garden. The door to the mausoleum was open.

There wasn't anyone there. The tomb was nothing but a small stone house.

Inside were two coffins covered in green prayer rugs, with gauze over the head of one and a fez and prayer beads over the other. They had to be husband and wife. Generally these kinds of tombs were reserved for men. This was the first time I'd come across one for a man and woman.

It was dark inside.

I sat across from the door that opened out into the garden. There were carpets on the floor. I could see the hills in the distance.

It was a black iron door that opened from the darkness onto the world of light.

I sat there looking at the hill until the sky darkened.

I don't know why.

It was as if I was visiting with the deceased.

They lay there peacefully in silence.

The three of us rested there like that, without saying a word, and if they happened to be speaking to one another I didn't hear it.

When night fell I left.

In the garden of the coffeehouse colourful lights were strung up through the trees. There were mounds of grass outside and a dirt floor inside where a few people who had nothing to do with the wedding were busy playing cards. Long, wooden tables were lined up in the garden.

The bride and the groom sat side by side in silence at one of the tables under the trees.

They had surprisingly grave expressions on their faces.

They were very young.

Now and then the groom would turn his head and say something to a friend. He was the centre of attention and this evening would probably be the only time in his life he would experience such a thing. You could see that he was struggling to hide his happiness.

It was a happiness born of all the attention but no doubt the idea that he would be sleeping with his wife that night played a part in it too. He was relishing every moment of it. And every so often he would stand up and visit another friend, a composed look on his face, his arms close to his sides, bright new shoes on his feet and little red cuts on his face from a fresh shave which no doubt smelled of lemon cologne. I couldn't help but smile at how seriously he was taking it all.

They met me at the door and told me how happy they were that I'd come.

There was a place for me in the middle of a long table.

At another long table just opposite there sat a group of large men in dark suits, with rough-looking faces. They were the VIPs.

I turned to Centipede, who was sitting beside me. 'Who are those guys?'

'The bride is the cousin of one of Muhacir's men. Those are his guys.'

Two men were standing guard at the door. A little beyond the wedding party.

'Who's standing guard?' I asked.

'Ah. Last summer a yellow minibus pulls up at the front door of a wedding and, well, you saw what happened in our coffee-house. Someone gets out and shoots one of the guests and just walks away. So they're taking precautions.'

Initially the crowd was calm. People spoke in hushed tones.

Then came the meat, rice and salad.

The men were on one side and the women on the other.

Then bottles of rakı were opened.

In little time the men had loosened their ties and the women were giggling and then the music kicked in.

The men got up to dance and the women watched them from their seats.

They danced a zeybek.

With their arms swirling up into the air, and rising and falling onto their knees, they moved slowly around in a circle.

During the dance the groom's father came over. He was a wizened little man, tired and drunk, and with a loosened tie. We had greeted each other at the door but he took my hand as he sat down and said, 'Welcome. We are proud to have you here.'

'It's a beautiful wedding,' I said.

'Thank you very much. He's my only child . . . We did everything we could for him, of course.'

'May God grant him much happiness,' I said.

'Indeed . . . our son, he's a good boy, peaceful, wouldn't hurt a fly, and the girl – well, let's hope God grants everyone someone as lovely as her, she's a true lady, pure-hearted. Now we wait for our grandchildren as we grow old.'

'Oh, stop there,' I said. 'Why get old so soon? You're still a young man.'

'Our hearts have grown old,' he said. 'Every morning I hit the road at six and I never come home before ten at night. It's not easy, life's taken its toll.'

He kept his cart of chickpea pilaf at the minibus stop, pilaf that he 'made with the missus'.

'I've even offered my pilaf to Mustafa Bey and he devoured it and said, Oh what a fine dish indeed. What else would such a great man say? He's a true gentleman, would never throw the poor to the dogs. Now, you see he has a brave heart, and may God always fill it with courage, he's not afraid of anyone, and you see he feasted on my rice and said, What a fine dish indeed, I've never had anything tastier, he said. Yes, he gobbled it right up, the great Mustafa Bey, but what more can I say but that he's stolen our hearts, yes he has, and God willing we'll be able to tell the story for years.'

I wasn't sure if he was always so garrulous but the more rakı he drank the smaller his eyes grew and the more he talked: 'We couldn't find the buried treasure. But someone did, that's for sure . . .'

And he pulled a golden coin out of his pocket and lowered his voice, 'This here I found up at the church. Who knows what else you might find if you dig up there.'

I turned the coin over in my hand. I thought it resembled a Carthaginian coin but I was no expert. Maybe Phoenician. Truth is I had no idea when it was made but I was pretty sure that it was old.

'Do you always keep this with you?' I asked.

'Always. Ever since I found it more than twenty years ago I've kept it right here in my pocket . . . This golden coin is our share of God's treasure. Many have told me to sell it but I never will. Why would I? I'll never find anything like it again.'

The people at the table across from us stood up. The music stopped and everyone was still.

'Oh, I need to show our guests out,' said the pilaf pedlar as he stood up and scrambled over.

They all greeted me with a nod as they filed past, though not one of them had acknowledged me earlier in the evening.

'I've become famous in this town,' I thought.

It was as if I'd found everything I was looking for.

Later I would come to learn that I would find even more.

I went home in a good mood.

Zuhal was waiting for me at home.

I realised how much I'd missed her.

And I couldn't get that golden coin out of my mind.

It was the first time I'd seen an actual piece of the treasure.

Perhaps all this talk of the treasure was true. Who knows, I thought.

XXIII

'about a month ago i overheard the women at the hairdresser's
. . . there's a woman, şükriye . . . she tells you everything . . .
even names names . . . i couldn't believe it . . . aynur told me
she'd been there and that the woman really knows her stuff . . .
then she said she wouldn't go again . . . the woman told her the
date her father would die . . . they made an appointment for me
. . . months later . . . i forgot all about it . . . when i came out
of a meeting today they called to remind me about it . . .

'we went to the ground floor of a house . . . the woman had
just arrived . . . she was in her fifties, red hair, a strange look in
her eye, talked a lot . . . just wait a little she said and if you
speak amongst yourselves please don't mention names . . . it
doesn't work if i hear names . . . then there was a knock on
the door . . . a man in a suit walked in . . . where have you
been, sister, you're not answering your phone, he said . . . the
woman leapt to her feet and led the man to a back room . . .
they stayed in there for half an hour . . . we expected some kind
of apology but the man just left without even looking at us . . .
the woman said forgive me, he was a businessman, i didn't do
a reading, it was just an interview . . . i couldn't believe it.

'nezahat went in first . . . who . . . my hairdresser . . . good
for me . . . then another group came . . . men and women . . .
they asked me if it was my first time . . . i said yes . . . we're
regulars they said and laughed . . . they had a young child with
them . . . i didn't like the look of them them and I went into
the kitchen opposite the front door . . . and i stood there and
waited . . .

'someone was always knocking on the door . . . two men came in . . . and left right away . . . i started to feel restless . . . i waited like that on my feet for an hour . . . but it seemed even longer . . .

'they finally came out of the room . . . nezahat's face was a mess . . . i asked if she was ok . . . she nodded . . . she had a glazed and frightened look in her eye . . . she looked funny . . .

'the women looked inside and then led me in . . . we sat across from each other at a table . . . my skirt fell open as i sat down . . . you are one sexy thing, my sweet, she said . . . i laughed and said i wasn't . . . come a little closer and she looked me in the eye . . . she had little eyes darting about in all directions . . . i was really uncomfortable . . .

'it began with my father . . . she tried to find his name . . . first she spelled the letters of his name . . . there's a t . . . i can't say there's a u . . . there's an a . . . i can't say there's an o . . . there's an e . . . and i just stared at her . . . occasionally she would scold me if i looked away . . . it's tamer, she said . . . aynur for my mother . . . she told me about both of them . . . you're an only child . . . and you studied economics . . . but not here . . . abroad . . .

'i took her hand . . . i couldn't believe it . . . at that moment it seemed like something entirely different . . . something extraordinary . . . she told me that i'd never wanted to be an economist . . . and so many other things . . . you've been through a bad break-up . . . but never had a child . . .

'tears began to well up in my eyes . . . you would have found it funny . . . i asked her if i would ever have a child . . . no, you won't . . . i must have asked her this at least five times . . . there's a man . . . there are two a's and a u . . . and m at the beginning . . . but not mehmet . . . mustafa, she said . . . and i felt like i was on fire . . .

'i've never felt anything like it before . . .

'he is an agriculturalist . . . can't give up on you, thinks about you but can't love anyone else but himself . . . has serious personal problems . . . selfish . . . strong-minded . . . it won't work out between you two . . . you always get stuck in the same places, you never move past them . . . you weren't fated to be together . . . if so it would've worked out by now . . . but you'll see each other again . . . but still it won't work . . . you'll get married . . . fall in love . . . at a moment when you weren't hoping for it . . . i started to cry . . .

'it lasted more than an hour . . . she told me so many things . . . i won't tell you what she said about you . . . nothing bad but i just don't want to tell you . . . in the end i was almost begging her to stop . . . and she smiled as i cried . . . she had no teeth . . . i'm not joking . . . no teeth . . .

'i don't ever want to go to a fortune-teller again . . . really . . . i just don't want to . . . up until now it was always just for fun but this was different . . . she scared me . . . a lot . . . i still can't believe it . . . i called nezahat . . . she left before me . . . i told her to tell me that she had just made it all up . . . she doesn't make anything up she said, she knows everything . . . maybe she got the letters from my eyes, i said . . . zuhal, the woman knows . . . well, you are going to call me straightaway if it doesn't come out the way she told you i said . . . ok, she said . . . and that's that . . .'

'were you really scared?'

'terrified . . . i wanted to call you when i left . . . but i didn't . . . i called hasan . . . who's he . . . my cousin . . . i was in tears . . . i think i just needed to cry today . . . he thought i'd been in a traffic accident . . . why . . . i don't know . . . then he got really angry with me . . . he said i was spending too much time alone these days . . . and that's why . . .'

Before I could write, she continued, 'are our fates sealed? . . . i mean are we just going through the motions, playing our parts? . . . what will become of us?'

'our fates aren't sealed . . . i think God writes it all out in the beginning . . . but he rewrites destiny every day, adding this and that . . . sometimes he changes the ending he had in mind at the start, depending on how things develop . . . imagine yourself as a character in a book . . . it's something like that

. . . could your fate be clear before the book ends? . . . anything can happen until the end . . . sometimes he adds things he didn't think of at first . . . sometimes you help him through your actions . . . characters in novels still have the right to speak up for themselves . . . a writer cannot do it all . . . after a point the characters determine what the writer will put down on the page . . .'

'so if i were a character in your book, what would be my fate?'

'how would i know if the book were still being written? . . . the fate i have in mind might change . . . you might do something to change the course of the entire book . . . even a fortune-teller can't know what lies in store for you.'

'are you sure that your fate is always written again and again? . . . that it changes? . . . i believe you . . . there's no way that God could have come up with a fixed fate for his creations . . . then what point would there be in living, you know?'

'he wouldn't write it . . . and if he did, i would change it . . . i have enough power to change your fate.'

'i believe that too . . . i believe everything you tell me.'

'believe me.'

'i'm telling you everything . . . are you bored?'

'you're not telling me everything . . . you're still keeping some things from me.'

'how do you know that? . . . are you a fortune-teller? . . .'

'i'm more than that . . . i'm the man who will determine your fate.'

There was no response and I felt her fear. Sometimes she was truly frightened by this kind of language.

'don't worry . . . i'm only joking . . . and i'm very happy with you . . . and even if i were to determine your fate it would only be a good one . . . of course providing you don't do anything to make me mad.'

'you would never be angry with me . . . you already said that i could be sure that you never would.'

'i won't be . . . never.'

'i can't tell you how much i miss you.'

'i miss you too.'

I really did.

'i suppose i'm making the gods angry these days . . . must be furious because i went to a fortune-teller . . . i'm always trying to help while he's doing nothing but scrambling the situation . . .'

'are you doing it yourself?'

'sometimes it seems as if i am . . . it's as if i'm wrecking everything deliberately . . . i feel like if i just leave things alone life will be that much better . . . but then i always end up doing something . . . it's strange . . . i don't know why.'

She started writing again as I lit another cigarette.

'today the birds aren't singing the way they were yesterday . . . strange, isn't it? . . . but it's just as warm . . .'

XXIV

Mustafa called me one Friday evening. 'Let's have breakfast together tomorrow,' he said. 'My place is beautiful in the morning.'

Since our lunch at the Chamber of Commerce we'd become good friends.

There was no one else he could talk to about Zuhal; he couldn't get close enough to anyone to really share his troubles. And chatting about books now and then helped put a little distance between him and the town, giving him a respite from the oppressive climate that had become his natural element, which was difficult to ever leave.

But to my mind he missed Zuhal, and if nothing else being with someone who was close to her helped relieve the anguish; that was the most important thing.

I knew the feeling all too well.

Because I missed her too, and I felt some kind of consolation when I saw Mustafa.

'Of course,' I said.

In the morning I went over to his house.

There was a stylish two-person granite table on the terrace, with flowers, freshly squeezed orange juice and little dishes filled with unusual jams.

Mustafa had good taste that could take you by surprise.

He would carefully hide this in his daily life, trying not to appear different from the others in town.

But he wanted to show me he *was* different from the townspeople. On the one hand he condescended to me but on the other he was genuinely afraid that I looked down on him.

We listened to the sounds of the waves breaking on the shore. It reminded me of Zuhal's voice. Maybe Mustafa thought the same thing.

'Have you ever been up to the church?' I asked.

'Oh, many times. I've been up there a lot.'

'What's it like?'

'A little church . . . But we can't have it restored. Everyone's afraid to even touch it, because the moment that happens people will say it's all about the treasure.'

'Ever since I came to this town people have been talking about that church, going on and on, but I've never actually seen it. I'm really curious.'

'Well, let me take you up there and we can have a look,' he said.

I was taken aback.

'Isn't it forbidden to go there?'

'Forbidden for everyone else. Come on. Let's go.'

I stood up right away, hoping he wouldn't change his mind.

We went in Mustafa's jeep. It was probably the biggest jeep I'd ever seen.

We drove up along the back roads without going through town and then turned onto a dirt road.

There were olive and fig trees along the road, and bushes of yellow broom. The strong smell of ripe figs was heavy in the air.

We wound back and forth up the hill.

At the top there was a plateau surrounded by a wooden fence. And right in the middle was a little domed church of darkened stone. The cross was still standing on top. The windows were broken.

I saw grating on the ground as we approached.

'What are these?'

'They probably lead down below the church but have been covered with stones. There's no entrance and no one knows who covered them.'

Two gendarmes were standing watch a little further on. Mustafa greeted them as we passed. Clearly they were used to seeing him there.

'Come,' said Mustafa as we both leapt up the two steps leading to the church and went inside. There were planks of wood that had probably been pews once upon a time, birds had nested in the dome and rotting timber from the ceiling had fallen to the floor. It was filled with the scent of wood, stone, dust and hay. On the opposite wall there was a small statue of Christ on the cross.

'This is it?' I said, disappointed.

'This right here is the heart of the town,' said Mustafa.

He pulled up a lid on the floor right under the statue.

And he jumped inside.

I jumped in behind him.

It was a room without windows, no door, no way out.

'Now, I'm sure there's a secret passage somewhere in this room. But no one has found it yet. We checked every inch of the place and couldn't find it.'

'Maybe it's just not there.'

'I think it's there all right, but we can't find it. Maybe we need to tap out a certain code somewhere but until now no one has been able to come up with it.'

I looked around.

It was a little stone room, completely empty. Stone floors.

It was nothing like what I had imagined.

This 'legendary' place which captivated the imagination of a town, and for which people had died, was nothing more than a rundown little building.

I stepped outside and took a deep breath.

In the distance the sea stretched out as far as the eye could see.

I sat down. Mustafa came and sat down next to me.

'That's what people always say when they first see it,' he said, laughing. 'What did you expect? Chests full of emeralds, silken drapes? If it was easy to find then someone would have found it long ago.'

'There's nothing here, Mustafa,' I said.

He looked out at the sea before answering, plucked a blade of grass and started chewing.

'You can't understand, outsiders never do. For you it's just a church, a heap of rubble you've heard people talking about and which you come to see with all these expectations and then you're only disappointed . . . It's not like that for us. This church is what makes this town. Even if there isn't a treasure, well, there is as long as we believe in it. It's the soul of the town. Without it everything would fall apart. And then of course you see there really is a treasure here.'

He spat out the bit of grass in his mouth and plucked another blade. A forlorn expression fell over his face.

'You know that golden coin you saw the other day at the wedding, the pilaf man's coin?' he said.

I realised that he expected me to show surprise but I didn't. I was getting wise to his game.

'Yes,' I said, waiting for him to go on.

He pulled out an ancient coin that looked just the same.

'Once upon a time many different people found coins like this up here . . . Then they disappeared . . . But we all know there's more underground.'

'And if not?'

'And if there is?'

'None of you will ever be able to find out . . . You're all stopping each other from getting that far. Why don't you come together and dig? If nothing else you'll get to the truth.'

We were sitting there together like two little boys watching the sea. It was a strange relationship: I was the only one who knew how this woman had brought us together. He slapped me on the back.

'Maybe we don't want to know,' he said.

'You're right, maybe you just don't want to know,' I said.

'But we do. Be sure of that. It's just that we can't come together. Someone will find the deed to this place. In the end someone will find it. And if need be, there will be − how should I put this – some unsavoury procedures, but someone will find it. Maybe you don't really understand but the person who takes control of this place takes control of the town. Outsiders don't get that. Whatever it is that makes a man a man, well, it's the same in that this treasure makes this town. It's the centre of power. And power is never shared. If it is, well then it isn't power. We're not interested in getting rich, we already are. I'm talking about the people who are powerful enough to find the treasure. We don't want money, we want the town, and everything in it. The deed to this treasure is the deed to this town.'

'If it's not the treasure you're after but the deed then why are you secretly digging here in the middle of the night?'

I thought he might deny it but he didn't. He laughed.

'After I find the treasure I'll have an easy time finding the deed. Or rather the treasure is the deed itself.'

'What will Raci Bey say about that?'

He sighed.

'That's an important question. I don't know what I'm going to do with him. We'll meet and discuss the matter but I don't think we'll be able to come to an agreement. The guy has suddenly thrown himself completely into the race for power. But first he should keep an eye on his wife . . .'

Then he stopped, embarrassed at what he'd just said. 'Anyway,' he muttered. 'I think Muhacir is putting him up to it, getting him to rattle his sword at me,' he went on, 'but no need to worry about him. Never mind Muhacir. He's just a low-grade gangster, a brute, what good will come of him? Thinks he's going to take the town, and who will let him have it? My fear is that these guys will get lost in their insane fantasies, mess up the whole operation and kill each other in the end.'

Whenever he talked about the treasure he adopted a different manner of speaking, becoming once again the mayor of a small town. Gone was the urban intellectual.

Then it dawned on me. We were confidants.

But it was a one-way street. He shared his secrets with me

but I hid my own from him. If I told him my secrets we'd no longer be friends.

'You know, sometimes I think I should just give it all up and leave. I get so tired sometimes, and everything seems so meaningless. I want to go somewhere and just read history books.'

He had slipped into his other personality. With me he was always switching back and forth between the two roles.

But the strange thing was that I found his mayor persona far more interesting: this was a type of person that I didn't know and that I found fascinating.

'You could establish a town in the middle of the forest and make yourself the mayor.'

'That's also true. This kind of work makes you sick. And when you sit like this watching the sea and talking it all sounds like nonsense. So what if you get to be the mayor of a town, you say to yourself, but then when you go back and see the people there . . . The sickness comes back . . . It's like seeing the woman you love but can't have . . .'

I kept quiet. I couldn't be sure if he wanted to bring up the subject or not.

I didn't know if he wanted to tell me something in particular.

On the one hand I liked playing the role of the villain, listening to a man talk about his relationship with a woman I was sleeping with, learning all the details from both Mustafa and Zuhal, examining the feelings they had for each another which they couldn't share openly, with a power unbeknownst to them that allowed me to possess them.

In a strange way I had become the stronger one in the relationship and although this pleased me it was an exhalted feeling. Every new detail I learned about Mustafa and Zuhal made me stronger but also weaker. Every bit of information was a blow. None of which were strong enough to knock me out, but when they came one after the other I could feel that I was losing my resistance.

After a few moments of silence, Mustafa continued as if answering a question I'd never asked: 'We're talking about it but I don't know,' he said. 'She tells me she loves me but then sometimes even this makes me angry. I know that she won't agree if I ask her to marry me, and so what kind of love is this? Doesn't a woman want to marry the man she loves?'

And then he asked me the same question.

'Doesn't she?'

'Maybe she's mad at you too. Maybe there are things she assumes the man who loves her should do.'

'What, for example?'

'How should I know?'

I was about to say, 'You should ask Zuhal,' but I would have been caught revealing just a little too much, and I stopped myself just in time.

'You should ask her.'

'She doesn't really tell me anything . . . I don't know what she wants . . . And sometimes I think that she doesn't know herself.'

And that bright smile of a dashing young man was on his face again.

'Our love is just another treasure. We say it's there, but no one really knows if it is.'

I answered him with his own words.

'If you say it's there, then it is.'

He made a sad face.

'Love's not like that. When you say it's there it actually isn't. And sometimes when it is you can't even say it's there. I said it was and what happened? I looked up and she was married to some other bastard. No, it's not like that. Not at all.'

'But what does she say?'

'She's insane, in my opinion. You know what she said to me yesterday? That she wants to have a kid with me. Fine, let's do it, I said. You know what she said? You can't even imagine . . . that we're going to have a kid without getting married. No way, I said and I hung up.'

I nearly broke out laughing. He could see that I was holding back a smile but of course he didn't really know why.

'It's funny, isn't it? Of course it is. I would laugh too, if someone told me that.'

He turned to me and said, 'Now tell me the truth, what would you say if the woman you loved asked you that?'

'"No problem and let's do it in the courtyard of a mosque," I'd say.'

He thought for a moment with two fingers on his lower lip. 'That's good. Hold on a second.'

He took out his phone.

'What are you doing?' I said, a little worried.

'I'm going to send her just that. I wish I had said that to her yesterday.'

He tapped out the message and then showed it to me.

If you want to have a kid with me well then let's do it in a mosque courtyard.

'Let's see what she says,' he said.

Suddenly it was all just a game for him, and he looked like a naughty little child.

His phone beeped. A new message.

He held it out so I could see too.

Together we read her message.

Fine and I'll leave you there like the heartless animal you are and take our baby with me.

He burst out laughing. I couldn't help but laugh too. We were like two little boys taunting their mother. But this was a woman we both loved and we had both made love to.

'What should I say? Let's write something.'

'I don't think you should. You'll make her really angry.'

'Who cares, she deserves it. She's the one driving me mad. Let's get her back. Come on, just tell me what to write,' he said.

'Okay, write this,' I said.

He was already poised to tap out the words.

'It'll be just like an old Turkish movie.'

'You're incredible, man,' he said, and wrote out the message. As we both waited for the answer, I imagined Zuhal taking all this quite seriously. I thought she'd be pretty surprised by the last message. It wasn't Mustafa's style.

The phone beeped again. We read the message together.

Are you drunk? At this time of day?

Mustafa was having a great time. 'Come on, what do we write now?'

I told him to write, 'Can I call you my wife, dear?'

He had already finished and the message was gone.

It was fun for me to watch the two of them go at it.

Go and say that to your Russian whores.

Now, this wasn't a message I expected. I'd heard her using much stronger language at home but I never thought she used those words with him.

It was a little surprising.

Their relationship went deeper than I'd imagined. That message wasn't from a woman showing anger at a man she was in love with but a woman fighting with her husband.

She would never say something like that to me.

Even if she was in love with me she wouldn't say that.

This was a different kind of veiled intimacy, buried but occasionally surfacing. It wasn't just love. This was something more. Something that would last.

I didn't really want to see this.

When I learned that Zuhal cried with Mustafa in his hotel room, and when she told me that she loved him, I felt something I couldn't quite define. It was the feeling that there was more to what she said, feelings that she had not entirely explained.

'Come on, let's go,' I said, abruptly.

The game wasn't fun any more.

XXV

The rains came on suddenly. And lasted three days.

Never in my life have I seen such angry rain as I did in that town. Large, hard raindrops fell down from the sky as if it was battling the earth. The swollen drops smashed violently to the ground, unable to contain their anger as they bounced off the ground and splintered into a thousand shards.

It was as if we were under attack from the air. There was a constant din.

Everyone had fled, taking refuge indoors.

The streets and little squares were empty.

Life in the town had been arranged for people who were accustomed to spending their lives outside, and the indoor spaces where people took shelter suddenly seemed very small.

I can't stand crowded places so I didn't leave the house for three days.

I listened to Hamiyet chatter away at the furniture.

There were objects she liked very much and there were those she 'didn't get along with'. She got along fine with the wingback chairs, and they would share their troubles, but I imagine she had problems with smaller items: she never really liked ornaments, glasses and plates and the like. 'Now, you just won't stay in your place,' she would say.

Every so often I would hear her break a glass or a plate and every time she blamed the object: 'If you're going to keep moving around like that, well, then you'll get what you deserve. Now look and see what I'm going to do. I'm going to throw you out.'

She spoke with these things more than she ever spoke to me.

She didn't speak to me much but then again we always felt each other's presence.

It was a difficult relationship to describe.

Between a man and a woman in the same home, who never touched, there was an unnamed, invisible, intangible current, like a draught blowing in one window and out the other, that you could never catch but always felt.

There was this current between us. We both felt it and we delighted in it.

Generally she worked around me. Sometimes we passed close by each other, and sometimes she would roll up her skirt and sweep the floors right in front of where I was sitting, allowing me to watch her. I could see that she enjoyed provoking me.

Not every woman would do this but it came naturally to Hamiyet; her instincts pushed her in that direction, always conjuring up that 'current' between her and the men around her, like a bird building a nest or a spider weaving a web.

I knew it.

I knew her, far better than she thought I did.

I saw that wherever she was and whomever she was with she couldn't stop herself from creating that current.

With the rains the activity online was out of control.

Like the radio chatter between soldiers on the brink of an assault, everyone was in contact or trying to reach one another, but the current that surged between me and Hamiyet was more powerful than anything online.

I knew almost everyone in town and despite the usernames they hid behind I knew exactly who they were.

I was always turned on by what the wives of civil servants in town would write on their cheap computers, the way they would talk to men and make love, using words they would never use with their husbands, overwhelmed by tides of pleasure.

I would see some of them on the street. It was nearly impossible to believe that the woman I spoke to on the internet was the same woman I saw on the street, but it was her, shut out from the male world, belittled and left in a corner; I watched these forgotten women's secret insurrection.

They gave me the most specific details about how their husbands made love, making fun of them.

Almost all of them had something in common with Sümbül and it was something that I also saw in Kamile Hanım. In fact they all often used the same line, 'Good God, I can finish him off in five minutes.'

I spoke to every woman I managed to catch, telling them that I was a twenty-eight-year-old engineer – they liked 'educated' young men – and they didn't just belittle their husbands, they also harped on about men on the internet who were crude and impolite. Almost all their conversations began with them denigrating these men.

The internet had started an incredible underground revolution among the women.

I spoke to almost all of them but there were three people in particular who caught my attention: Hamiyet's relative, and a husband and wife who were pharmacists.

The pharmacist was a quiet man in his forties. Whenever I went to the pharmacy he was there writing away on his computer, and his wife was always there beside him knitting. When someone walked in she would look up for a moment and then return to her knitting.

They were looking for a couple.

They wanted a couple from the city.

They were afraid of running into someone they knew.

I told them that I was a thirty-five-year-old banker and that my wife worked with me in the same bank.

When I asked the pharmacist to describe his wife's body he gave me a fully detailed description. He described her quite accurately. That's when I realised they were serious. They weren't just playing games online. They were indeed looking for a couple to have sex with at the weekend.

It seems that the pharmacist's wife was strongly against the idea and said that she would never do anything like that. He wasn't really happy with this and asked me if my wife would be game. I said, 'She'll do it.' He was very pleased.

But the detail that would truly startle me came later. It seemed the pharmacist's wife enjoyed certain activities very much.

After finishing these conversations I would practically race over to the pharmacy. I looked at the woman. She was busy knitting, her head bowed. I looked at her mouth. She had thick lips.

I thought about it. If this were a novel, and I was writing about the pharmacist's wife, some of these things she supposedly had a penchant for would never have occurred to me. I would have written about how she behaved in the pharmacy, about her knitting, but I never would have imagined she had such desires; indeed it would have been difficult to imagine she had any kind of sex life at all.

She always wore a sweater buttoned up to her neck. And very little make-up. She never looked at the men who came into the pharmacy.

I wondered how they dressed when they went to see a couple they'd met online. Surely the woman had a few dresses and loose blouses in her wardrobe. She would put on make-up. She would speak to the other man. She would flirt. She would become someone else.

There were two women: the woman she was and the woman she wanted to be.

Which one was real?

After a tryst you could ask the man who slept with the pharmacist's wife about her and he would describe a very different woman, completely different from the woman in the pharmacy who dealt with customers like me. He wouldn't believe we were talking about the same woman.

Life was insipid and boring for those who didn't know the 'underground'.

That secret world full of sin was where all the fun was.

I'm grateful to God for all of the immoral acts he created for us.

He was a good and intelligent God.

He came up with such entertaining transgressions that life was effectively transformed into a festival of secret sins, the only flaw being that evildoers would be burnt to a crisp in the 'other book'.

But those who delighted in reading this book were ready to forget there was a second volume. While this book was engaging, the second volume seemed all too boring; but there is nothing to be done.

I got on well with the couple in the pharmacy.

Twice we decided to meet.

On one occasion they cancelled and on the second, when I realised that they were serious, I cancelled.

I went to the pharmacy after the first cancellation – my drawers were packed with aspirin and cold medicine because I went so often – and I suppose they thought I had a bad case of the flu that just wouldn't go away. But those bottles of pills were souvenirs of the foursome we never had.

When I went that day I could see that they were quite troubled.

When we chatted the next day the pharmacist told me how very sorry he was.

I knew that they were really upset.

But indeed the big fish for me was Hamiyet's relative.

I reckoned that his story was more sinful than all the others.

After reaching out on many occasions I managed to persuade the young boy to tell me about it on the day when the rain was at its peak.

Terribly ashamed, he began.

It all came pouring out.

It was hard to believe what that young kid had to say but I knew it was all true.

'Did you ever touch your aunt?'

'Yes.'

'How did it happen? After you saw her in the bath?'

'No.'

'How, then?'

I was pushing him but now I felt that I was getting close.

Once he started there was no need for me to jump in with any more questions.

'It was two days after I saw her in the bath. I'll never forget what she looked like. I'm not sure if she saw me. Maybe.

'One night when I came home she was watching TV. She was wearing her nightgown. I put on my pyjamas. She always gets angry with me when I wear my normal clothes at home. She says I bring all the dirt and grime inside.

'She was watching a series. I can't remember which one. But she was totally lost in it.

'I sat down next to her. She stretched out her legs. Her nightgown opened a little. Then she said that her legs really hurt and that she was really tired.

'I said that I could rub them. Go ahead then, she said. That'll help.

'I started rubbing her ankles.

'Then I started rubbing a little higher. She was still lost in the show.

'I rubbed a little higher. I held her legs with both hands as I rubbed.

'I held her under the knee and started rubbing there. Under the knee. Behind the knee.

'She stretched out her legs a little more, but I wasn't sure if it was on purpose, and she was still watching TV. I was watching her. Watching her legs. And I was watching the TV too.

'I rubbed her knees for a while. I didn't know what I was doing and she didn't say a word.

'I lowered my hands a little. And I rubbed and caressed between her ankles and her knees.

'Then I took her knees again and I rubbed them.

'And behind them.

'I didn't know what else to do but I didn't want to stop and I was afraid she would tell me to stop and get angry. When she's angry, she really loses it.

'I started rubbing a little higher, above her knee. She didn't say anything.

'Then I held her a little higher. With both hands I held her legs above her knees and I started rubbing. I rolled my hands up higher, I pulled them down to her knees.

'She was lost in the show. She didn't move. She stretched out her legs a little more.

'I grabbed her legs four fingers above her knees and started to squeeze.

'Sometimes going a little higher. Then back down again. Then a little higher.

'Then her nightgown opened a little more but she didn't notice. There was a belt. It was loose.

'I started rubbing even higher. Not looking at her at all . . . I kept my eyes on the TV. She was watching too.

'One leg was completely open. I ran my hands from the very top down to her knee.

'I rubbed the very top of her leg.'

Then he stopped.

'I need to go now.'

'What's wrong?'

'I just need to go. My time is up.'

'Are you coming back?'

'Maybe we can talk tomorrow.'

'Ok . . . talk then.'

Either he was afraid of telling me those things or his time at the internet café was really up. They rented the computers by the hour.

I was curious to know what happened next.

What did Hamiyet do, how much had she not even noticed as she was watching TV, or when did she pretend to notice and what did she say?

As I wrote to her nephew she was dusting the big mirror

in the room, and I could see that occasionally she would lift her head and look at my reflection.

I wondered how she would react if she knew what I was reading.

If she knew that I was on the verge of uncovering her deepest secret.

What would she do?'

Run away?

Shrug her shoulders?

Laugh?

Cry?

I had no idea.

Ever since I'd entered this secret world I could never be sure what people were capable of, in their real lives, on the streets, at work; were they wandering about as someone else only to suddenly slip into another persona? Anything about them could change: the way they spoke, the sound of their voices, their clothes, the way they smiled.

I had never known that people could change so dramatically.

It would have been impossible to guess that these people were obsessed with the very things they described as 'shameful' or 'sinful' in the presence of others.

It is forbidden for the millions if not billions of people who obssessed with this other world to disappear and become someone else and openly discuss their experiences; it's like an underground organisation: everyone worries they might be revealed and no one acknowledges the group's existence.

No one shows his or her real face in the light of day.

Sin pulled these people in and despite the many punishments and threats they continued to commit their heinous acts.

They weren't afraid of God but of other people.

Jesus Christ uttered what were perhaps the most honest words in the history of humankind when he said, 'Let him who is without sin cast the first stone,' and it seemed to me that no one online was willing to throw the first stone.

I suppose the situation hasn't changed since the creation of the human race.

'As Jesus entered the temple the scribes and Pharisees brought in a woman who had committed adultery. They spoke among themselves, saying, "If he pardons her he will be contradicting the laws of Moses and we can condemn him, but if he condemns her he will be acting against his own principles because he advocates compassion." So they approached Jesus and said, "Teacher, we caught this woman in the act of adultery. Moses commanded that the punishment for this is to be stoned to death; what say ye?"'

Hearing these words Jesus lowered his head and drew a mirror in the sand and all who looked saw their own evil deeds reflected in it. When they pressed him for an answer Jesus stood, pointed at the mirror and said: Let he who is without sin cast the first stone.

And again he leaned over and drew a mirror.

Everyone who had looked inside, starting with the oldest, one by one, left, for they were ashamed to see their vile deeds.

Jesus stood again, and when he saw that the woman was the only one there he asked, 'Woman, where are those who shamed you?'

The woman wept as she answered, 'Teacher, they are gone. If you forgive me, God is alive and I will never sin again.'

Then Jesus said, 'Praise God! Go peacefully on your way and do not sin again, for God did not send me to condemn you.'

So it is written in the Gospels of Barnabas.

Would the Lord Jesus have stoned Zuhal, Hamiyet, Sümbül or Kamile Hanım?

Who among you will cast the first stone?

And Jesus drew a mirror in the sand and saw the sins of those who looked.

And I will draw a mirror for you, look at the glass and you will see your sins.

Is there someone among us who will throw the first stone?

Look at the mirror revealing your sins.

Read your sins in the glass.

Why did God have his son say those words? Because he alone is the one who can throw the first stone, he alone is immaculate.

In this world, where he who created sin and sinners is the only one without sin, I am a murderer, I am a sinner, and I will be punished for my sins.

In this book and in the 'book to come'.

The cradle-maker said, 'People come together to share their sins. If not for them, people would live alone on mountaintops.'

Come together, people!

Gather.

Share your sins.

I have watched all of you, I have seen you all.

And I drew a mirror for you.

In a little while the dawn will break.

In a little while they will come to kill me.

The most sinful will cast the first stone.

XXVI

'whatever he does and whatever i do we respond to each other in the same way . . . we pick at each other's wounds . . . never tiring of it . . . never giving up . . . never considering the costs . . . and most of the time never even aware of what we're doing . . .

'in my opinion we don't even know if we actually love each other . . . we don't trust each other . . . we can't give up on each other . . . we can't help but surrender to one another . . . we both think the same thing, that if we let go the other person won't do the same . . . i think more like that . . .

'maybe we're the same . . . we both suffered the same disappointments . . .

'i don't know, i'm afraid of being alone . . .

'but that's not really what it's called . . . it's so strange . . .

'what i fear is hidden beneath the loneliness and it's staring right at me . . . i know it so well . . .

'i want to call mustafa . . .

'it's like a junkie after a fix . . .

'first I say ok, this is going to kill me, and i decide that i need to give up . . . that i won't call him again, that i'll somehow push him out of my life altogether . . .

'for the last few days i've been wandering around in this void . . . normally i'm upbeat . . . and determined . . .

'then the void keeps growing and traps me . . . and everything is turned upside down . . . i start to feel such a terrible longing that i can't get my mind out of the past . . . i'm more afraid of him dying than of never seeing him again . . . i start to fear everything else . . . it's like pulling the trigger of a gun . . . of the future, other people, losing my job and having no money, getting sick, being alone . . .

'i lose my resolve . . . and then i spend several days struggling with the urge to call him . . .

'then i can't stand it any longer and i send him a short message or an email or he calls or we don't call each other for months . . .

'and when it goes on like that i'm always the one who gives in . . . good on me, eh?

'it's been like that for years . . .

'it just goes on like that, and who knows where it all started, and where it will end and where it's going . . . sometimes I feel that it never even began and will never end . . .

'and my mind tries to convince me that this is just an ordinary sickness and not a love story . . .

'i've been going through the same thing for years . . .

'i must be insane . . .'

Alone in a room lit only by the light of my computer screen, drunk on cognac and the endless din of the rain, I read Zuhal's confessions.

I didn't know how these two lovers had chosen to confide in me. We must have been the strangest threesome in the world.

'you won't believe it but i've only slept with three men,' she wrote, 'my husband, mustafa and you.'

I leaned back as I read her words.

'i'm sleeping with you and i still love him . . . and not feeling the slightest bit guilty . . . sometimes i think of you when i'm with him . . . but still no guilt . . . good on me . . . i've only ever slept with three people and i succeeded in becoming a whore . . .'

I smiled when I read this.

'you must be the most innocent of them all,' I wrote, 'an innocence that will be the end of me.'

'i really miss you, i always want the best for you, i burn for you, you turn me on, i want to know more about you, i worry

· 202 ·

about you, you make me happy, make me laugh and fulfil me.

'it's as if good sides of everything named was combined and emerged as something nameless.'

I waited for her to go on.

'sometimes as we make love i can hear in your voice what i see in your eyes . . . it's frightening at first . . . but then it passes . . . and i like it . . .'

'are you afraid of me?'

'sometimes . . . but when i am it's nothing like the fear i feel with others . . . why . . . i don't know . . . but i like the feeling with you . . . i'm most afraid when we make love . . . i think that's why whenever i experience that fear it comes with an overwhelming desire to make love . . .'

I lit a cigarette and she went on.

'every time we make love i get this feeling that's a little like dying . . .

'as if I'm nearing death . . .

'sometimes it's as if you take me to the shore to show me something before we come back . . .'

'when we make love you get that death-like feeling, yes?'

'yes,' she wrote back right away, 'every time it's so powerful.'

'good.'

'you know you should put that in your novel.'

'what should I write?'

'the only connection between a man and a woman should be lust . . . this single bond should be so strong that it supersedes everything else, startling in its ability to sweep away anything that lies in its path . . . indeed even in a passionate love that has grown into an obsession over the years . . . and even at a time when a woman wants to reunite with an old flame . . .'

'how can we explain something like this?'

'how can we? . . . i don't know . . . we could give little clues . . . notes written by the man or the woman . . . internal monologues . . .'

Zuhal had taken to the idea of writing a novel. Now, in her mind, this was a shared endeavour, and when she set her mind to something she attacked it with her entire being, giving herself fully, never calculating the outcomes, only applying her mind to the work at hand.

Now she was thinking about how we would write 'our book', searching for the solutions to the problems we would face along the way.

It warmed my heart and I felt that much closer to her but then again I couldn't get certain things out of my mind: the image of her crying with Mustafa, the words she wrote to him and the imperious way he spoke to her when I first met him.

I was becoming like him.

The rain was crashing against the window panes like wild birds.

'how did you fall in love with mustafa?'

'the second time we met . . . in america he loved me more than i loved him . . .

'there were so many problems when we met for the second time . . . we were always arguing . . . and always leaving each other . . .

'every time we broke up because something was lacking in our relationship and our dreams i became more strongly bound to him . . . . i don't know when i started to fall in love with him . . . he asked me the same thing . . . he was never quite sure if i was in love with him . . . he didn't believe anything i said . . .'

'are you jealous?'

'i was, a lot in the beginning.'

'then less?'

'over time, yes . . . both of us became less jealous . . . and to care less . . . we'd defeated each other . . .

'i couldn't deal with it any more . . . in the middle of the night he would get a call from a woman and talk to her for ten, fifteen minutes . . . or he would get all these messages from them . . . i was doing the same thing . . . once in the middle of the night i spoke with an old friend from university for forty-five minutes all the while looking right into mustafa's eyes . . . i didn't even like the guy . . . i got him back for every single thing he did . . . it turned into a full-blown war . . .'

'did you ever regret those things later on?'

'i always went through a whirlwind of different emotions after trying to make him jealous . . .

'the joy of victory . . .

'remorse . . .

'a devastating sadness . . .

'the desire to throw my arms around him and apologise . . .

'helplessness . . .'

'what do you feel now?'

'i don't know . . . i suppose i'm thinking about you.'

'good.'

And then we made passionate love amid the sounds of the rain, invisible lovemaking in which we did not touch each other's bodies, hear each other's voices, taste each other's lips, love that existed only in our minds, forged in our imaginations.

There was something powerful between us.

As she'd said, a nameless thing we'd fashioned from things with names.

This gave rise in me to a virile, shameful confidence: I had taught her things she'd never known and I had given her fantasies to dream about and with a scalding iron I had branded her with a mark that she would never be able to erase, which she would have no choice but to carry with her for the rest of her life. Never again would she be able to erase that mark from her body and her soul.

But I never told her that.

I never told anyone.

XXVII

It wasn't the day the sun first came out, but the day after. After the rain the oleanders were an even richer shade of red, glistening in the sun. The palm trees seemed a little taller and greener. The sea was dark blue and the flickering gold of the station dome made the town seem like something out of a fairy tale.

People were back out on the streets again and in the gardens.

The town was alive.

Instead of taking my usual shortcut, I decided to pass by the cradle-maker's shop and have a coffee and a chat with him.

When I got to the coffeehouse, I sat down on a little wicker stool and leaned back against the wall.

The cradle-maker was sitting in his spot, his head bent over a cradle he was carving.

I decided not to say anything, or disturb him, until he looked up.

The tea boy came over to me. He either had a wardrobe full of Barcelona uniforms or he just wore the same one every day.

I ordered a coffee.

And then I began watching the man carve out his cradle, digging into the wood with a broad, sharp chisel with a wooden handle.

Without lifting his head, he said, 'Are you going to have your coffee without saying a word?'

'I was waiting for you to finish,' I said.

'My work's never done . . . until they finish theirs,' he said, and with his head he gestured to the nearby houses.

The boy brought me my coffee. As I began to drink the cradle-maker raised his head and said, 'You write books then. You never told me.'

'It never came up.'

'Are you someone who always waits for the right opportunity to speak?'

'Not really,' I said.

'I didn't think so either.'

'Have you ever been to the church?' I asked.

'I went a couple times in my youth.'

'It's just a ruin. How can people believe there's treasure up there?'

'Do you only believe what you see?'

'What else would I believe in?'

'I don't know. People decide for themselves what they'll believe in. It's not for us to say.'

'Do you believe in things you haven't seen?'

'There are ways to not see. Not everything can be seen with the naked eye. Do you only write down what you have actually seen and then expect me to believe only what I've seen? You write books because you want to tell people about things you believe they haven't seen, things they can't see. Our eyes deceive us . . . The truth is hidden in the unseen.'

I thought of all those people on the internet and how the truth lay in the hidden aspects of themselves.

'I suppose our intentions are different but I'm of the same opinion. I believe that the truth is found in the unseen. But what we do not see is different. I'm interested in the unseen aspects of people. You're interested in creating things that can't be seen at all.'

'How do you know they can't be seen?'

Laughing, I said, 'I haven't seen them. Have you?'

He looked up at the sky as a bird left the branch of a tree in the little square. 'Look,' he said.

'A bird,' I said.

'It's flying,' he said.

'That's what birds do.'

'That's what birds do,' he repeated. 'When you look at a bird you see a bird in flight. When I look at a bird I see that which gave it the power to fly. It's your choice: will you see the bird or that which gives the bird flight? To see it all you need are your eyes but also a mind to see that which gives it power. Question with your mind and answer with your heart.'

'When I look at a bird I only see a bird.'

'When you look at people what do you see?'

'Sin.'

'Is it something you can see?'

I paused and said, 'Sometimes you can.'

'Can you see every sin?' he asked.

'Not all of them.'

'Then how do you know that the others are there?'

He was smiling under his moustache.

'So you believe they can't be seen,' he added.

'If not the actual sin then the clues that lead to it.'

He looked up at the sky again and watched the same bird alight on the tree.

'It flies and you're still looking for other clues?'

He leaned over the cradle in his lap. I turned the subject back to the treasure.

'You told me that there wasn't any treasure . . . Have you changed your mind?'

'Oh no . . . There's no treasure up there . . . They stripped the place clean long before our present idiots arrived . . . But it distracts them.'

'They're not just distracted,' I said, as if I knew what was to come, 'they're killing each other.'

'They aren't killing each other for that.'

'Why, then?'

'Because in this fleeting world they only want more power than the next man. That's why they're killing each other. As if they could really have any power over anyone.'

'They do, though,' I said.

'Are you speaking of the rich?'

'Yes.'

'Have you ever seen a rich man walk around this town without protection? Why do they need to have all those people with them? Because they're afraid. Can a man with fear in his heart ever rise above another? Is he better than someone who isn't afraid? They are proud and then they pay the price with fear. It is when you set out to be superior that you feel the claws on the back of your neck. Fear is the price you pay for pride. To be superior you acquire things you do not need, and then you begin to fear losing them. Why should one who possesses only what he needs fear anything at all? Will they come and take my cradles? Let them have them and I will just make more. Will they take my money? Let them have it and I will just make more. Why should I be afraid? Because I've never wanted more than I could make for myself. You can live in a villa with forty rooms but you can only ever inhabit one of them. What will you do in the others?'

'What you don't see can bring pride and arrogance too,' I said.

'He granted those birds power of flight but you don't go jump off a cliff. This means you have the power of choice. So choose wisely, not foolishly. If you choose foolishly you have no one to blame but yourself.'

I finished my coffee and stood up. I always felt refreshed and purified when I spoke to the cradle-maker. More than what he actually said it was the way he spoke, the clarity of his belief, and I suppose the way he never asked the creator for anything in return for it. He made me feel as if I had been purged.

I had always enjoyed chatting with him, I enjoyed his whimsy; it wasn't as if he was giving advice but rather making fun of fools.

As I said goodbye the bird was still up in the tree.

'The bird can still fly,' I said, trying to rile him up.

And without looking up, he said, 'You only think the bird can fly. You don't see what makes it fly.'

I made my way down the hill in a good mood.

When I arrived at Centipede's place, I sat down in my usual spot, and like every other day I went through the daily papers.

Everything was calm.

It was just another ordinary day.

I planned to have lunch with Mustafa. I would meet him at the town hall.

I set off in that direction.

The building is by the sea. There's a road that runs from the centre of town down to the shore, broadening in front of the building and turning into a little square before it narrows back into a road.

It was almost one.

When I turned the corner into the square, there was hardly anyone there. Most people had finished their errands and gone home.

I would be the only witness to what was about to happen.

Soon I saw Sultan standing alone in the middle of the square, waiting. He was looking up the road I'd just come down. He seemed to be waiting for someone inside the town hall. I could see his telephone glistening in the sun.

Just as I turned towards the main entrance of the building a yellow minibus appeared on the shore road, slowly and silently making its way forward; or perhaps everything simply seemed silent from the moment I caught sight of it.

I knew what was about to happen.

The minibus stopped ten metres away from Sultan, who was still looking in my direction, unaware of what was happening behind him.

The door of the minibus slid open.

Two men got out.

The door still open.

'Sultan,' one of them called out.

Sultan calmly turned and reached for his hip, but he was too late. The men had already drawn their guns.

They fired one round after another and Sultan reeled as he walked towards them, unable to lift his gun. The men emptied everything they had into him and then reloaded.

Sultan fell three feet away from them.

His white shirt was ripped to shreds by bullets.

Blood sprayed from the bullet holes in his body. A seemingly endless flow of blood.

He was still holding his phone in his left hand.

People had turned at the sound of gunfire. And together we watched them. The men hopped back onto the minibus and they were gone.

Then came the screams.

Killers and spies have their own particular sense of humour, and ways of getting their message across, their minds working in curious ways.

They had worked out that Sultan was interested in a girl, and they had taken her phone and sent a message asking him to meet her in front of the town hall. Sultan was no doubt too excited to wonder why she wanted to meet him there. It had never occurred to him that someone else might be using her phone.

They'd lured him right in front of the window of Mustafa's office and shot him dead.

Sultan was the one to die but they were threatening Mustafa.

They had sent him a message in the form of a corpse filled with precisely fifty-six bullets, saying, 'You're next. Back off.'

As Sultan lay there in his shredded shirt, still dripping in a pool of blood, police cars filled the square and the police chief soon arrived in his blue Mercedes. They cordoned off the square and took statements from everyone there.

The chief grimaced when he saw me and said, 'You're at every murder scene. You some kind of banshee?'

'Do you need a banshee in a place where a man is killed every other day and the killers are never apprehended?'

I was annoyed by the gutless bastard's ungracious talk and I saw him bite his lip and raise his hand but he stopped – I was a friend of Mustafa's and that had saved me. For whatever reason the man never liked me. I suppose he didn't like the fact that I was a writer.

'We'll find the perpetrators,' he said, icily. 'There is no need for any concern.' He turned to the policemen and said, 'Get his statement. Let's see what he's seen.'

I told them everything: I described the minibus and the men and how Sultan was standing there and the telephone in his hand, and how the men called out to him, and how he turned, and their shots, the way they reloaded and how Sultan stepped towards them before he died.

'What did the men look like?' the officer asked. 'Did you see their faces?'

I paused.

I couldn't remember their faces. I remembered everything else but I had absolutely no recollection of any facial features. I assumed I never looked at their faces, more at Sultan stepping towards them as he took all those bullets.

'I can't remember,' I said.

The officer was a plump man with red cheeks and a greying head of hair.

'You remember everything except the very thing we really need from you, old-timer.'

He had an absent air about him. Maybe he called everyone 'old-timer'. He didn't seem bothered by the fact that a man had just been killed; he didn't seem like a bad man but he'd grown immune to all the killings. Animals killing animals. The important thing was to keep the forest from 'burning down', the philosophy imparted to me by the chief of police the first day I got here.

As I was signing my official statement the chief of police came over to me again with an entirely different attitude: 'Forgive me. We're all a little on edge. I hope you didn't take what I just said personally.'

'Of course not. These things happen,' I said.

'Indeed they do, but this is an exceptional case. It hardly bodes well to see Sultan shot like this. He was Oleander's favourite nephew, that boy. This won't stop here. There will be more after this, and we won't have an easy time stopping it. And then they do it here in front of the town hall. Pumped fifty-six bullets into the guy. You should see his body, it looks like he was ripped to pieces by a lion. Fifty-six bullets isn't easy . . . And in a place like this. These people know what they're doing and everyone gets the message. It's not so simple . . .'

'What will happen now?' I asked.

'God knows. We'll go after them. But it's no longer in my power to put out the fires. That's a job for the lords of the jungle. It's beyond me. My job is to find the killers, and that's it. If there's a war in this town how can I stop it?'

'Will there be?'

'Seems so. You should be careful, everyone should be. We did everything we could to protect the town until now but once the elephants go on a rampage no one can escape to the meadows. They're already on the move . . . Until now, only the jackals skirmishing but the stakes are higher . . . the elephants are here . . . anyway . . . you've already given us your statement but if anything else comes to mind give us a call.'

He jumped into his blue Mercedes and was gone. It was the first time I saw him truly flustered and afraid, that much was clear. Evidently there was no one left you could trust.

Thinking that Mustafa had enough on his plate, I went back to Centipede's.

Everyone rushed over.

I told them what I'd seen.

They all said the same thing: 'He was Oleander's favourite nephew.'

Fear swept through the coffeehouse; the entire town was stricken with it.

Never before had I seen an entire town gripped with fear, as if it were a single person.

No one went out that night.

Only police cars circled through the streets.

XXVIII

The village of Göllü, literally 'of the lakes', was roughly an hour and a half from town. To get there you climbed up and over the mountains. There was a large lake at the bottom of a valley between the two mountain ranges. The hotel was almost identical to the one we had stayed in before but here the village and the hotel itself were on the shore of the lake. The village stretched up into the mountains and was renowned for a nearby source of thermal waters. It was filled with tourists from all over the world.

On one of those dark days when the town was full of fear, I got a message from Zuhal.

I'm going to Göllü tomorrow night. Come.

Of course, I wrote back.

Something occurred to me as I read that message: she had never invited me to her home, and she never came to mine, which meant she was exhibiting the very behaviour towards me that Mustafa kept complaining about – we only ever met in hotels.

The only difference between me and Mustafa was that I never complained.

I set out in the early evening.

As I wound slowly up through the mountains, passing through all the villages and then driving down the other side to the lake, she messaged me the number of her hotel room.

The hotel was a complex of bungalows along the lakeshore in the middle of a vast garden just outside the village.

She always chose hotels where the guests rarely bumped into one another.

Her bungalow had its own private garden surrounded by a wooden fence.

The room was painted a bright green and was on a slight slope, the shimmering waters of the lake reflecting off the walls.

Again she greeted me in a long white nightgown.

We'd missed each other.

I wrapped my arms around her.

When we finished it was dark outside.

'I'm starving,' she said from the bed, stretching and mewing like a cat.

'I'll order something for you,' I said.

She had planned everything in advance. 'They say there's an excellent restaurant in the village. Let's go there. It shouldn't be too crowded this time of year. But only if you want to go. We could also eat here in the room.'

She was set on going out and I couldn't imagine a man saying no to that soft, imploring voice. I don't think she ever met with any opposition in those moments.

We got dressed and walked along the shore of the lake to the restaurant, which stretched out over the lake on a wooden pier. The place was empty and they were about to close so we ordered what they had left.

We sat down at a table by the window.

The full moon was bright above the mountain, so clear we could make out the craters on the surface.

'Look at the moonlight. We're lucky,' I said.

She smiled and said, 'I arranged for that too. I picked just the right night.'

The lake quivered under a soft breeze, the colour of blue moonlight.

'I missed you,' I said.

'I know,' she said, laughing, 'I won't let you go for so long next time. It kills me when you're away for so long. I feel like I'm recovering from an accident.'

She said these words in her shy, feminine voice, which was strange to hear when she was dressed and we were speaking face to face.

'Is the night over already? Have I used up my allowance?'

'Hardly. I'm completely yours tonight.'

It was that voice of surrender.

Surely she knew how that voice drove me out of my mind.

I wanted to stop eating right then and race back to the hotel with her but I didn't say a word. The food had arrived and she was eating with a full appetite. I'd never seen hunger so elegantly manifested.

We talked a little about the news in town.

Once again I told her how they had shot Sultan.

'I'm afraid they'll do something to Mustafa,' she said.

It was as if she was speaking about her brother and not the man she was in love with, her voice full of compassion and concern.

'Will they do something to him?'

'I don't know but it looks as if things are spinning out of control.'

'How did things get to this point?'

'Raci Bey,' she said.

'What about Raci Bey?'

'Raci Bey has always been strong and influential but it seems that he's now trying to push Mustafa aside and take control himself. They say that he's close to Muhacir.'

'Mustafa told me that he's trying to provoke Muhacir,' I said.

'I know. He told me the same thing.'

I looked her in the eye and she looked back and strangely we both understood, and we laughed. It was maybe the first time the ghost of Mustafa was driven away.

'I'm concerned about you.'

'What's there to be concerned about?'

'I don't know but you're too exposed, and there's no one protecting you. Everyone else has someone on their side but you don't.'

'That's just why there's no danger. Why would they shoot someone who isn't on either side?'

'The town's gone mad. Lost its mind. I don't think it's ever been like this before.'

'In my opinion it's always been like this. All this talk of the treasure has long since infected everyone.'

'Do you think there is such a thing?' she said. Sometimes she would ask me questions as innocently as a child.

'I don't know. But from what I could tell, I don't think there's anything to be found in those ruins up on the hill.'

We talked about the town but without really caring, and as we spoke it seemed more and more remote, and Mustafa and his kingdom drifted even further away and we felt even closer to each other. I felt we were finishing off Mustafa and the town over dessert.

'It's beautiful here, isn't it?' she said

'Very much,' I said. 'And especially with the full moon . . .'

'I knew you'd like it,' she said.

She wanted to make me happy. It gave her such pleasure to see me that way, and I felt the same.

It was as if we had planted our own seed and it was growing into a tree that was ours alone, growing steadily, this unnamed source of joy.

In silence we sipped our coffees as we gazed out over the lake.

We were captivated by the anticipation of what was to come when we got back to the hotel.

We left the restaurant. The village streets were quiet and empty, scattered street lamps casting strong beams of light over the road, moonlight blanketing the backdrop.

She put her arm in mine as we walked, slowly leaning into each other. It was the first time she'd done something like that and I could feel the softness of her body against mine.

We walked on in silence.

Then far from the hotel we saw a man who had collapsed at the foot of one of the hills leading up into the village. He was crumpled up on the ground, leaning to one side.

She stopped.

She pulled her arm out of mine, leaned over the man and asked if he was all right. He mumbled something in English and they had something of a conversation.

I couldn't really make out what the man was trying to say. I watched them from a distance.

She came back over to me. 'He's really drunk. We can't leave him there.'

I sighed.

She went back and leaned over the man again. 'Which hotel are you staying in?' The man could hardly speak, garbling every other word. 'I have a house here,' he finally managed.

She came back over.

'We have to take him home, we can't leave him here.'

'How are we going to find his house?' I said. 'The guy's three sheets to the wind. He's in no state to give us directions.'

She turned back to the man.

'Where's your house?'

'Up there.'

'Up this hill?'

'Yes.'

She put her arm around his shoulders and tried to help him stand.

I went over and pulled him up, and he fell back against the wall, swaying for a moment on his feet.

'Are you going to be able to make it home?' I said.

'Yeah, I can make it, yeah . . .'

He stumbled off, wavering all over the road.

Zuhal watched him go.

After he had taken a few solid steps I turned to her and said, 'He'll make it. Come on, let's go.'

Zuhal seemed reluctant to let the man go in that state. She watched him a little longer and, sure enough, after a few more steps up the hill he turned and starting walking towards our hotel.

Then we heard a thick, muted thud. We turned and looked. The man had fallen and cracked his head on the road.

Zuhal rushed over in a panic.

She took him by the arms and sat him upright.

'Are you all right?' she said.

'I'm fine,' he said.

He had just smashed his head on concrete and the guy said he was all right.

As she struggled with him, I gently pushed her aside and pulled him up to his feet again.

Again she asked him where he lived, and he said, 'Up there.'

Zuhal turned to me and said, 'Go back to the hotel if you want. I'm taking him home.'

I couldn't help but let out a deep sigh. 'Let's take him then,' I said.

I put my arm around his shoulder and together we dragged the poor man up the hill, almost carrying him.

We climbed some way, the man's full weight against me, nearly unconscious.

'Where's do you live?' I asked.

'Up there,' he said.

Zuhal was so intent on helping him that my unwillingness was beginning to look a bit churlish.

Though it was a little sad to see the state of the poor man. He was drunk and all alone in a remote village.

He couldn't really walk but I suppose out of embarrassment he kept mumbling, 'I can make it now.' But he would have tumbled to the ground if we'd let go of him.

Finally he pointed to a house on the top of the hill. 'There it is.'

Zuhal took his house keys from his pocket and helped him unlock the door. Now I assumed we'd be heading off but the moment we let go of him he collapsed.

So we took him up to the second floor.

'I'll make you some coffee,' Zuhal said, and in no time she was back.

He seemed to have pulled himself together. He was probably in his fifties, unshaven, unkempt and fairly frazzled.

'What do you do here?' I asked him.

'I live here,' he muttered. 'My dad has a company here.'

I was surprised to hear a fifty-year-old man talk about his dad's company like that.

He repeated, 'My dad has his own company, and I live here.'

Finally we managed to get him down on a couch. Zuhal draped a blanket over him. Then we left and closed the door behind us. I was a little on edge: we had just gone into a man's house – someone we didn't even know – in the middle of the night and left him there conked out on the couch. If something happened to him, we'd be the ones to blame. But Zuhal didn't seem at all concerned.

Making our way down the hill, she said, 'That poor man.'

I'd never seen such pure and honest goodwill.

Later I would see her help others in times of need. Often she would stop to help the poor and disabled, putting aside everything else. She would become completely absorbed, and focused on the task at hand.

'Poor man,' she said again. 'I guess that's how he spends his evenings. His father's company must be some kind of burden for him. Look how he's taken refuge here.'

When we got to the shore she put her arm in mine.

At one point when she was helping the man I actually wondered if she had had second thoughts about having another intense round with me in the hotel. Had I been too rough?

But I was wrong. The lake shimmered on the bright green walls of our room in bluish waves, and it seemed as if we were under water.

Pale and naked, Zuhal was a mermaid in blue light.

Hoping to be ravished, hungry for more violence and more savagery.

She grew more and more diaphanous in the light.

Twisting, writhing, arching, moaning and wailing.

'I'm yours. Do whatever you want with me.'

'I'm your woman,' she whispered in my ear, 'and you're my man.'

She was mine.

My woman.

My slave.

Surrendering herself to me with all her heart.

And taking me with her as she did.

She followed my every order without hesitation, submitting passionately to my will.

She embraced me with desire, submission and tenderness, making me her master, my entire being melting into her tenderness, binding me to her.

When we stopped she was soaked in sweat, her hair dripping wet, her body glistening, the light on the walls reflected on her shimmering breasts.

We threw open a window and wrapping ourselves in sheets we sat opposite each other in the broad windowsill. With one leg bent her inner thighs lay in shadow.

Our knees were touching.

We felt a cool breeze off the lake.

She took my hand and pressed it against her cheek.

I saw tears in her eyes. 'I'm your woman. No matter what happens, don't forget this night, this moment, this lake, this room, that I am your woman. No matter what happens.'

I was silent.

I kissed her fingertips.

'I'm tired. I'll sleep a little now,' she said.

She went to bed and drifted off to sleep.

I leaned back into the window and watched her sleep, thinking that love was something like this: watching a woman sleep with your heart full of compassion and desire.

The way she slept reminded me of her in the waking world. She slept calmly and peacefully, like the unhurried nature of her voice, the curves of her feet under the white sheet like puffs of smoke.

She was bathed in the light of that room, a light I would only ever see that night.

A light that was hers.

Later, during one of our talks at home, I wrote about what I'd felt then.

'in my life you hold a place illuminated by a light that is yours alone.'

Later, I'd always think of her in that light.

In moments like these a woman pulls another soul into her own, into her very being, losing herself in a sacred communion, slipping into a world of creation, and gives thanks for the light, for the chance of abandonment, the chance to become something more than what you are.

I felt myself dissolving.

I watched her.

I knew that she was dreaming, she always did, and once she told me that she loved to sleep because it gave her the chance to dream.

I didn't know what she dreamt and she would never know what I really thought.

A little later she would wake from a deep slumber refreshed and alive.

And for a fleeting moment she'd look up, startled, wondering where she was, like a child who'd come to this world from somewhere far away, and then the expression on her face would change into the face of a woman.

'Come,' she said.

And in the time it took me to walk from the windowsill to the bed we were both changed again, once again we were a single body.

I took her by the back of her neck and kissed her on the lips.

When we drifted off to sleep together the sun was coming up over the mountains.

We woke around noon and over breakfast I asked, 'Is it possible to have your car sent back to the city? Could they find someone to drive it back?'

She looked at me, puzzled.

'I want to take you somewhere. But let's go together. I don't want to go in separate cars.'

'All right.'

After breakfast she got dressed and went to speak with the hotel receptionist. I knew she'd be able to work something out. She could solve anything.

'All settled,' she said a little later. 'They found a driver who'll take my car and leave it at my office.'

I'd taken a shower while I was waiting for her. 'Come on, jump in the shower and then let's go,' I said.

I heard her softly singing to herself as she went.

Then we were off.

Climbing back up the mountains again.

'Where are we going?' she asked.

'You'll see when you get there.'

We could feel the heat of the sun in the car.

She was curious to know where we were going but she didn't ask again.

An hour later we arrived in Şeftali.

XXIX

The town is twitching in a restless slumber.

I am weary.

My entire body aches.

I know I need to get up from this bench but I can't.

Every night the people here go to their homes and sleep but a brief and restless sleep, and in the morning they are tired; it's nothing like the long and blissful sleep of the seven sleepers who slept for hundreds of years in a cave, as symbols of faith.

I can see the restless dreams of the town.

God grants peace of mind as a reward for faith.

You say that you reward those who are faithful.

I am not faithful.

Maybe his punishment is for me to sit here alone on this bench.

I am paying the price for my lack of faith, condemned to sit and wait to die.

But who is faithful?

Have you ever known pure faithfulness?

Look, here I am sitting in the final hours of my life and I'm thinking about your book, how your words have brought me here, and now as my novel finishes every word you write takes on more meaning in my eyes, and I want to know which parts I may have misunderstood, which parts you may have got wrong.

In your novel you wrote of betrayal as well as faithfulness.

What magnificent discoveries.

What incredible suspense, what dramatic contradictions.

Then tell me, have there ever been any faithful heroes?

There has never been anyone who showed you perfect fidelity.

They struggle to seem faithful in your eyes because they fear you. Why would they feel compelled to show it if they merely loved you?

Can faith and fear coexist?

As we read your book must we believe that only cowards have faith?

What do you want from such miserable heroes as us?

Is it fear you want? Or is it love?

I'm not afraid of you.

I love you, your creativity, your mighty power in the act of creation, your imagination and indeed I even love the cruelty that is the fruit of your imagination.

I didn't follow your commands.

But did you really expect me to? When you created a hero like me you must have known I wouldn't obey your orders?

Did you know this when you created me?

Will you see me as a traitor because I do not fear you and disobey you? Or am I faithful in your eyes because of my bond to your creative powers, my eternal love for you and your creations, my admiration in the face of your unrivalled imagination unseen in any other writer?

What is faith for you?

I have no idea.

No hero knows.

We don't even know that. You don't tell us and so how should we?

You shower praise over fidelity yet you never write of faithful heroes; you speak of betrayal as the greatest sin but you write glowingly of heinous traitors.

In every chapter of your work betrayal takes on yet another form.

Since the creation of humankind, we see betrayal in every chapter and on every page; your heroes are very quick to take that path.

Where is fidelity?

Where is the kind of faith we see in the Seven Sleepers?

Even those young exemplars of faith betrayed the kings around them to remain faithful to you.

Betrayed the kings with whom they broke bread.

Is it absolutely necessary to betray to remain faithful to another?

Are there any stories in your novel in which fidelity is not tainted by betrayal?

Can a writer praise faith like this yet reward only betrayal?

Is your inability to create a faithful hero not a flaw in your book?

And so here on this desolate night we are left alone together.

Can you tell me about a single hero who has remained faithful?

There are billions but which one lived without betraying?

I suppose that in this novel faith is more complicated a concept than you had initially conceived. And do you know why? Because just as in the story of those young men, faith only comes through betrayal.

I know this all too well now.

You must betray one to stay faithful to another.

What are we to make of a hero like this?

Do we call him faithful or a traitor?

In this 'second volume' you said you've written only to show mortals when they've died, will you burn your hero or reward him?

Do you know the answers to these questions?

They say that you know everything in this book, so why not tell us?

Tell me.

Is it an act of faith or betrayal to sacrifice one to save another?

You always leave your heroes with the same dilemma.

But let me say this, in your novel there is no faith without betrayal.

That's just the way it is.

I wish that we had more time to talk about this earlier.

Time is now running out for me.

But if indeed you have set aside a place for me in the second volume then perhaps we will continue.

The time I have left in this book is counted out in hours.

And there's so much more I have to say.

I suppose I won't be able to put it all in tonight.

In my life I have seen so many people praising and exalting faith, so many desirous of being faithful, and I have not met one among them who has not betrayed another.

Sometimes it occurs to me that you don't spend that much time thinking about us, setting aside time for us in your novel, as there are so many other books in the universe that you, like Alexandre Dumas, are writing. So many at the same time that no doubt you'll have to leave drafts, assuming you don't have a good editorial team.

Fidelity and the desire for it are generally not innate in us.

A chain of betrayal is born.

But betrayal arouses the desire to betray.

Have you seen a chain of fidelity in your novel?

I can show you a thousand chains of betrayal in your novel.

Like all novelists, you are unwittingly drawn to evil.

This is why you have always defended the very opposite of what you have created.

Good, in your books, is only something talked about.

While evil is victorious.

Even today, if a writer like myself were to take what you said as principle, and begin to craft a character with the kind of absolute fidelity and absolute goodness you teach, he would soon realise he was conjuring up an idiot.

How can we get out of this corner?

If even you can't find a way out, what chance do we have?

Especially me.

As you drily spread praise, you provide such stellar examples of evil and it is simply not possible to resist being swept away.

I am the hero in such a novel.

That is how you wrote me.

Or did I write myself like this?

Whose work am I the product of? Yours or mine?

Who wrote what I've lived through?

You or me?

Who's responsible for Zuhal's actions, for her most unexpected behaviour?

You or me?

What a faithful woman she was.

How many acts of betrayal she committed.

But let me say this, the day I took her to Şeftali, in that chapter there was nothing but sheer goodness.

There are such chapters in your books that we should not be remiss in praising.

And no matter how fascinating I find evil, these chapters are dear to my heart.

This is a contradiction in my novel, and what can you do about it?

XXX

It was afternoon by the time we arrived in Şeftali.

The village was quiet and hardly anyone was out.

In the distance I could see a village woman leading several cows back to a barn. When I spotted the minaret in the distance, I turned.

We drove up to the mosque.

It was on the top of a little hill.

The road ended there.

It was a plain, little, white mosque.

With a little courtyard in front.

I stopped the car and told Zuhal to wait for me. 'I'll be back,' I said.

I stepped into the courtyard.

Three kids were playing there, and an old man was sitting in a corner with theology books lined up on a little counter in front of him.

There was a one-storey house attached to the mosque.

I asked the children where I could find the Imam efendi.

Then the old man got up and came over to me.

'Did you need something?' he said, eager to help.

'I'm looking for the Imam efendi,' I said.

'What for?' he asked.

'I need to speak to him about a matter.'

'He lives over there,' said the old man, pointing to the little house, 'but he's probably not there.'

Just then one of the windows opened and a young woman in a white headscarf leaned out. 'Who are you looking for?' she asked.

'I'm looking for the Imam efendi,' I said.

'He went to check on the bees,' said the woman.

'Where are the bees?' I asked.

'In a grove at the end of the village.'

'Okay, then. Thank you.'

I went back to the car and Zuhal asked me what was going on. I told her that the Imam efendi had gone to look after the bees. And that we were going to find him.

Zuhal had understood what we were going to do.

I turned and headed for the grove at the end of the village.

A young man with light brown hair and a bright face was tending beehives under the trees.

I got out of the car and as I walked over to the Imam I felt as if I'd already written the scene, and wondered which words I'd used to describe it. I couldn't quite remember, and I wondered if all my life I'd dreamt of getting married in a mosque, or if I was always going to meet a woman who wanted to marry me in a mosque after every new book I wrote.

Lost in thought, I knew I was taken by the idea of marrying Zuhal, forming such a bond with her. It brought a smile to my face.

The Imam saw me coming and stood up. 'Are you the Imam?' I asked.

'Yes. How can I help you?' he said.

'I would like to get married.'

'You need to get papers from the mufti. There's no other way. It's prohibited otherwise.'

'How can we find the mufti? Could you not perform the ritual?' I asked. 'Who would even know? I'm simply asking you to perform an auspicious deed, nothing ill-willed. To bring two people together.'

'I can't do it . . . I really can't. I would help you out, of course, if I could.'

I turned to look back at my car and we both looked at Zuhal inside.

'But you're going to let her down. Is it worth it in the name of some silly restriction?' I said.

Zuhal was watching us closely.

The Imam closed his eyes. I could see he was distraught, searching for a solution, and without saying a word I waited.

'I can't marry you but . . . There's a retired Imam in the village. He can. I won't go into the mosque but I'll wait outside.'

'Thank you very much. You're doing us a tremendous favour. How can we find this Imam?'

'I'll have someone call him.'

I offered him a ride back with us but he said that he'd follow us on his bicycle.

We returned to the mosque and waited. Zuhal was excited. She stepped into the courtyard. A little later I saw her speaking to a young woman who was the Imam's wife.

First the Imam came over.

Then came the retired Imam with a man beside him.

'You want to get married,' said the robust old Imam.

'Yes,' I said.

'Well, then bring the lady over here and let's go inside.'

I turned to see the young woman tying a thin white scarf over Zuhal's head.

It made her look stunning.

I'd never seen such an image of pure and innocent female beauty. She seemed a part of the mosque.

We stepped inside. It was immaculate, bright and silent, strips of light streaming through the windows, the mihrab serene and unadorned.

We knelt down in front of the retired Imam.

I took Zuhal's hand as the Imam read his prayers. And I squeezed her hand. She didn't let go until he stopped.

We were married.

The Imam and I rose to our feet. But Zuhal stayed kneeling.

'You go. I want to stay a little longer.'

I thanked the witnesses and the retired Imam and they left. Then I thanked the Imam, who disappeared into his home.

Alone I waited for Zuhal in the courtyard, birds circling over the mosque.

She came out a little later and tapped on a window of the Imam's house to return the headscarf. The young woman looked out and they spoke briefly, embracing each other before they said goodbye.

'What's up?' I said.

'They wouldn't take back the scarf. It's your wedding dress, they said, you should keep it. So it's my wedding dress and I'll keep it for the rest of my life.'

She was crying.

We drove out of the village.

'You see all this as just a game, don't you?' she said. 'You don't take it seriously like me.'

I recited the first part of a verse from the Qu'ran for her. And then I said, 'Don't forget this world is nothing more than games, having fun while we're here.'

She went on.

'Of course the hereafter is a better place for the timid, the people fearful of God. Are you still unwilling to understand?'

I had forgotten that her grandfather had sent her to Qu'ran classes when she was a child.

'But now we're here in this world,' I said.

She was quiet, only nodding her head. I didn't know what it meant. She probably wanted to say something but I couldn't work it out.

I felt as if I'd hurt her feelings.

'I take it seriously too,' I said.

But she remained quiet. She only smiled.

For some time she didn't say a word, gazing out of the window. At one point she took off her headscarf and tied up her hair.

'What did you do by yourself in the mosque?' I asked.

She looked at me.

'I pleaded for him to accept me the way I am and to forgive me.'

XXXI

The town went berserk after Sultan was killed.

It was such a groundless, meaningless flight of rage and madness that I couldn't help wonder if people simply needed to go mad from time to time.

They needed to lose their heads and were looking for the right excuse.

Suddenly the town was split into two camps.

Those with Mustafa and those with Raci Bey.

I couldn't tell just what it was that put people on one side or the other. I simply didn't know why the sausage sandwich vendor I met in Centipede's coffeehouse supported Mustafa and why the minibus driver who occasionally came to drink tea was a big Raci Bey man; and why they were always throwing punches at each other.

But what really surprised me was the way the town became so divided even though there was no clear and obvious evidence pointing to a conflict between Mustafa and Raci Bey, no sound reason suggesting any such thing.

Whenever I asked why Mustafa and Raci were fighting, they would all say the same thing, 'The treasure.'

'But we don't even know if there is a treasure up there,' I said.

They would stare at me blankly and then turn right back to their heated discussions.

So there were fights that brought people to the brink of death over a treasure that probably didn't even exist, a treasure that no one knew what to do with if they even found it, which was something that people never openly discussed.

But what frightened me more was the way the town was divided, with Mustafa's people supporting Oleander and Raci Bey's fans supporting Muhacir, making the clashes between the rival gangs an everyday part of life.

This is what I could never understand: was the conflict turning more violent because there was a fierce exchange between Mustafa and Raci Bey, or were Raci and Mustafa sparring because the conflict in the town had flared up?

I never knew, and no one ever would.

I was a friend of Mustafa's but I wasn't on either side; I stayed out of it.

And this made me even more valuable.

After the second big event in the ongoing struggle, though, it suddenly became extremely important to determine which side I was going to take as the stranger in town, the writer, the city boy.

But as there was no clear reason for war, everything beyond the real took on a new level of importance.

Those were strange days.

We were in the middle of real war without a real reason.

The generals were divided. The judge, the district governor and the police chief all supported Mustafa. The gendarmerie commander supported Raci Bey.

Or rather that was the word on the street but there was no sound and clear evidence suggesting this.

Suddenly the number of bodyguards in town shot up, and I never worked out where the men came from; all the fat cats had three or four bodyguards with them as they sped through town in their dark Mercedes.

They feared for their lives.

And the same fear swept through the poor neighbourhoods.

Everyone was afraid of getting shot.

People were heading home early in the evening, keeping a close eye on what was happening around them, always looking over their shoulders.

There was no reason for any of them to be shot.

But everyone thought they might be the next victim.

The anger fed fear and that fear only turned into rage.

The void had created a vicious cycle and in the end I was really worried that they would in fact start shooting each other.

It was then that Raci Bey's son Rahmi invited me to dinner. We met in a little fish restaurant on the far side of town. Rahmi was already there when I arrived. I noticed a crowd of men in black suits hovering by the door.

The restaurant was empty.

Rahmi was sitting alone at a table by the window.

He stood up when he saw me.

'Are all those men at the door yours?' I asked.

'Yes.'

'There's an army out there.'

'These are troubled times,' he said. 'You should see my dad's place. They were practically ready to pull me off the streets and stuff me in there.'

'What's happening, Rahmi? I can't work it out.'

Rahmi smiled mournfully.

'Nobody knows what's going on. Mustafa has lost his mind and now the entire town has gone mad too.'

'What's he done?'

'He tried to get to the treasure on his own, pushing everyone else away, showing disrespect, bad manners . . . He doesn't want anyone to have any control so that when he starts digging again no one will be able to stop him.'

'Rahmi, you don't even know if there's any treasure up there.'

'It doesn't matter,' Rahmi said, shrugging his shoulders. 'Once he takes control of the hill, he's the only man who controls it. The treasure's there or it's not, but the town is yours . . . No one could challenge you then. Even his decision to forbid people going up there was a challenge to us all . . . Who is he to tell us what's off-limits? Are we nothing but food for the dogs?'

'Is it really that important?'

I didn't think Rahmi was the sharpest knife in the drawer but considering the way he was looking at me I understood that he didn't think I was all that bright either.

'My family has been living in this town for hundreds of years. And there are many other families like mine who have lived here for that long. Are we now going to be enslaved by this one guy? Is he going to chew us up and spit us out just like that? How can the people here accept something like that? Everyone here has their reputation to look after, so are we just going to bow down and get chewed to pieces? Are we going to tell our friends that Mustafa singlehandedly crushed us all? He would never allow something like that to be said about him.'

The waiter arrived with our fish.

'The fish here is excellent,' I said. It really was delicious.

'Their fish is always top-notch.'

'Isn't there another solution? Apart from all this fighting?' I asked, returning to the topic.

'For now, it doesn't look like there's any other way. If Mustafa doesn't back off then no one else will.'

'There's always another way.'

'And what's that?'

'Start telling people there's no treasure up there and over time the fighting will subside.'

Rahmi was silent, weighing the thoughts in his head. Then he scowled.

'And if there is?'

'If there is, does there have to be a war over it? If things are going to be this bad then there should at least be a sound reason for it.'

'When did a war ever have a sound reason? Who ever engaged in one with the guarantee of winning? Wars are either already ongoing or just about to start.'

'And then?'

'Then someone wins.'

'And the people who die along the way?'

'They'll die anyway. Do people only ever die in war? Might as well die in war than, say, typhus. If nothing else, people can feel that they died for a cause.'

'So you don't mind the killings?'

'Those who do will lose the war. Is there any example in history that proves me wrong? Saints, guardians and writers have always worried about deaths of others but if commanders and leaders feared that then they would be the ones to die.'

I was on the brink of saying, 'Indeed the subject has enlivened your mind,' but for a moment it occurred to me that his father would probably have similar thoughts about war.

'You seem to have quite a few ideas on the matter,' I observed.

'I studied history at Columbia,' he said.

'Are you serious?'

'Why not? I don't seem like someone with a degree?'

'Oh no, I didn't mean that. I just didn't know that you'd studied history. But you don't work in the field?'

And he laughed in such a way that I couldn't be sure if he was making fun of himself or me.

'No, I work in the olive oil business . . . but it's a very old trade, one you might consider history.'

Suddenly I was angry at how this man, whom I had taken for a fool, was toying with me. I was angry with myself for being wrong about him. The wealthy young generation in town had a strange make-up: on the surface they exhibited hundreds of years of tradition and habits that came from a routine life of tedious gossip and meaningless banter; but when they conversed with an outsider and needed to impress they could draw on the knowledge and refinement of their educations, which lay dormant under a rough façade. I found it impossible to understand how that wealth of knowledge never softened the hard outer shell.

'You seem to know so much but still you don't understand that there's no need to fight for a treasure that's not even there.'

'No one knows that for sure.'

I was confused about why he'd asked me to meet him; surely not to speak about all this.

As we sipped our coffees I felt that breath of air that came with the arrival of important people and soon there was a flutter of activity, doors opening and closing, chairs thrown into place.

A cheerful man well over six feet tall strode into the room. He had wavy brown hair and good health was beaming from his face.

Rahmi stood up and I followed his lead. The man seemed deferential in Rahmi's presence but still very much aware of his own importance. As they greeted each other, he put on a display of respect he was in no way obliged to give.

Rahmi introduced the man to me as Nazmi Bey and, a little confused, I extended my hand. He said, 'I'm better known as Muhacir.'

'Ah, that's you,' I said, surprised.

'Ah, yes it is,' he said.

Suddenly I felt as if everyone in town was having me on.

Muhacir was probably the only man in town who seemed unmoved by everything that was going on. He turned to the waiter and said cheerfully, 'Tell the chef to throw a fish on the grill. I'm starving, so make it a big one.'

Then he turned to Rahmi and said, 'I haven't eaten anything since morning.' Then to the waiter, 'And bring us some rakı.' And back to us: 'Aren't you drinking?'

'We're having wine.'

'Ah, not partaking in the drink of the riff-raff?'

His massive gold 'riff-raff' watch was easily worth as much as the entire restaurant.

'We were just talking local news,' Rahmi said.

Muhacir sighed and said, 'The town. Man, things are out of control.'

He turned to me as all the lines on his face suddenly hardened. The look in his eye was one of a man ready to kill. The change was terrifying.

'Oleander learned about his worthless nephew's death from

me. Why the hell would I kill your nephew, I said to him. Sultan has a thousand enemies in this town, there's not a person here he hasn't messed with. Now, if you were a real man, you'd look after your nephew. Does he expect me to look after this kid? The freak son-of-a-bitch says he'll cut Muhacir's head off and hang it in the square. The dishonourable cretin, the day he even touches my head the world will spin the other way round. He might scare shopkeepers and drug dealers, and even shoot the poor fools, but he needs to know his limits. Now, you see, the moment I heard those words I swear I nearly lost my mind. I'm going to cut off both of his ears and shove them in the bastard's eyes. I'm going to drag that clown Oleander through town like a blind donkey. My conscience is clean. This is just God's will.'

There was no doubt in my mind that he was set on killing Oleander at the first opportunity but I also sensed desperation in his rage: Oleander and Muhacir were always talking trash to each other, putting each other down, but both knew their opponent's strength.

It wouldn't be easy for either of them to kill the other. Both were surrounded by bodyguards and both had men gathering information. Both might be equally cruel and indifferent to human life but when it came to their own lives they were more careful than anyone else. And they both knew this.

For now they were just putting each other down, acting as if they weren't plotting, looking for a window of opportunity.

Muhacir's colourful introduction made me laugh. But the fact was they only spoke this way to send a message of fear. There was no particular benefit or aim in striking fear in someone's heart; it was in their blood. Their very existence, everything they had created, was hinged on this network of fear.

'Oleander's spoiling Mustafa,' said Rahmi.

I looked at Muhacir; he didn't say a word.

Rahmi or Raci Bey might put Mustafa down but Muhacir knew the limits, he knew where to stop.

'I don't know anything about Mustafa,' he said. 'Oleander is playing up to him, but I doubt he'd really give the guy the time of day.'

Rahmi was afraid of Mustafa and was only prepared to confront him if there was no other option. Now he was careful not to say anything that might push Mustafa too far.

Muhacir looked at me again.

'This Oleander's a dishonourable viper. You never know where and who he's going to strike. It's chaos in town. Now, you're a good man so you might not understand how low we've sunk. And we can't allow any old punk to get the better of you. Our people should protect you. They're solid. You can trust them.'

Now I understood why we'd met.

Accepting Muhacir's protection meant taking a side, choosing one over the other; like the regulars in the coffeehouse, these people thought I was important and they wanted to get me on their side.

As far as I could understand, I was another kind of unseen treasure; in the struggle for power I was nothing but another pawn in the game.

'Thank you,' I said. 'But no one is going to hurt me. And in any case I'm not sure how much longer I'll be staying. I might actually leave some time soon. Thank you for thinking of me but there's really no need.'

Muhacir looked at Rahmi as if to say, 'What more can we do?'

He tried to push it one more time.

'The town's unsteady right now, full of all kinds of nutters, and the best thing for you to do would be to take cover under a strong shelter.'

At that moment I realised one side might shoot me and blame the other. I was a prime target for either side. I suddenly felt they should fear me.

'No one is stupid enough to hurt me. If something happens to me the public order would never recover, the incident would rattle everyone, and no one would be better off for it. I'm convinced that people here are bright enough to know this. And that there's no need for me to change my routine.'

'The choice is yours,' said Muhacir.

When I finished my coffee, I asked Rahmi if he was staying.

'I'll stay a bit longer. Keep Nazmi Bey company.'

'Fine,' I said. 'See you, then.'

When I got back home I started to seriously think about leaving.

Everything that had happened was absurd and it was getting increasingly dangerous for me to stay.

There was no point in me getting mixed up in a struggle between the locals, a struggle I couldn't understand.

It took me half an hour to pack my bags.

I hopped in my car and was ready to go.

Sitting there thinking about where I would stay that night, and where I might be able to see Zuhal again, I heard my landline ringing.

I went inside and picked up.

'I see you had lunch with Rahmi,' said Kamile Hanım.

'We did,' I said.

'Have you finished all my sweets?'

'All done.'

'I'm coming into town. Can I bring you more?'

'I'm home. I'll be waiting.'

Now, on this bench, I am wondering if I would have left town if Kamile Hanım hadn't called just then. Had a call from a woman who seemingly meant nothing to me changed the course of my life? Thinking about the indescribable rush I felt when I heard her voice, I suppose it did.

There was something about that woman that moved me.

I was willing to let the course of my life be shaped by lust and the games that come with it.

Perhaps everything changed for the chance to make love. That night a person died, that night I became a killer, and all because of a telephone call?

I don't know.

I don't have a definitive answer but what I do know is that before I could leave I received a call from Kamile Hanım, and she changed my mind. The next day I would feel less inclined to leave. Her call had stopped me then and after I'd made love to her again my fears about everything that was happening around me had dissipated. Life always seemed less important after a bout of passion.

Kamile Hanım may have allayed my fears but she condemned me to another fate.

She was wearing a skirt and jacket again, and was holding a package.

'I brought you sweets,' she said, with a coy smile, stressing the word 'sweets' in a way that only we could understand.

She sat down in the armchair.

I sat down across from her.

She threw one leg over the other.

'Would you like something to drink?' I asked.

'Cognac was just right last time. I'll have the same,' she said, lighting a cigarette, and I poured two glasses of cognac.

Then I couldn't help but ask her a question that had been flitting about in my head.

'Everyone's watching each other closely. I'm sure they know you came. Doesn't that worry you?'

'They know the way I am. And they're always gossiping but they still never believe I'd actually do something. And people don't really care either way. They make up so much about me, saying all these things I never actually did that there's nothing left I actually didn't do.'

'Raci Bey?'

'I told him I made you sweets . . . He would never suspect me of anything.'

I was quiet.

'Pull the curtains,' she said.

The trees in front of the house already blocked the view from the street but we were both turned on by the way she said those words.

I pulled the curtain shut and sat down again. She put out her cigarette and pulled up her skirt, showing me her thighs. Then she stood over me the way she had the last time and sat down on my lap.

I took her to the bedroom upstairs.

I satisfied her selfish, wild and dark desires.

'Let me know when you've finished the sweets,' she said on her way out.

'I certainly will,' I said.

I was addicted.

They were delicious enough to make me forget what was happening outside.

XXXII

'i just got into bed but i'm still awake . . . something was eating away at me . . . i don't know why . . . it was such a moment that . . . like i felt a breeze across my face . . . like when you open the door and feel that sudden rush of cold air . . . i could swear there was someone wandering around the room . . . leaning over my face . . . it was like i could hear the sound of the quilt over me moving . . . i could feel the weight of this intense feeling . . . i wasn't sure what it was . . . but i could swear it was there . . . then the room suddenly felt empty . . . i waited in bed without moving for some time . . . listening for any sound . . . nothing . . . i was scared . . . i switched on the lights . . . i locked the door . . . i opened the shutters . . . the security guard in the apartment building next door was doing his rounds . . . i couldn't work out what it was . . .

'something like this happened to me before . . . it was as if someone came over to the edge of my bed and leaned over me . . . i saw someone . . . a black hat . . .

'i thought i was going insane . . . you probably think the same . . . but i'm telling you the truth . . .'

'how are you now?'

'a total wreck all day and dead tired but i'm better now. these things scare me.'

'don't be afraid.'

'the same thing used to happen when i was a child . . . i used to feel this strange restlessness . . . i wasn't sure exactly what was happening . . . it was always changing shape, sometimes sweeping through my entire body, sometimes settling in a spot in the room and rattling my nerves . . . i can't explain it, it's difficult to describe . . . it was like something soft and slippery, sometimes it let out this low moaning sound or at least that's what it seemed like to me . . .

'and sometimes it came out so quickly and took me so much by surprise that i thought i'd lose my mind if i couldn't get free . . . i was afraid of being alone . . . i can't remember when it stopped . . . sometimes i was afraid it might come back . . . that's why i'm afraid of the night now . . .

'when i was young i had all these up and downs . . . when i stayed with my granddad i got what was nearly a religious education for some time . . . i already told you, my dad's dad was a land owner . . . in the summers we would go and stay with him . . . and my mother tried to raise me like a princess . . . but i was neither of those things . . . but i didn't want to challenge them . . . because i didn't know the right way to be . . .

'i don't really know where i got this belief in the supernatural . . . i always felt so alone when i was little . . . sometimes i thought they weren't my real mother and father . . . in the secret world i created from my loneliness there were things i exaggerated and got worked up about without knowing where they'd come from and they were probably worse than the hang-ups i got from my family.'

I worried about her when she told me these sorts of things. I felt an overwhelming compassion and a profound desire to protect her.

It seemed she had experienced a vast dark empty space swirling outside her immediate life, a part of it that no one could see, an emptiness that not even she could fill, let alone anyone else; I don't know why I feel this way but I do – the thing that makes her feel so very alone and that sets her apart from everyone else, that comes between her and the rest of human society, was this void.

It was a void filled with nightmares, dark dreams, the supernatural and monsters.

It was a heavy burden to bear.

I wanted to rescue her from it.

I truly did.

Sometimes it seemed to me she poured her negative experiences into this dark void only to later refill the space with her hopes and dreams.

This was the source of her near-manic need to help people, to suddenly take on a project to the point of forgetting everything else in her life, to throw herself into situations that would frighten others.

To save herself from that horrible dark loneliness. That's how I felt.

And feeling that way tied me to her.

Every time I saw that dark void in her heart, every time I imagined it, the sadness and anguish there poured into me.

But then she would come to me with a smile on her face as if nothing at all had happened, as if we had never even spoken of it.

And I was always surprised.

In those days she had appointed herself the task of helping me write the novel I would write. And every day she wrote to me with ideas and suggestions.

'fact and fiction . . . two people getting swept away in their dreams . . . the writer is a man with experience in the matters of the heart . . . and the woman is madly in love with him . . . now she is a slave to him and no longer struggles to break free . . . it even gives her a twisted pleasure . . .

'the two carry on with their real lives as they grow a secret passion for each other . . . there is real life on the one hand and then this love in their dreams . . . and unbelievably they even get married in this fictional world . . . and the woman calls the man her husband . . .

'they know the boundaries between the two worlds . . . but their experiences in the dream world never lessen the passion and lust they feel for each other . . . they both play the part perfectly . . . it's a conscious game of love they play, fully aware of the consequences . . . .

'but after some time fact and fiction inevitably begin to clash
. . . and they are forced to give up one . . . the real or the
imaginary . . . what they experience in the real world is "real
life" or "real love", whereas in the dream world nothing is real,
maybe not even themselves . . .

'is it absurd? . . . so be it . . . in my opinion you explain it
so well . . . and if there has to be a murder you can kill me if
you can't decide, or if I can't decide . . .'

It was true that there was a kind of 'imaginary real' to our
relationship, our bond mainly perpetuated by our written words
alone. Later, we would slip into the real world devoid of these
'words', without 'writing', as if they had never been there, and
what we experienced in the real world seemed like a dream;
but we never mixed the two – one world lay beneath the other,
unraveling secretly in the dark.

I was fascinated by what she was saying but I didn't know
how I could describe such a relationship.

Indeed I was thinking of writing a standard thriller and not
getting involved in these games.

While she was helping me write my book, I assumed that
she was also helping Mustafa with his work in town. I suppose
she felt the need to help not only people in town but everyone
on the planet. She would never hesitate to help someone if it
was in her power.

She ran to the rescue of so many others but neglected
herself.

The day after I met Rahmi, Mustafa invited me to breakfast.
We met at the restaurant in the Chamber of Commerce. There
was no one else there.

The entrance was full of men in dark suits.

Mustafa seemed a little stressed.

'Are you all right?' I asked.

'I'm fine, just a little tired of all these people.'

'What's happened?'

'Nothing. Just a lack of imagination. They're just a bunch of
idiots, always blocking any attempt at any kind of innovation.'

The table was covered with all kinds of jam and olives; I'd never seen such variety.

I tasted all the different jams but Mustafa didn't seem to have much of an appetite.

'I hear that you met Rahmi,' he said and I nodded as I stuffed a piece of jelly-smeared bread in my mouth.

'Did Muhacir come too?'

'Yes.'

'And what did they want?'

'They wanted to provide me with protection.'

'From whom?'

I smiled.

'I supposed from everyone. They're afraid I might be killed.'

'Who's going to protect you?'

I looked him in the eye; this kind of talk was starting to get on my nerves.

'I can protect myself. I have never needed anyone to look after me before and I don't need anyone now. I'm getting tired of everyone expressing a sudden interest in me. It seems to me you all should be looking after your own skins. Everyone here is far more dangerous than yours truly.'

'We have men protecting us, but you don't.'

I told him what I told Muhacir and Rahmi.

'If something happens to me it will be a national event. The murder of a writer will only attract attention. And I don't think that's something any one of you would find favourable. Of course I could just leave, there's nothing keeping me here. I'm not a permanent fixture in this town. No olive grove or factory keeping me here.'

I could see Mustafa was getting annoyed, looking at me with an absent glaze in his eyes.

'I was only thinking of your well-being,' he said.

'I know,' I said. 'But it's just that all this talk of death and dying, even though it's said with good intentions, is starting to get on my nerves.'

An unexpected smile stretched across his face.

'You used to be a quiet man but now I see that you're growing tense. Same goes for all the others here'.

'You turned this town into a living hell. And what for? You could all have been happy together. And I would have written my book in peace.'

'Is it that bad? We're giving you all the material you need.'

'Who would want to read about all the nonsense that goes on in this town? Even I can't work anything out. What would a reader make of it?'

Everyone was going on about my novel. We were both silent for a minute or two.

'There's no one else in this town I can talk to. They're all such morons.'

We were silent again.

'Last night I met Raci Bey,' he said abruptly.

I looked up at him. I was curious and he knew that I was.

'He doesn't understand a thing,' he said.

'Why not?'

'He doesn't understand anything, no one does. They only see this as a power struggle. I told him that too.'

He leaned over the table to give me the impression he was about to say something important.

'Look. This is the world's most beautiful town. Just look at the coast, the mountains, the olive groves and orchards, all the fruit. Have you seen anywhere more stunning? I don't think so. Every morning I wake up even more devoted to the place. Every morning before I go to work I go up on that hill and look out over the town.'

He was beside himself as he said all this.

'Then look at all those nasty buildings in town. Do they complement the surroundings? Do we have the right to sully God's beauty?'

He sighed.

'Add to the natural beauty the church on the hill, and its legend, that Jesus Christ was laid to rest there. If we tore down those ghastly buildings, turned the coast into an endless beachfront, restored the church, found the treasure and spent the money on the town, would this place still turn heads, would it still be a place for all the world to admire?'

'It would.'

'And you see it's just this I can't get across.'

'Why don't they understand?'

'They don't want anything to change. They don't want anything to change. They think I'm only doing this for power, because I'm mayor.'

'Then do it with them. Bring them into the process. Why are you trying to do it on your own?'

'They're not willing to accept that. And if they were, that wouldn't be enough. They would want to raise ugly buildings again. I even drew up my own new plan for the town. Prepared the blueprints. You should see them. I'll show them to you when you come over one day. They're all laid out in a big room. It's my vision for the town.'

'Mustafa, they'll never let you go ahead on your own. You have to persuade them. Now I don't know politics but if you're bent on going it alone then a lot of people are going to die. That much I know. You all offer me protection but all your lives are in danger. Don't you see that? Don't you see that you're driving each other mad? The way they arranged for that kid to stand just outside your window and then . . . Everyone else got the message, but did you?'

'You're a novelist, so let me ask you this. If you were to write the most magnificent book in the world, an unrivalled work of art that people would remember for hundreds of years, a book people would forever return to and reread, would you be willing to die for it? Or if you had to kill someone for it, would you commit the crime?

Then he added, 'But give me an honest answer.'

Smiling, I said, 'I don't know.'

'You do. It's just that you don't have the courage to tell me the truth.'

He looked out at the sea for a moment. 'You see, this town

is my novel,' he said. 'I want to do something here that will last hundreds of years, something that people will talk about for years to come.'

There was an expression on his face I'd never seen before. In the lines of his face I could make out the exhilaration of a man full of the passionate desire to achieve things others never dreamed of, possibilities other people would never see; it was a belief in reaching a goal indeed more important than life itself, and the confidence that he was the only man to do it, whatever the cost; and a decisiveness and a pride that told him he was cleverer than all the others. His face was set like a statue but full of the ferocity of a stormy sea. The lines were fixed but powerful emotions were flickering in his eyes.

In those eyes you could see the will of someone who believed no obstacle was insurmountable, that he was the only one who could help others; a frightening display of willpower prepared to crush anyone in his way. It was a belief in his superiority.

He had never told me these things before.

And he probably never said so much to anyone else.

He knew what he was going to do and he felt no compulsion to explain, indeed it only boiled his blood to feel compelled to explain himself. He simply couldn't understand why they didn't trust him, why they were questioning his actions.

When things got out of control he assumed that speaking the 'truth' would appease them but events only unfolded in ways he never expected and his surprise grew with their suspicions and then their rage.

I asked him what Raci Bey said when he heard all of this.

'What's the point, he said. We've been living here for hundreds of years and we've seen it all before so why not turn this town upside down? That's just what he said. He's convinced I'll push them aside and run the show singlehandedly. If you have a better vision then come and do it, I said, and he really should. But he doesn't and he has no intention of allowing anyone else to have one. And so then I need no permission. And whom should I ask for permission anyway? I'm the mayor. I already have a public mandate. I tell the man everyone will make more money and he says they don't want money. It's not enough for peace of mind.'

'Peace of mind is important, Mustafa.'

'I'm not saying it isn't. But if they weren't challenging me like this then there wouldn't be a disturbance in the first place. They oppose everything, meddle in everything, gun each other down on the street and then say there's no peace of mind. If there isn't, well, it's not my fault.'

'Perhaps you shouldn't have issued that restriction?'

Grimacing, he said, 'So what if we issued the restriction. If they weren't griping about it so much we would have lifted it. Is the future of the entire town more important? Does bringing in the ban mean I'm bent on destroying the town's future?'

'They feel you've pushed them aside. That you're doing all this because you want complete control. That's why they're so angry.'

'They're small men, you see. Next to my vision, what does it matter who runs the place, or who has power? They should look to the end result. I'm going to build a stylish, modern town, you see, planes from all over the world coming in and out of our airport. I'm talking about the big picture and they're still going on about this town.'

'What does the woman we exchange messages with have to say about all this?'

'She says they're going to shoot me. We talked about it a little last night. She says I should make a blow-up blueprint of my plan for the town and put in the main square where everyone can see it, so they can understand what I'm trying to do.'

'She's a clever woman. Not a bad idea in my opinion.'

'True, but it seems a bit much to me. I'm already telling them about it. Why should I up and show them my plans and then beg? Even if I did it they'd still come up with excuses. I know what they'd say. They're fixated on bringing me down. They're stuck and can think of nothing else.'

Last night he spoke with Zuhal and just as I'd expected she was worried about him and trying to help.

'What's happening with the marriage plans?' I asked.

He let out a troubled sigh and mumbled, 'She's another idiot. Says she's in love with me but that she can't marry me. And that she'll never get married again, whatever that means. I have no idea what the difference is between not getting married and never getting married.'

'So who's it going to be, this town or the woman you love?' I asked.

'Why would I have to choose? What's stopping me from having both?'

'If something was, which would you choose?'

'I don't know,' he said, letting out another sigh.

He smiled and I smiled back at him in the same way.

'You know, courage isn't always all you need to tell someone the truth,' I said.

XXXIII

It's getting cooler.

It's still dark outside but this must be the chill that brings in the dawn.

The scent of the eucalyptus is now heavier in the air.

People are hopeful in the morning – no doubt a result of hundreds of thousands of years of fearing the dark, afflicted by the terror felt when the sun first set over the horizon.

But for me it's just the opposite.

The morning will bring nothing but pain and death.

I should run but I can't move.

It seems they'll find me one way or another. I have no real hope of escape now. But I actually want to get away, save myself, although that seems completely absurd.

Maybe it's the fatigue that's drained me of all my strength, that's made me feel this way. My thoughts are blurry and so are my decisions – I probably just don't want to have to make this decision that will shape the course of my life.

I have no strength for that.

I still have the chance to decide my future but I just can't do it.

I suppose I want something outside me to drag me away, though out there I can only imagine dying.

It is to be willing to die instead of making a decision to act now, and to know this.

Maybe I've already died before death actually has arrived.

Perhaps the very idea of death has killed me.

Perhaps just the feeling of it coming is enough to kill.

Perhaps my body is slowly preparing for death, slowly breaking down, coming to an end.

And perhaps when death arrives it will find nothing but a corpse.

That's what I want.

I want to confront death as a dead man.

The first police car speeding around the corner, sirens blaring, will perhaps find nothing here but a dead man, sitting on this bench, smiling, puffing away on a cigarette.

The idea is comforting.

Why is it that we're so fearful of death?

Why am I afraid?

Indeed I am so afraid of it that I am willing to die before it actually comes.

This fear of death is one of the pitiful contradictions in this novel penned by God.

Throughout the book there is all this talk of the second volume, which he calls the hereafter, as the current volume strikes the fear of death in all its readers.

With all due respect, you're not quite believable in this regard.

Maybe you haven't even written the second volume; you tell us that you have but we have yet to come across a reader; and sometimes I do the same – I tell everyone that I'm writing when I'm actually at home laughing up my sleeve, and I wonder if you simply do the same. Many novelists do it: they ask all these questions and in the end they choose falsehood over truth – and so perhaps you have been deceiving us all along.

Perhaps we're sceptical because of the stirring in our hearts.

If you were truly capable of making us believe, I would not be so fearful now; all these people would not be so afraid, they would be at peace in the world.

But what can be done? It is but another flaw in your book.

Let's say it's your talent talking, merely the deft turning of your pen that can erase the fear of death in your characters. Well, then the book goes on, because you have linked the desire for life to the fear of death, and the moment you erase the fear of death the desire to live goes up in smoke and so does life.

This thing you call the desire to live is nothing more than a state of panic, a furious race against death, the desperate need to round up as much pleasure as we can before we die, for we all seek some kind of pleasure, and in that part of your book there is colour, as you have created so many ways to achieve ecstasy – making money or love and or in prayer – but these are only possible when we are in the race against death.

Eradicate the fear of death and your book no longer bears meaning.

We must have fear in our hearts to read it.

Of course there is your unrivalled talent manifested with such outstanding flare: tremendous contradictions (you see, I must admit that I am an adoring fan). For what you do is this: you take that dreaded fear of death and place it in the heart of a hero and deep into what we deem the 'subconscious', an immutable form, and you say to them that they will die, and you see I know all this too well from experience, I know that fear then becomes the executioner. But by far your most dazzling display of talent is how you instil disbelief in a man's heart despite his fear of death; an inescapable truth is swept right out of his mind.

It is his false belief in the notion that his death belongs to another; indeed his knowledge of this very falsehood.

And this is precisely the brilliance of the novel.

No matter how many different, contradictory and conflicting emotions exist simultaneously, the bearer of these emotions is aware of them all, knows how they push and pull against each other, but nevertheless he carries them all with the same conviction.

I now think I might escape death even as I am dying. On the brink of death I have trouble believing, indeed I don't believe.

The most brilliant game in the book is your invention of the subconscious. I've always said there's nothing else quite like it.

When you bury these two conflicting emotions deep in the mind of your protagonist – the fear of death and the desire to live (a rejection of the reality of death) – no matter what he consciously thinks he cannot destroy those two emotions you have planted in him.

You can maintain the existence of the two conflicting emotions in the secret and closed cabins of his mind.

You don't let anyone in.

Our consciousness belongs to us, your heroes, but the subconscious is completely yours, where the God particle dwells, and whatever thought takes shape there is blended with you, turning into the complex set of emotions you desire.

And of course after fixing these opposing forces in the human mind you can conjure up all sorts of other trivial contradictions which are highly entertaining.

I wonder why you didn't place this matter of the hereafter, which allows us to believe so staunchly in the second volume, deep in that untouchable part of our minds.

Was it to lessen the fear of death and consequently the desire to live?

Or was it because when you began book one, you weren't all too sure about what would happen in book two?

All right then, so what is my fate in this book?

How close am I to death?

What was written for me?

To my mind, that section is not yet done, for, like me, you too are unsure of what to do with me: will you kill me or employ the mighty powers and wizardry of a novelist and create a clever way out?

Indeed it seems a challenge to save me now.

Are you of the same opinion?

I know you don't have a problem with credibility but then again you keep breaking the rules in your work – for example, men here will never fly, apart from the angels around you, and so like all other novelists you are condemned to your own belief system. You know your boundaries.

This is why the coming dawn seems dim.

All the same, my respect for the power of a writer is boundless.

I cannot be sure of anything until this book is done.

Not even of this approaching death, which will kill me before it arrives.

But I'm afraid.

Though I believe in the writer's power, I cower.

I don't know if I would be so afraid if I knew what was coming next, but I have seen the terrible fear of those who believe in the hereafter.

Belief will not overcome the fear.

For you have planted fear so deep in our minds.

Even the belief in your powers fails to eradicate the emotion.

Well, then show me your writerly powers and save me from it.

What a pity.

You do not even have the power.

You too have limits in your narrative.

God's limits.

And so that is where I am now.

At the edge of your limits.

And in this world there is nothing more horrifying. Do you know?

XXXIV

I got a message from Sümbül.

Just three words.

How are you?

I got the drift right away: work was slow, she needed money and she was proudly asking if I was going to call for her.

She would never disturb me.

If 'work' was that bad, and she needed the money, she would send a message like that. And I would call her over.

I called her up.

'How are you? What's up?'

'Oh, nothing, just lying around on the couch watching TV.'

'Come on over if you're free.'

'I'll be there in half an hour.'

She was at my house in exactly thirty minutes, her hair still wet, fresh from the shower.

Before I knew it she was stark naked in a chair.

And before she could say a word, I had poured her a whisky-cola.

'How's work?'

'It's never been like this before. If I get a couple of customers a week I'm ecstatic. So yeah, I'm calling up the old stalwarts, the ones who always pull through, and you know they don't even call me back any more.'

'Why the sudden change?'

'The town's on edge, gone mad, something's up . . . these bastards have lost their minds, and there's nothing but fighting and power struggles and all this nervous energy. And now no one's even leaving the house at night. And if they do there's no point.'

She paused and let out an adorable laugh before saying: 'Who was this bastard of yours with the cat?'

'Which bastard with the cat?'

'You know how the man with the cat, put him in the box, you remember when you were talking about the treasure . . .'

'Ah, you mean Schrodinger's cat.'

'Yeah, that was it. It's just the same with these bastards, they have the cat and they don't. It's there, right between their legs, but nothing for me. These brutes can't handle their own treasure. The idiots keep going on about the treasure and they lose sight of the real treasure.'

She placed her hand between her legs. 'It's right here. You could have millions, but what would that be worth without this?'

Sümbül could always make me laugh – whores always have the last laugh.

'Do you believe in fate? Is such a thing possible? If there is such a thing then everyone has one. If it's to be poor then there's poverty all around you. My neighbour is worse off than me, and more beautiful, but why am I the whore? There's something in me . . . I like my work, and I enjoy it, and earn good money. But there are those who never wanted to end up like this, pushed into a corner, had no other option but they never lasted long, and got out the first chance they got. But the real whores do the whoring, and they like it! You know how there are the whores who aren't really whores, and they get out quick, they're doing it just to get by for the time being. You have to have it in you.'

She laughed again.

'I have no pity for the whores who aren't really whores – they get some pleasure out of it, they'll feel bad about themselves, make a little money and leave. But I pity the ones who want to become whores but can't, dying to know how to do it, willing to die for it, but how? They have the real problems.

It's like a cancer eating at away at her from the inside. Because prostitution is food, it's living off many men, not just one, and if she can't do this she eats her heart out.'

'The philosophy of prostitution. You're the Madame Descartes. I put out, therefore I am.'

Laughing, she said, 'I swear I didn't understand half of that but the second bit is true.'

'What's happening in town?' I asked.

She winced.

'The place is in bad shape. I haven't heard anything for a while now, because the bastards aren't even coming to see me. But I've heard that something big is going to happen in the next couple of days.'

'How big?'

'God, how should I know? I just heard it's going to be big.'

Then she put down her glass.

'That's enough of the chit-chat. Come on, let's have some fun.'

I took her hand and sat her down.

'Forget it for now. Let's just talk today, we're having a good time just doing that.'

I paid her when she left, and she hesitated a moment before taking the money – she probably really needed it – and as she stuffed the bills in her pocket she said in a serious, courteous tone of voice I'd never heard before: 'Thank you.'

Stepping through the door, she turned and said, 'You're a good man.'

'We're friends. You know who they are when times are tough. Is that enough? Or do you need a little more?'

'It's enough. This will be enough to send to Mum.'

She hugged me and kissed me on the cheek.

When I went to Centipede's place in the morning I found everyone locked in a heated wrangle.

There was no longer the same rush to get the tables next to mine as people didn't have time for the papers any more. It seemed everyone was now completely cut off from the outside world, obsessed only with the gossip, rumours and confrontations in town.

They spoke about it all like they were discussing a football game. If you didn't know Mustafa and Raci Bey you might even think they were teams, as regulars went on evaluating what each person said as if statements were goals, like football commentators analysing strategic positions or fighting over whether a goal should be disqualified for an offside.

Centipede came over with my coffee.

'Seems like they don't talk about anything else any more,' I said.

'They've all lost their marbles, slipping off the rails, running straight out of control.'

'Who do you support?'

'I'm just running a coffeehouse. I don't support either side.'

'We're probably the only two people who don't.'

'Why worry about it, brother? What difference is there between one side and the other? As long as they pay me for coffee and tea, that's all that matters.'

I started reading the paper.

No one in the outside world even knew what was going on in this little town; the country was busy worrying about other issues.

It was strange to read through the paper while still listening to people in the coffeehouse; it gave me the feeling I was living in two worlds at the same time, two planets that didn't even know the other existed.

I lost myself in the paper.

Suddenly there was a clamour.

Everybody was up on their feet, screaming.

I called Centipede over.

'What's going on?'

'They raided Raci Bey's factories.'

'Who?'

'The police and the municipal officials. They say they're carrying out inspections.'

I realised this had to be the big event Sümbül had told me about. Mustafa has gone too far, I thought.

'This has never happened before,' Centipede said. 'Raiding Raci Bey's factory.'

'What's going to happen now?' I asked.

'No one knows,' he said with a sigh.

I decided to have lunch at the Çinili because I wanted to get the opinions of the rich set. I was curious to know what was going on; indeed the town had a tight grip on me, and was pulling me in.

The restaurant was completely empty.

No one but me.

I sat alone under the magnolia tree and had lunch.

The emptiness and the silence in a place that was normally bustling with activity was enough to demonstrate the gravity of the latest disaster.

The waiters were on edge, with scowls on their faces.

Mustafa thinks he's going to breathe life into this town when he's only killing it, I thought.

Like a bloated animal, this town is going to kill itself in the end.

I had my lunch in the suffocating silence and in a foul mood.

Then I went back to the coffeehouse, where more news was coming in.

Unlike the restaurant, the place was teeming.

News kept fluttering through.

'Rahmi Bey supposedly drew his gun on the municipal police, and they had a hard time restraining him.'

'Muhacir's men surrounded the factory and were battling with the police.'

'Kamile Hanım went over too, and supposedly slapped an officer at the entrance.'

One bit of news after another, and there was no way to know what was true and what wasn't.

Police were on watch outside the municipal building.

'The gendarmerie came to the factory and told the police

that they were out of their jurisdiction, told them to scram.'

'The commanding officer of the gendarmerie was knocked about.'

'The police wanted to close the place down but the municipals stopped them.'

The town was at a breaking point.

People were clustered about the coffeehouse, chattering away, waiting for more news.

'The gendarmerie closed off the road out of town and aren't allowing anyone in or out.'

Then a fight broke out in the coffeehouse and someone drew a knife.

Centipede stepped up and shouted, 'That's enough, you bastards!', before jumping into the scuffle, pulling the two men apart.

There was no point in me staying there any longer. I was curious as to what was going to happen but felt that anything was possible and that it wouldn't be wise to stay out on the streets.

I went home.

Hamiyet was cleaning the house.

I went online.

There was no one there, at least no one from town. They were all too busy with the unravelling situation.

Bored and surfing the net, I noticed the username 'my aunt'. No doubt he wasn't at all interested in what was going on, far away from the immediate turmoil in town. I couldn't help but think that he was only interested in one overwhelming reality.

Ever since our last chat he had been avoiding me, and he'd changed his username, and so I'd left him alone. He was probably scared of what he'd told me, disturbed that he had shared his secret with someone else, and now he was acting as if nothing had happened. But I had the feeling that he wanted to tell me more.

Once I saw the old username I waited, because I knew that he had seen mine.

I gave him time.

Then finally he wrote.

'How are you?'

'Fine . . . you?'

'Fine.'

'You haven't been around for a while.'

'I was travelling.'

He was lying but we were in a place where no one cared about the truth.

'Sightseeing?'

'No, work.'

'How did it go?'

'Fine.'

'Did your aunt miss you?'

'She did.'

I was expecting him to throw up a smiley face at the end but he didn't.

'We never finished our talk last week.'

'I told you everything.'

'No . . . you were telling me how you were rubbing her legs.'

'What did I say?'

For a moment I thought he'd made it all up. Anything was possible in this world.

'You said she was watching TV and you were rubbing her legs but you left before telling me the rest.'

'Yes.'

'Yes?'

'Yes, I remember now.'

'What happened next?'

'Nothing much.'

His hesitation made me even more certain he was lying.

'You don't have to tell me if you don't want to.'

'No, it's not that I don't want to.'

'So . . . ?'

'Just trying to remember.'

'I'm waiting. Tell me when you're ready, and if not don't worry about it.'

He decided to go on.

'I started rubbing the top of her legs and then inside . . . her robe was open . . . and loose.'

'Yes.'

'She was watching TV . . . it was one of her favorite serials . . . she was really into it . . . I went back down to her knees and then back up to her thighs . . . Then she moved her leg and I pulled my hand away . . . and her robe fell open even more . . . I was excited and squeezed her even harder . . . Then she suddenly asked me what I was doing . . . and I was scared . . . Just rubbing, I said . . . Fine, but don't hurt me like that . . . And I went on.'

Hamiyet was cleaning the mirror again, just like the last time I was online with her nephew, and occasionally I'd look up at her to catch her looking at me.

We were reliving the same scene.

Looking directly at Hamiyet, I wrote: 'And then what happened?'

'The front of her robe fell open even more . . . She wasn't wearing a bra . . . and I couldn't help but squeeze her upper thighs . . . She looked at me . . . What do you want, she said . . . I didn't say a word . . . I kept quiet . . . But I kept rubbing her thighs . . . pressing my fingers inside . . . Then she said again, What are you doing? . . . And that was it . . .'

'And what does that mean?'

'That was it . . . I need to go now . . .'

'Ok, see you later.'

'See you.'

The username disappeared.

I spent a little more time online; it felt as if everything that was happening in town – the eerie tension and terrifying madness – had given rise to my desire to take shelter in the underground world: I wanted to fling open the door and rush inside.

But that day I couldn't find anyone to have an interesting conversation with.

I had also been infected by the restlessness sweeping through the town.

I wanted to do something. I couldn't sit still.

I left the house.

I headed for the main avenue. There was hardly anyone out on the streets.

I saw a blind man sitting in the corner of a narrow street. Singing a folk song.

The current plight of the town seemed lodged in his plaintive voice, restless and full of sadness.

I suddenly wanted to see the pharmacist's wife. I don't know why but I just needed to see them. It was crowded inside the pharmacy and the pharmacist was chattering away with a group of men, his wife quietly knitting in a corner. She was an accomplice of mine in the underground world – though she didn't actually know me – and it always gave me a thrill to see her.

One of the men said, 'They've arrested Rahmi Bey.' A little later someone told me that it wasn't true but since morning I'd heard a lot of talk about Rahmi Bey. It seemed all the trouble was rushing his way. I wondered why all the talk was about him. Maybe during the course of events his dad was the most aggressive, angrily sparring with all the others.

There was hardly any talk of Mustafa.

The streets emptied out early.

People were exhausted from all the frenzy of the day, afraid and eager to take cover at home.

In the evening the municipal officials succeeded in shutting down Raci's factory, citing certain laws the company were not obeying.

War had been declared once again and there was no turning back.

That night a fire broke out in Mustafa's olive grove outside of town, ravaging acres of land.

The firemen struggled to put it out.

As the trees cracked and moaned under the stress of the heat, the town watched the flames rise up into the sky, the bright crimson light in the sky reflected in the shopfronts and their eyes, all the houses and the squares steeped in the colour of fire, the smell of burnt olives wafting through the streets until morning.

That night Zuhal wrote to me: 'come to the city.'

It was the first time she asked me to come.

'I'll take the morning plane.'

XXXV

There wasn't really a morning plane, as there was just one plane per day that happened to leave for the city in the morning and came back at night, but the locals liked to call it that.

I was the only one on board.

The pilot lifted the plane off the ground as if he was in a hurry to get out of town.

We wobbled a bit as we rose into up into the sky but we soon levelled out and arrived in the city right on time.

I left the airport and sent Zuhal a message as I hopped into a taxi: *I'm here.*

Come to see me then, she wrote back, with her home address.

I gave the driver the address.

I was going to see her house for the first time.

It was an enormous house overlooking the sea, without much furniture but still tastefully decorated. It didn't seem like her style, more like a temporary home. I'm not sure what gave me that feeling, maybe it was the small amount of furniture or the way the decoration didn't seem quite finished.

She had set out a full breakfast on a big table.

She was wearing a white nightgown and high-heeled slippers.

'I really missed you,' I said as she let me in, and I meant it.

It was almost noon before we managed to sit down for breakfast.

I had really missed her.

When I got out of bed she gave me one of her robes then looked me over and laughed.

It was really too small for me.

'Last night I suddenly felt I had to see you,' she said as we had breakfast, 'and I knew I wouldn't be able to hold out for another day. I cancelled all my meetings.'

'You knew that I would come,' I said.

'Didn't you?'

'I did. I'll come whenever you want me to.'

'There's something else I've been thinking about.'

'What's that?'

'I'll tell you tonight.'

After breakfast we left the house with the peace of mind that comes with all the time in the world and together we wandered the streets, visiting antique shops and her favourite strange little markets and coppersmiths. We had a kebab lunch in the back streets before going into more shops selling strange and unusual things, and she made friends with the owners. Then we had tea in the courtyard of a local teahouse.

We were like two young lovers discovering a city.

I was a little surprised that no one here knew anything about what was happening in the town – the madness, the murders and the struggle for power. They couldn't care less.

I soon forgot about everything as well.

And for whatever reason Zuhal never brought it up.

She probably knew more about it than I did but simply didn't want to think about either Mustafa or the town.

In her voice, in her touch, in her smile and in the way she walked, there was a powerful sexual energy I couldn't describe, and I felt as if we were locked in an endless bout of love-making; even drinking tea together was sensual, everything infused with sexual pleasure: her elbow gently touching me; her breast brushing up against my arm; it sent shivers down our spines.

There are days like these in our lives but they don't come often, so I savoured the pleasure of each passing moment.

All of a sudden the town seemed so far away.

And meaningless.

We wandered through the colourful confusion of a sprawling city.

I realised how much I had missed it: the clamour, the confusion and the chaos that came with the anonymity, the indifference and the surge of energy. I had missed the way people on the streets seemed both inscrutable and familiar.

Zuhal had put her arm in mine, leaning lightly against me.

There was no need for her to fear someone seeing us.

The city offered us a new freedom.

No one was watching us, making notes of where we had lunch or coffee, or the people we spoke to.

The oppressive air of the town was gone and we felt a new liveliness and lightness of being, almost as if we might take flight.

Stepping out of a shop, Zuhal suddenly kissed me and then smiled, and pressed her breasts into my arm.

We bought food for dinner at home and picked out a nice wine.

The city had blessed us with an intimacy we had never felt before.

She turned quiet over dinner.

Clearly something was on her mind.

We were sitting across from each other in armchairs beside a broad window looking out over the sea.

She was silent. I was silent too.

She looked up at me and I saw a deep reflection in her eyes and she whispered softly those two words that echoed in my head.

'Sell me. Just for tonight.'

I looked her in the eye.

And she added in the same soft voice: 'You promised you would do anything I asked.'

I would have done it even if I hadn't made that promise. She had chosen me that day we met because she felt I was the one who could go this far. I could awaken the slumbering desires in her heart, bring them to life, make them real, without ever judging or offending; I was the man who could fulfil all of her desires. With me she could wear whatever she had packed away in her wardrobe, become any of the women she wanted to become in the wildest of adventures.

I was the promise life had made to her and with me the great passion of her life was gone. I possessed the woman in her who wasn't in love, the woman who was incapable of love. I was the man of her dreams. I'd been sent to make her dreams come true.

'Get ready then,' I said and nothing more.

She went inside.

I took a sip of wine.

We were preparing ourselves for a night in which anything could happen, facing danger and potential calamity; and she trusted me completely. A trust stronger than love. Stronger than anything else. It was the strongest bond between a woman and a man.

When she came back in her new outfit I could tell she had prepared it in advance, thinking closely about every little detail, excited to buy every item.

She was wearing a tight red mini skirt, a black transparent blouse with an extra-low *décolleté*, fishnet stockings like the ones you see in cheap films, and red, high-heel, hooker shoes with open toes – other women had told me they were called come-fuck-me shoes. I could see bright red toenails through the fishnet stockings.

She had pulled together an ensemble of all the sartorial clichés of a whore.

And clearly she had done so with painstaking care. She was proud of her work.

She put on a long, black overcoat.

She pulled her hair back into a bun.

After she buttoned up her coat, she looked like a perfect lady. And when she opened it: the perfect image of a whore.

Just wearing the outfit made her tremble, and as we walked down the stairs to the street I could feel her faintly shivering with excitement.

'You drive,' she said, passing me her car keys.

On the road she sat frozen in her seat, silent.

We parked on a main street near the cheap taverns, nightclubs and brothels, and she put her arm in mine and we walked into the back streets.

She whispered into my ear: 'You bring out all my demons.'

Maybe it was true that she wouldn't have done it without me; all her life she had been searching for a man she could do this with.

And we both knew that Mustafa wasn't that man.

We turned the corner.

Scattered among the shuttered shops on the ground floors of narrow old buildings there were dim little taverns with signs in the windows that read 'chanteuse' and pictures of women dancing and names in neon light and bouncers hovering outside. Scantily clad women waited the tables inside.

We took three steps down into a little tavern.

The place was empty except for three women around a table, all nearly fifty and dressed in slit skirts, and another slightly younger woman with purple bags under her eyes. Behind something that resembled a bar there was a burly man.

Zuhal took off her coat when we were inside.

The women shot us glances but quickly lost interest when they realised we were looking for a man.

The man behind the bar came over and took our order. Two rakıs.

There were arabesque songs playing that I'd never heard before.

We noticed a hotel just opposite the bar.

The lights inside were low; five or six steps led up to a glass door that had been painted a dirty yellow years ago; the paint was peeling and the glass was covered in stains.

There was a sign above the door: Anton Otel.

She looked over at it.

'I want to stay in a place like that,' she said.

'Fine.'

Unlike me, she seemed quite comfortable.

A little later she went over to the women, sat down and started talking.

I saw one of them caress her hair.

She was completely at ease with them.

Then she came back over to me and without saying very much we finished our drinks, and not a single man came in.

We sat for a little longer and then left. She put on her coat again but left it open.

Out on the street I saw a short man eyeballing her.

'He's looking at you,' I said.

She turned and said, 'No way, not him.'

I didn't ask any questions. She could do whatever she wanted, she was free to choose whomever she wanted — it was her night.

We went to a slightly bigger tavern. It was almost the same as the other one. They were playing the same kind of music. But the tables were more crowded.

She looked the men over and said, 'Let's go somewhere else.'

We left without having a drink.

As the night went on and the scene livened up she became even more relaxed and more confident, but she couldn't decide on a man.

We wandered through the street and many others like it, going into different taverns, and we peered into one of the nightclubs.

Towards dawn, she said, 'Let's go home.'

I looked at her and didn't say anything — she really wanted to go.

'All right then,' I said.

She didn't say anything in the car.

When we got home we went straight to the bedroom.

I quietly undressed her.

I took off her fishnet stockings.

But she wouldn't let me take off her garter belts. 'Leave those on,' she said.

I was the customer that night, a cruel and savage customer who pressed her face into the pillow so the neighbours wouldn't hear her screams.

The pain brought tears to her eyes and she cried out for me to stop, but I didn't.

When I woke up in the morning she was making me breakfast and softly singing.

I couldn't make out the song but I think it was probably one of the songs we had heard last night.

We didn't say a word about it.

During breakfast she said, 'I'm happy when I'm with you. It's just that sometimes I miss you so much.'

She had a meeting in the evening and she got ready, choosing the right clothes to hide her bruises.

I left before she did.

I'd thought about staying in town but she didn't ask me to.

I could have stayed all the same but I wanted to go.

I went back to town on the 'evening' plane.

I missed her already.

It was going to be hell in town.

XXXVI

Driving home from the airport I passed Mustafa's still smouldering olive groves.

In the twilight I could make out the burnt stumps, all that was left of the trees. They were sprawled out over the landscape like dead soldiers on a battlefield.

My phone rang as I was nearing town.

It was Mustafa.

'Are you back?' he asked in a tense voice.

'Yes, I am.'

'Can you come over to see me? I'm at home.'

'Of course. Just let me go home and change and I'll be right over.'

'Come straight here. I have food ready. We can eat together.'

I didn't know why he was in such a hurry but he sounded impatient and on edge so I agreed to go and see him right away.

When I got to his house I saw that it was surrounded by men in dark suits, and two police cars were parked outside.

Mustafa was sitting in the living room. He wasn't wearing a jacket and he had loosened his tie. His gun lay on the coffee table in front of him. He had dark bags under his eyes.

'You went to the city?'

'Yes.'

'Why?'

'I had some errands to do.'

'What errands?'

I didn't like the way he was interrogating me. 'Just errands,' I repeated, trying to keep it at that.

'What kinds of errands could you possibly have?'

He'd never been so rude and aggressive with me before; all his courtesy and good humour had disappeared, and in place of the man who enjoyed discussing life and literature was a crude, angry, impatient brute.

He had let himself go so completely that he no longer had the strength to show respect or kindness and as he spoke I saw his other face – the one he always kept hidden in my company. It was the primitive face of a savage deep inside him which sought only to destroy anyone who crossed his path.

I was exhausted, and in no state to tolerate such behaviour.

'What are you talking about, Mustafa? My errands are none of your business. You should take care of your own problems.'

And I stood up and said, 'I'm tired too. Let's talk some other time. You're in no state to talk right now.'

He took my arm. 'Forgive me,' he said. 'I'm just a little stressed. That's all. I didn't mean to offend you. Please sit down. I'll pour you a drink and we can have something to eat together.'

I sat down.

He brought me a drink.

'But really, why did you go?' he asked, in a friendlier tone of voice.

That's when I realised he'd called me over because he wanted to know not just where I'd gone but who I'd been with; the curiosity had practically driven him out of his mind; he seemed obsessed. To the point where nothing else mattered. He was jealous and desperate to know if I had been with Zuhal. Now I realised who had been messaging her when we were in the city.

He was racked with jealousy. But I didn't know why. It never seemed to bother him before, and he never perceived me as a real threat, but in the middle of this terrible power struggle he'd spent the last two days in a frenzy of jealousy. Zuhal might have provoked it. Any slight innuendo would have set him off.

He was a version of Napoleon, deliriously writing letters to Josephine in the middle of war. 'I'm forty-two years old and

I'm the mayor of this town. Tomorrow I'll burn it to the ground but what does all that mean when you're with that writer, Zuhal?'

I couldn't help but smile.

I pitied him.

I knew that I could wound him with just one word, scarring him for the rest of this life.

But I didn't.

He was already sufficiently afflicted by his anger, his cruel attitude and the desperate jealousy that was eating his heart.

'I met with my publisher,' I said.

'Is there a problem?' he asked. He needed more details if he was going to believe me.

'I signed a contract for a new book deal,' I said.

'Have you finished it?'

'I've started . . . I sent him the first chapter.'

The tension left his face, the lines softened, and he smiled. At that moment the torment he had been enduring the last two days must have seemed meaningless, or at least diminished. I had the power to hurt or heal him with a single word.

He leaned back.

'Nice gun,' I said to change the subject.

'Do you know guns?'

I leaned over and picked up the pistol, a Glock 17 with a recoil compensator.

'It's a good weapon. With a compensator to reduce kickback, seventeen-bullet capacity. The only thing is, you can see the flash from the barrel at night, which can throw you off if you're not used to it. Glock lovers are always arguing about whether the standard or the one with the compensator is better. I prefer the standard. If you want, you can max up the clip capacity, and there's an add-on that makes it automatic.'

'So you're a real enthusiast then.'

I held the dark gun in my hand.

'I am. I especially like these Glocks. Though I must admit I have a hard time choosing between a Glock and a Sig Sauer.

The Sig Sauer sports model is fantastic. In my opinion the trigger is a little more sensitive. But it's hard not to marvel at this gun, my friend. My dad was really into guns. We would shoot together when I was a kid.'

'Are you any good?'

'Not really. Though not that bad either. As Kemal Tahir says, I do all right.'

I reluctantly put the gun down on the coffee table.

He picked it up and passed it to me. 'Take it. A gift. I have another just like it.'

'No, thanks. I couldn't accept it.' Though I wanted to take it.

'Why not?'

'I don't have a licence.'

He started to laugh, a deep hearty laugh from his gut.

'Who's going to ask you for a licence round here? And if anyone does, you can tell them I gave it to you. Go on and take it. I won't tell you to enjoy using it. I hope God doesn't put you in a situation where you might need it, but it'll make you feel more comfortable. And we can go shooting together one day. I love doing that.'

He stood up and said, 'Wait. Let me give you a few extra loaded clips. You won't be able to find ammo at a time like this.' He went inside and soon came back with an extra clip and a bag full of cartons of bullets and a fancy leather holster. He handed it to me, 'Try this on.'

I threaded my belt through the holster. I normally don't like to wear one but it was a gift and he seemed so happy that I couldn't refuse. I placed the gun in the holster and the extra clip in my pocket. I was actually quite pleased. And it made him happy to see me that way.

'Come on, let's eat,' he said, as if he'd forgotten all his troubles after convincing himself I hadn't been with Zuhal.

He had a table set out on the terrace.

There was a cool breeze blowing in from the sea. Dark sand stretched out into the distance and the scent of lavender and jasmine floated down from the mountain, mingling with the scent of the sea and seaweed.

'Why did you shut down Raci Bey's factory?' I asked.

'He was asking for it.'

'Maybe you could work something out if you talked to each other.'

'There's no talking to him. I tried but it was no use. Now I'm speaking a language they understand. They can understand this.'

'Raci Bey is from an old local family, he has a lot of supporters. Won't it stir up the whole town if you close down his factory?'

Furrowing his brow, he said, 'We're past that now. Raci Bey is finished and we're the new order. My family has shed blood and tears in this town, working for hundreds of years to better this place.'

'All right then. But what was the reason for shutting it down?'

Smiling like a child, he said, 'They didn't have fire escapes.'

'Oh come on, Mustafa. There isn't a single building in town with fire escapes. Not even the town hall.'

'What can I do about it? Rules are rules. The rule is that the factory must have fire escapes or it will be shut down. Do they have them? No. And so? We have no choice but to shut it down.'

He laughed again. He was pleased with himself.

As we sipped our coffee, one of the men in dark suits walked over and Mustafa scowled, 'What is it now?'

'Your olive groves on the other side of town are burning.'

Mustafa flushed bright red. 'Sons of bitches. I am going to set fire to every one of them.'

He quickly walked over to the armchair on the other side of the room, grabbed his jacket then said to the man, 'Get ready. We're going.'

'What are you going to do?' I said.

'Tomorrow I'm going to close down everything they have, factories, shops, businesses, warehouses and branches, the whole lot! I'm going to show those bastards! They're burning down trees. Have they no conscience? It's disgusting.'

'I don't think you should take this to the next level. Are you sure this is a good idea?'

'From now on this is how it's going to be. Seeing as this is how they want it, this is how it will be. Power against power.'

Car engines started up outside, their headlights glaring, all the men waiting for Mustafa.

Before getting into his car, he said, 'Do you need someone with you? To take you home, just in case? It's getting late.'

'Thanks, but there's no need. I'll be fine on my own. I'm sorry to hear what's happened. Terrible news.'

'I'm going to show them,' he said, getting into his car.

They sped on down the road in a trail of lights.

And I watched them go.

They looked like a motorised infantry unit.

XXXVII

'we found each other on common ground going through different stages in our lives and leading completely different kinds of lives . . . i guess . . . we call it lust . . . you did . . . i don't know if there's another name for it . . . if you want me to describe it . . . it's not a shallow or fragile emotion but a powerful, unique, overthrowing of other feelings . . . a swirl of emotions made up of miracles . . . seems overly proud of itself . . . thinks it can compete with love . . .'

When I got back to the house Zuhal was waiting for me.

She was describing our relationship, something she couldn't name, and I suppose she was trying to better understand it herself.

This unnameable feeling, a feeling we were afraid to name, lingered over our naked bodies but later we felt it deep inside us, trembling, filling us with an indescribable rush of pleasure and fear. And when this mysterious feeling moved, it drove all other emotions, acts and people aside, ripping open a place for itself in the deep and settling there.

'you entered me and left parts of yourself there and then slowly became a part of me . . .

'we have grown comfortable with each other and long for each other.'

I sat there reading her words.

'i constantly miss the feeling i have when i'm with you . . . it's the feeling of someone pulling you out of the bottom of a well . . . the feeling of emerging from yourself and setting off on a journey . . .'

She continued to write.

'do you remember telling me that in your life you kept the light on in a place that was mine? . . .

'it's the most beautiful thing i ever heard . . . i'll never forget it . . . i want someone to whisper this into my ear when i die . . .'

For a moment the screen was blank, then she started again.

'can I ask you for something?'

'of course . . . what is it?'

'describe for me a house and a life we share together as if it was really there, a real house we share together . . . don't worry . . . i don't really want it . . . and i won't later on . . . i just want to hear you tell me about it . . . is that ok?'

'a house on a hillside . . . one floor . . . or maybe two . . . but the top floor would just be a loft . . . a wooden house with high ceilings . . . a big living room . . . maybe a fireplace . . . and in front of that maybe the biggest and most comfortable armchair you've ever seen . . . an antique . . . maybe velvet . . . a little worn . . . sometimes the two of us far away from one another, on the other side of the room, sometimes just opposite each other . . . while i'm reading something or watching tv you'll be sleeping right beside me . . . and when you wake up we'll make love right there . . . there is a town in the distance . . . and on the hillside above there are vineyards as big as the town itself . . . and a path running up through them . . . and a forest on one side of the town . . . and a river on the other side . . . where we swim . . .

'we plant vegetables behind the house . . . sweet-smelling tomatoes and peppers . . . i water them as the sun sets . . . it smells of green tomatoes and moist earth . . . and we look out over the vegetable garden from the kitchen window . . . and as i water the vegetables i see you cooking dinner . . . and sometimes i stop what i'm doing and watch you for a while . . . and you feel me watching you . . . and now and then you'll ask me for another tomato or some dill and i hand you them fresh from the garden . . .

'and cherry trees around the house . . .

'and an enormous magnolia tree in front . . .

'next to the main entrance and on the other side of the house is a back door with a little cloakroom . . . a place for our boots and raincoats . . . and when it's raining we put them on and stomp outside . . .'

I stopped.

'thank you . . .' she wrote, and then added, 'now i'm going to bed . . . to dream about our home.'

'goodnight.'

Puzzled, I sat there staring at the screen.

Suddenly she began to write again.

'there is a God . . . and for some reason he helps us realise our dreams and the dreams of others . . . most of them are beyond our wildest dreams . . . in fact some of them don't belong to us at all . . .

'for example, i could never have imagined such a beautiful mosque . . . i could only have imagined a little mosque among the trees . . . maybe he arranged that little mosque just for us . . .

'and it was the first time in my life that i got sick so late . . . today . . . after you left . . .

'our lovemaking isn't my dream . . . i could never have dreamt up a fantasy so beautiful . . . this has to be yours . . .

'do your best not to lose that scarf i bought you yesterday when we were wandering through the street market in town . . . maybe it will help to remind you that all of this was real . . . i'll do my best not to lose the ring you gave me . . . to remember everything we've been through.

'i suppose all my life i've wanted the impossible . . . and i never believed that there would be another person who wanted the same things . . . in the same way that sometimes i don't believe you exist . . .

'but sometimes i believe that you do exist . . .

'and that what we've experienced is real . . .

'and that together we long for the same things . . .

'once you told me that you felt close to me . . . and i feel the need to be with you . . . it is the most glorious need . . .

'thank you for the house . . . i will always cherish the dream . . .

'now i can really go to bed.'

I pottered about the house before I went to bed.

I had never before dreamed of happiness – I could say I never even really thought about it – as I have only ever thought about writing books and seeking pleasure where I could.

I have always cherished my loneliness.

I have never needed to be happy.

That night was perhaps the first time I sensed what it was to be happy, and I imagine it was the chance to dream with another person, and to believe in that dream.

That night I understood why people so badly needed happiness.

XXXVIII

As soon as I got up in the morning I had breakfast and raced out of the house. I was eager to try out my new gun.

I needed time to digest the conversation of the night before, and for this I needed to be alone.

I drove out of town quickly.

I rolled down the windows, put my foot down, and as the wind rushed through the car I felt a little lightheaded.

I made my way up the mountain road.

The forests grew thicker.

I found a spot in the mountains where I could make out the sea in the distance. There wasn't a sound, only the creaking of the trees and the air heavy with the scent of pine.

I pulled my bag out of the car.

I had my gun in my belt. I couldn't be bothered with the holster.

Getting the gun out of a holster, flicking your index finger on the little strap that holds the gun in place, is an extra movement, and sometimes that costs a life.

I pulled out my gun and weighed it in my hand, feeling the grip panel in my palm.

I hadn't fired a gun in some time.

Firmly grasp the handle. Place the butt of the handle in the palm of your hand. Then wrap the fingers of your left hand over your right hand clenching the gun.

Place your index finger on the trigger. If you place it after the first knuckle, the gun will jerk to the side when you fire, so place your finger on the edge and leave a little room on the trigger. Breathe in, don't squeeze the gun too hard but then don't be too loose. After you fire, let the barrel rise up easily into the air like a horse rearing up on its legs.

Fire. Missed.

The sound of the gunshot was deafening, causing a ringing sensation I could feel throughout my body.

I was angry with myself for not bringing ear defenders.

I pulled my shirt out of my trousers and cut off two shreds with the penknife I always have with me and stuffed the cloth into my ears.

I was firing at dried cones dangling from a pine tree ahead of me.

I was out of practice.

One more. The shot was wide.

I could feel that I was tense.

I let both my hands fall by my side.

I took a deep breath, closed my eyes and relaxed my entire body.

Then I raised the gun.

I gently pulled the trigger.

And the pinecone flew off the tree.

Oh, now that's more like it.

I stretched.

And then another, and another and another . . .

I emptied the first clip. Twelve pinecones were destroyed in the first skirmish.

I was on fine form.

I could now take aim at the ones a little further on.

I popped in a new clip.

But before I fired, I reloaded the empty clip.

It felt good to be shooting again. I could remember the last time I'd gone shooting in the forest like this – I was with a young woman, a champion marksman. It was another one of those strange relationships I quickly find myself embroiled in: you see, we were neither lovers nor friends, but we had sex often, we had fun together, and we used to go shooting too.

One day we went out to shoot in the forest and as a target I placed a packet of cigarettes twenty metres away – it looked like nothing but a speck in the distance. As I took aim, she said, 'If you hit it, I'll take off all my clothes and we'll make love right here.' It wasn't easy hitting a cigarette packet twenty metres away but I suppose I was amply motivated and I nailed those cigs on the first shot. And she kept her word. And we learned just how painful pine needles can be. Later I took up the habit of spreading a blanket over the back seat of the car. Just in case I might hit another pack of cigarettes.

I levelled my gun on a pinecone twenty metres away. Missed. One more. One more. I shot until I made the mark.

After going through more than half the ammunition Mustafa had given me, I sat down under a tree. I leaned back against the trunk. My hands smelled of gunpowder. I absently looked out over the sea. Just like the moment before you fire, holding your breath and emptying the mind, I sat there silently.

Then I got in my car and slowly made my way back.

Smoke was still rising above the olive groves set on fire the night before.

The tension in the air was palpable, as if the entire town was a taut muscle and everyone out on the street afflicted by a nervous tick, frantically, needlessly twitching.

When I got home Hamiyet met me at the door. 'You've heard what's happened?' she said.

'What is it?' I said absently.

'They've shut down Raci Bey's factories, his shops, everything he owns, and Rahmi Bey cursed them all, saying that he would drag Mustafa out of this town on his knees.'

'Raci Bey or Rahmi Bey?'

'Rahmi Bey, silly, the young one . . .'

'Well, then why are you so agitated about it?'

She stopped to think about it for a moment. 'They're the

backbone of the town. If they destroy each other then they'll destroy everything here.'

Smiling, I gently put my hand on her shoulder. 'Hamiyet, you're the backbone of this town. As long as you're healthy and sound the town will still be here. Come on now and make me a cup of coffee. One of your special cups.'

The fact was she really wasn't that interested in what was happening in town.

A few minutes later she came running out of the kitchen screaming, her telephone in her hand.

'They got my son,' she cried, 'they knifed him in the coffee-house.'

'Wait a minute. Your son isn't the kind of kid to get into fights like that, maybe there's been a mistake and they have the wrong person.'

'He wasn't involved. Those blind dogs stabbed him by mistake while they were fighting each other. I have to get over there right now.'

'Where are you going?'

'They took him to the hospital. I'm going. Oh my dear, my lovely little boy, how could this happen? God damn them. What did he ever do to hurt anyone?'

'I'll take you there. Just calm down. Maybe it's nothing serious.'

We got into my car.

We raced over to the hospital. Hamiyet was white as a sheet, clutching her telephone. 'Oh my son, my son,' she lamented again and again.

She flew out of the car before I could even park.

Outside the two-storey emergency department men were smoking next to a blood-stained stretcher.

Walking over to them I saw Centipede and asked him what had happened. 'How should I know, brother?' he said. 'I was inside when the fight broke out. The kid tried to get away just when someone drew a blade and he got knifed by accident.'

'Was he seriously hurt?'

'I have no idea. They're not telling us anything.'

'Where was he cut?'

'The thigh.'

I went inside, where Hamiyet was screaming through her tears, 'Where's my son?' A long-faced orderly told her to keep her voice down, took her by the arm and led her outside.

'What are you doing?' I snapped at the orderly. 'Leave the woman alone.' The startled orderly let her go. 'You need to be quiet,' I said to Hamiyet. 'Let's see what's happened. They say he was stabbed in the leg, so it's probably not that serious.'

'Where's the doctor?' I asked the orderly, who, realising from the way I spoke and held myself that I wasn't from the community and wasn't challenging his authority. He softened and said, 'He's inside with the patient.'

'Isn't there another doctor?'

'No.'

'A nurse?'

'There's the head nurse.'

'Well, then could you call her?'

He looked at me, trying to work out if I was someone worth calling the nurse for.

'What are you waiting for?' I said, and he hurried inside.

A little later he came back with a nurse who was irritated at having been disturbed. 'What's the matter?' she said, angrily.

'They just brought in an injured kid. And I'm here with a relative who would like to know his condition.'

'The one who was stabbed in the leg?'

'Yes.'

'It's nothing serious. The muscle was torn and the doctor is giving him stitches now. You're free to leave with him if you like.'

'We'll do that then,' I said.

Hamiyet was listening to her attentively but she didn't seem herself.

'What's that?' she said.

'Weren't you listening?'

'I was, but what's happened?'

'All right. The situation isn't serious. His upper leg was cut open a little and they're stitching him up now. We can go and get him in a little bit.'

'Oh, thank God,' she said, throwing her hands over her face as she cried. 'I dedicated a cockerel to Saint Horoz Baba so God would keep him safe for me. I'm sure he heard my prayers because I promised to sacrifice a cockerel to him.'

I sat her down on a bench and said, 'Now, sit here for a bit and stop crying. Your son is fine. In a little while we'll go and get him. I'm going outside to have a cigarette.'

I went outside.

After the gloom inside the hospital, I was startled by the bright light.

'What's up? How is he?' Centipede asked me.

'He's fine. We'll go and get him in a little while,' I said. 'What's happening in this town?'

'Oh, don't ask. This morning they shut down Raci Bey's factories, shops and other businesses.'

'I heard, Hamiyet told me. But what's happening now?'

'I swear everything's going up in smoke. There's no end to the fighting, no end in sight from now on. I tell you, there's nothing good about this place now. They say Rahmi Bey has sworn to take revenge.'

The same words over and over again.

Like a bolero, the same words and the same music running round and round, growing more and more violent, repeated by more and more people, the voices rising higher on every turn, and even if Rahmi hadn't said those words eventually everyone, including himself, would believe he had.

The increasing violence of the music influenced them all, shaping reality, building a new truth that was imprisoning them all.

'All this talk of the treasure is going to be the death of this town,' I said.

Centipede angrily threw his cigarette on the ground and stamped it out with the tip of his shoe like he was crushing a vile bug.

'To hell with the treasure. What treasure? Sometimes I think we would all be saved if someone would just drop a bomb on that hill and blow the whole thing up.'

We lay Hamiyet's son down in the back seat of the car and Hamiyet sat next to me in the front, giving me directions to their house.

We passed through parts of town I'd never seen before.

'There are a lot of gypsies living here,' she said, looking much more composed after seeing that her son was all right. 'They say bad things about them but they're good people. They never bother their neighbours.'

Carpets were draped out of the windows and some were even spread out on the streets.

On the top of a tile roof there was a full sofa set, a three-seater and two armchairs.

Who knows why they'd put them up there on the roof. The pieces were so big I couldn't imagine how they got them up there. And they were perfectly arranged. I suppose they thought it looked good, adding a little style to the rooftop.

On the top of a one-storey house there was a wonderful statue of a mermaid that looked as if it had just fallen from the sky. It was stretched out watching the passing cars. I nearly had an accident. They must have nicked it from one of the rides in the amusement parks that came through town.

Hamiyet lived in a little two-storey house in the middle of a strange and lively neighbourhood. 'Come and have tea some-time,' she said, but I didn't go inside.

'Don't come tomorrow,' I said. 'You should be with your son.'

'No, I'll come. You don't know how to make breakfast and you'll mess up the house. But I'll leave early.'

'Whatever you want,' I said.

Within a couple of hours the town had its tentacles around

me like a giant octopus; this place I had forgotten all about in the city was now fully a part of my life again.

I was curious to know what was happening.

The conflict was rushing ahead at breakneck speed, leaving unforgettable scars in its wake.

No one would be able to forget the burning of Mustafa's groves and the utter shame of seeing Raci's factories shut down like that.

Both sides were brimming with anger and the burning desire for revenge.

On the walls of every home in town the words echoed, 'Rahmi Bey has sworn to take revenge.'

How could either side take a step back at this stage of the game?

The struggle was ostensibly about capturing a hill that supposedly held buried treasure, but there was no sound argument for any one person to possess it; and inevitably the problem spread throughout the town, seeping into daily life – I don't think it was something that either side had bargained for.

When they started the fight they were under the impression they were invincible and that no struggle would actually cause them any harm, but now they were face to face with the truth – the reality that no one was invincible – and they were in shock; the real fight would be born of this shock. I could feel it: neither of the two opposing sides would suffer a financial blow devastating enough to knock them out entirely. Raci could have his business reopened the following day and Mustafa hardly even felt the loss of his olive groves when he owned such a vast estate. It was simply not possible for either to ever swallow this idea of vulnerability, to easily accept a collapse of confidence built on a hundred-year tradition, to replace their bravado with fear and forgiveness.

There was nothing left for them to prove in merely protecting themselves because once they received a blow there was no point in continuing to play defence. And so the only option was to inflict even more damage on each other; no other option but to show how the other might buckle under irreparable damage.

They would come to learn the story of the wizard's apprentice who cast a spell he did not know how to reverse. The will of one man was enough to start a fresh battle but it took the will of more than one to finish the war that had been set in motion.

They had started something they couldn't finish, and from now on the violence would only escalate and the strength of the rival gangs would only grow.

It was inevitable that in the struggle one of them had to die.

Was that why I was still in town?

To observe the ultimate murder?

Was that why I couldn't leave?

Was I waiting in the front row to watch the execution like the drunken vultures at the guillotines of the French Revolution?

I didn't know the answer then and I don't know now.

Perhaps I stayed because I had this groundless, meaningless belief that if I left town I would lose Zuhal. There was no logical explanation for this. I knew that it was illogical but I couldn't stop myself from feeling that way.

I knew we had to be in the same place. I knew it would only be possible for us to either separate or be together in the same city. Now I am no longer in a position to choose one or the other: I cannot leave her and I cannot be with her, and the same goes for her.

We were in a place where we had no choice but to wait.

Every impatient step took our relationship a bit closer to its end and until we said to each other, yes that's it, we had to keep some distance between us. But the day of reckoning would come. I was going to wait till then.

I felt that I wouldn't ever wait for her anywhere else.

An important part of Zuhal was here: the man she loved. If she disappeared one day she would turn up with Mustafa at her side, because she couldn't stay away from him for long.

I was afraid that something might happen to him.

If he were to die then my relationship with her would die with him.

This absurd place made everything else seem all the more absurd.

And I was now a part of the madness.

XXXIX

The next two or three weeks were eerily quiet.

It was as if the town had woken in a daze, its head still spinning, trying to work out what was going on.

People were struggling to adjust to a new way of life, to the changes, trying to grasp what had happened and the nature of what they had experienced.

There were the familiar troubles, joys and routines, and they were even accustomed to the dreariness, and their regular complaints.

But all of a sudden everything had been turned upside down.

Their relationships had changed, along with their troubles and fears.

It wasn't easy settling into this new life in which all the boundaries were redrawn, and habits had been shaken out of place, the rules of the game always shifting.

They wanted to understand.

To understand what had happened and what was going to happen.

That's why it seemed as if everything had come to a standstill.

The town was thinking.

And it wasn't only the town trying to understand the new situation, grappling with new emotions, struggling to reach some kind of verdict.

Zuhal was also keen to understand her changing emotions, to get a clear picture of what we were going through and what might lie ahead.

Those days I hardly ever left the house.

Nearly every hour of the day she would come home and I was always waiting for her there.

She told me things. She wrote.

Even the way she wrote had changed, everything had changed.

Something had charmed us but also left a fear in our hearts and we were both drawn in and tempted to flee.

But our desire to step closer grew stronger

She would come home between meetings and sometimes she would even cancel meetings so she could stay home.

She wrote more than I did.

On the one hand she was wrapped up in the idea of our novel, always giving me ideas on how we should write it. She was immersed in it.

At that time it was as if our shared life and our book were slowly coalescing.

We were coalescing.

'a writer meets a woman . . . and it's as if this woman is being imagined by all of the women in all of the books he's written . . . and every time he sees her he's with one of these women . . . not that he gets something different from each one . . . it's that he's with a different person each time . . . it's as if each of them had come to visit the writer in this woman's body . . . why? . . . i don't know . . . it's some kind of madness.

'the writer doesn't know what this woman or the others will do next . . . when he has given his soul to all of them . . . doesn't know why she has come, and why she is playing this game . . .

'he's trying to turn them all into a single woman . . . or the woman is trying to save herself from them . . .'

She leaves the computer for a while and then comes back a little later.

'the question is this . . . i get carried away . . . no matter what i'm doing, no matter what i'm trying to achieve . . . most of the time i forget what i've left behind . . . at the same time there are things i need to do . . . but this is all i can think about . . . everything becomes meaningless in its shadow . . . as i lose someone i come to have another . . . my life is full of these kinds of choices . . . i'm always sacrificing one thing for another . . . and sometimes i turn around and take it back . . . and then i leave it again for something else . . . but sometimes it's not there where i left it . . .

'i would never be a good writer . . . i would only write about myself . . . and because i couldn't find anything to write about i would spin all sorts of nonsense . . . and more and more . . . and i would be angry because people wouldn't really understand me . . . but i wouldn't even understand myself . . . and in the end i would go insane . . .'

There were times when she went on these kinds of flights.

'is loneliness something we are destined to feel? . . . i don't believe it's a choice . . . it seems as if some people are obliged to feel it . . . it's as if i don't feel close enough to anyone to really bring them into my life . . . i don't have the courage for that . . . or any real desire . . . sometimes i can't understand why . . . because i feel the need but i can't make it happen . . .'

There were times when she would misunderstand something I had said and she would take it personally.

'sometimes you suddenly feel so very far way . . . you drift away from me as quickly as you came . . . this isn't a thriller . . . it's my life . . . and what's more, you're a part of it . . . and i am destroying it . . . i am aware of that . . . you know it too . . . so then there is nothing wonderful and exciting left . . . only my silly thoughts . . . and the courage i have to spill them here . . . i don't want you to just sit there and watch them pass by . . . . you said that nothing would happen to me as long as you're here . . .'

In those times I tried to assure, I tried to explain to her that I hadn't drifted away; true, there were times when I feared that I wasn't close enough.

Then suddenly she would remember Mustafa and her love for him.

'it's a passion i feel for him and love and desire i feel for you . . . only the two of you can make me a complete woman.'

Then came the emotion she felt for me, something she called 'love'.

'i think this is why loving you is such a beautiful thing . . .

'i think i've found the answer . . .

'i have no expectations of you or of this relationship . . . apart from being happy and making you happy . . . and that's probably what you want from me . . .

'when you remove expectation from love, what remains is so utterly pure and magnificent . . .'

By this point I was eating in front of the computer and I would fling open the door to our home as soon as I got up in the morning, full of the hope of finding her there or a note she'd left for me while I was sleeping. There was usually something waiting for me.

'i like sleeping . . . probably because of the dreams i have . . . i slip into a secret world . . . which i adore . . . sometimes i feel so wonderful in the morning that i give thanks to him . . . for example, i give thanks for what i share with you . . . like other things, i suppose this is a stroke of good luck . . . a little earlier i made love to you in my dream before i woke up . . . one day i was terrified to think of it ending and never having such a dream again . . . that would be dreadful.'

In the middle of the day she would hurry out of a meeting only to write me a single sentence.

'sometimes it's everything, sometimes it's one thing that I miss . . . the look in your eye . . . your smile . . .

'but now i miss making love with you . . .'

When she said things like that I knew it wouldn't be long before she would drop everything she was doing to come and see me.

And we made love.

We made love with a desire that wasn't real.

'to feel lust and peace at the same time and with the same person . . . do you think it's possible?'

At the time I did think it was possible and so I told her so: 'i suppose such a miracle is possible . . . i suppose the authenticity of lust, independent of any other support, game or provocation, can bring about this miracle.

'and the confidence born of true lust brings peace of mind.

'is this the secret? there are things i only understand when i explain them to you . . .'

'maybe because we want both of them at once, lust and peace of mind, he won't be angry with us . . .' she answered. 'maybe he has his own games, who knows? . . .

'he's watching us from above with an enormous smile on his face . . . you think everything is a coincidence, eh? if you think you found that mosque on your own, you're wrong . . . years before, the villagers collected money so they could build it for you . . . the former imam had to die in a traffic accident three years earlier but i sacrificed his life so that you could marry . . . at this point you owe me for them . . . but from now on i want to see what you're going to do, he says . . .

'do you think he's angry with me for saying these kinds of things? . . . i hope not . . .'

Sometimes she wrote almost nothing.

Sometimes she went on and on.

She thought about what she'd experienced with Mustafa as much as she thought about our time together; sifting through the past, she would tell me all about it, hoping to discover something about herself in the telling, hoping that I would unearth something new.

She gave me her perspective on her past with Mustafa.

'he first started this ill-fated game . . . he fell madly in love with a woman and cared for her deeply . . . for years . . . every day he woke up with visions of her . . . and over time his unachievable dream turned him into a bitter man . . . and he wouldn't let anyone stop him . . . he wasn't used to anyone standing in his way . . . and whenever he had a problem he blamed his dream . . .

'sometimes they lived together in his imagination . . . they began again in the same way every time, embracing each other in the moonlight . . . those were the times he felt closest to her . . . the simplest gesture could bring him to his senses . . . he tried this . . . the woman didn't want to . . . and this is why it didn't make any difference if it was imagined or true . . . the man couldn't understand and was enraged . . . he took his anger out on his dream . . . he couldn't do anything for the woman . . .

'the woman alone held on to the dream . . . she suffered . . . such pain . . . she blamed herself . . . while others were realising their dreams, she was giving up on hers . . . she had to be insane . . . or there had to be a reason why . . .

'it was the first time the woman had encountered such pain . . . life had granted her everything others wanted and had treated her well . . . she dismissed her pain . . . in the same way she dismissed the truth . . .

'reality wasn't perfect, but dreams always are . . .

'the man knew his pain well . . .

'the woman touched her pain and tried to live with it . . . sometimes it came in the form of a faint but sharp fever and sometimes it came to life with such strength that it burned both of them . . . the woman began to experience pleasure in the pain, a dangerous game . . . and the man was swept away in a terrible rage every time the fever seized him . . . and in his own dream he wanted to kill her . . . . in their efforts to reach each other, they became obstacles . . .

'on the one hand there was this perfect dream and on the other the horrific pain that was the cost of keeping the dream alive . . . two people lost in the ebb and flow of misfortune . . . for years . . . so many partings and reunions . . . to fall so far away from each other after growing so close . . .

'the man gave the woman her last chance . . . but now she no longer had the strength to play the game . . . she didn't want to play . . . she wanted peace of mind . . . perhaps it was the first game she'd ever played . . . she was angry . . . ready to accept it all, ready to give it all up . . . he said to the woman, be mine . . . only mine . . .

'the woman wore a weary smile . . . i can't do that, she said . . . the man wasn't expecting such an answer . . . and again he asked her why . . . i don't know, the woman said . . . . i must be insane . . . or there must be a reason . . .

'the man left without any intention of returning . . . the woman didn't know that yet . . . she'd grown used to suffering because he would never return, yet knowing all the while that he would return . . .

'as he was leaving, the woman stood up . . . or she didn't . . . she sat down on a long white sofa . . . unwittingly brought her hands to her stomach and thought, where am I? . . . which city, which house? . . .

'why is reality never perfect like dreams? . . .

'why are we so afraid of pain? . . .

'why do we have to choose? . . .

'this is all nonsense . . . you're right . . .'

I didn't know if she was suffering under the burden of the two relationships or because of the pain she assumed Mustafa was feeling, as sometimes she wrote about how she wanted to be free of him . . .

'now i want to be free of him and his dream of me . . . i truly need to be free . . . can you do that for me? . . . can you save me from him? . . .

'do you know how difficult it is to bear such a pain for so many years, a pain you can't ever really understand? . . . living always with the pain in your heart . . . not knowing why you're doing anything . . . forever feeling guilty for what you do . . . i wonder why my heart has shut all other doors, taking revenge on me for what? . . . as if mocking every answer my mind comes up with . . . i just can't get to the source of the pain . . . if only i could be sure that this is love . . .

'and i don't know what can save me . . . asuman tells me

the only salvation is a great passion . . . and i'm not even sure
of that . . .

'if only we were madly in love . . .

'you and me . . . truly . . .'

Were those words 'madly in love' some kind of invitation, a
wish or a joke, I didn't really know. But sometimes I doubted
the reality of this pain she felt because of Mustafa, and I thought
it might be something she had cooked up in her own little
devil's workshop of a mind.

That's what I wrote to her.

'it seems to me that you have a strange relationship with
pain . . .

'on one hand you're addicted to the pain, even though your
emotions generally spur the pain into action . . . and then it
also seems that you are afraid of it . . .

'it's as if an artificial "fantasy" pain makes you fearful of true
pain . . . as long as you feel pain over mustafa you may very
well be keeping another pain at bay . . .

'an artificial pain protecting you from real pain . . .

'a kind of inoculation . . .

'sometimes i think that in your life mustafa symbolises a
kind of protector . . . a dream that protects you from reality
. . .

'maybe i got it wrong . . . but what i said might be true . . .

'but the fact that mustafa is an imaginary emotion doesn't
lessen his importance . . . just the opposite . . . it makes him
all the more important . . . because you need that shield . . .

'or that's how it seems to me.'

Once she asked me a question I thought about a great deal
later on.

'what do you think is a more wonderful feeling? . . . to
realise your dreams or the dreams of another? . . .

'will it make you happy to help me realise my own dreams?'

From time to time I would share with her my thoughts
about Mustafa, and I never knew if they were laced with a hint
of jealousy. I doubt it. I think that in our home I was always

completely honest with her. I never polluted the dream with slanders and lies. Maybe sometimes. An insignificant distortion . . . perhaps . . .

'it seems to me that he's living out a part from a scenario in his head . . . and because real life didn't fit with the narrative there, he was convinced that something was wrong . . . and believed that everything would work out and unfold according to his script . . .

'it seemed to me that everyone who believed in this script would end up getting hurt . . .

'i suppose i experience these fleeting moments of enlightenment . . . . and i would see the truth, moments when i experienced terrible pain and sought consolation . . . and it's at those moments i feel i have to call you.'

Sometimes she would miss me. In fact those terrible moments of longing sometimes caught us at the same time.

'i have such strong feelings for you now . . . it's like what i feel for him . . . an overwhelming love . . . different from what a woman can feel for a man . . . or both feelings intertwined . . . . and a similar belief . . . nothing will happen to you as long as i'm here . . . he will see everything, know everything and you won't let it happen . . .

'perhaps when you're with me i don't want to be with anyone else . . .

'but i'm afraid that when you're not with me i don't want anyone else either . . . strange, isn't it? . . .

'but don't worry . . . it will probably pass . . .

'what surprises me and strikes fear in my heart is that i don't want the feelings to go away.'

She went on: 'i don't know the reason why . . . i don't want to touch anyone else or him to touch me . . . what was that i told you? . . . loyalty to lust . . .

'there is definitely such a thing . . . i don't want to lose that feeling when you touch me . . .'

She kept giving me suggestions for my novel, as if part of her mind was always working through it. She wanted to help me write a good book and she adopted me and my work and my writing, as if she had become a part of me.

'maybe you should write about what it is like to realise another person's dreams . . . someone outside your family . . . in fact the dreams of someone you're not in love with . . .

'maybe in realising this other person's dreams it will eventually become your own . . . you'll write about the extraordinary nature of someone's miracle . . .

'are you my miracle? . . .

'now i'll pray that nothing happens to our home . . . nothing will happen to anyone's home . . .'

In the middle of the night she surprised me with these words: 'i love you . . .'

If I am to believe she loved me, and made me happy even though I didn't love her, why was it even important if I loved her or not?

We didn't see each other but we never left our home, and I never went out, and she came when she had time off work or she cancelled her work, and we would message each other until morning.

Without ever seeing each other.

Without ever hearing each other's voices.

We never called each other, even when we missed each other the most. Though we had never openly talked about this, we had made some kind of silent pact.

We were living in a fantasy world, waiting for the dream to ripen and then turn into truth, and as we waited, so happily drenched in the dream, it was as if we were wondering which aspect of 'reality' might damage the dream, fearful that it would finish it.

We both sensed the greatest threat to the realisation of our dream was exposing it to the real world too soon.

The truth of that moment was the enemy of a reality we both expected and desired.

The truth of what was and what was to come had lodged itself into our dream and we waited.

One night I woke up to find a single line:

'i've gone insane and you're not telling me.'

In the morning I understood why she thought that way.

'there was a ring on my finger . . . the one you bought for me . . . i feel good when i wear it . . . but asuman took my hand and asked me what it was . . . i said, a ring . . . so it means something? . . . it does . . . zuhal, you're driving me mad, she said . . . i smiled and said no . . . then tell me . . .

'since yesterday morning i can't understand why i did it . . .

'i told her i was getting married . . . i said i wanted to see what the ring would look like . . . then i thought this was just another game . . . i don't know . . . as long as they don't know who it is, if they don't have a name, it's a harmless game . . .

'she said she didn't understand . . . when did this happen? . . . it was someone i knew and we decided to get married . . . God, when? . . . next month . . . which day? . . . at the beginning of the month . . . next week . . . i suppose so . . . where? . . . in italy . . . don't be ridiculous, why are you getting married, are you mad? . . . i don't know, he wants to . . . (don't laugh but you can divorce me if you want, i deserve it) . . . well, did you even ask if he was serious? . . . don't think so but he's a bright guy . . . who is this guy? . . . some guy, a printer . . . married before? . . . yes . . . we need to meet right away, invite him to dinner . . . the game finishes here . . . my shoulders slumped and i realised what a foolish thing i'd done . . . of course we'll come, i said . . .

'she took my hand, her eyes tearing up (she must have been making that part up) . . . you look happy . . . yes, i'm very happy . . . please introduce him to us . . . i was just starting to come round but too late . . .

'i really don't know why i did it . . . i knowingly throw myself into these corners . . . as i left, i didn't even think to tell asuman to keep quiet about it . . .

'can you tell me why I did it? . . . i'm dying to know . . . i wanted to do it and knew the consequences . . . but believe me that i don't know why . . .

'maybe i was jealous of other married couples . . . i really don't know . . . do you think that's why? . . .

'would you tell me if you thought i was insane? . . .

'ok, i'm the one who started all this but i don't know why . . .'

'in my opinion,' I wrote, 'for some reason (which we need to work out) you like to provoke people and create incidents . . . to scare them . . . as if you want everyone to look at you and cry out . . .'

She interrupted.

'i don't like scaring people but i do like to see their limits . . . my boundlessness versus their limits . . .

'then i convince them of the possibilities . . . that's the fun part . . .'

I went on.

'your quiet front makes for a delicious contrast with the provocateur that lies beneath . . .

'you terrify some people who don't know your temperament . . .

'but more interesting is . . . while you're busy devastating a scene, you're already busy coming up with the solution to clean it all up . . . if things spiral out of control now, you know what needs to be done in advance . . . i know that you know . . .'

I could sense that she was smiling as she read these words and then replied. How? I don't know.

'it seemed like the truth when I told them . . .

'but if it were, i wouldn't have been able to hide my true feelings . . . i couldn't lie to them . . .

'i suppose sometimes i'm a little bit afraid of myself . . .

'i don't know what's happening . . . in a way, i can't decide . . . and then whatever springs to mind at that moment . . . i end up doing whatever i feel like or want to do then . . . and there's nothing that comes after . . . or even before . . . when i get to that point, i can't assess anything . . . i feel like i'll either disgrace myself or die . . . and i couldn't care less . . . i do whatever i feel like doing then . . .

'and i don't think about anything at that moment . . . it's dangerous . . . i suppose i get some kind of thrill out of it . . . i don't know . . .

'in an instant i want everything to change . . . to turn my life upside down . . . to go off the rails, off in an entirely new direction . . .

'does any of this make sense? . . . it all seems empty . . .'

'what you're saying makes sense . . . i think i know the way it makes your head spin . . .

'the power to take control of life and change it if only for a moment . . .

'even if you have to pay a high price for it . . .'

'i don't think about that . . . i could pay with my life . . . my future . . . my career . . .

'you asked me what i feel at that very moment . . . i think it's superiority . . . i feel above the others . . . strange . . . but true . . .'

I think it was the next morning when she wrote those words again: 'i love you.

'whatever happens . . .

'and you're lucky . . . really . . . because it's a beautiful feeling to be loved by me in this way . . . whenever i think of you, i smile . . . and i feel warm inside . . . i always want the best for you . . . i always pray for you . . .'

I suppose that over those days I had no sense of time, cordoned off from the real world. I didn't know where I was, the time of day and what was happening around me, and I didn't care. I only stayed at home with Zuhal, reading her words, answering, turning in a kaleidoscope of emotions.

I had lost myself in a dream, a virtual world, and one that made me happier than any other.

As she was working as an advisor to several different companies, she was actually quite busy, always had to 'run' somewhere, but generally she ran faster and further than she ever had to. I wrote to her about it.

'yes, you're right, i have a busy life . . . i was thinking about it this morning . . . i want to stop but I'm afraid . . . it seems as if everything else will stop with me if i do . . . it's as if i won't ever really think, feel excitement again . . . i know that's ridiculous . . .'

Sometimes she carried on writing without having given me the beginning of her thought, like a child, no beginning and no end, sentences that dangled in mid-thought, of an unknown origin.

'i want to be everything you aren't . . . nothing you have already become . . .

'to live in places you have never lived, to live lives you could never live . . . and i want you to think thoughts i cannot think, do things i cannot do, say things i cannot say . . .

'where is all this coming from now? . . . i don't know . . .

'just something that popped up in my mind . . . so not something we should worry about as i suppose we're already like that . . .'

But she went on describing this marriage she'd told her friends about.

'it was a fun meal . . . i told them about you . . . really . . . i told them how clever and funny you are, and how much you know, and how you're so kind and understanding with me . . . and how you make me so happy . . .

'it gave me such pleasure to tell them all this . . .

'they were all entranced by what i had to say . . . it was as if i was speaking to them of their own dreams . . . i was every-thing they were not and what they could never do (God forgive us, for i know that we will be punished for all of this and i am going to blame you and i am assuming that you will not deny the sins of your wife . . .)'

'what did your friends feel when you told them all this?'

'some of them were sad . . . slipped into bad moods . . . i don't know why . . . maybe they were thinking of their own marriages . . . their hopes . . . . their dreams . . . the beginning of everything . . . maybe they were reliving something through me they felt they would never experience again, something far away for them . . . i really don't know . . .

'but they were far more confused in the end than they were at the beginning . . .

'and so am i.'

'and what did you think?'

'i'm probably afraid to think about what i'm feeling . . . and sometimes of what I'm doing . . . until then it's as if i'm not thinking, just living . . . i know that if i was doing all this alone i would go insane . . .

'i like mixing fact and fiction, i prefer a dream reality, most of the time i feel that reality can only be tolerated with dreams, but this is too much . . .

'this is how people get lost . . . it's bewitching . . . in the past i could still make out reality and dream, even when i had mixed them up, but now i can't . . . i don't know if this should frighten me . . . madness is something like this . . .

'have you ever experienced something like this? . . . can you understand all this? . . . tell me . . .'

In the morning she wrote to tell me that she wasn't going to work.

'i feel sick . . . and i don't want to get out of bed.

'i can't understand why.

'i probably should ask you this . . .

'am i important to you?

'because i realise that in this game i get all my strength from you . . . when you can't play the role then i take over . . . or i don't know . . . i'm just not sure . . .'

Then she dashed off a series of sentences that made me begin to tire of the dreams . . .

'we have to decide if we're going to live in reality or stay in the world of dreams . . . isn't condemning one thing to the world of dreams the same as being a prisoner of your own dreams? . . .

'maybe we need to understand that when we are close and touch each other it's not actually what we want, we only make new dreams . . .

'maybe reality is far more beautiful than dreams . . .

'or we have trapped ourselves in dreams . . .

'but this time it will be our own conscious choice . . .'

Reading those lines, I felt we'd grown so close that we now had to make that decision.

This mysterious 'dream' relationship had reached the point where it could not contain all our other dreams. It was ripening. It wanted to become real.

Then she asked me.

'have you ever written about a real marriage?'

Once she had a dream about Mustafa. In the morning she told me about it.

'i dreamt about him again . . . and so many other things i can't remember . . . there was a bed right in the middle of the room . . . it must have been for me, and i was about to go to bed but i noticed bugs crawling all over the bed . . . one of them was a scorpion . . . then they disappeared while i was wondering how to get rid of them, but i still felt them in the room . . . i sat in an armchair with my feet tucked under me . . . i was exhausted . . .

'he was just about to tell me something when i woke up . . . it was as if i didn't want to hear what he had to say and i woke up . . . but i was curious . . . or maybe not . . .

'that's the call to prayer . . .'

Once again it was a sentence I couldn't understand, a conversation with herself that I happened to overhear.

'i don't want to turn into someone else . . . i can't do it . . . i'm not even trying . . . i think i only like the changes inside me . . .'

Then again a short sentence.

'i want to tell you everything i see . . . i want to always speak with you . . . is it strange? . . . so what . . .'

I started to detect a strange sadness in her words, an enigmatic restlessness she was avoiding.

'i'm living a life that belongs to a stranger . . . i don't know if i will ever have a life that i'll be able to call my own, in which i can be myself . . .

'you're right, i can interact with all kinds of people, at every social level . . . searching for clues that will lead me back to my own life . . . but i belong to none of them.

'are there times when you suffer too?'

How many days had we spent at home, how many days since I'd stepped outside, how many days had I lived steeped in this honeydewed dream? Now I don't know.

Things had changed in those few days.

It was as if we'd come to a door and it was now for us to decide if we were going to open it.

Indeed now I know that I'd already decided to open the door.

I just wanted to enjoy the last few minutes, to be sure, and so that I could fling it open with even greater pleasure.

I was full of a swelling desire to turn everything we experienced at home, all our dreams, into reality and to live in a home that was a little more real.

Because what we experienced in our home was happiness.

Or maybe it was that I believed the recipe for happiness was something like this.

That's what I believed.

XL

On one of those days when everything in town was quiet, I received a telephone call in the afternoon.

'Have you finished all my sweets?' she said, teasingly.

'All finished,' I said, but once I heard her voice I was captivated.

'Do you need any more?'

'Why, yes I do.'

'Let me bring some of my tastiest over then,' said Kamile Hanım. 'But it's a little hard for me to get through town at a time like this. It's tense out there. We have a summer place about an hour outside of town that we never really use. It's quiet there. No one around. Come and pick up your sweets there.'

'Okay. When?'

'Be there in two hours,' she said.

'All right.'

Although my mind was filled with thoughts of Zuhal, my body had suddenly surged to life when I heard Kamile's voice, alluring, and steeped in her crude and selfish desires.

What's more I knew this would never happen again, that it would come to an end if Zuhal and I started a real life together.

True, I wanted that life with Zuhal, especially during those insane days when we were shut in at home, writing to each other constantly. She had practically taken possession of me, pushed me into another world, making me believe in the perfection of that place.

It's hard to explain my belief in it.

It is a feeling of warmth, the softness that comes with a woman's body, which, even when she isn't there, envelops you, and you feel an unending glow.

It's a feeling of touch and wholeness that stays with you.

I didn't want to lose that.

But it wasn't easy to give up my own life and my solitude. For a long time I'd been happy living that way – I'd become used to a life in which anything could happen. It wouldn't be easy to forget old habits. I would have to push myself.

It was going to take me time to convince myself that I could love a person more than my time alone, that I could experience the confidence of this solitude when I was with another, that I could lead a life that would allow me to forget the freshness that came from the freedom of solitude. I wanted a woman, I wanted to be with her, I wanted to spend time with her, but my solitude was another woman, someone I loved just as passionately. It was a curious dilemma. To love two different things that could not coexist, to want both at the same time.

I kept imagining that scene in which I would watch her in the kitchen cooking as I whiled away my time in the garden; back then the vision was more appealing than anything in the real world.

I was going to change.

I knew myself well enough to know just how hard it was going to be.

As I set off to meet Kamile Hanım I thought about how it was going to be this last time, a goodbye, the last chance to taste her unrivalled sweets. It was my last journey, one more thrilling adventure inspired by the sin of lust.

It wasn't easy to understand how this woman on the brink of old age had such a power over me. It was lust, her desire for pure pleasure and her selfishness, and I could only understand it if I worshipped at the altar of her lust.

About an hour's drive out of town I followed Kamile's directions and turned off the main road onto a dirt road shaded by palms trees, making my way down to the sea.

There was the house: two floors and the shutters closed, in a garden surrounded by high walls.

The red iron garden gate was open.

I drove in along the gravel driveway and the gate let out a mechanical creak and automatically closed behind me.

Kamile Hanım was already there.

I felt an overwhelming desire to touch her right then.

I've met people who say that making love is the same with every woman, but it's not like that at all. With every woman you enter a different world, making love to them uniquely, because she will ask something remarkable of you and you will rise to the challenge; she will touch you in her own way and this will change your touch. But this is not as easy as it seems, and choosing is distressing because when you decide on this man or that woman you will have to make sacrifices in return, and the weight of the decision can knock you to the floor. The real then is not enough, it will not lead you to make these sacrifices, and so you turn to dreams. Dreams like the dream of watching Zuhal through a window.

It was a beautiful garden.

I crossed a broad veranda to the front door, which was ajar, and as I pushed it open I stopped for a moment to adjust to the darkness inside, a stark contrast to the shimmering daylight.

'Shut the door,' Kamile Hanım said.

I shut the door.

The bright light outside streamed through the shutters, casting strips of light on the carpets.

When my eyes finally adjusted, I saw Kamile Hanım.

She had taken off her jacket.

She was sitting in an armchair with her legs crossed.

And her skirt was pulled up over her knees.

Looking at me with that teasing smile on her face, she said, 'You came for your sweets?'

'Yes,' I said.

'You've come a long way for them.'

'I would have travelled further.'

She stood up.

'Come here,' she said.

I followed her out of the room. The door to the bedroom was open. 'I changed the sheets. They start to smell of mould otherwise.'

My hands were almost trembling as I undressed her and laid her on the bed.

She'd learned to surrender; she was quick to learn anything for the sake of pleasure.

At first we groped each other like hungry animals, and it took us some time to sink into it.

When it was over, we each lit a cigarette.

'How are you?' I asked. We finally had the time for small talk.

'Fine,' she said. 'Considering the circumstances.'

'Is it that bad?'

'Terrible. Mustafa has lost his mind. And he's driven Raci and Rahmi mad too. He's shut down Raci Bey's huge factories, which is unheard of. The boy's gone insane in his lust for power, lost his head, and there's no way to reason with him any more. He's not thinking clearly. If you're going to challenge someone whose family's been here for hundreds of years, someone everyone respects and who no one would challenge, well then you're in for trouble. The boy's lost his senses. He starts a feud with Raci Bey and he ends up burning down the whole town. But the day will come when Mustafa will have to pay for everything. Anything can happen now. I wanted to send Rahmi to the city but he won't listen to me and his father's telling him to stay. Rahmi's really on edge. I don't know what I'm going to do, I'm really depressed about it all. Everyone is.'

'They're fighting over the treasure?'

She laughed and said, 'No. That's a thing of the past. Now the fight's over who's got the biggest rod.'

She could be a lot like Sümbül sometimes.

'They set fire to Mustafa's olive groves.'

'Well, whoever did that was an idiot if you ask me. The town is full of olive trees, so burn a few and there's only more and more to burn. And what does it take to do it? Just a match. You tell some guy to go do it and he does. I mean, forgive me, but these boys have no brains. They're half-arsed wasters who can't even sit still, just have to fidget, get up and break something.'

'What's going to happen now?'

'God knows. Most likely Rahmi will appeal to a higher court, but if someone with some sense doesn't step into the fray and stop all this I don't know what will happen. In the end I'll have no choice but to send my kids away. They can't get to Raci easily, and Rahmi's become irritable, which is starting to scare me. He needs to get out of town, if only for a short while. Let his father put things back on track, then he can come back. I'll be much more comfortable once he's gone. Anyway, I guess I'll send him away soon. But I tell you, they'll ask you over for dinner one more time before I can do it. It turns me on, seeing you in public.'

Her leg was up against mine and she put her hand on my stomach. 'What's wrong?' she said. 'Are you full? Seems you're more interested in town gossip than my sweets.'

Her breasts, stomach and inner thighs were glimmering in the dim light, fully exposed. She knew how much I loved her body that way, and her casual style.

When we stopped this time the sun was setting.

My telephone beeped as I lit a cigarette.

A new message.

I got up and looked.

It was from Zuhal.

I really miss you. I'm in town. Where are you?

Out of town. But back in a couple of hours.

The phone beeped again.

Where are you?

I didn't know what to write.

Out of town.

Silence for two minutes as I waited by the phone. Thinking

what more I could write as I walked back to bed, the phone beeped again.

How's Kamile Hanım?

I can't describe the fear and panic I felt just then; panic was no exaggeration, considering the rush of emotion that seized me.

To this day I don't know whether Zuhal knew when she sent that message or if she was simply having me on.

But I was swept away in such panic that I suddenly felt we were being watched.

I felt Zuhal was standing there at the garden gate, looking at my car.

She's fine, I wrote.

Later I would tell her that I was joking, that I assumed she'd be amused by the absurdity of it.

I waited a bit then went back to bed.

Kamile Hanım needed to get home before dark, and I was feeling restless, and so the next session was a little rushed.

I left before she did.

And as I did she gave me a packet of sweets.

'Here you are then. Are you happy?'

'Very,' I said but panicking inside. I knew the feeling wouldn't pass until I saw Zuhal.

I took a shower once I got home, hoping I would see Zuhal a little later.

I called her on the way.

Her phone was switched off.

I called again and again. In a frenzy, I kept calling. I don't know how many times but I never got through.

I drove past her house when I got to town.

No lights on inside.

I didn't know if she was even in town or if she'd left for the city in a fit of anger. Then later it occurred to me that she might be with Mustafa.

Maybe she'd gone to that hotel she never liked.

Sometimes just a word can change the course of your life,

everything that lies ahead; nothing was the same after I wrote that word: *fine*. I was paralysed by the thought that the door to our future would never open again.

I called her all night but she never answered.

Then I waited at home until morning but not a word from her flashed on the screen.

She had suddenly vanished from my life.

I had never thought that just a few words could lead to something so bad, from good to something utterly dark.

At first I thought that her anger would fade over the next few days.

But it never did.

I imagine there was much more than anger.

Something deeper.

Something that could not be repaired.

XLI

A pinkish smoke is emerging in the middle of a dark silhouette, a barely perceptible brightness between the mountains.

This light will bring me to darkness.

We are approaching the end.

There's no time to escape now.

I have two options: surrender or die.

And I still don't know which one to choose.

Will I change my mind at the last moment?

Am I afraid?

Will I be afraid?

The initial fear has subsided.

I feel a strange numbness, as if every part of me is slowly separating, and as the parts leave me I feel less and less.

And not only pieces of me but pieces of my life, floating away. It seems that I am ready to bid this world farewell.

From the moment you accept your fate all emotions change, and you no longer want to drag out the farewell.

A strange smile appears on your face, as if you've discovered an amusing secret no one knows, and you feel mature and disdainful of those who will remain alive.

I don't know why I feel this for them.

Perhaps because I'm past the initial fear, the terror, and in time they'll all have to face it too.

The part that has fallen to me in this epic novel has come to an end.

I am preparing to leave this book.

Is God aware of this?

Or is he somewhere far away in the universe, receiving plaudits for a book that was far better written? Does he even care about this book?

I wonder if this book was nothing but a draft.

Truth is, it gives that feeling.

In the beginning he clearly wasn't thinking of a draft, but somewhere in the middle he might have said, This isn't working.

In the beginning there was the appendix he sent to the prophet Moses, in which he proclaims that the heroes of his novels are created in his image.

Then God said, 'Let us make mankind in our image, in our likeness, so that they may rule over the fish in the sea and the fowl in the sky, over the livestock and all the wild animals, and over all the creatures that move upon the ground.'

God made human beings in his image. And so humans were created in God's image.

The Book of Genesis.

Do you remember your own words?

I forget some of the things I've written and I wonder if the same happens to you?

I suppose it doesn't.

Was I created in your image?

Am I a part of you?

Do you know the part of me that was capable of murder?

Doesn't it bother you?

A murderer forged in your image now sits here on this bench, an image of you that waits for an imminent end.

Indeed they say that something of the author always lives in his heroes.

In some of his books the hero is clearly the author himself.

Bearing in mind that you say 'All heroes are made in my image', I must conclude that there is an autobiographical element in your work, for in your book you're telling your own story.

I wonder if we should call these diaries and not novels, as you follow one day after another. Isn't it merely the day in a life put down in a diary?

What will you write tonight?

Will you write the section 'I killed a person' tonight, or did you write it in advance?

You killed a person tonight.

And because I was made in your image they will take me for a killer and punish me.

Who knows that I was made in your image?

No one would believe me if I said so.

Am I the only one who believes in you?

Is there no one who takes your novel as seriously as me?

Maybe one needs to love literature to believe in you; one needs to know the value of a novel to marvel at your ways; for I know the value of your book.

But it seems that there are times when you falter in your choice of words.

Your heroes might very well come to the wrong conclusion when you say, 'let them have dominion over all the other creatures on this earth'. To me, one might extract the wrong message here, and indeed people do.

For there is nothing they will not do to have dominion over others.

Simply look at what's happening in this town: what have they become for this dominion?

Maybe it is a word you never should have used.

Here we are on an infinitesimal planet far from the centre of the universe. Is that why you dashed off this novel without taking any care?

Have you only lingered here a little while because you have more books to come? And so the adventures here on this planet are of little importance?

Is this planet nothing more to you than this miserable little town is to me?

Is it only a place for you to pause while you dash off your first draft?

To impress your readers, you said 'These heroes are made in my image' – a crafty way to keep your readers on their toes, dying to know more about the author's personality.

And so you have a good beginning, a fine entrance.

'The people in this book are made in my image.'

But what do these images of yours get tangled up in? Do you know?

They delight in everything you have forbidden them to do.

And you delight in breaking all your rules.

You are an author making fun of his readers.

You delight in sowing confusion, pretending to talk about serious matters when you're just having fun, presenting dramatic twists as if you're being lighthearted, meddling a little in other people's minds, having fun while you pretend.

Perhaps it's only possible to reach a decision about you after reading your other books.

Here, in this novel, we see brilliant creativity.

Do you love me as much as I love you?

Do you admire me as much as I admire you?

Do you praise my novel as much as I praise yours?

I am but an image of you.

I am you.

I write, create and kill just as you do.

I am a writer and a killer.

They'll be coming soon.

I know.

I won't say to them, you are killing God.

I won't say a word.

I will remain silent like you.

I never hear your voice and so they will not hear mine.

XLII

If I were to search for a word to best describe those days it would surely be grief, for those were days of mourning.

When I experienced the void Zuhal left behind, I realised that she had held a greater place in my life than either she or I had imagined.

That word – *fine* – had taken on a completely different meaning in my life.

It made me wince to even hear it.

I don't know why I went to Kamile Hanım.

In fact I knew this was a lie the moment I said it.

Despite all the pain it caused me, if I were to live that day over I would make the same choices again and again, and it would end the same way.

Not because God wrote the day like that, forcing it to unfold in no other way, no, but because God made me like that and I would never be able to change.

Because I would never be able to change.

Indeed I wanted the impossible. I wanted there to be two of me: one part would live with Zuhal, create a home together where we would be happy, and the other part would remain alone, would wake in the morning to decide on his own what he would do that day, asking no one, telling no one, speaking to no one.

I imagine this is what everyone wants.

And this is why I suppose there's no such thing as pure happiness.

We can't fit a whole person into one life.

This life we live is too small for all desires.

God has planted too many of them in our little minds and bodies.

We go through life denying this but I now accept the truth.

But accepting doesn't lessen my suffering.

I missed Zuhal.

I missed our home.

I missed the home I'd told her about, the home we were to make together.

I wanted to know where she was and what she was doing.

I was in mourning.

I sought consolation in two completely different people: in the cradle-maker and in Sümbül.

In the morning I would go and sit on a short little wicker stool opposite the cradle-maker, and the young boy at the coffeehouse, dressed in his football uniform, brought me coffee: and sometimes I would sit there for hours and watch the cradle-maker without saying a word, studying the way he carved, working out a groove, preparing his cradle for a human being, unborn, yet to be created in the image of God, yet to walk this earth.

Watching him work, I was fascinated by the cradles but I was mostly moved by the feeling of little human beings getting ready to walk this earth; and it seemed that if those cradles were never made, if they never came to be, those babies would never be born.

He worked so calmly and quietly, watching him gave me a sense of peace.

As he held the wood in his lap and slowly shaped it into a cradle, I could see an infinity stretching out into the future, an infinity that reminded me of the insignificance of every passing moment in my life, and in every chip that fell to the ground my troubles became less and less important, as did my entire life.

I just sat there and took him in.

Occasionally he would glance at me from under his eyebrows.

I wondered what he saw. What did my face tell him? I saw an infinity reaching out into the future in him but what did he see in me? Hopelessness, pain, maybe the swirl of all the emotions inside me.

Occasionally we spoke.

He never asked me questions.

Once he said, 'How can we know the true value of joy without knowing sorrow?'

'Isn't it a little tiresome to ascribe value to things in terms of their opposites?' I said, 'Isn't your frame of reference a bit oversimplified?'

'You would get bored if it was otherwise,' he'd said.

'Why is that?'

'Living with a single emotion would bore you. The same feeling every day, morning, afternoon and night. Is that what you really want? You would just get used to that one feeling . . . The secret lies in action. Can't you see that? Babies are captivated by anything that moves. Why would they stare at something still? How are we any different from them? For something to keep our attention, or distract us, it has to move. Give praise for anything that moves. For if it stops, you won't even have the strength to cry, no desire to cry . . . Even joy would eventually bore you if it went on in the same way for long enough. Because you get used to it. The secret to it all is movement . . .'

'But now there are times when I want it to end. I want it to end already.'

'That's what you say, but how are you to know where it should end? Would you be willing for it to stop right now?'

'No. I don't want it to end just now. It should either have ended earlier or it should end later on. I just want this to pass.'

'Of course it will pass. It will pass. That is the wisest thing to know, that it will pass, the most precious wisdom. The greatest truth. All things will pass. Don't pray for it to end, pray for it to pass.'

When I spoke to him I wasn't hoping he would calm me

down or change my mind, but seeing him embrace life the way he self-assuredly embraced a cradle in his arms gave me a sense of peace and tranquility.

Sümbül's methods of consoling me were of course altogether different, but there were times when she said similar things in another way: 'Oh come on, everything passes. There's no point in letting any of this get you down. I don't let anything get me down any more. Wallow in your troubles as much as you like, but he'll do what he does anyway, and you wallow and fret and then you forget. If I'm going to forget in the end anyway, well, then why should I even fret in the first place? There's so much we forget, it's all gone, and I'm left having worried for nothing.'

She told me about what was happening in town.

It was as if I'd cut all my ties because I was actually getting ready to leave, mustering my strength, trying to get used to the idea that I wasn't going to see Zuhal again; in my mind leaving had come to mean that I would never see her again — I equated her with the town itself — and so leaving one meant leaving the other. But at that point I didn't have the strength to leave both. I did my best to gather strength to get better, and then I would leave.

Sümbül was making fun of the men in town.

'I've never seen the place like this before. It's like they're all numb. Whatever happens to the town happens to me in the end. These bastards' pricks are sensitive and when they're stressed out they can't get it up, they go brain dead, shell-shocked, and it doesn't even twitch, and what is Sümbül supposed to do all on her own? How is she supposed to elevate something brought down by the mayor? I swear I would have died of grief if not for you.'

'Isn't there anyone else?'

'There are the snitches. Thank God for them, but there are only so many. Business just isn't the same any more.'

'What's happening in town?' I asked, indifferently.

She grimaced. 'With Muhacir's help they're going to take

down one of Oleander's guys, but God knows who it's going to be.'

I can't remember exactly which day it was because back then I would get up in the morning and stubbornly go and check our home, used to finding nothing, but that day I received a message from her.

I couldn't read it right away.

I was too overjoyed at first.

And at that moment I knew it was going to be the last chat we would ever have at home.

I sat down to read.

'i don't know what's happening, it's as if i am crippled. and i don't know what it was that did it . . . or even whether it's something new . . .

'there's this ancient olive tree in the garden, its trunk spilt in two. it wasn't pruned this year and there are little olives on the branches hanging close to the earth . . . last night i lay there still under the tree like an invalid and eventually i began to feel like a part of the tree . . . and i reached out and touched the little olives it had produced despite its old age, and the leaves as if they were miracles . . .

'a cricket hopped over . . . it looked like a bit of bark with legs, and I watched him, listening to the cries that came from his tiny little body . . . i wanted to touch him and he raced away . . . everything around me must have sensed my sadness . . . i had contracted some terrible disease but they were acting as if i shouldn't know what it was . . .

'i don't know what it is within me that's lost . . . the strange thing is how i felt i'd been there for so long . . . as if i'd always been sitting there under that tree.

'are you sad? . . . don't be . . . i feel oddly at peace . . . as if i could spend the rest of my life leaning against the trunk of this tree . . . i wanted to shelter under this ancient tree tonight . . . right now i feel such an affinity with that tree . . . like the closest friend i have in the world . . . i don't know . . .

'ok, in a little bit i'm going for a swim and i will start to see everything again . . . i will pull myself out from the deep water . . . promise . . .

'i watched the sunrise . . . so beautiful . . .'

I read her words. And then again.

I knew that I would never see her again.

Knowing was one thing, and understanding was something else, and I simply knew that this was going to happen; I was in pain but I still had hope. Now I know with certitude.

Not once again in my life will I see her face, hear her voice, touch her.

She had closed the door behind her softly and decisively.

At the same moment the real and the unreal, a real life and a fantasy life, had come to an end. For when the real life was tampered with both of them were doomed to die, and there was nothing left but a vast and looming void.

All that remained was the faint smile that appeared on her face when she whispered softly and touched my cheek with her fingertips.

Nothing more.

XLIII

Hamiyet was in high spirits. Her son was getting better but he was still at home. She was once again the same old Hamiyet.

She was chattering away with the furniture, rolling her skirt up over her knees as she waddled about the house cleaning.

The strange current between us had returned.

It made me smile to see her carry on like that with a vase.

She would make me food but I wasn't hungry, and she'd say, 'You're a big man, if you don't eat you'll shrivel up and die.'

Life was like a switched off TV, and if you turned it on everything was right there where it should be, but I no longer found anything interesting – not a movement, not a flicker, not a sound.

If I reached out and hit the button it would spring to life but I didn't have the desire. I didn't want to do anything at all.

I was walking myself like a man walking a dog, my body a beloved creature that wasn't my own. I felt estranged from my body, like I was someone else. A life form that was waiting to be taken out, tended to and fed.

On one of those days Rahmi called.

'Come over for dinner. We'd all like to see you.'

'Of course,' I said, smiling. Amidst all their troubles, I doubted that they really missed me. I knew exactly why they were inviting me: Kamile had come up with some reason to get them to do it.

You might expect me to feel nothing but anger and hatred for Kamile Hanım, as she was the source of all my troubles, but life isn't like that. The game doesn't work that way – the mere mention of her name excited me.

If this was a bad novel everything would seem clearer, more in focus and by dint of that dull and boring. But I was wandering through the novel of a masterful author in which nothing was clear, contradictions were rife and the most unexpected thing could happen, stirring the most unexpected emotions.

In one of the writer's appendixes I had read with my own eyes how life on earth was nothing more than a game, a *divertissement*; and even if I was no longer entertained the game aspect of the affair continued.

I was a player and I would continue to play; it would be like that until the end of life on earth.

The game would carry on.

I went to have dinner with them that evening.

I only went because Kamile Hanım was going to be there, as the fat cats in town no longer interested me.

The sun was setting as I left.

I'm not exactly sure just how this happened, but as the last beams of sunlight streamed through one of the windows of the church on the hill – or was it a glimmering piece of glass or a stone – it seemed as if the church was flashing me an ironic smile.

'And Jesus drew a mirror in the sand,' I thought, for us to see our sins, every transgression that we rejected and denied, and our pains – clearly a part of the game – because sin was part of the game too.

I was full of grief and the world seemed steeped in sadness.

Passing the bodyguards outside, I stepped inside.

Raci Bey and Rahmi were on edge, oblivious to the real reason I'd been invited and annoyed that they now had to deal with a guest, while Kamile Hanım sat in an armchair, legs crossed. I looked at her carefully. Her skirt wasn't pulled up above the knee. She knew how to carry herself in every situation.

The girls were more cheerful: no doubt they were tired of

the oppressive atmosphere and the endless fighting, enlivened by the slightest change of scene or a guest.

As we waited for the food to arrive, we started talking, and the conversation inevitably turned to Mustafa and the town.

'He's smashing everything up like a drunk, only thinking about keeping a hold on power,' Raci Bey said. 'Nothing else on his mind but himself and his position. There's no one he hasn't hurt or turned against him.'

'But people like him. At least a good majority of them.'

Rahmi's words were laced with ire, a repressed fury, and this made him seem desperate and powerless.

'They like him because he's in power,' he said. 'The day he falls from his throne you won't see a single servant of God keeping company with the likes of him!'

'But it doesn't seem as if he'll fall from power any time soon,' I remarked.

'You never know,' Raci Bey grumbled, relatively calm compared to his son. 'There are many different ways to relieve a mayor of his duties, and if he's going to take things this far then we will have to explore one of these options. No one is willing to allow the town to be ravaged like this right before our eyes.'

Then he added: 'I don't know how it will happen but it will. Whatever happens, there's a limit to what he can do. Mustafa has crossed the red line.'

He said he didn't know but I was sure that Raci Bey had long since looked into the various ways he could spring to action to bring Mustafa down. Generally the bigwigs in town didn't like outside interference and preferred to handle problems amongst themselves, but it appeared that this time Raci Bey was planning to avail himself of all possible solutions.

'And they set fire to his olive groves,' I said.

I saw Raci Bey glance at Rahmi.

'That of course wasn't a wise move. Everyone has olive groves. You can't control the fire and before you know it you've burnt the entire town to the ground. If you're going to be angry, do it intelligently. You want revenge but you have to protect yourself while you carry it out.'

'Oleander's eating at the Çinili every day now,' Rahmi said. 'He never used to show his face there, he couldn't take the risk, but now he's breaking bread with all the bigwigs. And there are dogs all around him. What's all this about? Where does he get the nerve? Was it possible for him to do something like that before?'

'That's also an unwise move, and you have to pay a price for it,' Raci Bey said.

Oleander was indeed parading himself about the streets, which meant that he was making a display of confidence, a challenge to Mustafa.

It was clear that Mustafa was trying to drive everyone mad. He was pushing the boundaries.

As we were eating, Gülten asked, 'What's your take on all this as an outsider? You probably have a fresh perspective.'

'It may seem strange to say this to you openly but I think that this phantom treasure is driving you all insane,' I said. 'If so much importance hadn't been attached to that hilltop then none of this would be happening.'

Once again Rahmi angrily leapt into the fray.

'That hilltop has been there since I was born and no one has tried to take control of it until Mustafa lost his mind. Yes, everyone is looking for the deed but he goes and stuffs the place with gendarmes and hauls in excavators.'

'What if someone finds the deed?' I asked.

'Now?'

'Yes. What will happen if it turns up one of these days?'

'Anyone with brains who finds it wouldn't let it be known now,' Rahmi's wife said timidly. 'They would set fire to anyone who found it.'

I don't know why I said the words but I suppose they'd been banging about in my head for some time and they suddenly just slipped out. 'In the Barnabas Bible it's written that the Lord Jesus drew a mirror in the sand in which people could see their sins. Sometimes it seems to me that the hilltop is like a mirror reflecting all the sins of this town.'

Silence. They weren't used to such remarks.

In a cool and distant tone of voice, Kamile Hanım said, 'The sins aren't up on the hill. They are right here in town. So one must draw a mirror for the town. Is that right?'

I looked at her, and as I remembered our shared experiences her face seemed composed. But I knew her well enough to know that beneath the veneer she was smiling. She was having fun.

'I don't know about that. You know the town better than I do,' I said.

With the same cool expression on her face, she said, 'That's right. You can be sure of that.'

I decided to play along.

'Are you still making those fantastic sweets?'

'Well, of course. I always do, providing there's someone who appreciates the flavour.'

A flicker of lust flared up in her voice – one that only I could understand – and then vanished; in that moment I was sure she wanted to make love to me again.

As we were eating the main course, Raci Bey managed to forget about Mustafa for a moment and said, 'This lamb comes from our farm. You can taste the thyme because the sheep graze in fields of it,' and before he could say any more Kamile Hanım cut him off.

'Mustafa is going to marry Zuhal. I heard from the manicurist.'

I didn't look up from my food, but a little later I said to Gülten: 'Could you please pass me the bread?'

I knew that Kamile Hanım was watching me and I knew that only she could see the pain in my face. I managed to recover relatively quickly and turning to her I said, 'Now, I might be wrong but I think it was Winston Churchill. He was told that one of his commanders on the front line had recently married, and smiling he said, Well, then he'll be fighting on two fronts from now on. Seems Mustafa is in the same boat.'

Once again Rahmi was unable to restrain his rage. 'And who does he think will come to his wedding?' he cried.

'They're planning to have a rustic wedding. And everyone is invited,' Kamile said. Turning to me, she added, 'I imagine that you will be going too?'

'It would rude of me not to go if I was invited,' I replied.

'Oh, they will, they will indeed,' cackled Kamile. 'Why wouldn't they invite you? What kind of issues would they have with you?'

Did she know or was she simply guessing? It was hard to know but she had stuck in the knife, drawing blood. She was probably jealous and that surprised me. I never expected her to feel such an emotion. Or was she merely amused by my suffering? That was more likely.

'What are you going to do about the factories being shut down?' I asked Raci Bey.

'We sent the workers home and we'll continue to pay their salaries while the factories remain closed. And we've appealed to the Administrative Court. I have also informed the Chamber of Commerce, explaining that if my factories are not reopened I will have to report the conditions of all other factories in town. They don't have fire escapes either. We've never seen them in the history of this town. As if Mustafa's factories have them . . . despicable, shameless and immoral . . . No shame left . . . He wasn't always like this and I have no idea what changed him. He has lost all humility. Even in war there's a code of honour. And he doesn't have it. No respect for his elders any more.'

Grumbling through his teeth, Rahmi said, 'You're not listening to me, Dad. At this point we need to speak the only language he understands.'

'Everything in due course, my son. There will come a time for that,' Raci Bey said in a hurry, making it clear he wasn't interested in continuing the conversation just then.

'If the time hasn't come yet, I don't know when it will,'

Rahmi sputtered to himself and added: 'Are we going to wait for the bastard to come and shut down our home?'

Trying to calm down her brother, indeed the whole family was trying to do it, Gülten said, 'Dad knows what he's talking about, Rahmi. He's more experienced than all of us.'

Kamile Hanım seemed the calmest and most collected of all of them. But I didn't know exactly why. I sensed that she might be the one who issued the final verdicts to do with this war against Mustafa, as she was shrewder and more powerful than everyone else there. She could do things they couldn't, take risks they could never take. That much I knew. I knew she wouldn't waste time complaining. But when she felt the time was right she could deliver the cruelest verdict on Mustafa, and the others would carry it out.

As I left she stuffed a package in my arms. 'The sweets you like so much,' she said, with such a cold and blank expression on her face that I trembled with pleasure. I felt her hand touch mine as she passed me the package.

In that fleeting touch the curtain between us fell and I saw her naked, moaning. No one there would ever even dare to think that she had that hidden side.

Sometimes the truth is so far from what we see on the surface that we can't help but doubt our eyes. I wanted to lift the façade like a blanket and slip inside. That was where the life I loved took place.

Humans will always be drawn to the forbidden.

Only the commandment has changed.

'Don't commit your sins in the open.'

And like everyone else I obeyed.

Thanking her for the package, I said, 'I'll go through these in no time. You see, I am addicted.'

'Let me know when you're finished and I'll make you more,' she said.

Those sweets were the source of all my pain but I couldn't give them up. And compared to what I had lost they seemed so insignificant. It was impossible to compare the two.

My addiction to those sweets was a curse.

It didn't stop.

I ripped opened the package on the way home and popped one in my mouth.

It was delicious.

XLIV

There are things you know you'll do even before you've decided to do them, before you've even thought about doing them, as if part of your mind has made the decision already, never informing you.

When I called Mustafa in the morning I had not yet decided to do it.

I don't even know how it happened.

Suddenly I heard his cheerful voice. 'Hello?'

'How are you?'

'I'm fine. Heading to the town hall now.'

'I never really thanked you for the gun you gave me the other day, so I thought I should call. I went out shooting by myself. I'd missed it. Thanks.'

'Don't mention it. My pleasure. We should go out together one of these days,' he said, speaking with the gentry's centuries-old tradition of refinement and politeness. Gone were the crude manners that expressed themselves in statements such as 'What could it possibly have to do with you?'

He had changed.

'How are things?' I asked.

'Fine, all fine, we're getting things done.'

'Great. I'm glad to hear it. Then give me a call when you have some time and we'll go out shooting.'

'All right.'

'See you, then.'

When I hung up I knew.

He was back together with Zuhal. So the news about them getting married was true.

Only a woman could instil that kind of joy in a man's voice. In his voice was the energy of a happy man, full of confidence, with the woman he loved; he was so pleased, he'd forgotten all about the troubles that plagued him. Speaking to him then, I got the feeling he would have been happy to cede control of the town to his enemies.

Now, some claim people are easy to understand but I have never felt that way. When I heard the cheerfulness in Mustafa's voice, and understood his situation, I felt that sharp pain in my stomach but I also felt a happiness, peace and lightness of being, indeed I might even call it delight.

Initially it was a sharp pain.

Then came a sense of peace and contentedness.

Why would a person feel this way talking to a man who loved the woman he loved and desired? A woman whose absence caused such pain in his heart?

What is this?

Why did I feel that way?

And it wasn't just a fleeting emotion. I waited for it to pass, thinking I was deceiving myself with emotions that only served to dull the initial pain that rushed through me. But no, the sense of peace was still there. It was real.

I walked to the veranda, feeling an overwhelming desire to slap Hamiyet on the rump as I passed her.

I sat down and put my feet up on the veranda railing.

And I looked out over the town.

It was a bright, beautiful day.

The dome of the train station was shimmering like a rival to the sun on earth, beside the palm trees, the oleander, the beach that stretched as far as the eye could see, the dark blue sea, the eucalyptus between the buildings, the plane trees and flower beds, and the scent of honeysuckle and jasmine.

'Could you make me a coffee?' I asked Hamiyet.

When she returned, I said: 'How's your son?'

'Better. The wound is healing.'

'He's not leaving the house?'

'No, not yet.'

I thought about asking her what she was up to these days. I still didn't know the full story of why he'd been stabbed.

I was thinking. I was trying to understand.

Why was I so pleased? It had to be the wrong emotion. There had to be a clear explanation.

I wouldn't feel such bliss simply because I was a good person with a good heart. I wasn't that kind of person. Moreover, when it came to women there wasn't ever a man who would feel like this, I thought, and so I needed to find the source of my happiness amidst all that had gone wrong.

In spite of Mustafa's happiness and his reunion with Zuhal, I felt joyful and I think I knew the source.

Weighing the sadness that came on in the wake of Zuhal's final words to me and Mustafa's joy, Mustafa's situation only seemed pathetic, and I could sense that Zuhal wasn't as happy and full of joy as he was, because reading through her last words, probing her feelings, I knew that she wouldn't easily get over our separation.

She had gone to Mustafa with the sadness born of the void in her life that my absence had created and, despite this sadness, Mustafa was happy. On the one hand I was pleased to know that Zuhal was safe: Mustafa would protect her, from everything, indeed even from herself. Although she had gone to the man she was in love with, she had done so with me on her mind.

She had gone to him with me in her heart; she had taken me there.

But Mustafa couldn't see that.

And so I pitied him.

I wouldn't have changed places with him. Perhaps other men would. Men who might very well say, As long as the woman is by my side, I don't give a damn what she feels. But I wasn't one of them. What she was feeling was important too, more important than who she was with.

Mustafa was happy with a woman still thinking of me, and this didn't sadden me.

I would rather she be with Mustafa than with any other man. Someone I knew. With someone she was once in love with. With someone who was in love with her.

So I know where she is. I don't need to worry about her any more. I will never have to think of something happening to her.

No longer would I be plagued by that obsessive sense of responsibility, protecting her, the urge to always wonder where she is. The responsibility was gone.

This had given me a lightness of being far greater than I could have imagined.

There was the pain of not having her in my life, there was my dream of watching her in the kitchen, but now there was nothing for me to do but accept this pain. I had been freed of burdens far greater than this pain.

Those are heavy burdens indeed.

But I can carry them.

I can be distressed by the troubles.

But freed of these burdens, light and at ease, I was left bare with nothing but the lingering pain.

I had my solitude to console me.

A magnificent solitude I could never renounce. It was everything.

I decided to go to Remzi's and feast on his fine köfte.

And wash the meal down with a cold beer.

My appetite was back in full force.

But this is going too far, I thought to myself. I shouldn't feel better so soon, but that's how it was – it was the surprising truth. Struggling to convince myself of the wonders of this strange reality, I said to myself, Don't worry. In any event it won't be long before you're seized by an even greater pain, and all the memories will come flooding back.

That was true. Such pain simply didn't vanish into thin air, and so you might feel this way today but who knows about tomorrow? But it was clear that I had been freed of the burdens.

And that was enough for now.

I despised those burdens; I couldn't simply shrug them off; they were so terribly heavy.

This is a common idiocy in men: when they break up with a woman they assume that something terrible will befall her – I don't know why – and they rack their brains just to know what she is doing, desperate to know if something has happened to her. This foolishness had made me the prisoner of so many women.

And so never underestimate the power of shrugging off these burdens.

It was a salvation.

And I went to celebrate my newfound freedom at Remzi's.

After starving myself for so long it was good to tuck into a plate of grilled meatballs, grilled tomatoes and a frosty mug of beer.

If I'd told someone then that I was celebrating the return of a woman to the man she loved, a woman who had caused me such terrible pain when she left me, he would surely have said I was a fool.

But I didn't tell anyone.

I was celebrating.

I bought Remzi a beer and he joined me.

Finishing our second beer, he said, 'Trouble's on the way. Bad things are soon to come.'

I didn't care.

XLV

I can only explain what I experienced that day as one of God's horrific coincidences. I don't think there's any other way to express it.

During those days I carried in my heart a pain free of all responsibility.

And despite the pain and curiosity, I felt a strange bliss that came with the freedom of not having to worry about Zuhal. Worry could bind me to a woman and bring about dark humours that over time hardened the bond, which grew stronger, and my love for her could then spark concern that later turned into anger and finally a dull weight on my back that I wanted to throw off. It was a ghastly progression of emotion. Relationships could be like that for me: in the end my beloved was nothing but an overstuffed bundle of rags. The love was tainted.

It became distasteful in the end.

I was open to any emotion as long as it was free of burden. Passion, longing, lust, pain, grief. Whatever it was, but no burdens.

When I began to feel concerned for someone else in a way I never felt about myself, I felt a kind of injustice. I was a restless horse tied to a stake, kicking and struggling to be free.

Perhaps this was one of the main reasons I treasured my solitude.

Thanks to Mustafa, I had freed myself from the burdens of my relationship with Zuhal, but that didn't take away the pain. Yet the change did provide a sense of comfort and a fresh state of mind.

After breakfast that morning I read through my papers and

then, after wandering through the garden, inspecting the trees, touching the odd flower and bantering a little with Hamiyet, I left around noon.

I set out on foot.

I wanted to see the cradle-maker, chat a little with him, whittle away at the pain within me through the infinite future I saw in him.

When I got to the little square, he wasn't in his usual spot and his shop was closed.

I asked the coffeehouse boy what had happened.

'I don't know. He didn't come today.'

'Has this happened before?'

'No, never before. This is the first time he hasn't come.'

I collapsed onto the little wicker chair.

Suddenly I felt an odd sensation, something like dread. I had no idea why. Some things you just get used to, the important fixtures in the fabric of life, which help define who you are. I needed to see the cradle-maker in his usual place.

Like the rising sun . . .

What would you feel if one morning the sun didn't rise? That was the feeling I had when I saw the cradle-maker's shop closed. The order of the world was disturbed, as if the definition of the world had changed.

He was supposed to always be there; he would be there every time I went to see him.

But he wasn't there that day.

Suddenly I felt the urge to go and see him at home, and I asked the coffee boy where he lived, but the boy didn't know. Maybe I could have found him if I really tried but later I realised I had no right to do something like that.

Our friendship didn't give me the right to go and find him if he didn't ask me to. If he wanted me to find his house he would have mentioned where it was, but he never did. I had never even imagined his home. It was as if he lived there in the square; like the enormous plane tree, he belonged here.

But the tree was now gone and life suddenly seemed empty.

Shocked and lightheaded, I stood up and started to make my way down into town through the maze of narrow back streets.

It was almost noon.

It seemed as if everything had shifted, something had swept through town, uprooting life itself.

I didn't know what it was.

I felt something akin to a landslide within me.

We don't always know how important a place some people hold in our lives, and they don't know either, and then they are gone and we know this from the tremors that come in their wake. We understand what they meant.

The cradle-maker had been my connection to the future. Somehow he connected me to the infinite, reminding me of tomorrow and easing the pains of today.

I felt that I no longer had a future. Not seeing him there in his spot snapped the tender bond that linked me to the days ahead.

Perhaps I had such a reaction because my emotions were so fragile and tumultuous at the time. Perhaps. But that's how I felt then.

I felt dizzy.

As I made my way down the hill, the town seemed so very far away.

I was on the main street into town but I felt so far away.

It was hot. I started walking. I paused for a moment and then carried on.

A long convoy of black cars passed by. Then stopped a hundred metres ahead. And like a train, the entire convoy of cars started to slowly back up.

It was a spectacular sight.

It was like a shimmering mirage: I was a baby giant playing with a train set, holding the row of cars in my hand, pushing them forward, pulling them back.

The lead car stopped next to me.

The window slid down.

Rahmi.

'What's wrong? What are you doing so far out of town? Are you lost?'

I felt the urge to say 'I've been lost for some time', but settled with: 'Just strolling.'

'Hop in,' he said and pushed open the door.

I got in.

I saw there was someone with him. Muhacir.

'Hello,' he said. He was on edge, a frown on his face, leaning up against the other door. But Rahmi seemed unusually lively and full of energy.

'What are you doing around here?' Rahmi asked.

'Just walking. I must have taken a wrong turn somewhere and ended up on the main street.'

'Where are you going?'

'Nowhere in particular. I was going to eat something and head home.'

'Come on then. Let's eat together,' he said, slapping my knee.

Muhacir was silent.

'Where are you planning to eat?'

'At the Çinili.'

I discreetly looked over at Muhacir, who was staring out the window.

'Well, I won't disturb you then. You must have a lot to talk about. I'll just head over to Remzi and have köfte.'

Rahmi insisted.

'You can go to Remzi's any time. Come on. I'll have them make you a superb fish. We can eat and talk.'

It was strange of him to insist like that.

Then it dawned on me. He knew that he was misbehaving, unconsciously seeking an unwitting partner in crime; he wanted to put on a show at the Çinili, and in front of both me and Muhacir. As he had said to his dad, 'It's a place we always go to. What's the problem with going there now?'

I recalled the anger he'd expressed when he heard that Oleander was going to the Çinili every day. Mustafa would surely respond to Rahmi's effrontery with a good dose of his own.

He would only rise to the challenge with a greater challenge.

It was clear that Muhacir was aware of just how dangerous this was going to be, but apparently he had no choice other than to agree to go if Rahmi insisted.

I couldn't be sure if Rahmi was aware of the consequences; he was now swept away in the heat of the moment, and the wild and overwhelming emotion of punishing the object of his anger was blinding him, shutting him off from reality.

I don't know why I didn't say no, even though I'd sensed the possible outcomes and could guess what might happen. I imagine I felt it would be rude if I declined after he'd insisted so firmly; or maybe I didn't have the will to resist then, as for the most part I allowed myself to be swept along by the tides.

The Çinili garden wasn't very crowded. Fewer people were going there then. Most likely Oleander's frequenting the place discouraged some of the other bigwigs in town.

There was no sign of Oleander.

So much would have been clear from the absence of body-guards at the door.

We sat down at one of the tables at the end of the garden. Muhacir kept his back to the wall, choosing a place from which he could keep an eye on the door, his men settling down at the surrounding tables.

The others formed a group at the door.

Muhacir didn't say much during the meal. It seemed he was waiting to get out of there as soon as possible, his entire being exhibiting a frustration with Rahmi, but he didn't say a word.

I was nervous too.

Rahmi did all the talking, pleased that he had come with Muhacir to challenge Mustafa; no doubt he saw us getting in and out of there without an incident as a great success.

He talked about his childhood, the way the town used to be, and how they would go swimming in the sea, dig up mussels and cook them over a beach fire. It was all trifling dross that only showed how nervous he really was.

And so it was a meal at which Rahmi spoke and we were silent, waiting for it to be over.

I was angry with myself for coming

Something terrible could happen any moment, and it just wasn't the most flattering thing for me to be doing: having lunch with Mustafa's enemies out in the open like that, and just after having spoken to him the other morning.

It annoyed me to be doing something I knew I shouldn't be doing.

Muhacir relaxed a little towards the end of the meal and started sharing some of his childhood memories too.

He told us how they used to steal fruit from the orchards, how he formed a gang and about the time he first smoked marijuana behind the wine factory, how when he was thirteen he and his friends went to the open air cinema together and stabbed a local gangster and then got arrested. 'We were rebels even back then,' he said.

At one stage he was on good terms with Oleander but then they drifted apart over the sale of a carpet shop, and it had been the same ever since.

Muhacir laughed as we sipped our coffees.

He was in a good mood.

He was enjoying the fruits of having avoided a terrible disaster while making an open challenge to Mustafa.

Today the entire town would be talking about how Rahmi and Muhacir had lunch at the Çinili restaurant.

'Mustafa thinks his dad owns this town,' Rahmi said at one point, not bothering to tone down his anger. 'Well, he needs to know who really owns this place.'

We all got up together.

Rahmi greeted people at the other tables, and as he was approaching the door I heard the sound of cars pulling up to the restaurant, and so did Muhacir. Rahmi looked up and said, 'What's wrong?'

'Cars just pulled up,' I said.

Even inside you could feel the buzz of activity at the door.

Muhacir kept an even stride, slow and steady.

He gestured to the others around him.

The men formed a kind of ring around us.

I saw him bend his elbow to check the gun on his hip, and I was sure there was a bullet in the chamber. A quick draw and a pull on the trigger. They would leave nothing to chance as the others came into the garden.

We reached the door.

Then a large group of men stepped inside, Oleander in front, and they glared at each other.

I could see that neither group was looking for a confrontation.

Oleander's men moved a little to the right and Muhacir's men a little to the left, leaving a gap in between.

Both sides glided past without making any contact.

I could feel beads of sweat on my brow.

We stepped outside.

There was a wave of tension as the bodyguards of the rival gangs sized each other up.

'Let's go,' Muhacir said to his men.

We made for our cars.

We were nearly there, and one of Muhacir's men had already opened the front door.

Suddenly a scuffle broke out between two of the youngest bodyguards trailing behind. I don't know who started it but most likely they knew each other and had an old beef. One of them cursed the other and guns were drawn.

Shots were fired and one of Muhacir's bodyguards pushed him into the car, saying, 'Let's get moving, brother,' but then Muhacir turned to see what was happening.

And I saw a bullet tear into his throat.

A thick fountain of blood spurted out from beneath his Adam's apple as he clasped his neck, the blood pouring out between his fingers.

Then shooting erupted from both sides.

It was a horrible clamour.

I could hear bullets crashing into the car windows, the walls around us, human bodies, and there was screaming, cursing and moaning.

Rahmi was standing there, frozen, watching it all, so I grabbed him and pushed him under a car, then took cover behind the back wheels.

I didn't know why I'd even wanted to protect him.

Perhaps I was simply trying to protect the person closest to me, or perhaps it was because he was Kamile Hanım's son, or perhaps simply because he was standing there between two cars, looking for cover, and I pulled him down with me.

But I had saved his life, and as we huddled behind the tyre bullets shattered the windows of the car in front of us.

I don't how long the shootout lasted.

Eventually I heard police sirens.

One of Rahmi's bodyguards said, 'Come on, Rahmi Bey,' and dragged him to his car.

'You come too,' Rahmi said. But I stayed put.

'You go,' I shouted.

I scrambled over to one of the back streets.

Apart from Muhacir, three men had been killed right there at the entrance to the restaurant, one of them Oleander's cousin. Twelve other men were injured and seven were in critical condition.

The wounded were taken to the hospital.

Muhacir and Oleander were not just leaders of rival gangs, they were the heads of important families, and many of the gang members were relatives.

Later I learned that people from both sides gathered at the hospital and that there weren't many policemen among them.

The entire town was on its feet.

Thirsting for revenge.

As expected, the first conflict broke out at the hospital and rapidly spread, hitting the poorest neighbourhoods the hardest.

Watching from my veranda, I heard the gunshots and could see flames rising up into the sky, spreading minute by minute, as people set fire to each other's shops and offices.

They even stormed the police station, smashing all the windows.

There weren't enough police and gendarmes to contain a conflict of this magnitude.

I kept my gun by my side.

The town burned until morning, and all the shops were looted.

The death count rose to nine and there was no limit to the number of wounded.

Towards dawn people of neighbouring villages and the gendarmerie surrounded the town.

They went through every neighbourhood.

And the fighting settled down.

Soon there was a gendarme on every corner.

This time the 'morning' plane arrived from the city, because they'd sent the plane to the city before dawn to pick up those leading citizens of the town who lived there.

By dawn all the bigwigs had gathered at the Chamber of Commerce.

I don't know what they discussed in that meeting.

But in the morning I learned that Mustafa had resigned.

And Raci Bey had reopened all of his businesses.

After the sun came up I closed all the windows and shutters and went to bed, thinking of Zuhal.

Wondering where she was.

I was curious.

Drifting off to sleep, I heard my phone: it was a message.

Are you ok?

It was Zuhal.

Fine, and you?

Fine.

I waited for her to write more but nothing came.

XLVI

The pinkish smoke between the mountains was rising, becoming thicker and casting a purple hue over the darkness in the distance.

It was dawn.

The sun was readying the world for its arrival.

As it rose over the horizon, the prophet Abraham said, 'My lord this is greater than all else.'

I remember Zuhal's final words at home.

'i watched the sun rise . . . it was so beautiful.'

I still don't know if I will see this last sunrise.

It will rise soon enough.

The purple clouds over the mountaintops will turn silver.

I am ready now.

For anything.

Will I be able to say, 'It was wonderful'?

I don't think I will.

For I have died.

I died here today.

I was swifter than death. I died even before it came.

I can't feel my body.

I am nothing but a thought.

A thought sitting alone here on this bench.

I sat down on this bench as a person, and died on this bench as one, but now I am drawing out the last few minutes of life as a thought.

Everything seems a little strange and amusing, probably because of the sense of superiority my thought feels in the face of everything else.

I look down on life and death.

I now find myself in such a place that I am far away from both, neither of them can touch me now, and in the last few minutes of my life, far away from life and death, I will embrace the two with even greater power and invincibility.

I am face to face with God.

God and his image.

You and me.

You must be something like this, far from life and death, and greater than both.

And you have put me in such a place tonight that from this vantage point I can see where you have paused.

This is why I must die before I surrender to death, and move far away from life while I am still alive.

This you have given to me.

You have praised me with fear and horror tonight, and you have tamed me with horror and fear, and I was frightened to the core and I suffered deeply, and I couldn't bear it so I changed shape, making a blue diamond from a lump of coal. You have made a blue diamond out of a lump of coal. Am I now a blue diamond because I am no longer afraid, because I am a dead man, or is it because I am thinking beyond the grave, not living while I am still alive?

Tell me.

Speak to me.

Is it because the most precious moments in life are the ones I am experiencing now?

Or is it because, as I sit here on this bench, I have become like that little wisp of cloud that I thought of taking as my own?

You know who I killed, don't you?

Only the two of us know.

And no one else.

The others will soon find out.

Your novel is full of secrets that will remain unearthed for thousands of years to come but accept this: that a novel in which the killer is revealed does not suit your idea of a good time, your beloved understanding of a secret.

My story has come to an end.

But yours will carry on.

My body is dead, and soon enough my thoughts will die too.

But let me tell you this before I die.

In these final moments I'm thinking of the novel you wrote, as there is nothing else for me to ponder, for I was brought here by your words.

I know that they could have been revised endlessly – you refer to the burning of a rough draft as an apocalypse, and if you burn it and rewrite it yet again the novel that takes place on this little planet would be better.

Do you know that on this earth I could create a masterpiece to rival yours with just one word?

Just one word.

'Some.'

That word is missing from your book.

You wish all your heroes to be perfect but none of them have been created that way; either you should overhaul them all or throughout the story you should expect some success rather than complete perfection.

Why do you create heroes who can never achieve perfection but still strive for it? Why do you think of yourself as a writer who can never realise what he truly wants in his books?

You say that the best and the most beloved heroes are perfectly good, that they are free of sin; but no such hero exists.

You have created millions of protagonists and not one was created in this way.

Why do you ask of your heroes that which they can never do?

You would have done so much if it was indeed in your power – you would have created a hero who was good and law abiding, you could have done it, but you didn't and you could not.

Because such a hero doesn't fit the template of your novel.

Sometimes it happens, sometimes it can befall a novelist.

He thinks of another work, and his own book slips away from him, and something else altogether comes out.

Is this that kind of book?

This book cannot be the only one on this earth.

There has to be more.

I wonder how you wrote them.

More carefully crafted?

More painstakingly edited?

With a plot and characters more cleverly in sync?

I wonder how these heroes found the word 'a little', something that you never asked for, a word you perhaps never cared for – how did it end up here in your book?

How is it that your entire novel came to be based on this word when it is a concept you so resoundingly reject?

There are no absolutes, my beloved writer.

You fill the hearts of people with such longing and desire, and so much ambition and so much good and evil, but then how can you expect a perfect hero?

Are you angry with me for saying all this?

Will you have me punished?

But if we are to assume that I am but a character in your book then what I am saying is nothing but self-criticism.

I became a killer in your book.

When did you decide to make me a killer?

We have returned to the original question.

Who is the killer? Who is responsible for this crime?

You?

Me?

No one can give a verdict.

This is how we began and this is how we will end.

Never knowing.

Every novel is a reflection of its author and we are reflections of you.

We were made in your image.

As a writer you show little mercy to your heroes, and you say that you will show them in the second book, where we will need your mercy.

I am not seeking an absolute mercy from you.

But in the passages you will come to write I am merely begging you for a little mercy.

Your poor heroes.

Look, here's one now, waiting for the sunrise, which humans perceive as a miracle, a moment when everything will be erased and then gone.

You know that I have also done good.

And evil . . .

I am a hero in your book.

I am a human being.

You wrote this.

And those you write about cannot be other than what they are.

They cannot.

XLVII

When I woke that fairy-tale town was gone.

The shimmering golden dome, the beach, the sand-coloured houses, the palm trees, the oleander, the olive trees, the vineyards, the little squares and narrow streets, the plane trees, the flower gardens, the jasmine and honeysuckle and the clementine trees, this perfect town was dark under a cloud of thick black smoke. It was now nothing but a ruin that reeked of smoke and ash.

Even the sea was dark.

Columns of smoke rose from all corners.

And a terrifying silence reigned.

The town was now no different from the ruined church up on the hill.

I'd slept through the whole day and the sun was now setting.

Hamiyet hadn't come.

The house was steeped in a crepuscular gloom, the caramel-coloured stones darkened and cold.

It seemed abandoned.

I threw on some clothes and instinctively put my gun in my belt; there was something eerie about the smoke-scented silence.

I went out onto the veranda and ate a little stale bread and cheese that I'd scraped together in the kitchen.

Then I shut and locked the door to the veranda and went upstairs to pack my bags.

In pursuit of this chimerical treasure they ended up burning the actual prize.

There was nothing left for me to do here.

It is difficult to explain the sadness and grief I felt then as

I knew I was on brink of leaving not only the town but Zuhal – I would never see her again.

As my life was barrelling forward in one direction, the word *fine* had switched the tracks and like a train I was off in another direction.

I'd grown fond of the place.

There was something enchanting about it; you had the feeling of looking out over it from a distance when the surroundings were actually quietly drawing you in, making you a part of them.

I had become a part of the town and it had become a part of me.

Like an ice breaker, Zuhal had cleared a way forward for me and I was consumed by the entire town and all its people and their struggles and their lies and the murders and dark desires. To leave a place knowing that you would never return, that you would never see the people there again and that among those people there was a woman with whom you had shared dreams and with whom you had imagined a future, makes the moment of departure that much more difficult.

That moment suddenly seemed so difficult that I actually considered staying.

It was enticing to think of sharing an intimate moment with Zuhal again, meeting her on the street somewhere or in a restaurant, but at the same time I knew how painful this would be, stripping me of all my strength, turning me into a wretched fool.

And Zuhal would sense this.

In fact that would be the moment I would truly lose her.

I knew that not seeing her didn't mean losing her. I wasn't going to see her again but I was always going to be a part of her life, hidden behind a secret door, resting like a place of worship, and sometimes she would come in to look at what we'd lived through together.

I suppose the fear that I would ruin this place weighed heavily on me.

I was all the more resolved to leave.

I wondered what they would do with my books after they were married. Would they burn them? Throw them away? Or would Mustafa simply dismiss them, tucking them away in some corner of their home?

What strange thoughts people have.

How much importance is placed on the trivial in moments like these.

It was one of the rare moments when solitude was painful.

Like an empty hotel room, the bed in disarray after love-making and empty plates strewn over the table.

The memories remained there but the creators of those memories were gone.

Darkness was falling.

The town was sinking into the darkening sky.

The last wisps of daylight seemed darker.

I don't know why but I wanted to slip into the dusk.

I felt so helpless and so powerless then that I was seized by the horrific thought that those emotions might stay with me for the rest of my life. I suppose I wasn't thinking clearly, or perhaps I wasn't thinking at all. I had given in to fragile and feeble emotions, and they were driving me to make all the wrong decisions.

I put my suitcase on an armchair and sat down.

'I'll leave in the morning,' I said.

No doubt I was fooling myself, hoping that in the morning I would change my mind and stay; in deciding to go I had actually decided to stay but I couldn't admit this to myself, as conflicting thoughts and emotions waged a civil war in my head, a war in which I could not take a side.

There and then I understood why people cannot tolerate solitude for very long and have a pressing need for the company of others. I understood this as the town vanished into the smoke and the encroaching darkness, and in the twilight a giant serpent slowly wrapped around my body, pressing down on me, and with the coming darkness I felt the need to find another human being, someone to push this oppressive weight off my shoulders.

Someone to save me.

I was in no state to get up and go or wait till morning.

I was collapsing into darkness, like the town.

Collapsing in on myself.

I couldn't breathe.

There have been very few moments in my life when I felt so helpless and alone.

I would have sacrificed nearly anything simply to hear a voice.

Did God then hear the bartering in my mind? I don't know.

Was he listening and then came to an agreement without consulting me?

The phone rang.

I remember that the last red dot of the setting sun was just disappearing into the sea.

I was so jittery that I dropped the receiver.

When I finally got it up against my ear I heard that teasing voice.

'Oh, so excited you dropped the phone then?'

'Yes. I really did.'

'What are you doing? Getting ready to go?'

The woman had spine-chilling intuitive powers.

'Yes.'

'Raci just called to tell me that their meetings would be going on till morning. Gülten's in the city and I sent our bodyguards and servants to tend to their families. So you see, I'm all alone in this big house. Come to say goodbye if you want. Would you like that?'

'I would very much.'

'But no sweets . . . We'll just have a chat and say goodbye. Still want to come?'

'Yes.'

'Well, then come over. But don't come by car. The place is swarming with gendarmes and police, and the car will only attract attention. You can take a minibus from the neighbouring village. They pass through. And if you can't find one now then you can walk. Are you willing to walk that far?'

'Yes.'

'But I'll say it again, no sweets . . . Still willing to walk?'

'Yes.'

'Fine, then. Come on over.'

I didn't know then that I had come to the end of my life on earth. A little earlier I'd felt dead to the world, suffocating in grief and solitude, but after this conversation my emotions were sent into a tailspin, whipping up such an overwhelming feeling of joy and excitement that I wasn't sure if what I'd felt just two minutes ago was real.

Human emotions can turn on a sixpence, flitting from one extreme to another, swinging from branch to branch like an ape, forgetting altogether the tree just left behind.

I put on a thin jacket and left the house.

I made my way down to the centre of town through the narrow and deserted back streets; the curtains of all the houses had been drawn and the streets were dark.

The centre of town was full of burned out shops, charred bits of boards scattered over the streets and broken glass that crunched under my feet. Columns of smoke rose up into the sky.

Soldiers and policemen were standing guard on the street corners.

And no one else was there.

Even the dogs were gone.

The streets were completely empty.

I headed out of town.

I estimated it would take me about half an hour to get there.

I heard a minibus behind me, and I started at first and stepped to the side of the road. Then I reasoned that with so many police and gendarmes around the hit men wouldn't be out.

I flagged the minibus down.

It stopped.

There were no passengers inside.

I got in feeling a little scared, as the driver and his assistant might very well be hit men.

I checked my gun with my elbow just to be sure.

There was a bullet in the chamber and it would go off with a single squeeze of the trigger. This put me at ease.

I kept my hand on the butt of my gun throughout the trip, watching the two men softly speaking to each other.

I got off near Kamile's place.

I had to pass a squad of soldiers.

The broad garden gate was open and it seem like no one was there.

I walked to the house and stepped up onto the veranda but the door swung open before I could knock.

She had a pleasant smile on her face.

'So you did come even though there are no sweets . . . Are you that lonely?'

'I don't need loneliness to feel the need to see you.'

'Oh God, always a quick answer. Come in.'

I stepped inside.

All the lights were on.

'What's it like out there?' she asked.

'Like a body torn to pieces.'

She grimaced.

'One idiot's stupidity . . . It's completely ruined.'

She sat down opposite me, her skirt rolled up far over her knees. I looked and she laughed: 'Your mind's on the sweets, no? But none for you tonight!'

'So be it. What's there to do then?'

I knew that it wasn't the right place for us to make love but she must have felt that anything could have happened in that enormous house; and I did too, though neither of us really wanted it. We both felt that strange rush of desire, a rising heat, as we sat there quietly across from each other.

I couldn't stop looking at her legs.

'If someone comes, you can say that you called to say goodbye and that I invited you over for a cup of coffee. And that you then stayed for dinner. Are you hungry?'

Looking at her legs, I said, 'Yes.' And she laughed.

'I'm talking about food.'

'Oh, I'm hungry for that too.'

This woman had a strange power over me, driving nearly every other thought out of my mind.

'I'll make something for us to eat then. I sent the girls away so I'll have to do it myself.'

'I'll help you,' I said.

I couldn't help but think of how we searched for coffee in my kitchen the first time she came over.

'Why not,' she said, and we went to the kitchen together. As we set the plates and silverware and warmed up some food, I was close to her, our bodies touching, and then she rubbed her hips up against me as she pretended to look for something on a shelf.

I couldn't resist: I stuck my hand up her skirt.

She grabbed my hand. 'I said no sweets tonight.'

But she had turned to face me and as she turned away she pushed her ass right into me; she was certainly having fun.

'Feeling the fire?' she quipped.

'Oh yes.'

'I can see.'

We sat down across from each other at a long table.

Suddenly she was serious.

'I wanted to thank you,' she said.

'For what?'

'For saving Rahmi's life.'

Then she became truly angry, a kind of anger I had never seen before.

'They were going to kill Rahmi. If you hadn't pulled him under the car they would have shot him, and I won't forgive them for this. They would have shot him there and left him for dead.'

Her rage was different from any of the others in her family. It wasn't threatening. It was eerily decisive. She wouldn't forgive them. It was clear she didn't leave any room for anyone to doubt her.

'I didn't do anything,' I said.

She smiled, turning back to her old self.

'Now, enough with your chivalry . . .'

'Really.'

'Why did you do it?'

'I hit the deck then pulled him down with me . . . Nothing more.'

'And not just him, you saved us all, the entire family, because if something had happened to Rahmi we would have been torn apart . . .'

She paused and flashed that teasing smile.

'Of course Rahmi will never repay the debt to you but I'll give you everything I have . . . Are you going back to the city?'

'Yes.'

'When?'

'Tomorrow morning.'

'Will you think of those sweets when you're there?'

'Everywhere I go.'

'Good. Then I'll make a point of going there often. We'll be more comfortable there. More time.'

She smiled. I had never seen a lustier smile in all my days. The smile reminded me of how she made love, insatiable, selfish lust swirling in her eyes.

We cleared the table together, our bodies touching.

Then we made coffee.

And she sat down across from me again.

Her legs crossed, she pulled up her skirt a little higher. 'Have a good look then. You like to look. So take a good look now because you won't be able to for some time.'

I sipped my coffee as I gazed at her legs.

I knew that it wouldn't be easy to find another woman like her, a woman as lusty and a woman who so openly showed it.

I felt strangely addicted to her.

Towards ten, I said, 'I should get going.'

She looked at her watch.

'Have another cigarette before you go.'

As I was lighting my cigarette, the telephone rang.

She picked up.

The expression on her face changed.

It was the same expression that fell over her face when she'd said, 'I won't forgive him.'

'Tell me when they leave,' she said and hung up.

'What's up?' I asked.

'Oh nothing . . . Mustafa and his people are going to the city tonight.'

'There's no plane at this hour.'

'They're going by car.'

Then I understood.

Indeed I had already sensed it: she was the one who was making all the decisions.

She was the one who wouldn't forgive them for what they had almost done to Rahmi.

They were informing Kamile Hanım, not Raci Bey, about Mustafa's movements, which meant she had her own foot soldiers. I had already seen how the family bodyguards were sensitive around her, the way they held themselves with her, and how she gave them orders.

Suddenly I panicked and said, almost pleading, 'Don't do it.'

She flashed me a stern look.

'Don't do what?'

'Don't do anything to Mustafa's people.'

'Are you mad? I wouldn't do anything to them. You think I have that kind of power? If I could, of course I would. I wouldn't let them fire at Rahmi like that and then just up and leave, but all the same I don't have the power to do anything.'

'He wasn't the one firing at Rahmi. The shooting just suddenly broke out and Rahmi was caught in the middle.'

'If Mustafa hadn't spurred them on, who would have even dared to start shooting in the first place?'

Beads of sweat were forming on my brow.

'Don't do it,' I said again.

'Don't do it, don't do it, don't do what? Just what do you

think I'm going to do? And then what's it to you? The guy ran off with your girl and you're telling me don't do it . . . You're really one of a kind.'

I wasn't listening to her any more.

'Please don't do it,' I said.

She looked into my eyes and suddenly seemed so far away, like a stranger.

'You're in love with that girl, aren't you? That's why you're so paranoid, thinking that I'm going to do something to them. You're panicking because you think something will happen to her. Now look, you should know better than to act like this. To fall in love with a girl like that. I can understand why you'd like her. You'd like any woman who's willing to have you in bed. But to fall in love with her . . . and with a worthless girl like that. She's pathetic. Mustafa this and Mustafa that, wandering about town, giving every man she sees the glad eye . . . God knows what she does with the men she consults for.'

'I'm not in love with her.'

'Then what's this all about? You've suddenly lost your mind, dreaming things up. Jumping to conclusions after one telephone call. You're insane.'

'I'm worried about Mustafa. I don't want anything to happen to either of them. Just let them go. You can stop this.'

'Look, let me tell you something, you're dreaming, making up all sorts of things, and anyway I'd only go ahead and do something about this if I had the power to do it. I'll never forgive him for what he's done. And if the men in this town have any balls they won't forgive him either. So many people killed, the place burnt to the ground . . . and he's just going to leave as if nothing's happened? And he is . . . Now, maybe I can't stop him myself but I would kiss the hand of anyone who did.'

She stopped and looked at me gravely, then smiled.

'You should go and get some sleep. Forget all this and so will I. Because I don't think we'll ever be the same now that I've seen you this way. Go now, so I can forget all this.'

I suddenly realised how ridiculous I was being and I felt ashamed; I was probably blushing. It was just that imagining Mustafa and Zuhal blown to pieces in their car made me panic. I was tired, and on edge.

I laughed.

'I'm sorry. It's just that so many people have been killed and I guess that's all that's on my mind. Will I never taste those sweets again?'

She smiled.

'Hmm. Not sure yet. But you'll need to work hard to help me forget . . . Will you do that?'

'Oh . . . you'd have to beg me to stop working at it.'

'Well, then I will forget. Get going. I'll call you later.'

I turned and stepped towards the door.

God's horrible coincidences.

The telephone rang.

I looked at her.

At that moment I saw that unforgiving expression in her face, fixed with an unflinching rage, a look that bristled with the knowledge that her son had almost died − but it was something I could never explain or prove in a court of law. I knew her conversation would be brief. 'Okay,' she would say, or simply 'Yes' or 'As I said', or something to that effect. She was determined never to forgive Mustafa and Zuhal. She probably had a man working as one of their bodyguards and the plan had already been put it in place; she only needed to give the word.

'Please don't answer,' I said.

The mocking smile on her face had disappeared.

'You need to go,' she said, and nothing more.

She reached for the telephone on the coffee table.

'Don't answer,' I said, practically begging.

She picked up the phone.

I stepped forward to take the phone away from her but she pulled her hand away.

'Put down the phone,' I shouted.

I could feel that Zuhal was moments from death; Kamile only had to answer the phone and give the order.

She brought the receiver to her ear.

I drew my gun.

I don't know why I did it. I suppose I wanted to frighten her because I knew that if she answered the phone everything would change. I wanted to stop her with a threat. Nothing more. But then I had no idea what to do after that.

She stood up.

The look on her face was firm, full of anger and derision.

She hit my hand.

I can't really remember much more after that.

I only heard the shot.

She opened her mouth to say something and then winced, one arm in the air and the other on her stomach; and then I saw her fall to her knees; but I didn't see any blood.

I don't know what killers normally feel but at that moment I felt tense and then a rush of fear, a fear like no other I had ever felt, in every fibre of my being.

I had promised Zuhal that I would change the course of her life, her fate.

And I had done just that.

And she would never know.

I left the house. The gendarmes were no longer there and the streets were deserted.

I walked back to town.

I came and sat down here on this bench.

At that moment I was sure that Kamile was going to order the hit, and my suspicions only grew as I walked, though I could never be entirely sure; but I had seen that expression on her face, and I wasn't wrong about that.

I saw her conviction.

But still I will never know for sure.

No one will ever know how much I'll miss Kamile. Now, more than pain, I feel a longing, and I can see just how important a part of my life she had become.

God uses dastardly coincidences in his novels and here one of them had saved one woman's life and killed another.

He had made me a murderer.

Indeed perhaps Kamile Hanım was the woman I could never give up, or that's how I feel now.

How strange to understand that after taking her life.

But that's how God pens his own work.

Sardonic and cruel.

I can hear the sounds of cars. Raci Bey must have gone home.

XLVIII

And so here they are.

At both ends of the street.

I'm tired.

But I won't surrender.

My gun's empty. I took out the clip and removed the bullet from the chamber.

But they don't know that.

They're approaching me with caution.

All of a sudden I'll stand up and point my gun at them.

'Life in this world is nothing but an amusing game.'

But this won't be any fun for me. Maybe it will be enjoyable for you, dear writer, for the fancies of an author are boundless.

But this will be my last game in this world.

And so I rise to my feet.

I hope you've finished volume two.

I hope it's a better book than this.

A NOTE ON THE TYPE

This book is set in Bembo, a humanist serif typeface commissioned by Aldus Manutius and cut by Francesco Griffo, a Venetian goldsmith, in the late fifteenth century.

This harmonious typeface has gone on to inspire generations of type founders, from Claude Garamond in the sixteenth century to Stanley Morison at the Monotype Corporation in the early twentieth century.